Forgive the Moon

Forgive the Moon

MARYANNE STAHL

CONVERSATION NAL ACCENT GUIDE INCLUDED

FICTION FOR THE WAY WE LIVE

Written by today's freshest new talents and selected by New American Library, NAL Accent novels touch on subjects close to a woman's heart, from friendship to family to finding our place in the world. The Conversation Guides included in each book are intended to enrich the individual reading experience, as well as encourage us to explore these topics together—because books, and life, are meant for sharing.

Visit us online at www.penguinputnam.com

NAL Accent
Published by New American Library, a division of
Penguin Putnam Inc., 375 Hudson Street,
New York, New York 10014, U.S.A.
Penguin Books Ltd, 80 Strand,
London WC2R 0RL, England
Penguin Books Australia Ltd, Ringwood,
Victoria, Australia
Penguin Books Canada Ltd, 10 Alcorn Avenue,
Toronto, Ontario, Canada M4V 3B2
Penguin Books (N.Z.) Ltd, 182-190 Wairau Road,
Auckland 10, New Zealand

Penguin Books Ltd, Registered Offices:
Harmondsworth, Middlesex, England

First published by New American Library, a division of Penguin Putnam Inc.

First Printing, June 2002
10 9 8 7 6 5 4 3

FICTION FOR THE WAY WE LIVE

REGISTERED TRADEMARK—MARCA REGISTRADA

LIBRARY OF CONGRESS CATALOGING-IN-PUBLICATION DATA:
Stahl, Maryanne.
Forgive the moon / Maryanne Stahl.
    p. cm.
ISBN 0-451-20633-9 (alk. paper)
  I. Middle aged women—Fiction. 2. Seaside resorts—Fiction. 3. Family
reunions—Fiction. I. Title.

PS3619.T473 F67 2002
813'.6—dc21   2002019647

Set in Centaur
Designed by Ginger Legato

Printed in the United States of America

PUBLISHER'S NOTE
This is a work of fiction. Names, characters, places, and incidents either are the products of the author's imagination or are used fictitiously, and any resemblance to actual persons, living or dead, business establishments, events, or locales is entirely coincidental.

For my mother, Cesita Biancardi

Acknowledgments

Forgive the Moon owes debts to everyone whose work I have ever read, of course to everyone in my family, surely to everyone I have ever loved or who has ever dared to love me. So these small notes of appreciation can never be adequate.

First, I thank my agent, John Talbot, for believing in me when I had only seven chapters written, surely an unusual and generous act of faith and encouragement, and my editor, Genny Ostertag, whose enthusiasm and prudent questions about my characters helped me understand my own intentions.

Next I must thank my friend and mentor, Carol Lee Lorenzo, whose integrity was and remains my guiding star; and our writing group, Katherine Harris, Kit Robey, and Marre and John Stevens, whose interest and intelligence sustained and motivated me.

Thank you, too, Rita Ciresi, whose praise for my first chapter sent me on my way and who embodies the generosity of spirit I am convinced all true artists harbor. And thanks, Les Standiford, aka Dr. Plot, who argued with me and challenged me and whose Seaside Writers Conference nourished my soul. To other writer friends—Andrew Nicoll, Bruce Dunlap, Charlie Sanders, Kim Whitehead, Dawn O'Dell, Devaun Kite, Jai Clare, Wendy Vaizey, and everyone at the Zoetrope Writers Studio—I thank you for reading me and, especially, for existing on this earth as though in answer to my prayers.

Special thanks must go to The Breakers resort in Montauk, Long Island, for providing the inspiration for my setting—with which, of course, I took tremendous liberty and license.

Finally, and most emphatically, I thank my family: my husband, John; my daughter, Heather; my son, Jack; and my siblings, Phyllis, Anthony, Andrea, and Billy, who are *not* characters in this book, but without whom I would never have begun to imagine any of it, nor had the heart to try.

CHAPTER 1

I STOOD BREAST DEEP IN THE ROLLING WAVES, past the breakers, past the rocks, my face tilted to the white August sun, breathing in brine. I had drifted eastward about fifty feet from the spot on the beach where our blankets lay, where my siblings and their spouses tended their children and their coolers and their grievances. Then, testing with my toes to see whether I was over my head, I had touched the soft ocean bottom and stood, facing land.

My son, Damien, swam up behind me, grasping my shoulders with both hands. He hung from me, nearly weightless, and instinctively, in counterbalance, I leaned forward and looked toward shore.

The sun's glare blanched the sand and everything on it, so that the shapes that were my brother and my sister and their families began to lose their boundaries. Something ran past them, a blur—a dog—then turned and disappeared up the path through the dunes. The vanishing animal reminded me of last summer, reminded me who was missing now. My mother.

My family had been coming to the ocean in August every summer since I turned twelve—the summer of my mother's first stay in a mental hospital—without her then as we were now. The last time I had seen her alive, in fact, was at this very ocean, just east of here, one year ago. She'd been what Lizzie, Jeremy and I called "good" last summer. (*Mom's been good*, we'd say, referring to her mental state, or *Mom has not been good lately*.) And yet there had been something in her expression that I didn't recognize, and about which I had endlessly speculated since.

Looking toward our enclave on the sand, I thought of the last photograph of her, our group shot, the one that had caught her looking sideways. I had memorized the image of her half-face.

"Mom, watch this!" Damien pushed backward off my body into an underwater handstand and then came up gasping. "Try it!" he said. "The water holds you up."

I pulled my mouth into an exaggerated grimace of fear, but in fact I loved the way he assumed I would try anything. "I'd rather watch you," I said, and he flipped over again.

Together, Damien and I co-represented the entire Kincaid contingent of this year's Sinclair family beach vacation. I watched my son as he cavorted in the waves, but in my mind the group shot reappeared.

Standing next to me in that photograph was my husband, Keith, the tallest of us, our bodies not touching. He, too, was absent now. I had come to the beach without him, had left him home in Atlanta for the week, immersed in the beginnings of an abrupt new business venture—and a trial separation I had told no one about. This week apart was to be an experimental hiatus in our marriage, though I wasn't sure what hypothesis we meant to test.

The two of us had been circling around each other these past few months, sniffing the air for hints of danger. I couldn't tell where our marriage stood amidst the chaos of the changes my husband desired, and I had boarded the plane at Hartsfield, hoping our time apart would clarify the connections we still had. Instead, away from him, I felt only the loss of him.

As I also felt the loss of Isabella, my eldest child. She, who in last year's photograph stood defiantly apart from her family, was absent from the gathering as well this summer. Instead of coming home after her freshman year at college, Isabella had chosen to spend the summer in Boston, working on an internship—and a man. Adjusting to her departure had been acutely painful, but the week she'd spent at home during spring break had been fraught with tension. I missed her daily, yet I dreaded the inevitable struggling that occurred when we were together.

Sad notes from a theme without resolution, I thought, like the musical compositions I'd attempted in college. I had been remembering them lately, as I thought about how I'd come to arrive at this place in my life.

My mother, my husband, my daughter—I was here without all of them, possibly carrying a life of which they knew nothing. This morning's queasiness had just returned, reminding me of my most recent worry. For the first time in years, my period was late.

I turned to Damien bobbing between the swells beside me, intending to ask whether he was ready now to head back to shore.

But as I began to speak, Damien jumped to catch a wave. He took it late, got tumbled, and came up coughing water.

"This one," he said, sputtering and pointing, and he leaned into the next quick curl before catching his breath. I followed him with my eyes as the wave took him, knowing the perils of an outgoing tide. But he caught it right.

His miniature man's body shot fearlessly over the surface of the water, and he landed on his feet, raising his fists in triumph. His hair, black and straight like mine, shone like a seal's; his whoop of delight was animal in its clarity. My heart expanded. This morning, only Damien had run immediately into the water, eager to brave the initial shock of cold and the fierce undertow that were the Atlantic after three days of storms.

"We've *got* to go swimming, Mom," he had insisted as soon as we'd set down our towels, and I couldn't refuse him—or resist. The Atlantic Ocean, with its ever-changing tides, had been the one constant in my life. It was one of the reasons I had been persuaded to abandon landlocked Atlanta and my standoff with Keith.

I needed to feel the pull of something more powerful than either of us.

"Watch this!" Damien called now as he flipped over a waist-high surge.

I smiled at his easy pleasure, but I cautioned him, "Be careful."

The undertow was strong, too strong to resist; you had to know how to go with it until it let you go. I remembered how to do it. I'd learned about letting go that first summer of my mother's illness, that August I did nothing but ride waves from morning until dusk, pretending I was a mermaid, pretending I didn't have a mother—or need one. "She kept herself busy the entire vacation," I'd heard my father tell a neighbor about me when we'd returned.

Two weeks later, when my mother came home from the hospital, fuzzy with drugs and shame, we showed her our softly focused pictures: Lizzie playing in the sand, Jeremy diving off the high board at the pool, and me immersed, elbow deep in the surf. I wondered if some dim, perhaps atavistic memory of ocean light and sound, genetically passed on, was now stored in the recesses of my son's brain.

Whatever the case, Damien learned quickly, bobbing past the curling crests, looking for the swells in the distance that would break just right. I swam beside him. While we waited for the good ones, we floated, finding the warm spots and speculating about currents, sometimes ducking under the whitecaps, sometimes springing straight up out and over them like porpoises. And all the time Damien waited for the one that would ride him in to shore.

There, Lauren and Lindsey, my sister Lizzie's eight-year-old twin girls, stood in the foam, holding each other's arms, and screaming with gleeful horror each time a wave splashed them. Lizzie had promised the girls and their three-year-old brother, Ryan, that Daddy—her husband, Rick Adamo—would take them all for a swim soon. Lizzie herself swam only in calm water.

In the past, our brother, Jeremy, had been the one to count on to supervise the nieces and nephews, taking them into the ocean in turns and organizing games at the shore. But those were the years before he'd had a child of his own. This summer, he was busy playing the conscientious new father ad nauseam. He and his wife, Frances, whom he called Froggy, had divided every bit of care for their newborn son, Jay, fifty-fifty. I swore they counted who got spit up on last. I was glad my cottage wasn't next to theirs; they kept a baby monitor on their deck.

Jeremy had taken care of the week's arrangements this year, renting cottages for each of our families and one for my father, choosing an unfamiliar resort, though we had come over the years to several other Montauk inns and motels.

Each of us had arrived at Laughing Gull Cottages separately the previous night, a Friday. I'd driven in late, more than three hours from

LaGuardia in a steady rain, and hadn't seen anyone as I unpacked my rental car. Someone had left a key for me inside the screen door of cottage number six.

Using my suitcase as an umbrella, I'd guided a sleepwalking Damien from the car into his bedroom—a narrow, musty space that held two creaking beds and little else. Then, after getting him tucked and settled, I'd returned to the car for my violin, wrapping its case in a plastic trash bag for protection.

I had only recently gone back to it and, though I knew I probably wouldn't get to play much here and couldn't say why, I'd felt I needed to have my violin with me this week. I'd carried it into the cottage and stowed it in what seemed the safest corner. Then I'd raised all the windows an inch or two for air and sat in the dark, listening to the rain and the crashing sea.

The waxing moon had cast a fragile light across the walls, out of which my mother's face appeared to me, dry and still as a wraith in the way she'd lain in the hospital, hovering in that place between life and death. I'd spoken to her apparition. "I might be pregnant," I had whispered, "and my husband is leaving me." Though I had never told my mother my secrets when she was alive, if I could have her back again, I thought I would now. I fell asleep on the sofa bed without opening it.

This morning, when the sun came up strong, and the gulls really did laugh us awake, Jeremy knocked on my door and announced that breakfast was being served—on my deck. My father stood behind him, carrying white-paper Montauk Bakery bags filled with rolls and coffee and looking grayer and wearier, older than I'd remembered him. His response to everything since my mother's death had been a kind of subdued alarm. Even now, when he saw I'd brought my violin, he'd warned, "Take care it isn't damaged."

And so, as Damien tested the joys of the ocean, I was glad my father had decided to spend the morning at the pool and wasn't around to shout to us that we'd gone too deep.

"Look!" I called to my son, pointing toward a blue-green rise at the horizon. "That's the biggest one yet. Probably all the way from England."

Damien raised his eyes and his whole face opened with excitement.

"That's the one!" he yelled, turning his back on the wave, positioning himself to ride. The ocean roared its approach.

I turned as my son had, catching the towering wave a second after he did, and then I was swept up in the roiling surf. Its force was a familiar shock, one that sent me tumbling over and over, arms windmilling as if I could somehow maintain balance while being wildly tossed. When I landed and the ocean withdrew enough for me to pull myself to a gasping stand, I looked immediately for Damien.

He'd been deposited farther in than I had, still not all the way to the beach, but it was the closest he'd gotten. He stood ankle deep in froth, at the first dip in the ocean floor where the rocks gathered. I'd been surprised this morning to find a section of round, smooth rocks about three or four feet into the surf, before the bottom turned sandy again as it inclined. These rocks were somehow new—I didn't remember rocks in this part of the water at Montauk—and I worried now whether Damien had been bruised tumbling on them.

"Are you okay?" I called, treading through the foam to reach him. He turned to me, his cheeks red as though he'd just been slapped. But he was grinning. My fingers snagged a long, slippery strand of seaweed.

"Did you see that?" he shouted. "That was the most awesome ride." He began trudging back out through the surf to deeper, calmer water, and I followed, pushing into the pull of the undertow.

We lay back in a cool current, listening to the ocean's low roar. A bubble moved inside me, deep in my belly. "I'm getting tired," I said, though what I felt was an enervating hollowness. "Are you ready to go up?"

"I guess so," Damien replied. His blue eyes were closed, but even the curve of his lids and the pattern of his lashes were recognizable to me as Keith's eyes. In profile now, with his head back and his chin pointed to the sky, he looked like a gentler, less-complicated Keith, a Keith I yearned to know. I wondered where Keith was at this moment, whom he was with, and whether he had thought of me. I had woken up dreaming of him.

Lizzie's voice came to me as if from a great distance. I looked up. She stood at the edge of the surf, calling my name, waving.

I waved back at her, waved her in. She laughed and shook her head.

"Come on!" I called.

She looked good, I thought, healthy. Younger than her thirty-four years. My ponytail felt tight, and I pulled the elastic band from my hair. I had been letting it grow since I'd turned forty, and it fanned out past my shoulders as I dipped my head into the sea.

Damien flipped onto his back and blinked. "One more wave."

"Okay," I said. "One more."

Damien waited, his body hunched forward, his head turned to look over his shoulder.

I paddled beside him and breathed deeply, willing my limbs to soften, my muscles draining tension into the sea, and imagined returning to an original, liquid state. I looked at Lizzie, shading her eyes with her hands, watching us, and waved again. I was eager for sister-talk, eager to ask her how she was, how things were with her and Rick. I wanted to tell her about myself, how my marriage was changing and my period was late and I was living suspended in a state of near panic. More than anything I wanted to talk to her about our mother, about my memories and my fears, to measure them against hers, to assess our danger. Wasn't it after the birth of Lizzie, her third child, that my mother's illness had overtaken her?

I had to duck under the next wave. It broke early and surprised me with its power, yet Damien caught it and rode it in. I sensed him being lifted, thrust away from me at the moment I went under.

When I surfaced, I again immediately looked for him, knowing this wave must have tumbled him badly. At first I couldn't see him and I felt a surge of alarm. I called to him, "Da-mien," the urgency in my voice cracking his name in half. Then I saw him rising, ten yards to the east of me in the rocky part of the water, blood covering his mouth. I moved as quickly as I could to get to him, my legs moving in slow motion as though I were running in a dream.

"Oh, my God," I cried as I reached him. "What happened? Let me see."

"I hit a rock," he said, lifting his face. "I think I broke something."

I took his chin in my hand, wiped blood from a cut on his lower lip, and then I saw it. His top left front tooth had snapped in a jagged diagonal—his recently grown, permanent, front tooth. "Your tooth!"

Damien's face crumpled.

Lizzie splashed up behind us. "What happened?"

"Damien broke his tooth."

He started to cry now at my words, fat tears rolling over his lashes and off the high planes of his cheeks.

"You're kidding," Lizzie said, and she bent to look.

With seawater cupped in my hand, I washed Damien's lip, and he winced at the sting of it. Blood flowed from the gash, even as he pressed it with his fist.

"Come on," I said. "Let's get some ice on it." I began walking him in to shore, my arm wrapped tightly around his shoulders. The undertow was so strong, if we hesitated between steps, our feet sank, covered in sand. Damien moaned that his tooth hurt, that he could feel his pulse in it.

Lizzie ran ahead of us. She stopped where Jeremy lay sprawled in a low chair next to the shaded blanket where his newborn son slept in his infant seat. Froggy sat opposite them in her own, more upright chair, still wearing her beach cover-up, reading *Parents* magazine. When we reached her, she closed the magazine, but kept her page with a finger.

"Damien needs some ice," Lizzie told them as she dripped water on their blanket.

"He's bloody!" Lindsey said, while Lauren made a face.

Jeremy reached for the closest cooler, the one that held Jay's bottles. Froggy kept them cold so they wouldn't spoil, then set each bottle in the sun for six minutes—she timed it with her watch—to warm the formula before she fed Jay. She was proud of having figured out this method for feeding an infant at the beach. Lizzie and I had nursed our babies.

"Not *that* cooler," Froggy said to Jeremy, still holding her place in the magazine as she leaned forward. "Take ice from the other cooler, the one with the Cokes and sandwiches."

Damien and I walked past them to our own towels. "I've got ice," I called back to them, feeling my eyes burn.

Damien had broken his front tooth—he would never grow another. If only we'd come in to shore a minute sooner. What if something worse had happened, if Damien had hit his head instead of his mouth, or broken his neck? Why had I let him ride the waves in such strong undertow? Why was I so careless with what I loved best?

A tear rolled down the side of my face, and I twisted my head so Damien wouldn't see it as I opened the Styrofoam cooler that held our cans of soda. The ice stung my fingers, sharp spines of cold. I grabbed a handful, wrapped it in a towel, and pressed the bundle against Damien's lower lip. He whimpered and sank onto our blanket. Jeremy came up beside us and knelt.

"What happened, big guy?" he asked.

"I hit my tooth on a rock," Damien mumbled.

"He broke it, a permanent tooth," I said.

"Let me see." Jeremy tilted Damien's head back and looked into his mouth. "Yup," he said. "You did. And cut your lip."

"Does it still hurt?" I asked and Damien nodded. He looked down at the white towel, red with his blood.

"Gross," he said, smiling a little as he removed a piece of ice and sucked it gently. "Ow."

"I've got to get him to a dentist," I said, searching my brother's profile, as familiar to me, in memory, as my husband's. "Do you think I can find one out here, on a weekend?"

"Sure," Jeremy said. "At Gurney's Inn down the road."

I frowned.

"Don't worry," Jeremy said, briefly touching my hand as he stood. "I really think it can wait. Why not call your own dentist in Atlanta? See what he says."

"*She,*" I answered. "I will." My dentist, Beatrice Fox, was elderly and slow moving, close to retirement, but she was experienced and kind. I would call and leave a message with her service.

Jeremy's eyes were on Rick, surrounded by his kids at the water's edge.

"Looks like Uncle Rick caught a sand shark," Jeremy said. He ruffled Damien's hair.

"I want to see it!" Damien lifted the towel from his mouth and examined it once more. The bleeding had slowed. "Look, it's better." He stood and lifted his chin. His upper lip bulged where he pressed his tongue to his tooth.

"Go ahead," I told him. "Just try to keep the ice on your lip for a while."

Rick and his kids were up the beach about ten yards. His tall surf caster rod stuck out of a piece of plastic pipe in the sand, and he was bending over, working at something. His three blond children huddled around him. They all had his coloring, though Lizzie was also fair. Her brown curls were tipped with gold, as our mother's had been.

Damien ran toward them, and I sat on the blanket, my head in my hands. Jeremy sat next to me. "He'll be okay," he said.

I sighed. "He might have damaged the root. He might need a cap. Ten years old."

Jeremy shrugged. "Maybe. But it could be worse."

"I know," I said, starting to cry again, and Jeremy rubbed my hand.

I wanted to call Keith, to tell him Damien had gotten hurt already. If he were here, I knew Keith would tell me I should calm down. He would say to Damien, "You'll live." But he wasn't here, and I wanted him to realize how suddenly harm could happen.

Lizzie's feet appeared in my bleary line of vision. Her toenails were painted pink, the polish chipping. I wiped my eyes and squinted up at her.

"Is Damien okay?" she asked.

"He's okay for now." I sniffed and rolled my eyes. "I guess."

"A freak accident," she said, without irony.

I swiped at my eyes.

"Let's start lunch," she said, looking away. "Dad's coming."

I turned and followed her gaze toward the dunes and the path to Laughing Gull cottages. There was our father, walking awkwardly in our direction, carrying one of the striped beach chairs from around the pool. He was slightly built, and since my mother had died, he had lost weight. He was dressed in old suit trousers and a shirt he'd owned for years—clothes were not something my father gave thought to—and as they billowed loosely around him, he seemed almost not to inhabit them at all.

Jeremy jumped up. "We'll put out the sandwiches and stuff on my blanket." Lizzie followed him.

I knew I should offer to carry my father's chair, but I couldn't go to him, couldn't let him see on my face the too many things that were wrong. Instead, I searched in my beach bag for my sunglasses and put them on. Then I looked back into my bag for lip balm. From the corner of my eye, beneath the stem of my glasses, I saw my father stop, run his hand over his bald spot under his fishing hat, and set his chair between my blanket and Lizzie's.

"Mom!" Damien was calling me. "Come see this."

I swiped balm across my lips and trotted over to where Damien stood in a semicircle with his cousins, examining a two-foot-long sand shark. Rick still hadn't gotten the hook out of the thing's jaw. It was torn inside its mouth and bleeding into the wet sand, twitching at the end of a piece of fishing line. Rick stood with his hands on his hips, half smiling.

"Mom, touch it," Damien urged as I bent at the waist beside him. I did. The shark's cool skin felt like sandpaper.

"Feel its mouth," Damien said, demonstrating by poking a finger at the gaping fish. "No teeth."

"Ooh," squealed Lauren, grabbing onto her twin sister's arm.

"Me do," said Ryan, kneeling on the sand and reaching five chubby fingers toward the shark's mouth. The fish gave a sudden twitch and flipped to its other side. It was covered in sand, like a cutlet. The girls squealed again.

"No, Ryan!" I warned, pulling his hand away. Even if it didn't have teeth, which I wasn't sure was true, the shark could snap its jaws. Ryan blinked up at me, probably forgetting who I was.

I looked at Rick chewing thoughtfully on a stick of gum, his eyes out to sea. "Are you going to put the shark back in the ocean?" I asked.

Rick pursed his lips and considered. "I can't seem to get the hook out."

"Won't it die if you don't do it soon?" Was I pleading with him? Rick, I knew from his years with Lizzie, was unmoved by pleading.

"The kids are getting a big kick out of it," he said.

I gazed at the huddle of them.

"Okay." I motioned for the children to give me room. "Time for the shark to go back to its home." With both hands, I lifted the torpedo-shaped fish, one palm flat under its body, the other hand grasping at its tail. The shark twisted powerfully, scraping me with its rough skin, but I held on. It had a lot of life left for a creature that had been out of its element so long.

"Cut the line," I said to Rick and, wordlessly, he sliced near the hook with his knife.

With the children close on either side of me, I stepped into the surf. I let the sand shark slide, half dropping it back into the water. For a second it lay motionless, as though unconvinced of its change in fortune, then it darted away. I wondered whether it could survive with a large hook jutting out of its jaw. I figured it would adapt.

Rick came up beside me, scratching his blond chest. "Amanda always was a bleeding heart," he said, chuckling. "Hey, that reminds me. Have you met our hostess yet? Althea or Anthea or something. Real time-warp, hippie chick, straight out of the sixties."

"I haven't met anyone yet," I said, watching Damien out of the corner of my eye. He had thrown his towel and ice aside and was holding Ryan by both hands, lifting him in and out of the shallow surf. The twins held hands beside them, jumping at each tiny ripple of foam.

"Well, wait till you meet Alfalfa, or whatever her name is." Rick laughed. "A real blast from the past. You'll appreciate her."

I looked up to see my father, barefoot now with his trousers rolled, coming toward us, waving to the grandchildren.

"Grandpa!" the kids called in a chorus as he approached, and he tipped his hat at them.

He shuffled over to where Rick and I stood. "Lizzie said you caught a shark." My father reached over to brush sand off my shoulder. I shifted my weight toward the water.

"Sand shark," Rick said. "Your daughter here couldn't stand to see the thing suffer."

"It still had the hook in its mouth!" I said. "The poor thing was bleeding, besides the fact that it couldn't breathe out of water."

"So you put a bleeding sand shark back into the ocean?" My father squinted into my sunglasses.

"What should I have done?" I asked, not wanting to hear.

"Well, I wouldn't swim out into that water anytime soon," he said, gazing thoughtfully toward the horizon. "You might attract a bigger shark now with that little, bleeding one."

"No!" I protested, looking at Rick.

Rick shrugged. "It's possible," he said. "Sometimes one small injury will create a feeding frenzy."

I looked at him, at the jut of his jaw as he stared across the sand, and was reminded of myself thirty years earlier. I felt my past beneath my present like an undertow, like a slow tide. My mother's illness had begun that way, with one small, nagging injury. Real or imagined, the results were the same. Something was destroyed—a tooth, a fish, a heart.

Rick's words echoed, inadvertently wise, and I suddenly understood how Lizzie could be persuaded by him. I wanted to grab his arm, to shake him and insist he tell me that in this specific instance the shark would survive, but instead I turned.

"Start lunch without me," I called as I began to walk. I imagined I could feel the air move as my father shook his head after me. I knew what he would think, what he always thought: Amanda was being temperamental.

Did he worry that one day soon I would come into my genetic inheritance, that I harbored in my very cells the imprint of my mother's illness? That those voices she'd heard would speak to me? Sometimes, especially recently, I wondered.

Despite those around me, I felt utterly alone.

I waded through the ebbing foam in the way I always had, toes curled up to make the most splash. I was furious with Keith for abandoning me, especially since I might be carrying his child. Look at what had just happened to our son!

But I hadn't told Keith I might be pregnant. I hadn't told my family about my marital estrangement. I couldn't speak of what I did not want to believe. And, despite my unhappiness, I couldn't believe my marriage would end. That I could lose my husband, or my life as I knew it.

All at once, I missed my mother, missed her as I had so many times before. I'd missed her that first beach vacation almost thirty years ago; missed her Saturday mornings when she couldn't get up to make us breakfast. I'd missed her at my hasty bridal shower; missed her when my babies had colic and kept me up all night; and missed her when Keith was out of town and I just wanted to talk. I'd missed my mother all the moments of my life when she hadn't been available to me.

And all those times, all those years, I'd always try to find a way to live without her. I would think I had found it and then, after a hospital stay or the simple passage of time, she'd come back. The bemused expression on her silly-sweet face would reveal that at least a part of her had returned, and I would be glad and need her all over again. I would depend once more on what I knew could never last.

But now she was truly, irrevocably, lost to me, just as my husband was lost to me, and I was lost myself.

CHAPTER 2

Late August—one year earlier
Long Island

Someone had taped a photograph above the hospital bed in which my mother lay, and it was the first thing I saw when Jeremy brought me to the room. Beneath it—our group shot from this year's beach vacation—my mother seemed almost asleep. Her undreaming face was a shell, particular as shells are, etched and shaped by the tumbling tides of the person she had been.

Except for the rhythmic, machine-induced rise and fall of her chest, she lay perfectly still, though some nuance in her fixed expression changed with each forced breath. Her cheeks grew minutely softer or perhaps they brightened. For a moment, I allowed myself to be fooled that those tiny modulations of flesh came from within.

My mother couldn't be dead.

The ventilator that supplied the air to her lungs was noisy; its hose resembled something that had been borrowed from a vacuum cleaner. I made myself look at where the tube entered the incision at the base of her throat. With each downward pump, the bellows seemed to express the tremendous effort required to keep a human being alive.

My mother looked dead.

She *had* died, having sustained a violent head injury in a car accident the day before, though her heart had been restarted and the ventilator kept her breathing. Her brain, however, was silent. Jeremy had explained this to me when he'd called me at home in Atlanta to convey the news: compressed by the trauma of the accident, her brain stem had been deprived of oxygen for too long.

I understood, but still some part of me would not believe it. How could it be true that my mother, with whom I'd sat on the beach only two weeks earlier, was gone? How could she be gone before I'd said good-bye?

I touched my lips to the place beside the bruise on my mother's forehead that was the one outward sign of the devastation within. Her skin felt dry and neutral, much as her kiss had felt against my cheek those times when her mouth had greeted me but her brain had been listening to other voices. A kiss without consciousness, I had described it once to Keith. Where was her consciousness now? Had it remained here with us, with her body; had it traveled somewhere else—or had it vanished entirely? I wanted to know, but no one could tell me. I wanted to know what she knew.

With my index finger I lightly stroked against the grain of the fine stubble of her shaved head, tracing a tiny arc in between the wires that led from her skull to one of several machines. Could she feel my touch? I wondered how the doctors had attached the electrodes those other times, when she'd had her hair. When she'd had her *treatments*. This ICU room was different from the psychiatric ward—that was a separate country.

I remembered with a sour twinge of guilt the relief I had felt as a teenager whenever she would go to the hospital. Then, for two or three or four weeks, our house would seem almost like other people's houses, almost normal—except we lacked a mother. But hadn't we lacked a mother even when she was there?

Those other times, in those other hospital rooms we visited, my father had acted oddly cheerful, planning her return home from the minute he delivered her bags. At her worst, he was at his best. I'd never forgiven him that.

Though I hadn't seen my father yet today, he was expected soon, and I dreaded that moment, dreaded his reaction to what had happened and what was to come. An old hostility stirred within me as I irritably anticipated his helplessness.

I fought the resentment, the residual anger that had been churning in me since my brother's phone call. My mother had done it again—

abandoned us—and again my father had done nothing to prevent it. I knew my feelings were unreasonable, but they were familiar and strong.

Now, stretching my neck over tubes and wires, I examined the photograph. I hadn't yet seen this year's group shot, hadn't even gotten my own roll of film developed. There we all were just two weeks earlier—Keith making bunny ears over Damien's head, Ryan laughing atop Rick's shoulders, Isabella angled toward Lizzie, and my parents crouched in front of all of us in the sand, my mother turned to speak to me. In profile, she looked distinct and undisturbed, not vague and tentative the way she photographed head-on. She looked as though something had just occurred to her, and she'd had to say it. What was it we had been talking about?

I said a few quick prayers now: that she not suffer in pain, that she return to us if she could but, otherwise, that she dwell in peace. I touched my mother's soft, gray-beige cheek and saw her haunted face as I'd seen it so many times before when her mind would leave us. My throat swelled. *Where are you this time?* I turned away.

In an unlit corner of the rectangular room that held only one bed, my mother's, but had been designed for two, Lizzie and Froggy sat on folding chairs, while Jeremy stood leaning against the window ledge. I walked over to them.

Lizzie was sitting forward, rubbing cream into her hands. As I stepped toward her, she offered me a tube of antibacterial lotion, which I accepted without thinking.

"Give it back to Frances when you're done," she said in a low voice. "It's hers."

I squeezed a grape-sized dollop onto my left palm, and snapped the cap closed with a thumb. As I rubbed, my hands grew warm, and I decided to massage some lotion into my mother's hands, just in case. Careful of the I.V. tube, I approached her right side, lifted her right hand, and lightly spread the cream. Her fingertips were chapped and nicotine stained, yet surprisingly soft. I held her hand in my own, hoping that somehow she knew I was there. I tried to recall our last phone conversation, searching her ordinary talk for clues that something was wrong, but found none.

I repositioned her right hand on the bed. For a moment, I had an urge to put a cigarette between her fingers.

Her left side intimidated me, with its more complicated tubes and wires, so I resisted lotioning that hand and returned to where the others sat. Froggy slipped the lotion into a plastic bag in her purse.

"That group picture came out nice and clear," I said to my brother as I wiped my fingers on a brown paper towel. I knew Jeremy had been the one to tape the photo to the wall.

Jeremy nodded. "Yeah," he said.

"I just got the film developed yesterday afternoon," Froggy explained.

I visualized her stopping at the camera store on her way home from work after hearing the news of the accident. *Frances is a very thorough person,* my mother had once said.

I looked back at my mother—at the body that had held my mother. I had never seen her so motionless. "Where was she going when it happened?" I asked.

Lizzie touched my arm. "We don't know," she said. Her puffy eyes met mine, and she broke into a small, nervous giggle. "No one knows. It's a mystery."

I turned to Jeremy. "Really?"

He shrugged, then shook his head. "She was doing well lately," he said, as though that explained something. "It happened at that light by the Texaco station on the turnpike, at the intersection there."

I envisioned her blue Ford, its hood collapsing like a folding picnic cup. "I know that. I just wonder where she was trying to go. Her destination."

Once more my brother shook his head.

The door clicked open and a stout, severe-looking nurse entered the room. We glanced at each other as she checked the machines, jotted numbers onto a chart, and then stepped toward Jeremy.

"Dr. Sanders has processed the health-care proxy and is ready for your decision whenever you are."

Jeremy nodded. "Thank you. My father will be back soon. And my sister just arrived." He extended his hand toward me.

The nurse assessed me. Her mouth was firm, but her eyes were kind. "The daughter from Georgia."

"Yes." I was impressed that she knew.

"A sad accident," she said as she smoothed the top page of her clipboard. "Your mother has no viable brain function." As though to prove her assertion, she leaned across the bed and raised one of my mother's eyelids. "Pupils fixed and dilated," she said. I stared with horrified fascination at my mother's hazel gaze.

"We know," Lizzie said in a voice that meant *stop*. She walked over to my mother's side and stroked her arm above the I.V. connection, as though to comfort her.

The nurse faced Lizzie. "Tomorrow, you'll be given the option of a feeding tube."

"No." Lizzie's voice was hoarse. Her head was bent, but it was evident she had started to cry. Her small hand cupped my mother's shoulder, causing her to tremble slightly. I was peculiarly grateful to see my mother move.

"We're going to discuss it tonight," Jeremy said. Froggy reached up to clasp his sleeve.

The nurse nodded, turned, moved toward the door. "It's never easy," she said. "But at least you have the proxy statement; at least you know what she wanted."

I pressed my palms against my eyes. *The last thing we knew was what she wanted.*

"So, we have decided." My father's voice was barely audible. "To do this . . . thing."

"Dad, it's your decision," Jeremy reminded him.

My father shook his balding head. "We must all agree."

We were sitting at a table for eight, though there were six of us, in the Greek diner across the street from the hospital. We had all turned out to be rapaciously hungry, except for my father, who used his fork only to move chunks of feta cheese around his salad.

"We do agree," I said. "There's not much choice."

My father moved the last piece of cheese so that each was equidistant from the rest. His left hand clasped his ice tea as though someone might take it away. His wedding ring slid up his finger, too big for him. Most men I knew found the opposite to be true, that their rings grew tight as they aged.

He looked up. "Are you sure we shouldn't wait?"

I glanced at Jeremy across from me, knowing he had been awaiting only my arrival to make the decision. "We were waiting for Amanda to get here," he said, taking my thought.

Lizzie was leaning against Rick's shoulder—he had gotten a sitter for the kids and joined us. We were all here now except Keith, home in Atlanta with Damien, and Isabella, who had just started school. They would come up for the wake and funeral. Thinking those words made my forehead tight.

"There's no hope," my father said. "I understand."

"She didn't suffer at all," Jeremy said.

"How do we know?" my father asked.

"The paramedics were on the scene within minutes and all her vital signs were shut down. You know this, Dad."

"Will they do it now, then? As soon as we go back?" My father's voice caught. He lifted his tea to his lips with a grimace as though it were medicine.

"Yes," Jeremy and Lizzie answered together.

"I spoke to the nurse about pain medication," I said.

"She isn't in pain. . . ." My father's voice rose.

"No," I answered quickly. "I mean during the . . . the stopping . . . just to be absolutely sure she feels no discomfort." I winced at my euphemism. *I can't bear the thought of her pain,* is what I meant.

"That's a good idea," Lizzie said. She had nestled under Rick's arm.

"Would they do that? Give her a painkiller?" Froggy wanted to know.

"The nurse assured me they would." I had approached her shortly after my father's arrival at the ICU.

"We'll need to get a few things," Lizzie said.

"Like what?" Rick lifted his head.

"Music and a tape player."

Jeremy nodded. "The *Three Tenors,* her favorite. We could light that sandalwood candle she liked."

The corners of my mouth tugged into a smile. Years earlier, my mother had fallen in love with the incense I burned and had asked for her own. "An open flame in the ICU?" I asked.

"Oh, right." Jeremy smirked. "I hate the stuff, anyway."

He'd always accused me of using incense to cover the scent of smoking pot, and he'd been right. I half wished for some now. "How about a bottle of wine?" I thought out loud. "We'd each take a small glass in her honor. She would like that." My mother enjoyed rituals, even those in which she didn't partake.

My father made a face. "We don't have any alcohol in the house."

"The anisette," Lizzie reminded him.

My father nodded. "We always keep a bottle of that."

"I'll go get it. I know where everything is." Jeremy stood and reached into his pocket for his wallet.

My father waved his hand at him. "I've got it," he said.

Froggy stood. "I'll go with you."

I watched them weave their way to the door, envious of their brief escape. My father got up to go to the rest room, leaving me his VISA card in case the waitress came. Rick began to finish the food on Lizzie's plate. She shifted to give him room and looked at me.

"I'm glad you're here," she said.

"Me, too," I said, giving her a small smile. "I just can't believe . . . of all her times in the hospital, it would happen this way."

"I know."

"Do you remember when she left that first time?" As I spoke the words, I recognized that the feeling I'd had then was exactly what I felt now: my mother was lost to me. Only this time was the last.

Lizzie shook her head. Rick stopped eating.

"You must have been four or five. She just disappeared. Took off for the city for two days. Finally she called and Daddy had to get her."

"Oh," Lizzie said, nodding, looking at her plate as though surprised to find her food gone.

I stared at nothing, at the young girl chewing her nails behind the cash register, at my father leaning against the wall outside the men's room. "All those times she wasn't there," I said out loud. "And now *we* have to do this."

Jeremy had forgotten to get cups. I noticed right away, but I didn't say anything. He'd remembered the anisette, the *Three Tenors* concert tape, and the tape player, and had returned quickly. We'd arrived at the hospital elevator just as he and Froggy did and we all rode up together, in silence, as though we'd reserved this three-floor trip to the

ICU in advance. As the elevator bumped to a stop and the doors whooshed open, I suddenly saw my mother on the other side. Or rather I saw her face, floating in the split-second vacuum of air created by the opening doors, and for a half-thought I was lost in time. It was the face I have carried with me from that moment on, the face I must have carried for years before: my youngish, soft-haired mother, her mouth a hard, broken line, her eyes two clouded marbles; the mother who sat smoking at the kitchen table while my father packed her suitcase for the mental hospital.

A new shift of nurses awaited us at the ICU. With the paperwork in place, we could remove the life support immediately. The nurses showed no surprise or alarm at our decision, but were efficiently complacent as they explained how and what they would disconnect.

"We need a few minutes," my father said.

"Let us know when you're ready," a young blond nurse answered in a sweet voice. Her manner reminded me of someone, I couldn't think who. Later in the car, I would realize it was my childhood neighbor and piano teacher, Gloria. The nurse left the room, which suddenly felt not airless and overheated but too cold.

We gathered in a circle around my mother's bed. Lizzie reached for my father's hand, he took mine, and I took Jeremy's. Froggy took Rick's and then we were all connected. "Our Father, who art in heaven, hallowed be thy name." Jeremy began the prayer, and we joined him. Lizzie said a "Hail, Mary" next. Then we were silent. All I could think of was *Now I lay me down to sleep,* the prayer that had terrified me throughout my childhood, but I didn't say it. Instead, I squeezed my mother's fingers. "I'm here," I told her silently, then turned toward the folding chair that held the tape machine. The tape was ready to go; I pushed "play."

Luciano Pavarotti's deeply tender voice filled the room. *"Non ti Scordar di Me,"* he sang—*Do Not Forget Me.* I tried to remember the English lyrics—*The swallows have left my cold, sunless country in search of spring violets.* My entire head filled with tears.

I uncapped the half-filled bottle of anisette, which had sat on a back shelf in my mother's pantry for probably ten years. She had offered me a drink of it once, which I'd accepted, on the afternoon I came to tell her I was moving to Atlanta. She hadn't reproached me for leaving the family—the only one who hadn't. I remembered the sun making the same four o'clock patterns on the kitchen table it always had and which I thought I might never see again. We'd drunk our anisette with cups of coffee that day.

Lizzie was bent over my mother now, whispering to her. Jeremy clutched his wife to his side, while his other arm hugged my father, a head shorter than he. I rejoined the circle next to Rick and tipped the bottle to my lips while the melody rose and fell. I could hear my mother humming the tune through the house on a good day. *There is always a nest for you in my heart.*

The sweet, licorice-flavored liqueur burned my lips, but I smiled through my tears. "This stuff is awful," I said, raising the bottle. "But you liked it, Mom. To you."

Rick took the next swig, then grimaced. "Bon voyage, Ma," he said, his face reddening, and passed the bottle to Lizzie.

Lizzie wiped her cheeks with her hand, and sniffed the bottle. "Yuck," she murmured before taking a tiny sip. She scrunched up her face, swallowed, and spread her fingers on my mother's arm. She whispered, "I love you, Mom."

My father's hands were shaking as he accepted the bottle from Lizzie. He took a noisy gulp, but he said nothing. Though I couldn't look at him, it seemed he held the liquid in his mouth a long time before swallowing, that it took all the effort he could summon to perform that simple, physical task. Finally, he bent to kiss my mother's cheek and passed the anisette to Jeremy, low and discreet.

Jeremy closed his eyes as though the bottle were a sacred vessel and stood holding it for a few seconds before raising it to his lips. "God bless you, Mother," he said. I heard the voice of the altar boy he had been, and suddenly I knew why he had been one and the tears ran down my chin.

Froggy gave him an odd look as he handed the anisette to her. I didn't yet know she was trying to get pregnant; I only noticed that she didn't really drink, just pretended to. Froggy moved her lips in silence, set the bottle on the floor beneath the bed where we ultimately would leave it, and bowed her head.

We were all touching my mother, our hands on whatever part of her we stood near, as Pavarotti's voice vibrated through our bodies—

Do not forget me—and the song came to an end. As I stood with my hands near my mother's feet, I wanted to lift the thin hospital blanket to see whether the nurses had put on her socks, but the possibility of her cold, bare toes—her bumpy, blue veins and thick, yellowed nails—wrenched my heart.

"I'll get the nurse now," Jeremy said softly, and another song began to play.

CHAPTER 3

THE SUN SHONE STRONGLY AND I LAY BASKING in it, my limbs stretched motionless on a chaise beside the pool as though I were trying to absorb clear light through my pores. I craved illumination, but for now I would settle for a tan. Even though I had gotten plenty of sun on the beach, I wanted to lie out, wanted to feel heat penetrate my bones, warming me to the core. My tightening skin signaled it was time to turn over, but at the moment I lacked the energy. If only I could lie still, I might dispel the queasiness at the bottom of my stomach.

"I had it first. Mom, make her give it to me!" Lauren or Lindsey's voice pierced the ambient splashing sounds from the shallow end of the pool, where Lizzie and her three kids struggled over the big float.

Froggy had gone to her cottage to put Jay down for a nap, my father had driven to town for the paper, and Rick had disappeared—probably to make a beer run. I should have gone back to my own cottage to unpack suitcases, but I couldn't face them or the melancholy dinginess of those cramped rooms. Why had I supposed I would play my violin here? I had hoped to lose myself in ocean sound and light, but instead, of course, I was surrounded by the very people who would never let me forget myself.

For now, I relished the opportunity to lie perfectly still and close my eyes, grateful Damien was at an age where I no longer had to pay attention every second as he practiced back flips off the diving board.

Soon enough he would call me: "Mom, watch this." I would turn over then.

We had come up from the beach after lunch and headed to the outdoor showers to wash the sand from our skin. Jeremy had jumped in the pool first, of course, followed by Damien. I detected a pattern emerging for the week, whereby Jeremy would play Damien's surrogate father and Damien would provide a practice son. I didn't mind, but I wasn't sure about Froggy's reaction once she caught on.

I had rinsed off, then succumbed to the lure of a sun-drenched chaise. Lunch, I thought, was to blame for my lethargy. I had eaten too much—one each of Jeremy and Lizzie's sandwiches, to please them; a dripping peach brought half jokingly by my father to remind me of my new home in the South, though I'd lived there eight years; and countless, absentminded handfuls of potato chips.

"Why don't *we* ever have potato chips for lunch?" Damien had asked, licking his lip where the salt must have stung his cut.

"They wouldn't taste as good if we had them all the time," I had answered, trying not to stare at his mouth, at the glimpses of broken tooth when he spoke.

"Everything tastes better at the beach," Jeremy said.

Lizzie agreed. "The salt air makes me hungry."

Then Rick had cracked, "What kind of air doesn't make you hungry?" and Lizzie had put down her sandwich and squeezed her eyes tight. She had always struggled with her weight, especially after each pregnancy, but she looked just fine to me. Her body had an appealing roundness I couldn't believe Rick didn't like.

My father had asked when I was going to call my dentist about Damien's tooth, and a discussion ensued wherein every Sinclair, born or wed, voiced an opinion about whether to cap the tooth or not. Even Ryan had a comment, "Toof bwoke," and briny tears had pooled again beneath my sunglasses.

All through lunch my father had watched me for signs to interpret in his quiet way and file in his silent system. I knew he did it—as a child I'd caught him watching me from the hallway outside my room or the basement stairs as I played piano—but what did he do with what he knew? How much could he tell from just looking?

Footsteps scuffed along the concrete pool deck, then a shadow

crossed my eyelids. I heard a familiar sigh to my right, opened one eye
a crack, and saw my father fold a newspaper in the lengthwise crease
of a New York commuter, a habit as old as I was. He hadn't taken the
train to work since the earliest years of his marriage, before he'd been
given the non-choice of running his father-in-law's business, but he'd
never changed the way he read his paper. I heard the scrape of metal
on concrete as he settled in an umbrella chair a few feet away.

I kept my eyes closed. My father was disinclined to make small
talk. He wouldn't be insulted by my quiet, but would be satisfied to
sit and read his paper in companionable silence. Only I didn't feel
companionable. I was, in fact, starting to feel that whatever I did, my
father was there, lurking in the corner of my vision, hovering but dis-
engaged. I felt a familiar irritation, and I winced. Forget all that for
now, I told myself.

Another shadow crossed my lids and stayed there, so I opened my
eyes. Jeremy stood over me, skin glistening from his swim, his straight
black hair, so like mine, slicked back and faintly striped with gray.

"You're blocking my sun," I said, squinting up at him.

"You're burning, anyway," he answered. "I want to show you something."

"Oh, no," I groaned as he pulled me up by my wrist. "No hurt animals, please. One bleeding shark a day is sufficient." I had always
been an animal lover, and Jeremy had always shown me animals: fallen
baby squirrels, stunned birds, stray dogs sniffing around the edges of
our yard when we were kids. My reaction was always double-edged:
eager, even excited to see something wild up close, and sad because the
creature was usually hurt or in danger and there was little I could ever
do.

"Christ, Mandy, when was the last time I found you an animal?"
Jeremy asked, using my childhood nickname as only he and Lizzie ever
did.

"I don't know," I said, my head heavy with sun. I reached beneath
the chaise for my sunglasses. "I guess I was thinking about Rick's
shark."

"Right. I can see how you would confuse me with Rick," he said.
His voice remained light, but now there was an edge to it.

"Would you keep an eye on Damien for me?" I asked my father, and he nodded, flipping green sunglass lenses down over his regular glasses.

He folded his paper in his lap and looked across the pool to the diving end. "He seems to be okay with that tooth," he said as I walked away.

Jeremy led me through the pool gate, up the slate path toward the white clapboard cottage that was the rental office. Someone had painted a life-size, black-headed gull on the front door. The artist had worked hard to get the bird's proportions right, but there was a child-like quality about the technique. I liked it as much as any painted gull I'd ever seen and wondered whether I would find its likeness for sale inside, perhaps on a T-shirt.

This cottage had only a crumbling stone stoop to welcome visitors, but it looked slightly larger than ours, increasing, if possible, the forlorn aspect of its sagging windows. Jeremy started up the steps.

"What are we doing?" I asked, thinking that in this way my brother was very like my husband—he liked to lead me places without telling me why, testing my trust.

"It's okay. I was here yesterday, when I checked us in. Athena *wants* the guests to visit, to scope out her stuff."

"Athena?" I asked. "Motherless daughter of Zeus? Virgin goddess?"

Jeremy laughed. "Well, she could be." He lowered his voice. "She has a son, though apparently no husband. She's our hostess. The owner of this fine establishment." He pulled open the door and stepped into a dim, mold-smelling room. A large golden retriever lay sleeping at the threshold, blocking the entranceway. It didn't budge as Jeremy stepped over it, only opened one eye and thumped its plumed tail against the sandy, wooden floor.

I followed Jeremy, stepping gingerly in my bare feet, wrapping my arms self-consciously around my bathing suit. A woman about my age, perhaps a little older, sat at a plain wooden desk to the right of the door. Her long salt-and-pepper hair hung in a thick, loose braid down her back. I wanted to look behind her and see if it reached her waist. She was wearing a gauzy, Indian print dress, a style that had been popular maybe twenty-five years ago.

"Hello," she said looking up, smiling at Jeremy. Her top front teeth crossed each other slightly, making her smile somehow more cheerful than had her teeth been straight. "I told you the weather would be good today."

"You were right," he said. "This is my sister." He stepped back, edging toward some lopsided shelves against the far wall.

"Amanda," the woman said before I could tell her my name. "The one I haven't met, from Georgia."

"Yes, hello," I said, starting to extend my hand. But her long fingers were woven together, her hands clasped on the desk in front of her, her wrists circled in silver bracelets. "Nice to meet you."

"I'm Athena," she said, smiling while her somber eyes examined my face. "Do you have children with you, a husband?"

"Just my son," I said. "Damien. He's ten."

"Oh, well, he'll have to meet Crosby, my son. He's eleven. You'll see him running around."

"Okay," I said. "Great." I bent to pet the dog. Its thick, caramel-colored fur was matted with salt and sand and the mustiness of this place. "Who is this?"

"That's Sunshine," Athena said, squinting slightly, seeming to evaluate something. "She's lazy unless motivated."

I knelt beside Sunshine to scratch her ears and she looked up gratefully, her large, brown, retriever eyes almost superhuman in their plaintiveness. Jeremy was kneeling, too, a few feet away next to a bookcase, rummaging through boxes.

"I wanted you to see this stuff," he said, glancing at me.

I stood up, wiped my dog-smelling hand on the hip of my swimsuit, and scanned the room. Something about this cottage reminded me of the basement of our childhood home, the house where my father still lived.

The phone on Athena's desk rang.

"Feel free to look around," she said, extending an arm that jangled with silver bracelets. "I make all the jewelry myself. Some of the other items are made by local artists, and some are from California, where we live during the off season." The phone rang again and she put her hand on the receiver as if to calm it. "Look around," she said once more before answering.

The dark room was crowded with dusty glass cases and cardboard boxes and tables piled high. At the far wall a doorway led into another room, and I made out that it was a kitchen, also crowded with stuff and clearly in use. Athena and Crosby lived in this cottage.

Sunshine sighed, shifted her weight, and stretched a front paw. I stepped over her. Jeremy was looking through a stack of board games. He glanced up as I bent over his shoulder, not wanting to kneel on the gritty floor.

"Look at this," he said, tilting a box cover for me to see. "Trivial Pursuit, Sixties Edition. We've got to play."

"I'm the only one old enough to remember anything from that time," I said. Keith would remember, I thought with a pang. I needed to call him, and Dr. Fox, but there were no phones in our cottages.

"*I* remember," Jeremy said, opening the box. "I remember the carefree days of the flower children. Here, ask me something."

I picked a card and read. "'Identify the following line: 'Excuse me while I kiss the sky.' "

Jeremy played air guitar, scrunching up his face. "Na-na-na, Na-na-na. 'Purple Haze,' Jimi Hendrix, of course."

"You were ten years old in 1968," I calculated as I returned the card.

"And you were twelve," he said. His green eyes locked onto mine. In 1968, our mother had returned home from her first stay in St. Mary's Psychiatric Hospital, three weeks that had turned into three months.

I moved away from Jeremy, toward the closest display case, through the heavy, stifling air that stirred like dust. None of the cottages was air-conditioned—the ocean breeze was enough if the windows were open, but these weren't. I touched my hand against the glass case, surprised to find it cool, and peered down at the jewelry. Most of the pieces were made of silver, some with semiprecious stones. It was the kind of jewelry I had once worn a lot of and Isabella wore now.

I spotted a ring with a deep blue stone, possibly lapis lazuli, that reminded me of a necklace of my mother's. What had happened to it? I had never thought to ask. My father had given me my mother's diamond engagement ring when she died, and Lizzie had gotten her pearls—jewels that neither of us wore. But what had happened to the blue necklace?

Athena finished taking a phone reservation, replaced the receiver, and crossed the room. She was sandaled in well-worn Birkenstocks. Her dress reached the top of her feet and seemed to sweep the dusty floor as she moved. Her braid bounced below her hips; she could probably sit on the tip of it. "See something you like?" she asked.

"That ring with the blue stone," I said, pointing. "How much is that?"

"Oh, that's a very special ring," she said, walking around behind the case to slide open the unlocked doors. She picked up the ring, slid it onto her own finger, and then held her hand out for me to admire. "I didn't make this one. Mostly, I make earrings and bracelets." She took the ring off and handed it to me. "Seventy-five dollars."

I nodded, turning the ring between my thumb and forefinger. The thick, silver band was plain, its only embellishment a narrow row of beading around the oval, deep blue stone. I liked the ring's simplicity. "Is it lapis lazuli?"

"Oh, yes," Athena said. "See the tiny flecks of gold? That's how you can tell."

I turned toward the window, examining the ring in the weak light around the edges of the dark curtains. The silver had tarnished to a muted gleam. I slid the ring down the fourth finger of my right hand where it stuck on my knuckle. Disappointed, but not wanting to force it, I took it off.

"The ancients used lapis lazuli for healing," Athena said as she came out from behind the glass case to stand beside me. "Why not try it on your left hand?"

I glanced at my wedding rings, platinum-and-diamond antiques Keith had bought at auction, then slipped them off. The lapis lazuli ring slid all the way down on that finger, the wide silver band filling the whole white space that my wedding rings had taken up.

Jeremy stood now, holding up a small box. "You've got some great tapes," he said to Athena. "Can I borrow this one? It's Crosby, Stills and Nash, the first album."

"Sure," Athena answered, moving her hands with a soft jingle as she spoke. "Everything in that bookcase is for the use of our guests. But please return it. I've had that one a long time." She began to move around the room, jingling, touching things, drawing my attention to ceramic mugs and T-shirts and plastic pails and shovels. I didn't see the laughing gull from the front door.

"Do you need anything else?" Athena asked me. "Some sand toys or sunscreen? You've gotten some sun."

Her own skin was pale, as though she spent every day inside. She probably did, in this cottage, with the ocean and the dunes and the sky right outside her door. I breathed in the room's mustiness, and my stomach grew queasy again.

I pulled off the lapis lazuli ring, laid it on the glass case, and replaced my wedding rings. "I'll have to think about it," I told her.

"All right," Athena said, setting the ring on the top shelf of the case. "Come back later, bring your sister."

Jeremy looked up from the box of tapes. "Maybe Frances would like something," he said, and a small stab of annoyance shot through me. He was too good, always thinking of what his wife would like. I couldn't imagine Keith making a mental note that I might want to buy a trinket, nor that he would need to.

"Oh," I said aloud at the thought of Keith. Athena had sat down again behind her desk, her long fingers folded in front of her. I approached her, the sides of my feet brushing Sunshine's thick fur, eliciting a low groan of pleasure.

"Is there a phone I could use with my credit card number?" I asked Athena, my fingertips resting on the smooth, worn edge of her desk. "I need to make a couple of long-distance calls."

"Around back, by the laundry building, there's a pay phone," Athena said. "But if you're going to use a credit card, you might as well use this phone here. Make all the calls you need to."

"Thanks," I said, trying to remember Dr. Fox's number. I couldn't. "I'll have to call Atlanta information first." I would wait to call Keith later in private from the pay phone. I'd tell him what Dr. Fox said, using her prognosis as the reason for my call. I would wait until tonight, when I hoped I would find Keith at home.

CHAPTER 4
June, Atlanta

THE NIGHT I FOUND OUT ABOUT KEITH'S NEW FRIEND, we were drinking Montrachet. He had just returned from a week-long business conference in San Francisco, and I had prepared a nicer-than-usual dinner of grilled shrimp and vegetable risotto. Keith ate as he always did, quickly and without speaking, which I interpreted as approval. As we finished our meal, Keith opened a second bottle of wine. Damien ran off to play outside with the neighbor kids—it was late June and the sun was still bright—and I leaned back, in no hurry to clear the table.

"So, what was your week like?" Keith asked, looking past me toward the French doors that led to our yard.

I shrugged, feeling my face glow with wine. "Nothing unusual," I said. "Spoke to Isabella. She seems to be settling in to her job at the lab. Damien has had swim team every day, a meet on Tuesday; his team won." I continued listing the news I thought might matter to him, leaving out most of what I'd done or thought. I didn't mention the book I was reading or the notecards I had painted or the dreams I'd been having about playing the violin. I had been thinking of picking it up again.

I studied Keith's profile and took a sip of the remarkable wine, one he usually saved for rare occasions. "And Lizzie called," I remembered. "About the plans for August."

"Ah," Keith said. "How is your family?"

"In character," I answered. "Rick is acting like a big shot now that he's officially running Dad's business. Lizzie can't bear it. Froggy is more anal compulsive than ever, though apparently Jeremy takes care of the baby more than she does. She really timed it right, giving birth just as my brother finished the spring semester. They still want to do the beach; Jeremy is handling all the plans this year."

I stopped myself there, though I could have gone on indefinitely until he stopped me, the way I did with Lizzie when we spoke on the phone. Keith was playing with the empty shrimp tails on his plate, peeling them apart and making two piles.

"Do you think you'll be able to come to the beach with us?" I asked.

Keith considered the shrimp tails, then moved several from one pile to the other, making them even. "I'm not sure," he said. He glanced quickly at me. "Depends on how things go."

I knew he meant at work. Keith was the chief actuary at Stone & Stone, a large corporate insurance company. He had just spent a week at a conference about team building and executive burnout. "So, how was the conference?" I asked, smiling. "Are you unburnt?"

Keith glanced at his forearm and frowned. "Not really," he said. "We spent most of the time inside."

I burst into a giggle, spitting wine over myself. "No." I laughed. "*Un*-burnt, as in un-burned-out, you know. Renewed." I was starting to feel lightheaded. I motioned for the wine bottle and Keith slid it across the table toward me.

"Better have some more," he said, his dimple flashing. "To clear your head."

I poured another two inches of wine and raised my glass. "To clarity," I toasted.

Keith smirked and the muscles in his jaw twitched; I knew he had been about to say something, but thought better of it.

"So, tell me about the New Beginnings Conference," I said. "Was it painful?"

"Not really," he answered, pushing his plate away and leaning forward on our old pine farmer's table. He traced a deep scratch with his finger. "It was actually not bad in some ways."

I moved my chair around the corner of the table so I was sitting beside him. I rested my hand on his thigh and leaned my head against his upper arm, breathing in my favorite combined scent of fabric softener and Keith's deodorant. "Like what ways?" I asked.

Keith shifted to face me, and I had to raise my head from his arm. "Well," he said. "You know I read that guy Dorsey's book, *The Nine Secrets to Unleashing Potential.*"

I nodded. I had seen it on his night table, assuming Tripp Stone had forced it on him. Our reading habits were typical of most of the couples we knew: I read only fiction, Keith read only nonfiction.

"So Dorsey was there—the guy's making a fortune on this thing—and he led the main stage sessions. Then we did breakout sessions, small groups to discuss issues or do team-building exercises."

"Uh-huh," I said, hurt because he had moved away from my touch. "So what was interesting?" I leaned across the table for my wine, and Keith ran his fingers down my back. I took a long sip and pressed up against him once more.

"Dorsey's ideas," Keith said, his chin moving against the top of my head. "Nothing really original, more like a distillation of major schools of thought. But the way he's synthesized it all into practical applications is pretty impressive." Keith took my glass from me and drained it.

"So tell me a secret," I said, sliding my fingers under the short sleeve of his polo shirt.

"What?" Keith's arm stiffened slightly.

"One of the secrets, one of the nine secrets to unleashing."

"Oh." The corners of Keith's mouth curled. "But that's the point of secrets. You can't tell them." He lowered his eyes in a gesture that alerted me.

"Tell me!" I said, squeezing his arm. "I'll tell you a secret, too."

Keith poured the rest of the wine into the nearest glass, mine, and drank it in one long swig. His face flushed. I touched his cheek with my hand: his evening stubble felt sharp. We had been married for nearly twenty years, but suddenly my husband seemed mysterious, male.

"Tell me, please," I said in a low voice, my mouth against his shoulder, acting drunker than I was. "Tell me something I don't know." I felt a pleasant tingle of thrill, like the split second before take off when flying or diving under a wave.

"Okay," Keith said, shifting again in his chair. "I'll tell you something." My stomach tensed at his tone. He picked up a shrimp tail and cracked it between his thumb and forefinger. "I met someone interesting in San Francisco," he said.

I pulled back, away from him, and looked at his face in disbelief. "Who?" I asked, searching the darkening blue of his eyes for signs of teasing. "Male or female?"

Keith looked away, out the French doors again, so that it was the back of his head I was seeing, thinking he needed a haircut, when he answered. "Female."

That night I was ravenous for Keith, unable to get enough of him, as though he were going off to war and I needed to amass a lifetime of memories in an hour.

"Do I know her?" I asked him as we climbed the stairs to our room.

"No," he said and told me about her. She was a senior account manager whose director position had been eliminated in a recent downsizing and now reported to someone who had once been her peer. Keith had met her in a team-building session; gradually, they'd found they had grievances in common.

"How is she interesting?" I wanted to know before I even asked her name. "Is she attractive?"

"It isn't like that," Keith assured me in a voice I found anything but reassuring. He hadn't slept with her, he said, didn't think of her that way. She was a colleague and becoming a friend, the first person at Stone & Stone who'd been honest with him in a long time. Her *ideas* were interesting, he explained, the things she wanted to do.

"What does she want to do?" I asked, forming ideas of my own.

But Keith wouldn't talk any more about her. "You're jealous," he said, as if he hadn't anything to do with it. As if that dismissed it.

I unbuttoned the top of his pants and ran my finger inside the elastic of his boxers. I bent to press my lips against the curls below his navel. "I just want what's mine," I said, licking him. He pulled me up and kissed me hard.

"So what does she look like," I whispered as he unhooked my bra. "Does she have nice tits?"

"Cut it out," he said. But I thought about her, about them, the entire time. I imagined how he'd been slow at first to recognize she was hot for him, how he'd tried to resist. How he'd been tortured.

"You're torturing yourself," Keith said when afterward I asked how old she was. But then he told me. Thirty-four.

We were still in bed when Damien came thumping through the front door from outside. I lifted my head and saw that it was dark. He probably wondered why I hadn't called him in. His footsteps trailed into the kitchen where the table remained laden with dinner dishes. Not like me to leave them.

"Mom?" he called. "Dad?"

I jumped up and scrambled into Keith's shirt. Keith groaned and rolled onto his side.

"We're upstairs," I called from the landing outside my room, tugging the shirt hem against my thighs. "Daddy's tired after his trip."

"Oh," Damien grunted, opening the refrigerator. "Do we have any ice cream?"

Keith was sleeping by the time I finished cleaning the kitchen and got Damien settled after his dessert and shower. My head was throbbing with wine and sex and smoldering anger, so I searched the bathroom for a bottle of Advil. Finding none, and recalling Keith's suitcase on the bedroom floor, I thought to check his toiletry travel kit. It did contain a bottle of Advil, along with the usual toothpaste, razor, and deodorant. But there was something else I didn't remember Keith ever using.

Breath mints. I ate one and began to cry.

The next morning he told me her name. Sarah. Sarah Stein. My spirit sank as soon as I heard it. *How alliterative,* I said. Sarah was one of my favorite names. If I'd had another child, a girl, she might have been called Sarah. But now I had to hate the name Sarah. I had trouble even saying the syllables out loud, so thereafter I referred to her as *your friend.* "Does *your friend* eat breakfast?" I asked, trying to catch Keith. He didn't eat in the morning.

"Cut it out," he said.

"Does *your friend* work on the seventh floor?" "Will you be meeting *your friend* for lunch?" "What color eyes does *your friend* have?"

"Please stop it," Keith said each time.

We were sipping coffee at the kitchen counter. Damien had gulped down a bowl of cereal, then gone to the basement to play video games. It was a beautiful, clear morning, and I wanted to do something outdoors, a family activity. I thought of the pool club, but Damien and I had been there every day this week for swim team practice, and Keith disliked the weekend crowd. I thought of bike riding; we should go before it got too hot.

"Do you feel like going for a bike ride, the three of us?" I asked Keith.

He shrugged. "I guess so."

"Did you bike at all in California?"

"No." He selected a piece of mail from the pile on the counter.

"Well, what fun things did you do while you were there?"

Keith looked at me with narrowed eyes. "I don't know," he said. "The usual company crap. I played golf. There was a boat ride."

"Did your friend go on the boat ride?"

"Everyone went."

"But did you go with her? Did you hang out together?"

"We talked, yes. Cut me some slack, okay, Amanda? Don't be a shrew."

My anger was palpable now: it was a hard fist in the center of my chest. I felt it expanding, the fist opening, and I wanted to scream.

"What are you doing?" Keith asked as he went through the mail. "Why are you pushing me?"

"What am *I* doing?" I replied, seething. "You're the one who dangles this new *friend* in front of me, then refuses to talk about her. What am I supposed to think?"

Keith threw an envelope against the counter and it slid to the floor, his American Express bill. "How can I talk to you?" he asked angrily. "I can't say anything to you without you overreacting." He strode to the door that led to the garage. "I'm going for a ride, alone," he said, lifting his bike helmet from its hook.

"Go," I said in a voice that he probably couldn't hear as I bent for the envelope. He pulled the door closed with a loud thud. I tore open the monthly statement and scanned it, looking for anything out of the ordinary and quickly realizing that the dates would be wrong. The San Francisco charges wouldn't have gone through yet. I tossed the pages onto the floor. Let Keith pick up after himself!

And then I felt my face drain white and I grew dizzy. I could have sworn I smelled a cigarette, could have sworn I stood in my mother's kitchen.

Chapter 5

RICK SURPRISED US ALL WITH A BUSHEL OF LOBSTERS he had bought down at Gossman's dock for our dinner. He'd gotten some local corn, too, the first of the white and yellow "ladies and gentlemen" variety we all loved best, and a case of beer. Maybe his true mission had been a beer run after all, I thought cynically as I opened a bottled water and tilted it to my lips. Then I reconsidered. Rick didn't have to bring back lobster—especially without collecting money from the rest of us. Maybe he was trying to make up to Lizzie for that crack at lunch about her hunger. She had seemed pleased, anyway, to let her husband take over the meal arrangements, pleased that he had made a gesture her family would appreciate.

Only Lauren seemed disappointed about something, frowning as she and Lindsey spread paper tablecloths over the redwood picnic tables we had pushed together. With Rick's help, Jeremy had carried over the table from his deck so that we could eat our meals all together, on my deck.

"Sinclair Central," Jeremy had dubbed my cottage for its location between his and Lizzie's (my father's cottage was near the road), and for its supposedly superior view of the ocean beyond the pool and the rise of the dunes. But Rick was sitting with his back to the view, drinking a beer and listening to the Crosby, Stills and Nash tape playing on Jeremy's boom box while the lobsters steamed in their seaweed wraps on the charcoal fire. Jeremy and Damien were shucking corn behind the cottage, and Froggy was inside feeding Jay his bottle. My father was inside, too, having volunteered to make the salad. I was counting out plastic plates from a shopping bag beside the door.

"I can't believe Daddy went to the dock without us today," Lauren whined to her sister as they pulled at either end of the paper tablecloth, trying to make the edges even.

"I know," Lindsey answered with an identical pout. "And we were stuck doing *nothing* all afternoon."

Rick ignored them, leaned back in his chair, and crossed one sneaker-clad foot over the other on the edge of the table, moving his toes to the rhythm of "Marrakesh Express."

"Daddy!" Lauren cried, and as Rick pulled his feet off the table, the paper cover tore.

"That's disgusting, feet on a table," Lindsey said, covering the tear with a napkin, and I could hear young Lizzie in her daughters' admonishments—Lizzie before she had learned to quiet herself. The twins ran off the deck, and around behind the cottage.

As I thought of her, Lizzie appeared, walking lopsided down the path from her cottage, with Ryan on her hip, though he was getting too big for her to carry. He was damp and scrubbed pink from his bath, and Lizzie was all pink herself, wearing an ankle-length, hot pink T-shirt that said *Laughing Gull Cottages* in italics across the front. It reminded me of something my mother might have had in her closet.

Lizzie and Froggy had gone over to peruse Athena's wares during Ryan's afternoon nap. "Going shopping," Lizzie had said, but I hadn't joined them. Instead, I'd staked a claim on a chaise by the pool, lazily watching Damien's perfected back flips. Now and then I'd thought about the lapis ring, envisioning it on my left hand. The daydream had developed—a small house near the ocean, a life without Keith—until it scared me.

"How are the lobsters doing?" Lizzie asked as she thumped up the two steps to the deck and plopped Ryan into Rick's lap.

"Simmering in their shells as we speak," Rick answered, smiling over Ryan's damp blond curls.

"A stroke of divine inspiration." I was moved by the sight of father and son in the fading summer light. Rick was nice looking. It was something I frequently forgot in my general distrust of him. I felt a pang for my son whose father was absent, and for the embryo whose cells might be dividing inside me at this moment.

I took the last gulp of my water and looked away from Rick and Ryan, across the pool, past the dunes, to the sea. How gentle it looked from here, how exotic. We could be in Marrakesh.

"Do you like my whatever this is, long T-shirt?" Lizzie asked me, spreading her arms.

"Beach cover-up?" I offered. "Yes, I like it. It looks comfortable." I felt the roughness of my own T-shirt against my sunburned shoulders, felt the skin of my face pull tight as I spoke.

"The color is a bit bizarre," Lizzie admitted, looking down at the fabric. "It was so dark in that office, I didn't realize how pink this really is!"

The screen door to my cottage groaned, and out stepped my father, carrying a large plastic salad bowl. He held the door open with his shoulder, and Froggy followed him out, carrying two bottles of Australian Chardonnay and a corkscrew.

"Jay's asleep!" she announced. "And I'm off duty. When he wakes up, it's Jerry's turn."

I had never gotten used to her calling my brother Jerry, but she did, as did his colleagues at the junior college where he taught biology. But then Froggy probably didn't know that Lizzie and I referred to her by Jeremy's pet name for her, nor that we knew its origins. (Her legs, long and shapely like a frog's, had been one of the first things Jeremy had told us about her, ten years earlier, when we'd all had too much to drink after visiting our mother during one of her stays at Saint Mary's.) We called Froggy Frances to her face, and Froggy to each other, almost always.

"My turn for what?" Jeremy asked now as he came around the corner of the cottage, carrying a pot of shucked corn. Damien followed, carrying an identical pot and arguing with the twins.

"I cleaned most of them, I get to carry them," he was saying, stomping up the deck. "Who asked you to help, anyway?"

Lauren and Lindsey were scowling on either side of him.

"Your turn for everything, the rest of the night," Froggy said suggestively as Jeremy walked past her into the cottage. "Could you bring out the wineglasses, please, Jer."

"I don't think this cottage is equipped with wineglasses," I told her, taking the pot of corn from my son. "We'll just have to use the same plastic ones." I nodded at the stacks of acrylic dishes and cups on the tables.

"These match the rustic decor," Rick offered. "And the ambiance." He chuckled, pleased with himself.

"Okay, young ladies, let's finish setting the table," my father said to the twins. "You know, tablesetting was your mother's specialty when she was your age."

Lizzie groaned, and I followed Jeremy into the tiny kitchen of the cottage. I put the corn on the stove to boil, while Jeremy rummaged idly through the cabinets. He would want to see whether my cottage held anything his didn't. Suddenly the screen door banged open and Damien pushed past me, tramping noisily through the kitchen and the living room to the back bedroom where he slept.

Jeremy looked at me, his eyebrows raised.

"Mom," Damien called from his room, "why is this baby on my bed?"

"Sssh!" I answered, hurrying back there. "Jay's asleep, Damien. *Please.*"

"Well, why is he asleep in my room?" Damien asked, and I pulled him through the doorway.

"Because, this cottage is where we're all eating dinner. The baby has to be close by so Aunt Frances and Uncle Jeremy can hear him if he cries."

"Why do they all have to eat at our cottage? Now I can't even go in my own room."

"You don't need to go in your room. We're having dinner in a few minutes."

"Will they move him after dinner?" Damien asked.

"I don't know," I said, doubtful. "Let's not worry about it right now."

"What's the problem?" Jeremy asked.

"Nothing," Damien answered, then stomped off.

"I'm sorry," I said. "He's probably tired."

Jeremy laughed. "Who isn't? Come on, those lobsters should be almost ready."

Out on the deck, Rick had moved the lobsters to one side and was grilling hot dogs for the kids. Damien was sulking on the bottom step, arms crossed over his chest. I knew he would want a lobster. He was used to going everywhere with Keith and me, used to adult food and adult attention and not having to share anything with siblings. He and Isabella were nine years apart, she having been the most memorable result of my senior year in college. It was as though I'd had two only children.

I lowered myself next to Damien on the bottom step. Immediately, mosquitoes began biting my ankles.

"Ow," I said, drawing my legs under me. "Are you getting eaten alive?"

Damien shrugged.

"How's the tooth?" I asked. "And the lip?"

"Okay," he murmured. He touched a finger to his mouth, as if to test it.

"Dr. Fox said it will be sore for a while, that it's normal. When we get back to Atlanta, she'll fix it to look just like the other one."

"I don't want it to look like the other one," he said. "I want it to look like it was."

I smiled. He was giving me a hard time—in Damien as in Keith, a sign of reviving spirits.

"I can't eat a whole lobster," I said. "Will you share it with me?"

Damien turned his face to mine, scowling. "Why do the kids get hot dogs?" he asked. "It's not fair!"

"Maybe your cousins don't eat lobster," I suggested. "Uncle Rick probably didn't realize how spoiled you are."

Damien slugged me in the arm, almost softly, then he let me lead him to the table where he graciously ate a hot dog, two ears of corn, and half my lobster triple-dipped in melted butter.

The light faded through the trees to the west behind us and the air cooled and the wine warmed our insides and we sat, eating and drinking and laughing about nothing that mattered, though I didn't allow myself more than half a glass of wine. For once no one was insulted or insulting, no tears were shed. We ate till we were full, lobster and corn and salad and crusty bread, till our fingers were so slippery with butter we couldn't hold on to our glasses. When the bottles were empty, Froggy brought out more.

Ryan fell asleep in his chair, and Damien, lacking alternatives, played card games with the twins at the far end of the table. My father found a couple of citronella candles under the sink, and he lit them, and we sat as the moon rose, a wafer of ice against the sky. We shivered in our thin cotton clothes and our sunburned skin.

Then Jeremy jumped up. "We need a bonfire!" he proclaimed, and I remembered that I needed to call Keith.

A white stone path led around the side of the Laughing Gull office, Athena's cottage, to the laundry, housed in a building that might have once been a guesthouse. I was carrying a flashlight, handed to me by Jeremy so I could find my way to the bonfire after I called Keith. "Just a backup," he said. "Since my bonfire will light up all of Montauk." In fact, I scarcely needed the flashlight, but it wasn't my brother's fire lighting up the path of crunching stones beneath my feet—it was the moon.

In front of the pay phone at the side of the laundry building, I lifted my face to the moon's radiance and stood still under its glow. I imagined I could feel its forces, pulling at me. The circle wasn't quite complete, not yet full. Maybe by the end of the week, by the time I returned to Atlanta, the August moon would work its changes upon my internal tide.

I laid the flashlight on top of the phone and punched in the numbers of my credit card, hesitating over the digits of my own number. For a moment my mind went blank and I couldn't remember what came last. Nine. That was it. After four rings, our answering machine picked up, and Keith recited our phone number with a slightly husky impatience. My heart automatically leapt at the sound of his voice.

Then, immediately, I flushed with anger. Where was he? I hung up and looked at my watch. Eight-thirty. He would be out having dinner somewhere. Would he be with her? I imagined Keith leaning forward across a small, round table, talking animatedly. I could see the way his forehead creased in thought, the way the corners of his mouth pulled up when he stretched the truth. But I couldn't see her, his friend, because I'd never met her. I hoped her hair wasn't long and dark like mine. Then I hoped it was.

I wanted to tell Keith about Damien, about the rocks in the ocean that had not been there before, although now that Dr. Fox had assured me the tooth could wait a week or two to treat, the news seemed less than urgent. What else did I need to say? All I could think of was what I hadn't said before I'd gone—why had I left without telling him?—but I couldn't talk about that now, on the phone. I couldn't leave a message on our answering machine. "Oh, by the way, I forgot to mention that my period is late." I pressed my abdomen against the hard edge of the phone cubicle, testing for bloat.

I dialed our number again, practicing "hello" out loud as the phone rang. I wanted my voice to sound casual, warm, to let the anger out of it.

"Hi, it's me," I said, smiling in the dark like an actress. I left a message telling Keith about Damien's tooth, saying I'd phone again tomorrow. Perhaps the combination of warm voice and bad news would make him feel guilty for suggesting this week as time apart. For not changing his mind.

I hung up the phone and picked up the flashlight, breathing deeply to relieve the tension at the bottom of my throat that was not quite nausea. My hand pressed my left breast, testing for tenderness, but feeling only sunburn. I shivered and decided to go back to my cottage for a sweatshirt before heading to the beach.

I walked past Athena's cottage. As though she had been expecting me, Athena stepped out from the back door, silhouetted against the yellow light from inside. The bulky shape at her side was Sunshine; I could see the wave of her tail as I came up the path.

"Another phone call?" Athena asked without greeting. I heard amusement in her voice.

"Yes," I answered, feeling caught. I pointed vaguely in the direction of the dunes, not wanting to stop to talk. "We're having a bonfire," I said.

"I know," she answered. "Great night for it."

I nodded and kept my eyes on the circle of flashlight beam in front of me as I walked.

"Amanda."

I stopped, looking back at the dark shape of Athena's braid falling over her shoulder as she leaned against the railing. Her bracelets jingled softly when she moved her hands.

"I meant to tell you," she said in a voice so low I had to step closer. "Lapis lazuli is a sending stone. It has wonderful properties for communication."

I stood, focusing my eyes on her face, not knowing how to answer. The waves beyond the dunes seemed to crash louder now, as though their sound was my own pulse, drumming in my ears.

"I just wanted you to know that," Athena said. "Stop by tomorrow, if you like." She turned and disappeared inside her cottage, Sunshine along with her. What was her point—that the lapis ring could help me communicate with Keith? That would require more than a blue stone.

I hurried toward the beach, my skin prickling with goose bumps, eager for flames.

The path to the beach followed the natural undulations of the dunes, so it wasn't until I came over the last rise and was almost upon it that I saw the fire—a brightness leaping up out of the dark, an eruption of light and heat. I stopped, thrilled and wary, taking in the scene. Jeremy was standing, presiding over the flames, while Froggy, Lizzie, and Rick sat on a log drawn up to face the bonfire and the nearly invisible, pounding ocean beyond it. Damien and the twins knelt next to Jeremy, blowing at toasted marshmallows on the ends of sticks.

I clicked off my flashlight as I joined them, sliding next to Lizzie, who moved closer to Rick to make room for me. Froggy sat at the far end, her long legs stretched out in front of her, bare toes buried in the sand.

"Beautiful fire," I said. "I thought the wood might still be wet after all the rain."

"Don't forget I have Boy Scout training," Jeremy answered, picking up a piece of wood from a stack in the darkness behind him. "I can start a fire under any conditions."

"Yeah," said Rick as he opened a can of beer. "As long as you bring dry wood from home."

Lizzie sighed.

"Did he?" I asked.

"I brought some," Jeremy answered quickly. "As backup. But most of this is driftwood I collected this morning."

"Who cares what wood it is?" Lizzie said, her frown lit by the flames.

Lindsey gave a little shriek and ran over to her mother. "My marshmallow fell!" she cried.

"Disaster!" Lizzie reached behind her for a bag. "Here, take the rest."

Lindsey snatched the bag of marshmallows from Lizzie's hand and skipped toward her sister, dangling it.

"Share them!" Lizzie warned.

"I want some, too," said Damien. "I'll toast one for you, Mom."

"Thanks," I said, though I really wasn't in the mood for anything sugary, except, perhaps, for the high, sweet notes of my violin. Those I suddenly craved. I decided to play when I got back to my cottage.

"I'll toast a marshmallow for Daddy," Lauren offered.

"I'll take one," Froggy chimed in, reaching. "Will you roast me a marshmallow, Jerry?"

I felt Lizzie stiffen, and knew she was rolling her eyes, though I didn't look at her. Her mood had darkened since dinner, the effects of Rick's lobsters worn off. Maybe I had missed something. I leaned back, my fingers splayed in the cool sand behind me. The fire's intense heat was hurting my sunburned face, yet my back felt cold. I tried to find the right position, some middle space between fire and night air, but it didn't seem to exist, or it was too narrow for me to occupy.

Jeremy's face was half in shadow, lit like an actor in a German Expressionist film. He was toasting a marshmallow for Froggy, turning the stick slowly, concentrating, I knew, on achieving a perfect, even brown without any burned spots. Damien, on the other hand, loved his marshmallows quick and black. He carried one over to me, the charred lump hanging dangerously from the tip of his stick. I plucked the gooey mass before it could drop, popping it whole into my mouth without thinking.

"Mmph!" The liquefied center of the marshmallow scorched the inside of my mouth. Lizzie lifted Rick's beer from his hand and passed it to me. "I'm okay," I said waving the can away. "Thanks."

Damien ran back to his cousins and the remaining marshmallows, and as he skirted the fire I remembered another bonfire, years earlier, when I had pulled a six- or seven-year-old Lizzie back from the flames as she leaned too close and her hair began to singe. I had been a young teenager, chronically sullen, irritated with my father for taking me to the beach and away from my friends. My mother had been with us that time, had been sitting next to me, in fact, smoking a cigarette under a star-filled August sky. But she hadn't been paying attention to Lizzie, only to the drama playing itself out inside her head.

"Remember the year you burned one side of your hair?" I reminded my sister. "Where were we that year, Hampton Bays? Dad cut the other side to make it even, but he made it worse."

"Sag Harbor," Lizzie said. "How could I forget? You made me do you favors the entire week, telling me you'd saved my life."

Damien stepped closer to the circle. "My dad saved my life once," he said. "I was two and a half, and I fell into someone's pool at a party at night. My dad dived in with his shoes on and saved me."

I pulled my sweatshirt sleeves down over my hands. Damien had the story right. Except that no one had seen him fall, and it was his own instinct to hold his breath that kept him from immediately swallowing water. Keith had happened to turn, reaching for an hors d'oeuvre, when he saw Damien's little body thrash. If he'd looked anywhere but exactly there at that moment, Damien might have drowned. As it was, he had been perfectly fine, not even particularly shaken.

"Were you scared?" Lauren asked.

"Nah," Damien answered. "I did the doggie paddle."

That was new to me.

Froggy stood, picking up a folded blanket she had been sitting on, draping it around her shoulders like a cloak. She moved next to Jeremy, who presented her with a golden-brown marshmallow on a stick.

"I can't imagine that happening to Jay," she said in a tone that made me think she meant she couldn't imagine herself ever behaving so negligently. She blew on the marshmallow, then sniffed it.

"All kids have accidents; everyone does," Lizzie said, then stopped abruptly. I knew she was thinking of our mother, of the accident that had killed her barely a week after our beach vacation last summer.

Rick crumpled his beer can in his hand and tossed it onto the sand in front of him. He shifted left on the log, away from Lizzie, taking up the space where Froggy had been sitting. "Kids are tough," he said.

"It's us parents who are basket cases," Jeremy replied.

"Too bad Dad isn't here for this fire," I said. I dug into the cool sand and let it sift through my fingers. After dinner, my father had offered to stay behind in Lizzie's cottage with the sleeping Ryan and little Jay. He was being nice, grandfatherly—or self-sacrificing? He loved bonfires.

"At least Dad's here," Jeremy pointed out.

"It's funny how much I miss Mom," Lizzie said. "Considering how many of these vacations she didn't make."

A log sizzled and shifted.

"We have to discuss something," Froggy said, licking her fingers and pulling the blanket tighter around her. She wasn't addressing Jeremy, but he nodded and then looked at me.

"We have a problem about the arrangements, Mandy," he said. He prodded the end of a log with his sneaker and sparks flickered up.

"What arrangements?" I asked, leaning forward. I had no idea what he could mean.

"Dad's cottage. He can have it only until Wednesday, then Athena has it rented out to someone else. She booked it months ago, last year maybe. Double-booked it by mistake."

"And she just discovered that?" I asked. That didn't seem to fit the Athena I'd seen.

"No, she told us a while back. We figured it would be okay; Dad could just share one of our cottages for the last three days. Frances's and my cottage, actually."

Lizzie got up and walked over to her girls. "That's enough," she said, taking the bag of marshmallows from Lauren. "We'll save the rest for tomorrow."

"Mom!" Lauren and Lindsey protested as one.

"Listen to your mother," Rick warned in a voice deeper than necessary.

"But your father can't stay in our cottage," Froggy continued. "It's just too much, with Jay waking up for feedings and the way your father snores. I can't do it."

"I'd take him," Lizzie said to me as she came around the fire. "You know I would, but there's absolutely no space in our cottage with the five of us. Dad's not the type to sleep on the floor."

Lizzie turned her head in the direction of the pounding ocean, where wave crests now shimmered in a funnel of moonlight.

"So, you're saying he has to stay with me?" I asked, understanding now and angry, mostly with myself, for imagining I could find refuge here.

"It's what makes the most sense," Jeremy said, putting an arm around his wife, rubbing her shoulder.

"Not really," I answered, feeling my face burn. "You have an extra bedroom, since Jay sleeps in a port-a-crib. It's so tight in Damien's room. What about *him* when Dad snores?"

"Yeah," Damien said softly behind me.

"I don't know," Jeremy said. "But Frances really isn't up to it. You must remember what having a new baby is like."

I did. I had been twenty when Isabella was born, cramped in married students' housing, trying to care for her and finish my last semester, living on coffee and tablespoons of liquid protein. I had given up my plans for pursuing a career in music, as had Keith, who had gone to business school. I reached for the crumpled beer can Rick had tossed down.

"It isn't fair," I said, unbending the can. "Everyone cooks at my cottage; everyone eats at my cottage. Now everyone sleeps there, too?"

"Not everyone," Froggy answered angrily. "Just your own father."

I threw the beer can hard at the fire, sending up a shower of sparks as a log broke in two. The children screamed, half with delight, and Rick jumped up as if to rescue, or attack, someone.

Then I heard crying, and at first I thought it must be one of the girls, that someone had gotten burned. But the sound got closer, an infant's sound, and then my father was standing there in the circle of firelight, holding a screaming baby Jay in his arms.

CHAPTER 6

I AWAKENED SUNDAY TO A LIGHT-FILLED ROOM and a knock at my door. Lifting my head from the thin pillow I'd squeezed into a lumpy mound, I squinted my eyes to focus and to remember where I was.

Another knock. "Yes?" I slid my legs from under the sofa bed's sheets. The cool touch of the pine floor against my feet made me wish for socks.

"It's Lizzie."

I rose, crossed the room to open the door, and stood facing my sister, shielding my eyes against the dazzling sun.

"Yikes," I said, blinking, my voice thick with sleep.

"I know." Lizzie handed me a Styrofoam cup of steaming coffee. "Today's even more beautiful than yesterday."

"Thanks," I said, blowing across the top of the cup and then breathing in its welcome, spicy aroma. "What are you dressed for?"

"Church," she answered with an almost invisible shrug. She was wearing a blue-and-green, flower-print dress, and black sandals. "The girls are going to receive communion next year, you know, so we're trying to go to mass every week now."

"Oh," I said. Except for weddings, funerals, and the occasional Christmas Eve, I'd stopped going to church in college. Last spring, Damien had wanted to take communion at my cousin's wedding, to see what it was like, he'd said. Keith had let him do it, and afterward at my father's house, Keith and Rick had gotten into an argument about whether Damien had committed a sin. I'd recoiled at the word as though it were an obscenity, hoping my children hadn't overheard from the next room. Neither Damien nor Isabella had received first communion, though they had both been baptized Catholic as infants, and neither had any serious religious training. Rick felt Damien hadn't the "right" to receive communion. Keith had been furious.

"Jeremy and Froggy are going to church with us," Lizzie told me now. "Actually, Froggy found the church. We'll probably go out for breakfast afterward, so you'll be on your own this morning." She smiled, as if offering good news.

"Is Dad going?" I asked, taking a sip of the strong, sweet coffee. It was surprisingly good.

"Oh," Lizzie shook her head. "No. I didn't want to wake him. He doesn't go to church anymore, does he?"

I shrugged. "He never really did."

We turned toward the sound of the Adamos' dark red minivan pulling up on the road behind the pool. I could see Rick's muscular arm bent out the driver's window, adjusting the side-view mirror. He honked the horn.

"Coming!" Lizzie called, then turned back to me, frowning. "He can be so obnoxious," she said.

Was I supposed to agree? Offer some platitude about men in general? I looked at her nose, already beginning to peel. "Have fun," I responded lamely.

"Right." Lizzie sighed. "See you later." She hurried down the path toward where Jeremy's white Jeep had just pulled up behind Rick's van. I waved, but he wasn't looking. Beyond the cars lay the dunes and beyond the dunes, the shimmering Atlantic. Ribbons of blue wavered, ocean against sky.

"Mom!" Damien called from within the cottage.

"Hi, there." I turned back into the front room to greet my son. He stood at the far end of the hall, squinting and scowling, and my heart melted as it did each morning at the sight of his tousled hair.

"I want breakfast," he said, then disappeared into the bathroom, shutting the door behind him.

"Yes, sir!" I called after him, but I was happy to oblige. Lizzie's coffee, the clear, bright sky, and the prospect of a morning to myself had started my day off fine, without any nausea. I glanced at my violin in the corner, and, touching my fingers together to feel my calluses, decided I would practice today.

Damien and I were sitting at the picnic table on our deck, just finishing our breakfasts, when my father came strolling up the path, an apparition from my childhood in a T-shirt, an old pair of pants, and a fishing hat. He nodded as he approached us.

"Good morning," he said with a quick, conspiratorial smile. He wouldn't ask why we weren't at church.

I raised my coffee mug—decaf, not nearly as good as Lizzie's. "What a beautiful day," I said.

"Hi, Grampa," Damien said without looking up. He was playing a hand-held video game, his fingers sticky with maple syrup from the frozen waffles I'd "borrowed" from Lizzie's freezer and served him. He left a film over every button he pressed.

"What've you got there?" my father asked Damien and pushed the thick Sunday newspaper through the deck railing. "Thought you might want this," he said to me.

"Electronic poker," Damien answered.

"Thanks," I said, removing the magazine section. "The sun shines, Lizzie brings me coffee, and now you arrive with the Sunday *Times*. What more could I ask?"

My father chuckled, or maybe he gulped a breath, as he climbed the steps to the deck and walked over to stand behind Damien. "Hmm. You're not going to stay with that hand, are you?"

Damien looked up. "I *was* going to." The game buzzed and Damien snapped his fingers. "Rats," he said.

My father patted Damien's shoulder. "That's okay," he said. "Better to learn now, before you go to college and lose your brand-new convertible in a bet."

"What new convertible?" I said, feigning indignance. My son smiled up at his grandfather, who grinned at him and winked.

"Let me have a section of that," my father said, pointing at the *Times* as he sank into a deck chair. A speckled gull landed on the railing, eyeing Damien's breakfast plate.

"Which do you want?" I asked.

"Doesn't matter," my father said, pulling his glasses out of his pocket. "I read them all, eventually." I smiled, remembering how he'd lay his sections across the kitchen table, while we kids sprawled on the floor with the comics and TV listings from the local paper.

I handed him the first section, the news. "Have you eaten breakfast? Do you want some coffee?"

He held up his hand. "I've had mine," he said. Then he lifted his hat and wiped his bald spot with his sleeve.

"I'll take the comics," Damien said.

"No comics in the *Times*," I told him. "Sorry." The gull inched clumsily closer, watching me sideways. I picked up Damien's plate and shook the sticky waffle crumbs onto the grass; the gull swooped down to get them and then soared away.

"Want the sports pages?" my father asked and Damien took them as I picked up "The Week in Review." We sat and read, hunched over our sections, quiet under a cloudless sky. Periodically, I glimpsed my son's tongue poking around his lip above his broken tooth, but he didn't complain and I didn't call attention to it.

After a while, Damien went back to playing poker; I traded my father "Arts and Leisure" for the "Book Review." An older couple, who had been sitting under an umbrella by the pool, began swimming laps, and the rhythmic sounds of their strokes made me want to close my eyes. Last year, my mother had done slow laps every morning. Then, dripping through the webbing of her deck chair, she had sipped coffee and smoked cigarettes as the grandchildren gobbled their morning doughnuts. Keith always made them save a Bavarian cream for her.

I moved from the picnic table to a chaise longue and lay back. I pressed the tips of my fingers under my sunglasses, against my eyelids. As I drifted on the brink of sleep, suspended, the sounds of this place—the distant roar of the ocean, the far and near cries of the gulls, the steady rhythm of the swimmers in the pool—all enveloped me, now and then pierced by the sharp, otherworldly beeps from Damien's game.

I began to visualize a tiny child, more homunculus than fetus, taking shape before my mind's eye. It floated as though it too were suspended, its arms stretched out from its body. I couldn't see its face.

A scraping sound from the right, and something cool and wet nudged against my hand. I opened my eyes and sat up to find Sunshine nuzzling me. Damien hurried to crouch beside her.

"Good dog," he said, extending his palm. She licked his fingers, no doubt grateful to find them sweet.

"She's called Sunshine," I said, and she wagged her tail at the mention of her name. "She lives here."

"She's mine," came a child's voice, and I looked up to see a boy the color of caramelized butter from head to toe, his long, uncombed hair pulled back into a ponytail. He stood on the grass beside the deck, wearing only a faded black Speedo.

"Hello," I said.

Hanging his arms around Sunshine's neck, Damien squinted at the boy.

"Sunshine is my dog," the boy repeated. His shaggy gold hair made him look as though he could be the dog's brother.

My father put down his paper. "What's your name, son?" he asked.

"Crosby," the boy answered, climbing the steps to the deck. He stopped at the picnic table and picked up the poker game. "What's this?" he asked.

Sunshine moved to Crosby's side and Damien followed. "It's electronic poker," he said. "It's mine."

"I know it's yours," Crosby answered. The two boys were about the same height, though Crosby was thinner, bonier. They eyed each other briefly.

"Wanna see how to play?" Damien asked. Crosby nodded.

Contrasted against Athena's beach-gilded son, Damien looked pale. I got up to put sunscreen on his face and neck. He handed the game to Crosby and winced as I rubbed lotion on his skin.

"Athena says for you to come over," Crosby said as his thumbs pounded buttons.

"Who?" Damien asked.

My father set down his newspaper and lowered his sunglasses. "I'll take some of that sunscreen," he said.

"I meant your mother," Crosby answered as the game buzzed. Then he looked up at me. "You. You're Amanda Kincaid, right?"

"I am," I replied, handing my father the tube of lotion.

"Athena said to tell you to come over to the cottage," Crosby continued, his eyes on the game in his hands. "She has a ring for you." The game chimed the signal that meant he'd won, and he grinned in triumph.

I gazed at this skinny, sun-baked waif who called his mother by her first name.

"Right," I answered. "The blue lapis ring." Had I said I wanted it? Perhaps that was just her way of getting me to her cottage; perhaps she'd had a message from Keith. "Does she want me to come now?"

Crosby shrugged. "Do you want to race in the pool?" he asked Damien as he clicked off the game.

"Okay," Damien answered. He peeled off his T-shirt.

"Wait," I said. "Let me put sunscreen on your back."

My father finished applying lotion to his bald spot, replaced his hat, and handed me the tube. He stood. "I wouldn't mind a swim myself. I'll go change and meet you boys in the pool."

I slathered sunscreen across Damien's back, resisting the impulse to kiss the top of his head. (A primary principle of motherhood: you didn't kiss children in front of their friends, especially new friends.) Though Crosby might seem different to Damien than the boys at private school in Atlanta, he was an available playmate, and for that I was grateful. The kid probably swam like a fish, but I figured Damien could hold his own, at his strongest now after a summer of swim team.

"Okay," I said, squeezing my son's shoulder, feeling how solid if still small he was. I wanted to ask about his tooth, but knew he wouldn't want me to bring it up. "I won't be gone long," I said and headed where I'd been summoned.

"Hello?" I called as I stepped through the door to Athena's cottage, squinting as my eyes adjusted to the dim light. The room smelled of cooking—something grilled or fried in butter, maybe pancakes—and I was glad to think Crosby had probably eaten breakfast.

"I'm in here." Athena's contralto came from the kitchen.

Stepping over more boxes than I'd remembered being there, I made my way back to her. She sat at a small, round table amidst an incredible amount of clutter, her long fingers wrapped around a mug of tea. Red Zinger, I saw from the tag. I didn't think anybody drank that anymore, if anyone ever had.

"Would you like some tea?" Her head tilted up at me, but the rest of her stayed perfectly still.

I shook my head. "No, thanks." Light streamed in through a bare window, falling across stacks of crockery and jars of herbs and open bags of flour and rice.

"I have many teas," Athena said. "Something for whatever ails you."

"I'm feeling okay," I said, wondering whether she had a specific ailment in mind. "I met your son," I told her.

"Of course," she answered.

I bristled, then flushed with embarrassment.

"Crosby always meets the guests," she continued. "Especially ones who bring interesting toys." A smile played at the corners of her mouth, reminding me for a split second of Keith. Then she stood, jingling. She was dressed in white today, a gauzy, shapeless dress that flowed to her ankles. In addition to her bracelets, she wore a necklace of tiny silver bells.

"I have a solution to your dilemma," she said, enunciating each syllable. "About the lapis ring."

So there wasn't any message from Keith; she really did want to sell me that ring.

She crossed in front of me toward her office, her braid a swinging pendulum across the round curve of her bottom. The visible outlines of her body when she moved made me suddenly wonder whether she was dressed for a lover. I followed her into the dim room to the glass case that held the lapis ring.

"You really should have this ring," she said as she lifted it between two fingers. "But I understand your reluctance to remove your wedding bands."

I considered what she might imagine she understood as she offered me the circle of silver and blue. I felt as though I were part of some college drama class improvisation. What would my character say next? "It is lovely," was all I could come up with as I slipped the ring onto the pinky of my right hand. It slid around loosely.

"You know, there is someone you need to meet," Athena said. "He'll make the ring fit where you want."

"Oh," I said. "A local jeweler?"

"Yes," Athena said, moving to her desk. "And more. A friend. I'll take you to him." She picked up a faded woven bag from the floor and extracted a set of keys.

"Now?" I asked. "On Sunday morning?"

"Yes," she answered. "Why not? He usually goes back to the city on Monday."

"I don't know," I said, gazing at the ring. Glittering specks within the inky blue reminded me of the night sky. "I have to see about Damien."

"Damien is fine," Athena said, and then leaned toward me as though in a parody of confidentiality. "You'll like this person." She turned before I could respond.

I followed her once more through the kitchen, quixotically choosing to see this through. Part of me winced at the ridiculous posturing game we seemed to play; but another part of me saw Athena as the accommodating hostess, a role to which she was somehow obliged.

"We'll pass the pool on the way to the road. We can stop there and tell the boys what we're doing," she said. She opened a back door that led to a little driveway beside her cottage.

Had I mentioned the boys were at the pool or did she just assume it? Or had she instructed Crosby to see to that, too? I frowned.

"Don't worry," she said as she led me to a bright orange Volkswagen beetle at the end of the drive. "We won't travel far."

I followed her, holding the ring in the center of my fist. It felt cool, like a pebble from the ocean floor that hadn't seen the sun for years. "I guess my father can watch over the boys," I said, as I walked around the VW to the passenger side and slid in across a torn vinyl seat. The latch clicked, and my pulse quickened—in anticipation of adventure, or was it folly?

Athena tilted her head and briefly met my eyes as if to check them. Then she turned the key, adjusted the mirror, and shifted into reverse.

"I haven't ridden in one of these in a long time," I said, remembering a college boyfriend, before Keith, who drove his black VW beetle with an unending supply of marijuana stashed in the elastic door pouch.

"Ah," she said, "then you're overdue." Lifting her foot from the clutch, she let the car roll down the slight incline of the drive. "This car is an old friend," Athena told me as she shifted into first and turned the wheel. "I call her my pumpkin coach."

Y FATHER CALLED HIS FORD THE "DOUGHNUT EXPRESS." Every
Friday, before any of us was awake, he'd drive to one of his
client bakeries, fill the backseat of his car with trays of sweet,
hot doughnuts and bring them home for breakfast. We were allowed
three each, though I never managed more than two. But mostly, my father got the doughnuts so that my mother could take a box to her
weekly meeting at the St. Mary's Mental Health Extension. This was
a support group for former mental patients, but that didn't prevent
my mother from treating it as a social outing.

Except for when she was feeling especially ill, my mother dressed
her best for these meetings, selecting from among the outfits in her
wardrobe that she called her "daywear," but which I never saw her
wear on any regular day. I'd hear the muffled scrapes and banging of
her rummaging though her closet about the same time the yeasty scent
of doughnuts would come wafting up the stairs.

Sometimes, if she sensed I was awake, my mother would call me
into her bedroom to help her dress.

"Which scarf do you like?" she'd ask, tossing brightly colored
squares of silk to the bed. I'd answer arbitrarily, at times absurdly, just
wanting to get away. Other times, I tried to choose well, to make it a
kind of test of my skill. But then she'd pull open another drawer;
she'd have another request. "Pick me out a pretty slip," she'd say, or

worse, "I can't find a pair of hose without a run in them. Would you look?"

I hated pushing my hands through the limp leg shapes of my mother's nylons, hated that my fingers had to touch the places her feet would go. But if I let her wear just any ripped pair, the whole town would see my mother with long ladders down her calves.

Much to my profound, fourteen-year-old embarrassment, my mother liked to walk the six blocks to the Presbyterian Church where the extension group meetings were held. I would cringe at the sight of her in her black-and-white houndstooth coat with the velvet collar, one wrist looped through the inevitable white bakery box tied with string, sniffing the air with pleasure as she left the house. I knew she'd wave to any kids who looked to be the same ages as her own kids (roughly, anyone from six to seventeen), thinking they might be her children's friends. I wanted to ask her not to, but I never could find the words.

Though she insisted she liked to walk, my mother lumbered along the streets of our small town, and I worried that she would strike people as lost. Or that she would talk out loud to herself, mumbling strangely as she trailed the scent of fried dough past the houses of my classmates.

Though I regularly boasted not to care what anyone thought of me, I was far less cool when it came to what was thought of my mother. I tried to estimate how many of those she passed on the street knew exactly where she was headed, and I wondered whether she might be the subject of local gossip. I was relieved on the days when my father drove her in the car.

When the weather was bad—when it rained or snowed—my father would arrange to go late to work so he could drive my mother to her meeting. "I don't want you traveling on risky roads," he'd say when my mother would protest that she could drive herself. The truth was that for several years after she began her medication, my mother rarely drove at all. For reasons I thought stupid at the time, my father refrained from pointing that out.

"Want a ride to school?" my father would ask me every time it rained, as though I might not. Lizzie got bus service to the elementary school, and Jeremy rode his bike no matter what, but I walked the mile to the junior high. So on rainy Fridays, I drove with my parents, and before we'd even turned the corner the car was thick with my mother's cigarette smoke. I wondered how my father could possibly see to drive, between the fog outside and the fog within, and I wondered if perhaps my mother wasn't proving some kind of point about relative safety.

Slouched in the backseat, with my arm pressed to my nose and mouth against the choking smoke, I tried not to listen as my mother spoke about her "friends" at the extension group. I pictured long, rubbery but invisible tentacles reaching from the psychiatric ward of St. Mary's Hospital, keeping its patients stuck to that place even when they weren't there. Mental illness, I had learned, was something you could never get away from. For years, I automatically assumed any program with the word "extension" in it was for crazy people.

One rainy Friday my mother turned around in her seat and caught me breathing filtered air through my sleeve. "Hmmm," she said as she lifted her velvet cuff to her nose in imitation of me, and the smoke from her cigarette curled around her kohl-rimmed eyes. For a moment her glance caught mine, her expression bemused as a child's. I slipped my eyes away from hers, toward the window, and she turned around again. Although it was raining hard—icy, slanting drops that hurt the skin—I rolled the window halfway down. For months afterward, whenever my mother lifted her hand to her mouth, I wondered whether she harbored a grudge against me or was trying to see what it felt like to be me.

My father never asked anything about the extension group beyond the odd details my mother chose to tell: a woman had cut all the tags off her husband's ties; a man had suddenly forgotten how to get to his job and spent an entire day riding buses. Though he seemed to consider it important that my mother attend the meetings, my father dropped her off at the entrance to the church basement without getting out of the car himself. To my knowledge, he never went inside the building. My mother could have been worshipping the devil and he'd never have known. At the time, I would have preferred that.

The extension group participants paid a small monthly fee to cover coffee expenses, and they took turns bringing in baked goods. I knew from my mother's conversation who baked and who store bought and who never brought enough for everyone. My mother, of course, contributed doughnuts every week, no matter whose turn it was. This I gathered made her popular. But in all the years my mother attended the group, we only ever met one of her friends, Dolores.

We heard about Dolores long before we met her. "Dolores brought Fanny Farmer chocolates to our group today," my mother announced to the three of us one night after dinner when my father had stayed late at the office. "And I saved some." She reached into the pocket of her apron and pulled out three misshapen blobs cradled in brown, fluted paper cups.

"Who's Dolores?" Jeremy asked as he carried his plate to the sink.

"A friend at my extension group," my mother said. She lit a cigarette, then touched the match to the cellophane wrapping from her pack so that it flamed up quickly and burned to nothing in the ashtray. Lizzie stared at her, awed by the dual spectacles of candy and fire.

Jeremy grunted and left the room.

My mother exhaled and pushed the candy across the table between Lizzie and me. "One each," she said.

After that, my mother would often produce three candies after dinner on Fridays, and Dolores became renowned in our family as the candy lady. At least to Lizzie and me. Jeremy never wanted any, and more often than not my father came home late on Fridays. We sometimes left the extra candy on the table for him, but usually Lizzie and I split it.

One Saturday morning, Lizzie and I sat at the kitchen table in our pajamas, eating cereal while my father drank his second or third cup of coffee and read through mail he'd read the night before. He was already showered and dressed in the clean but worn-out work clothes— the faded oxford shirts and baggy suit pants—he wore on weekends. Lately, he had been dressing early on Saturdays, perhaps because he never knew when Gloria, our next-door neighbor, might show up to "check on" us.

"I'm on my way to the A&P," she might say. "Do you need milk?" Or she would be headed to the shopping mall and offer Jeremy a lift to baseball practice. Her quick, sharp knocks on the door reminded me of the way she tapped out the time with her fingers on the side of the piano during my lessons.

Always she would ask, "How is Barbara doing?" in a low voice that suggested the answer would be a secret. My father would respond in a low voice of his own, and then he'd move toward the back door, sometimes going outside with her to finish their conversation.

"She's a big help," he'd say with a tight mouth when he came back in. I figured he was embarrassed to have a neighbor know about my mother's problems, and that annoyed me. I understood the feeling, of course, since I felt it myself, but I wanted him to be stronger than I was.

So on this Saturday, when he jumped up at the knock, ran three fingers flat along the receding edge of his hair, and tugged open the back door, I expected to see Gloria on the other side.

With her blond hair and slight frame, Dolores seen from a distance or through a wavering glass window might be mistaken for Gloria, but up close the two women were nothing alike. All Gloria's edges were round and soft; Dolores's were sharp and hard. She looked dry to me, brittle, as though if she bent an arm or leg too quickly she might break. I wondered whether she felt the way she looked and how the rubbery arms of the extension group could be of any possible help to her if she did.

"Is Barbara here?" Dolores asked in a smoker's voice raspier than my mother's. My father stepped aside to let her into our kitchen. Unlike most people, who looked around nervously the first time they entered a room, Dolores stared straight ahead, as though knowing exactly what to expect. My mother, who almost never came in to the kitchen when Gloria stopped by, appeared now in the archway to the dining room, our dog, Princess, at her heels.

"Vincent, this is my friend, Dolores," she said with uncustomary manners. Princess sniffed around Dolores's legs, but Dolores didn't pet or acknowledge her. A strike against her, as far as I was concerned. I opened my mouth to call the dog to me, but my mother pulled a chunk of cookie from her pocket and let the dog take it from her palm.

"Hello, Dolores." My father extended his hand, which Dolores accepted with small, white fingers. I could tell he had no idea who she might be.

My mother breathed deeply, noisily, and looked from her perplexed husband to this odd woman. And then Dolores reached into a worn Macy's shopping bag and took out a box of Fanny Farmer chocolates. Lizzie jumped up from her chair, but Dolores ignored her as she had the dog. She handed the box to my mother, who slipped it on top of the refrigerator between the fruit bowl and the paper napkins. Then my mother reached into another pocket of her skirt, pulled out her cigarettes, and offered one to her friend. I was amazed at the way they seemed to know exactly what to expect of one another. Amazed and envious. My mother and I had never shared so simple or direct an exchange.

I slid off my chair, grabbed the leash that hung on the hook by the back door and called the dog. With a last beseeching glance toward my mother, who ignored her now, Princess came to me and we went out for a walk. When we returned twenty minutes later, Dolores had gone.

After that, Dolores started coming home with my mother after their meetings on Fridays. She drove her own car—an incongruous red Fiat—and to repay her for the ride home, my mother would feed Dolores lunch. It became their habit, and my father seemed pleased with the arrangement. Though I never understood why he felt any more confident with Dolores's driving than he did with my mother's, I knew he had some weird notion of safety in numbers. Driving with a partner, to my father, was like swimming with a buddy.

Still, I don't think any of us except my mother ever felt comfortable or even entirely safe when Dolores was around. Arguably less crazy than my mother—a depressive rather than a psychotic—Dolores was scarier. On the rare occasions that I saw her—usually warming up her Fiat in our driveway—she looked about to burst out of her too-thin skin. Once, half curious and half snide, I asked my mother, "So what's Dolores's problem? What was she in for?" My mother told me that Dolores had been sent to St. Mary's when she tried to take her own life.

After that I asked nothing more. I was afraid to bring up the topic with my mother, afraid it would give her ideas. My mother hadn't ever talked about suicide—I'd never heard her say the word until now. Still, I knew how susceptible she was, how little things became stuck in her mind.

Although my mother seemed pleased to have a friend, I feared the danger in it. My father thought that discussing other people's problems helped keep my mother's mind off her own. I worried the opposite would occur. So while I avoided speaking to my mother about Dolores, I sometimes eavesdropped on their conversations from the dining room or the basement stairs. But all I ever caught was talk about what they were eating or some television special or a medication's side effects. I never heard any of the conversations I knew they must have about their problems. I wanted to know about their problems.

Maybe they could sense when I was there. Perhaps my mother thought to spare me. At the time, I wouldn't have supposed she gave my reactions a thought.

Halloween fell on a Friday that year. Scuffling down my street on my way home from school, I kept my head down, breathing in the rich musk of decomposing leaves as they scattered with each step. I didn't see Dolores's red Fiat until I was up to the house and my first reaction was to keep walking. But I wanted to hand out candy to the kids on our street, and I wanted to see Lizzie in her Raggedy Ann costume. So I turned into our driveway, and on impulse, I stopped to peek in the Fiat's windows.

I don't know what I expected to see. Something personal, I guess, a pile of objects I could read for clues to Dolores's madness. Perhaps I hoped by extrapolation to gain insight into my mother. But all I saw was a cardboard, Christmas-tree air freshener hanging from the rearview mirror. Otherwise, the car was empty.

I guess I'd expected that, like the kids I knew from the high school who drove cars festooned with stickers and hanging trinkets, and from whose backseats bottles of stolen Seagrams clinked at every turn, Dolores would carry her identity around with her. It didn't occur to me that she did and this was it.

So much for adult life, I thought. It either reeked of cigarette smoke and sickeningly sweet doughnuts, or offered nothing but a whiff of fake Christmas.

I walked around the garage and waved to Gloria raking leaves in her yard. She called hello and stopped to redo her ponytail. I pretended to look for something in my book bag so as not to have to talk to her. Lately, during our lessons, she'd been telling me what talent I had and how she wished she had a daughter like me. Gloria was nice, but I didn't want a second mother. I had enough trouble with the one I had.

I hurried up our back steps like I was late for something, opened the screen door, and tossed my backpack into the kitchen. Even though I had seen the Fiat, when I looked up I yelped in surprise at the person wrapped from head to toe in bandages, sitting at our table. For a second I thought it was my mother, that she had somehow been injured and just left there. But of course that was impossible, and it wasn't my mother. It was Dolores. She was sitting at our table in Lizzie's place, picking at a piece of orange cake on a plate in front of her, dressed as a mummy.

"Mandy? Are you okay, honey?" Gloria called from her yard when she heard me scream.

"Yeah," I called back immediately, not wanting her to come over.

Dolores just stared at me, the pale oval of her face and her thin white fingers her only exposed skin.

"Wow. You scared me," I said to her in what I hoped was a friendly way.

Her head seemed to vibrate, but she said nothing. Her eyes were so light, I couldn't tell what color they were. I looked around for my mother.

"She's getting Lizzie dressed," Dolores said. She picked off another piece of cake and took a small bite. I noticed Princess under the table, snout pointed toward Dolores's lap, waiting for crumbs. I doubted there would be any.

"Oh," I said as I opened the refrigerator. One good thing about Dolores coming on Fridays was there would be food in the fridge. I considered a bowl of leftover tuna salad, picked it up, and sniffed it. Princess padded over to me; I felt her tail wagging against my leg.

"Do you know why I'm bandaged like this?" Dolores's voice was trembly and strong at the same time. I put the tuna back in the fridge and reached for a small packet wrapped in white butcher paper.

Bologna. I took a piece and held it up. "Want a piece?" I asked Dolores, then threw it on the floor for the dog.

Dolores didn't answer. She was staring at me.

"You're a mummy," I answered her. "For Halloween." *Duh.*

"No, I mean bandaged *like this,*" she said.

I closed the refrigerator. Dolores was holding her hands up to her face, fingers fanned around her chin. I shook my head. *Just tell me.* "Uh-uh," I said. "Why?"

"So I can breathe," she said. "And so I can claw my way out if I want to."

The morning of Dolores's funeral, my mother called me into her room. It was a Saturday, and my first response was to yell to her, "I'm sleeping!" But then I remembered. I got out of bed and made my way down the unlit hall.

My mother was standing in the middle of her room in her black lace slip.

"Do you think this dress is okay?" she asked, meaning appropriate for a funeral. She pointed to a purple silk shirtwaist hanging from her closet door. She had worn it to the theatre for her anniversary. My father told me she'd fallen asleep during the first act—it was the medication, he said—and drooled for the rest of the performance. I thought I could see a dull stain down the front of the dress.

"I don't know," I said.

My mother looked worried. Her mouth was working the way it did and her stained fingers rubbed together as though feeling a delicate piece of cloth. "I have a good memory of wearing this dress," she said. "Your father and I had such a lovely time."

I walked closer to it. The stain was perhaps just a shadow. "I guess it's dark enough," I said.

"I want to wear something a little cheerful," my mother explained, as though preparing to visit a sick friend. But Dolores had finally succeeded in killing herself. She had put a plastic dry cleaner's bag over her head two nights earlier. Her sister had found her the next morning.

"Hmmm."

"This is what she wanted," my mother said, and I realized that perhaps she was *celebrating* for Dolores. "She always talked about it."

I stared at the fine scattering of freckles across her chest.

My mother sighed and reached for her cigarettes. Her eyes unfocused the way they did when she was listening to words inside her head. I wondered whether Dolores's voice would join the others now, and whether in a weird way my mother was luckier than the rest of us.

"Wear the purple," I said as I turned to leave. Then I walked down the hall and got back into bed.

CHAPTER 8

A THENA WAS TRUE TO HER WORD: we didn't travel far, only a few minutes down Old Montauk Highway before pulling into a gravel drive hidden among scrub. The house wasn't visible from the road, or even from the winding drive until we pulled right up to it, and for a moment I questioned my judgment. Did I trust Athena? Why was she going to so much trouble to sell a ring?

Then I saw the house and my misgivings vanished as my interest ignited. The thick scrub ended abruptly, giving way to tufts of tall grass rising out of drifts of sand, and the house appeared to rise from the dunes like an abandoned ship brought in by the tide. Constructed entirely of gray-stained wood—the color of driftwood—and large panels of glass, the house stood taller than it was wide, its roof pointing asymmetrically toward the sky. The ocean view would be spectacular from the upper floor.

"Wow," I said as Athena pulled her car around back to a small parking circle.

She glanced at me and smiled. "Well situated, isn't it?" She opened her door and I followed.

Small pebbles crunched underfoot as we crossed the drive. Now I could see the part of the house that faced the beach—three levels, almost entirely windows, overlooking decking and stairs, with a narrow boardwalk leading from the lowest deck into the dunes. Parked by the bottom steps was a silver motorcycle: a BMW, K1100 LT. That meant nothing to me, but Keith would know it. He had long coveted a motorcycle.

Someone was working at the far end of the lowest deck, a man digging in a wooden planter, transplanting yellow flowers from a nursery flat.

"Michael," Athena called out and he turned, shielding his eyes with his hand. Though not particularly tanned for someone with a house on the beach, he was shirtless, dressed only in loose-fitting denim shorts and deck shoes. His skin was naturally fair, his hair a flaxen brown, probably white-blond in childhood. As he stood to wave, I caught a glimpse of a long mark across his chest, but he turned quickly and reached for a T-shirt slung across one of the sleek, white deck chairs.

"Athena!" he greeted her cordially and with little surprise, tugging the shirt over his head and then wiping his hands down either side of his shorts. When we reached him, I saw that he'd been planting miniature sunflowers.

Athena took his hand, squeezing rather than shaking it. "This is Amanda Kincaid," she told him, indicating me with a jingling turn of her wrist. "Dr. Michael Burns."

He met my eyes and smiled in a way—as though he were truly pleased—that caught me off guard. "Hello," he said, extending his hand, and I found myself smiling back before looking away.

His eyes were blue, a shade close to Keith's, but different in effect, soft where Keith's were hard. Maybe it was their shape—Keith's eyes were long and narrow, where Michael Burns's were wide, large pupiled. Even in the strong sun, he had the look of someone who took everything in, for whom light was never too bright.

There was a tapping behind us, and a large dog appeared on the boardwalk leading from the dunes. It was a golden retriever, grinning and panting.

"Homer!" Michael Burns sang out in a voice boyishly higher than his speaking voice, reaching toward the dog with shapely but dirt-smeared hands. Automatically, I glanced down at my own hand, which had just shaken his.

Athena squatted on her heels and the dog loped over to her. She ruffled the fur of his chest. "Homer is Sunshine's half-brother," she said.

I bent toward her and patted Homer's broad head. Unlike his sibling's, his fur gleamed and was soft and smooth to the touch. Obviously, Michael Burns—or someone—was an attentive pet owner. I wondered what Athena thought of the difference between the two dogs, or whether she was aware of it.

Michael knelt now, too, and Homer panted happily, grinning from face to face as we all admired him. Then Athena stood, and Michael and I bumped eyes again—accidentally—for a suspended second over Homer's corn-silk back.

"I love dogs," I said, still squeezing the lapis ring in my fist. "I had one growing up, a mutt, Princess. She lived to be sixteen. But I don't have one now."

"Oh, that's too bad," Michael said sympathetically, as if he knew that life was harder without a dog. Was he a vet? I stood up self-consciously.

"Amanda is in need of your skills," Athena informed him.

Michael laughed. "Professionally?" He rose, resting his hands loosely on his hips. "Do you need an emergency appendectomy?"

Not sure how to respond, I smiled, then opened my fist. "I'd like this ring to be sized to fit my right hand."

He nodded, still smiling. "Is that all? No ten-year-old wart that must be removed tonight so you can dance at the Sea Sprays Inn? You don't have a sudden, serious need for Prozac or a few Tylenol 3's?"

"Do you do that?" I asked.

His lips pulled in. "Nooo," he said, shaking his head and glancing toward Athena. "But that doesn't stop them from trying."

Athena smiled wryly. "Michael is a big-shot internist."

He winced. "Hardly a big shot," he said, taking the ring from me. "But it's my artisan-self you're in need of."

Athena nudged the tray of sunflowers with her foot. "These need water," she said. "They're wilting."

"Right." Michael nodded. "I intended to water them as soon as I'd got them all planted. Which brings to mind—would either of you care for something to drink? Iced tea? A beer?"

I looked at my watch. "It's only eleven," I said, unable to stop a smile.

"A Bloody Mary, then," Michael suggested.

"Alcohol is hardly necessary," Athena said, "to fix a ring." Her tone was light.

Michael grinned. "Depends what you brought to pay for my services."

"Oh! I need to pay you," I said to Athena. "And I don't even have my purse with me."

"You'll pay me later," Athena said.

"And you," I turned to Michael. "I'm so embarrassed. I didn't stop to think." Michael ran his eyes over my face in a quick examination. I wanted to know what he saw.

"It's my pleasure," Michael said, rubbing his thumb across the blue stone. "As Athena's friend, you owe me nothing; in fact, I'm in her debt."

Athena smiled broadly, her crossed teeth glinting. "How gallant," she said. "Now I must get back to the Laughing Gull. I have guests departing and arriving. Shall I return for you later?" She turned to me, brushing a wisp of hair from her eyes.

"I shouldn't stay," I began.

"I can take you back. If you don't mind a ride on a motorcycle," Michael said. He was turning the ring over in his hand. "This is very pretty."

"I don't know," I replied. I felt my neck and ears grow warm. "I mean, I don't mind the motorcycle, but . . ."

"*Stay,*" said Athena so firmly that Homer looked up and wagged his tail.

Michael snickered softly.

"Your son is fine," Athena assured me, reading my face. "Relax. Tour the house. Watch Michael work; doesn't he have wonderful hands?" She turned and strode quickly off the deck, her white dress shimmering in the light, her bells tinkling as she moved.

I felt my skin grow hot—I *had* been watching his hands—and I averted my face from Michael, directing my gaze toward the dunes. From this lowest deck, I couldn't see above them, couldn't see the ocean, but I could hear the low roar of the waves. I hadn't been conscious of how their sound and scent filled the air.

"This is lovely here," I said, lifting my face to a breeze. I felt oddly happy and free, and breathed in deeply, filling my belly with air.

"It is beautiful," Michael answered. "I wish it were mine."

"It isn't yours?" I turned toward him.

He shrugged. "My soon-to-be-ex-wife is fighting me for it." He let out a long breath. "I'm going to give it to her, though she doesn't know it yet."

"I'm sorry," I said. "I guess."

"Yeah." Michael smiled a what-can-you-do smile. "Me, too. But it's just a house. And I'm getting my use of it this summer."

"You come out on weekends?"

"Every chance I can, given my schedule. *Carpe diem.* I'm staying till Wednesday this week."

Homer had wandered off earlier, and now he returned carrying a tattered tennis ball between his loose-lipped, bird-carrier jaws. He pushed the ball against my hand. It was damp and sand-encrusted, and I accepted it gingerly.

"He wants you to throw it," Michael said, amused.

"Okay." I lifted the ball in a two-fingered grip.

"But let me warn you: once you begin, there is no turning back. The consequences of even *flirting* with the idea of playing fetch with this dog are quite serious."

I looked at Michael sideways. He was teasing me. I felt a little thrill in the pit of my stomach as he took the ball from my hand.

"Here. I'm experienced in these matters," he said. "Plus, Homer and I have a history together, so he knows how little to expect of me." He threw the ball long and high over the dunes. Homer dashed after it.

"Actually, I bet he expects a lot," I teased back.

"You're quite right. I spoil him horribly," Michael replied. Then, gently touching my arm, he said, "Let's go in. I'll wash up and, if you like, I'll give you the grand tour and fix your ring. Or vice versa."

"Why not finish planting your sunflowers first?" I said. "I'll help."

Michael nodded. "Thank you," he said.

I showed him how to loosen the roots, spreading them gently before setting each plant in the rich, nursery-bought soil that filled his planters. Homer returned, dropped his ball, and sat with his head between his paws, watching us, demanding nothing. I asked Michael about fertilizer, and he showed me to a garden shed hidden behind the far corner of the house. It was filled with tools and chemicals and containers, but Michael didn't seem to know what any of them were for. Clearly, he had not been the gardener of the household.

I found some Miracle Gro, and we watered it in. Almost immediately, almost miraculously, the small plants revived, lifting up their golden faces, and the look of astonishment in Michael's eyes made my heart slip in my chest. He turned to me, took my soiled hand in his, and led me into his glass house.

CHAPTER 9

"THE MAIN FLOOR IS UP ONE LEVEL," Michael said, and he led me to a flight of narrow wooden steps. Homer squeezed beside me, his thick blond coat feathery against my leg. From the second deck, I could see above the dunes to the ocean, could feel the moistened breeze across my face.

Michael slid open a glass door, and we stepped into a soaring, sky-lit room that was clearly the heart of the house. Sunlight flooded the space, washing over the pale gray wood of the floors and walls, the pale blue fabrics of the furniture and rugs. A cathedral ceiling, two stories high, reached the roof's slanted apex.

I titled my head and looked up toward the large rectangle of glass in the ceiling, blue with sky like an object of art.

"We'll go all the way to the top," Michael said as he held Homer still with one hand and brushed sand from each paw with his other hand. "The view is great. I've got a telescope up there." Michael looked up to meet my gaze and smiled, a slow, satisfied smile.

"You look like a Cheshire cat," I blurted, surprising myself.

He stood and widened his grin, deliberately, appealingly. Something in my stomach did a tiny flip. "I feel like a Cheshire cat," he said.

I looked away. "You're very fortunate to have this."

"That's not what you meant, though," Michael answered. He walked over to a large, neatly cluttered desk and looked down at the flashing red light of his answering machine. A computer, phone, fax machine, stacks of books, papers, and medical journals shared space with various rocks, shells, even a small vase of feathers. I smiled at the juxtaposition of technology and nature.

Michael reached his hand toward the answering machine, but instead of pressing a button, he picked up a tiny scallop shell and handed it to me.

I wasn't sure whether he meant to show it to me or give it to me, but he started across the room without taking it back, so I kept it in my hand.

"Come on, I'll show you the house," he said. "I mean, if you like."

"Of course." Since childhood I'd been fascinated with houses. I'd often volunteered to walk the dog at night because I loved to stroll past the lighted windows of our neighborhood, looking in as other families moved around their rooms, imagining their lives.

Michael stopped in front of a massive, stacked-stone fireplace flanked by a pair of bookshelves. Two ergodynamic swivel chairs near the hearth could face either the fire or the ocean, and each was turned in a different direction. I imagined Michael and his wife, perhaps the last time they'd been here together, choosing alternate views.

He pointed to the painting hung low over the mantel, an oil rendering of fish underwater, done in muted blues and greens. The style was self-taught, but there was something dreamy about it. I liked it immediately.

"This is my favorite painting in the house," Michael said with evident pride. "It was given to me as payment by a patient, actually the mother of a patient, an eight-year-old kid. He's asthmatic and I treated him when he couldn't breathe in the middle of the night."

"It's wonderful," I said. "Almost like a Chagall."

Michael touched his fingers to his lips, nodding. "You're right," he said. "She's very talented, isn't she? I didn't want to accept it, but she insisted."

Without thinking, I blurted, "I paint. Watercolors." Then, flushing, angry with myself, I added, "They're nothing, really. Just note cards."

"I'd like to see them," Michael said as though we were going to be friends. I realized then I hadn't said I was from Atlanta, hadn't said I'd left a husband there. Instead, everything I'd said and hadn't said since we'd met had been a kind of playacting, a kind of dress rehearsal of myself as an unmarried woman.

Homer pushed his cool, wet nose into the back of my knee, and I jumped, then turned to pet him. I noticed a circular staircase at the room's edge, spiraling to a balcony and, apparently, to the second floor, to the bedrooms.

"Where do you sleep?" I asked Homer as I scratched behind his ears. He grinned up at me.

I heard Michael's snicker. "Anywhere he wants to," he said. "Like the proverbial primate."

We moved across the room, and Michael stopped in front of an antique medical-instrument chest, explaining how he'd come by it via the estate of a colleague's grandfather. As the burnished mahogany glowed in the light, I smiled at the realization that Michael was showing off for me. I expressed my pleasure as admiration.

"Why don't you touch it?" Michael said. "It's incredible wood."

"Yes," I agreed, but I didn't touch anything. Instead, I slipped the scallop shell into my pocket.

I realized as we headed toward the kitchen that I hadn't seen any photographs, not one. How unlike my house, with snapshot reminders of its resident family at every turn. This wasn't a family house, and yet I felt I could live here. Or perhaps another Amanda, a different-but-still-me Amanda, could live here.

Michael never mentioned his wife, and I didn't know how to detect signs of her. Nothing said overtly *this belongs to a woman*, but almost anything could have. The house and its furnishings were functional and elegant at the same time.

Even the kitchen, large and square with its driftwood-gray cabinets and green-marble counters, seemed androgynous. A well-worn farm table, something like my own in Atlanta, was angled between a brick fireplace and the ubiquitous glass doors. Copper pots hung from exposed rafters, and green-glass jars were filled with provisions I couldn't always identify. More stones and seashells and pieces of driftwood lined the windowsills and ledges, and I noticed they were artfully arranged, not haphazardly collected. His doing or hers? Or did he keep them as a shrine to the loss of her?

"I like this room best in winter," Michael said, and I nodded, imagining a pot of hearty soup on the stove, a fire crackling in the grate while a bitter wind whipped the long grass near the dunes. How wonderful the room would smell; how safe it would seem. I saw myself in a man's flannel shirt with the sleeves rolled twice, stirring soup, sipping tea.

"Of course," Michael added with a wistful purse of his lips, "I won't own this place come winter."

I felt bereft for him, conscious now of the grief and loneliness inherent in divorce. In the clear light of midday, a gravelly darkness lay beneath Michael's eyes. I wondered how visible was the duskiness of my own accumulated loss—of my mother, my husband, my equilibrium. Was recognition what drew us to each other? *Were* we drawn to each other? What was I doing, imagining myself in winter in a house that would soon belong to a woman I'd never met, the spoils of a man I barely knew?

Michael shrugged, bent to reach into one of the green-glass jars, then held out a cookie across the counter. I took it, thinking it meant for me, and had lifted it nearly to my lips before realizing its shape was a bone. With a little gasp I hoped Michael didn't catch, I offered the biscuit to Homer, who carried it into a corner to chew.

"Would you like something to drink?" Michael asked. Was he smiling?

I averted my gaze, in case he was amused about the dog biscuit. Had he deliberately teased me? My cheeks stung, from sun and foolishness. "Not right now," I replied. "Thanks."

We walked back through the central room, past the circular stair and a short hall. "The master bedroom," Michael announced in a flat tone, and he hung back, standing away from the door to let me pass. "Not much to see in here," he added as I poked my head into the room without entering. "Same view."

Though large, the room was spare, and I got the feeling items had been recently removed. A king-size futon bed, unmade, faced the doors of glass. A pine chest of drawers and a rush-seated, ladder-back chair stood against the long wall. From one corner, a tall, silver lamp crooked its neck like a wading bird. That was all the furniture, though there were piles of things—newspapers, books, a coffee cup, a pair of eyeglasses—on the floor beside the bed. The essential things, I thought, nothing more.

"A great view to wake up to," I told Michael, scanning the room for clues to his life.

Michael brushed past me into the room and reached above the glass doors to a long, blue casing. "I *don't* wake up to the view," he said, pulling down a pale blue, pleated shade, changing the color of light on his skin. "The house faces southeast, so the morning sun would shine right in my eyes if I didn't cover the glass."

I laughed and walked over to stand beside him as he tugged on the shade and it folded up into itself. I wanted to move close, to brush the pale hairs on his arm with the darker ones on mine till they all stood on end, but I didn't.

"The light is wonderful at this time of day," I said, looking beyond the deck, over the bleached-white dunes to where the Atlantic sparkled silver in the distance. I breathed the faint, sweet scent of salt and sun and sweat from Michael's skin.

"It is," he agreed. "The light is very special here. Like others who live here, it's what I treasure best about this place." He kept his gaze straight ahead.

"I understand that," I said, turning slightly toward his arm to breathe in more of him. "Everything looks different somehow."

"Clarified," he said.

"Resplendent," I answered.

"Radiant," he answered, a smile in his voice.

Standing beside him I felt, more than saw, his height. My head came just past his shoulder, which would make him several inches over six feet. Taller than Keith.

"Well," he said, turning. "Let's go up to the next level."

I followed Homer, his toenails plinking on the metal steps as we ascended the staircase to the balcony, then turned down a hallway to another, more tightly wound, circular stair. Homer stopped and lay at the foot of it, head between his paws. Michael stepped over him and I followed, my eyes fixed on a small, round place at the nape of Michael's neck. We climbed to a widow's walk and a tight, covered deck with room enough for just two people and a telescope.

The view from here was, as I knew it would be, phenomenal. We pressed against the railing and looked out across an endless ocean. I thought I could see all the way to where the earth dipped, to the place that curved around the sphere. A strong breeze blew back my hair, and I felt Michael looking at me—felt his eyes on the bend of my throat. I breathed in as deeply as my lungs allowed, relishing the sting.

"It's great up here at night," Michael said, and I thought I felt his breath across my hair, a stirring warmer than wind.

"I can imagine," I said, closing my eyes, reconstructing stars.

"I like to be alone up here," he continued. "To clear my brain."

I wondered about the kinds of things he needed to clear. As though I knew him at all! I shuddered and wrapped my arms around my chest.

Michael touched my shoulder. "Cold?" he asked.

"No. This feels good."

Michael made a small sound, half-sigh, half-laugh. "It's funny," he said. "This is such a great house. But I spend most of my time at the very top or the very bottom of it."

I turned my face up to his and he was looking at me and our eyes met. We both smiled. I knew what that meant; we'd smiled at how we didn't look away, and we kept looking.

I felt a swift contraction then, a pulling deep inside as though the walls of my belly had just collapsed. I must have blanched because something changed in Michael's face as well. I thought I saw a shadow cross his eyes.

A flash of nausea, and I remembered who I was, a possibly pregnant, still-married woman. I tilted my chin toward the sun, shaking my hair like a flag against the breeze. Just for a moment, I wanted to get stuck in time, in the now.

I felt a quick touch on my hand and looked to where my fingers rested on the railing. Michael pointed to my wedding rings.

"Antique?" he asked, his index finger hovering above my diamonds.

"Yes," I said. This was the moment he would ask about my marriage.

"Very nice," he said, and with that swift dismissal he turned toward the winding stair. "Shall we?" He led me down as he'd led me up.

"So, where do you make your jewelry?" I asked the back of his head as we descended. My sandals slipped from my heels and clanked against the steps. Homer, at the bottom, lifted his head and wagged his tail in greeting.

"Down below," Michael said. "On the lowest level, off the first deck, are several rooms. One is where I work—or rather, play." He paused, perhaps to smile; I was looking down on his neck. "Another is a kind of rudimentary wine cellar. Then there's storage, laundry, the garage."

"I'd like to wash my hands," I said when we reached the main level.

"Oh, of course," Michael said. "I'm sorry." He pointed to a door near the kitchen. "That's the guest bathroom. I'll go get cleaned up as well." He glanced down at his dirt-streaked T-shirt and grinned. "Guess I'll change into something less comfortable."

In the small, stone-floored bathroom, I sat on the elongated toilet and let loose a noisy pee, a welcome physical relief. Wherever I was lately, I worried I would need to find a bathroom, would be uncomfortable and unable to concentrate without one close by. But today I hadn't thought about my full bladder until this moment.

I scrubbed my hands and washed my face with a fragrant, fish-shaped soap. That *had* to be the wife's, I thought. Men didn't care about the shape of soap. I wished I'd brought my purse—some lipstick, a comb for my hair—but when I scrutinized my face in the mirror, I wasn't displeased. I looked good today with my new tan. My cheekbones stood out and my eyes seemed to shine. I shook my head. What was I thinking?

When I stepped out of the bathroom, Michael was waiting, leaning on his desk, Homer curled up beneath it. He had not only washed but changed his clothes and wet-combed his hair. In his white polo shirt and pressed khaki shorts he reminded me of Damien on his way to school—or a slightly older schoolmate of Damien's, on a date. I almost laughed. Instead, sliding my hands into the pockets of my shorts, I touched my sunglasses, and then, beneath them, the scallop shell.

Michael held up my lapis ring.

"Time to get down to business," he said with a quick smile and I remembered why I was here. How many minutes, or hours, had passed? I'd forgotten to put on my watch. I felt a stab of guilt. What had Athena said to Damien and my father about where I was?

Michael directed me through a door near the front entrance. Homer remained behind, asleep under the desk, and I felt oddly unchaperoned as we descended a narrow, carpeted staircase.

We emerged into a dimly lit room with a low ceiling of maybe seven feet. Compared to the rest of the house, this space felt womblike. Outside the doors on the lower deck, the sunflowers we'd planted blazed in the midday light, a patch of color against the muted hues of cedar planking and windswept dunes. The light didn't penetrate the glass, however, the way it did upstairs.

"My playroom," Michael said, tilting his head so that a lock of hair fell across his eyes.

I laughed. "Literally." I nodded toward a row of instruments, stacks of amplifiers, sound equipment, and a wall of stereo components. "Are you a musician, too?"

Michael grinned. "I was a musician *first*," he said. "Played lead guitar in a band all through college and med school. Now I just sit in every once in a while with friends. Mostly blues these days."

"I was a music major," I told him. "I played piano and violin." I walked over to examine his electric guitar, a Stratocaster, deep blue with subtle gold flecks.

"Your guitar is the color of my ring!" I blurted.

"We have much in common."

Towers of CDs, drawers of cassette tapes, and shelves of record albums lined one whole wall. "Do you really still listen to vinyl albums?" I asked, thumbing through the alphabetized covers: The Beatles, Beethoven, Paul Buchanan, Eric Clapton, John Coltrane, Cream, Miles Davis, The Doors, Duke Ellington, Brian Eno, Billie Holiday, Howlin' Wolf . . . An eclectic collection.

"Sure," Michael answered. "Vinyl sounds so much better, warmer; CDs have no soul." He ambled over to a table strewn with wires and beads, plugged in a soldering tool and switched on an intensity lamp.

"True," I agreed, selecting an album of Rodgers and Hart tunes. "But what about scratches? Do you mind if I put this on?"

Michael glanced at the album I held up. "Sure," he said, fastening goggles over his eyes. "Actually, I've had some of my favorite vinyl re-furbished—washed and re-coated. That's one."

I handled the record by its edges in the way I remembered from my college days, and set it carefully onto the turntable. How like me it would be to drop the stylus. My hand trembled as I lowered the phonograph arm to the groove, but the needle slipped soundlessly into place.

"Come, let me measure your finger," Michael said, and I reached his side as the opening bars of "Where or When" filled the room.

CHAPTER 10

July, Atlanta

I STARTED WALKING AT THE END OF JUNE. Every morning after I took Damien to swim team practice, I trekked the two-and-a-half-mile circumference of my neighborhood. I'd drop Damien off, walk my loop, and pick him up at our club without getting out of my car, and in this way I avoided the other mothers, who sat sipping coffee around umbrella tables, novels and newspapers open before them but never read.

I told those mothers, my erstwhile summer friends, that I was walking to get in shape, and they commended me when we passed in the parking lot. "You're so good, Amanda!" Maureen Pope cooed to me in her old-Atlanta drawl. "We miss you!" Susie Riley called, waving her tennis racquet as she lifted it out of her car trunk. "You're looking great!" Janet Currie insisted as she wheeled her baby stroller past. But the truth was, for once, I hardly cared how I looked. I wasn't walking to lose weight, though I had lost a few pounds, along with most of my appetite. I was walking because I couldn't talk.

I couldn't talk about my life, and I didn't want to listen to them talk about theirs. I didn't want to hear how Maureen's husband, Bruce, was a compulsive researcher, driving her crazy with the minutiae of his quest for a new computer. I didn't care that Janet's dry cleaner had lost Joe's shirts, and he was insisting she take the owner to small claims court. I certainly didn't want to know that Andy Riley was traveling so much, he and Susie hadn't had sex in over a month. Because if anyone asked about my husband, I might smash my sunglasses against the tabletop. I might wail. I might say Keith had told me he needed "space," but couldn't say what he meant by that, and I had to keep myself in motion until I found out.

So, I walked.

I walked without seeing anything at all except a kind of fluid murkiness, as though I were wandering underwater.

I thought about Keith, of course, replaying whatever "discussion" we'd had the night before or that morning. My chest would grow hollow with remembering, as though my rib cage were a thin shell, like those of the small, blue eggs in a nest I'd found while pruning crepe myrtle. I felt my insides would drain out of me, then, as yolk through a pinhole in an Easter egg, and that the slightest jolt would crack me. So I walked faster, trying to sweat, trying to fill myself with breath and fluid.

And sometimes, when I had walked myself beyond all thought, I would see the apparition of my mother's face. I longed for her at those moments, because I now realized she had been the one person to whom I could tell anything, the one person with whom I need not feel ashamed. I told her the story of my marriage in my head as I walked.

The night before swim team started, Keith went out for drinks with Sarah Stein. He had just returned from a three-day business trip to Houston, and I'd smiled when I heard the garage door opening, happy he was home early. Curled in my favorite wicker chair on the sun porch, I hummed a concerto as I sewed camp labels into Damien's T-shirts. Keith walked in through a haze of sunlight, and my face warmed at how handsome he looked in his dark blue suit.

"You don't mind if I go out tonight," he said after only a few minutes of catch-up talk. I remember at first feeling only a quick shudder of surprise; then my heart did a rapid time lapse, like an opening flower, to dread.

"Where?" I asked. I was holding my sewing needle straight up in front of me.

"I got a voice mail from Sarah." He unknotted his tie. "She wants to talk."

For a moment I was stunned silent. "Well, I *do* mind," I answered finally. "You just got home. We haven't seen you in three days. Now you want to go out on a date?"

"It's not a *date*," Keith said in a voice that made me feel small and wrong.

But he ended up going. He said he wouldn't go, and of course then I felt bad for keeping him, knowing the rest of the evening would be ruined either way. As I poured us each a glass of wine, I tried to explain myself, rubbing ineffectually at the detergent film on my goblet.

"Do you realize how often I've asked you to meet me for lunch in the last three months? But you never have the time." I thought that expressed a clear injustice: he didn't make time for me, but he wanted me to give time to someone else. I thought he would turn on his heel and say, "My, God, Amanda, you're right. I'm sorry."

Instead he said, "That's it. I'm going."

And I felt as though I'd been slammed against a wall, as though he'd been taken from me without warning, in some kind of accident. An accident I'd caused.

The next morning, I began to walk.

I walked and I prayed—prayed only outdoors for some reason, as though to do so I required the scent of trees. I prayed for Keith to love me, and then immediately thought, what a stupid, selfish prayer. I should petition at least for the well-being of my entire family: for Isabella, fifteen hundred miles away, green and tender in a grimy city; and for Damien about to leave for summer camp and the perils of open fires and overturned canoes and boyish hijinks in trees. I should implore grace in the name of my father, bereft without the burden of my mother. And surely I should plead for my mother herself, for her soul, if there was a possibility souls did exist, as well as for the tangled knot of my own grief. I realized I had to prioritize, to ask God for the right things. But I didn't know how to ask Him, any more than I'd known how to ask Keith for love.

And so I walked, day after day, and my legs began to get strong. One morning, after a rain, the street seemed narrower than usual, tunnellike. Out of nowhere, or out of someplace hidden, a dog I had never seen began to follow me. By follow me I mean that he seemed to accompany me, but he did so in a strange way—by running ahead. He kept several yards beyond me the entire time, trotting always in the direction I was headed, now and then glancing back. Once I almost caught up to him, and then he turned his squarish head to pant at me, tongue lolling out of his pink-lipped snout. At that moment, he reminded me of Keith. Something ironic twitched in his grin, the way his lips pulled back beyond his gums. Maybe Keith, too, was traveling with me by running ahead. Maybe I needed only to proceed along the route I was taking. I went home feeling almost calm that day.

One morning during the second week in July, Damien went to a friend's after swim team, and I decided to get all my housework done before taking my shower. I thought how nice it would be when I was dressed and alone to sit very still beneath the tall pecan tree in my garden, facing the red verbena by the southern fence, watching for hummingbirds. I straightened the kitchen, made the beds, and picked up clothing, then went around emptying trash. It's not that I was looking through the waste bin by Keith's desk, as he later accused me; it's simply that the receipt happened to flutter out. A receipt for Jacob's Tavern, a bar and grill downtown near Keith's office. A lunch tab, the amount too high for one person, dated the week before. I calculated: the date would have fallen on the previous Monday, the day I got my hair cut. I specifically recalled asking Keith where he'd eaten lunch that day because I had shared a sandwich with my hairdresser, a very good club sandwich from a new deli I wanted to tell him about. Keith had said he'd eaten in the company cafeteria.

I picked up the receipt and knew immediately what had happened. He had taken her to lunch, Sarah; he had paid for it. That was what was wrong, why he couldn't tell me. He was acting courtly to her, and he hadn't even had the decency to watch where he threw the evidence! I couldn't imagine anything—not Keith peeling off her black lace bra and kissing her palest flesh, not him nuzzling her downy slope farther and farther till she moaned in pleasure—nothing could give me more pain than to visualize him sitting across a booth from this other woman, talking to her, looking into her eyes, listening.

When Keith arrived home that night, a scotch on the rocks awaited him. I was on my second, and as I handed him his glass, I suggested we go out onto the patio. Damien was building a Lego fort on the kitchen table—something he hadn't done in a long time—and I didn't want him to hear our conversation.

I'd intended to act cool, detached, ironic, and irresistibly attractive. But Keith slouched in his chair. He had thrown his tie across the kitchen table and now he unbuttoned his shirt, revealing the frayed edge of his undershirt. He looked tired and forlorn—sorry for himself—and I grew outraged.

"Please explain to me what the hell this is," I hissed at him, pulling the receipt from my pocket and dropping it in his lap.

Keith picked up the thin rectangle, looked at it, then closed his eyes. "So, what?" he said in a low, exhausted voice.

"So what?" I asked, my voice rising. "So *what?*"

"So I took a colleague to lunch." He inhaled and held his breath. The sinews of his throat flexed.

"Oh, a colleague." I laughed meanly. "Sarah? That colleague?"

"Yes," he answered, then added bitterly, "I knew you would react this way."

"So you *lied* to me!" I was seething now, behaving the way I'd promised myself I wouldn't; behaving the way, in a film or a play, a character would act to prove herself worthy of the audience's disdain.

"A white lie," Keith grumbled, downing his scotch. Ice cubes clinked in his glass—such a civilized sound.

"A lie!" I shouted. "A run-of-the-mill, dirty little deceit!" I threw my glass to the brick at his feet, and it immediately shattered, one of my favorite tumblers, into a hundred slivers indistinguishable from ice.

Later, after I'd taken Damien out for pizza and rented him a video, after I'd swept the patio by the light of a Japanese lantern because I couldn't bear the sight of broken glass, after I'd cried in the shower until the water ran cool and my tears grew thin, much later that night I was ready to talk to Keith again.

He sat on the bed, fully dressed with his shoes kicked off, on top of our faded patchwork summer quilt, his hands locked behind his head, his eyes fixed on the slow-moving ceiling fan. He didn't stir as I opened the door from our bathroom and passed in front of him to take a nightgown from my dresser, didn't shift his gaze as I stopped to brush my wet hair in front of the oval mirror standing in the corner. The mirror was an antique, with candleholders on either side. I had always meant to light the candles, but I never had.

I sat on the edge of the bed, examining the pale blue ribbon that laced through the bodice of my cotton gown. This could be the nightdress of a young girl, I thought to myself, of a virgin or of an old woman.

Keith didn't move, but I sensed when he closed his eyes.

"I'll tell you about it," he said quietly.

I turned, a pinpoint of anger flaring like a lit match in my chest. "Do tell," I said.

"She—Sarah—is unhappy at Stone. As am I. You know I've been waiting to get into general management—been kept on a string. Well, for Sarah, it's the same kind of thing. Worse. She now reports to someone she should be supervising."

"If only I'd realized how much you two have in common!" I sneered. "I wouldn't begrudge you a blow job."

"Amanda." Keith leaned forward and raked his fingers across his scalp. "I have not had sex with her."

"But you want to," I said. "So you will."

Keith sighed and shook his head. I noticed the gray around his ears. All over, really, his hair had grown dull. "I don't want to. Or maybe I do, I don't know, but that's not the point."

"When do you think you'll know?" I asked, rising and walking to my dresser, just to go somewhere. I ran my fingers along the edge, checking for dust. There was dust.

"What we've been talking about, if you would only listen," Keith said in a stronger voice. "What we've been talking about, Sarah and I, is leaving Stone. Starting our own company. If we could take a few clients with us, we could get started."

I froze. No one left Stone, no one in his right mind or with any kind of decent career path. Stone was *the* prestige insurance company in the nation, arguably the world, solvent and stable when others of its kind had floundered. It had provided us a secure life.

"Why?" was all I could say.

"You know why," Keith said in a clipped voice. "If you've paid attention. I'm stuck in a staff position, given nothing but lip service and empty promises."

"You've had a terrific career," I said. "You've taken care of us."

He frowned and squeezed his eyes shut.

I knew Keith had been frustrated lately, underappreciated. We'd both been music majors in college, before Isabella. He'd gotten an MBA because we'd had a family to support. But I'd made sacrifices, too; I'd dedicated my life to Isabella, then to Damien, never considering the possibility of choice. Children *were* our choice. I'd felt some disappointment, occasional wistfulness about what might have been, but I'd assumed that was the human condition. In a word, adulthood.

"You're serious about leaving Stone?" I asked, tying the blue ribbon into knots.

Keith nodded, glaring at me as though I were a stranger. "I knew you wouldn't like it," he said.

"And you've been planning this departure, with her?"

Keith swung his legs off the bed. "We've been discussing options. Pooling our skill sets, our contacts. She has been director of National Accounts. If she can take one or two important clients . . ."

I looked toward the window, black beyond the filmy curtains. "When were you planning to discuss this with me, this change in our life. Or were you?"

"We're discussing it now." Keith rose. "I'm going to get a beer. Want anything?"

I shook my head, no, as my eyes filled.

When Keith came to bed, I was crying softly into my pillow. He touched my shoulder and I turned to him, passionate in my despair. We made love as though we were drowning, the both of us gasping, clawing at skin, lifting our faces as if toward oxygen.

When he entered me, I shuddered, and I knew he knew it was a reflex not of ecstasy but of grief. He also knew, without asking, that I hadn't put in my diaphragm. To have done so would have been an act of hope or of expectation, and how could I have summoned either? Keith had condoms in his night table drawer, but even to reach for them would have suggested a tacit faith, an acknowledgment of what we were doing. If we paused for a minute, we both knew, we could not continue. So we didn't use anything and he pulled out.

He timed it perfectly, ejaculating across my belly at the precise moment that ruined it a little for him and completely for me. My labia were tingling, almost humming with what felt like hollowness, and that's how I fell asleep, famished.

Thus went July for us. I was starving all the time for Keith, and he was unprepared for my voraciousness—literally; coitus interruptus became our method of birth control. When I thought about it, I couldn't help but see the irony: relying on Keith to pull out implied substantial trust on my part, and trust was at issue between us.

When we weren't fucking, we were fighting—I discovered several more lies of omission; he accused me of selfishness, of not understanding his need to, as he put it, "reinvent" himself. He denied he was sleeping with Sarah, but wouldn't deny that he wanted to. I asked him when he would know what he wanted, and he said he needed mental "space" to figure things out. Meanwhile, he kept meeting Sarah to discuss their treachery against Stone, sometimes telling me about it and other times not speaking at all.

Every night I wanted to ask him, "Did you see Sarah today?" But when I did, he was evasive, angry.

"Don't grill me, Amanda," he'd reply. "I don't need to face your hostility the moment I walk in the door."

So half the time I didn't ask, and the uncertainty wrenched me more than knowing would have. At the same time, I developed a taste for the pangs that made me feel alive. Uncertainty felt like hunger— a yearning, bottomless, gut-emptiness not unlike the experience of meeting someone to whom you are immediately drawn. Uncertainty felt like desire.

I figured we were experiencing similar sensations, Keith and I, hunger and uncertainty. He wouldn't say he wanted me or that he didn't. He wouldn't say our marriage would survive. All he would say was that he was going through a dark time, that this was about him, not me, and I shouldn't be so selfish.

"Don't be selfish," my father had chastised us children when we'd complained that our mother wouldn't be there for back-to-school night because she was in the hospital. "Think of how your mother feels," my father would say. "Think how bad it is for *her* to miss it." I tried to feel sorry for my mother on those occasions, but I never could, and I never knew how to explain. If you understood someone else's hurt, did you give up your own?

Some mornings I woke up angry, furious at Keith, although I hadn't gone to sleep that way. It was as though the small, shapeless clay bits of my despair had been slow fired overnight in the kiln of my subconscious. And I awoke to find them hardened into pointed shards, which I aimed his way.

"You'll be late for your meeting," I said as he toweled himself off from his shower and stared blankly at the row of blue suits hanging in his closet. "You're deliberately sabotaging your career."

"This is what I mean about you," he would say. "Whose side are you on?"

But at night, after a drink or two, I would turn to him, stroke his shoulder, smell his neck, press my lips against his ear. Sometimes he responded and sometimes he moved away. For a few days he refused to come to bed, falling asleep with the newspaper on the family room couch.

"This is unhealthy, Amanda," he said. "The way you're honing your pain. I don't want to be a part of it."

But he was more than part of it; he must have at least recognized that, and so after five days he came back to our bed and slept with me again, and again he pulled out. I believed he did not want to make me pregnant, not now. Though I knew, theoretically, that pregnancy could result from the tiniest drop of sperm, I said nothing.

What would I do? I thought about this as I lay in bed, remembering my Isabella-swollen body, my Damien-swollen body. I'd taken pleasure in those physical changes, the differences from my nonpregnant body, in becoming another self, in harboring new life. But a third child was the last thing we needed. I knew that much, even if I couldn't yet admit that our marriage would not survive.

CHAPTER 11

THE MOTORCYCLE ENGINE RUMBLED LIKE A GIANT CAT. Michael handed me a silver helmet.

"How do you get Homer out here on a motorcycle?" I wondered.

Michael laughed. "Why, that's *his* helmet you're borrowing," he said. "Actually, Homer stays with Athena during the weeks that I ride the bike from the city. He loves hanging out with Sunshine."

"Oh." I nodded and pulled the helmet on. It slid forward and Michael stepped closer to adjust the chin strap. His helmet bumped mine, awkwardly, like a first kiss, and I looked away.

"There," he said, testing the fit with his hands. Then he swung his leg over the long, black leather seat, and I climbed on behind him.

"Hold on!" he shouted over the sound of the engine as he released the clutch. My fingers rested on either side of his waist, seeking balance, but as the bike lurched forward into gear, I clutched at the belt loops of his shorts.

We went fast, very fast on that empty beach road, and I wondered whether Michael was trying to impress me or to scare me. Or maybe the ride just felt fast, with the big engine thrumming beneath us and the wind snapping through our sleeves. It felt wonderful.

I tried to lean away, self-conscious about my breasts brushing Michael's back, but the first curve pressed me forward, and after that I just leaned into him, eyes closed. That place where we touched, his back against my chest, grew warm, and I slipped my fingers from his belt loops to curl them around his torso. Engine, wind, and ocean roared around me as I hugged him and we hurtled through space, yet I felt protected as though in a capsule.

In a minute, we'd arrived and stopped, idling in neutral at the grassy berm in front of Laughing Gull Cottages. I found myself un-expectedly emotional. Something was over that hadn't begun, some-thing I couldn't name but fiercely wanted to go on, like a dream I struggled to finish though an alarm urged me awake. I unbuckled my chin strap and returned the helmet to Michael.

"Thanks," I said, turning my face as I disembarked so he wouldn't notice how ridiculously lost I must look. I would probably never see him again.

"My pleasure," Michael said in a louder-than-usual voice; his hel-met still covered his ears. He squinted and leaned toward me. "How long are you here?"

"Until Saturday."

"We'll see each other," he said simply. I looked straight at him then, not at his eyes or his mouth, but at the place where his unbut-toned collar lay open, at the tender rim of neck and chest.

"Okay," I said, smiling, and then he gunned the engine and took off, holding up his hand in a wave as he sped down the road. Hold-ing up his hand until he disappeared.

I started up the path to the cottages, lightheaded with the thought of seeing Michael again (how? when?), nervous about the reception I would get from my father and my brother and my son. It was mid-afternoon; I'd been gone several hours. Michael had sized the lapis ring, then polished it. Then I'd asked him to play his guitar. He'd ac-commodated me with gusto, demonstrating the lapis-colored Strato-caster, his Martin Acoustic, and a 1971, flame-finish Les Paul of which he was especially proud. I loved hearing him, observing him, discerning him through his chords. He played guitar exactly as he moved, I thought, in the cadences of his limbs and eyes and smile. He couldn't have explained anything about himself that would have told me more.

The sun was strong, and beads of sweat ran in rivulets down my back as I trudged up the incline to my cottage. There it was—Sinclair

Central—and sure enough, there were people on my deck, sitting at my table, lying in my chaise. As I approached, I recognized Froggy, propped backward against the picnic table, bouncing Jay in her lap. Lizzie was on the chaise, lifting her head, shading her eyes with her hand. The straps to her bathing suit hung down in front of her chest. She spotted me and waved, and I waved back.

"Hey," she said as I reached the deck. "So, you bought that ring."

"Yeah," I said, looking down at my hand. Oh, God. After fitting it, Michael had taken the ring to polish, and I'd forgotten to put it back on. I wiped the perspiration off my forehead and smiled sheepishly.

"Let's see it," Froggy said, turning toward me. Her peeling nose was a patchwork of red and brown.

"I don't have it," I groaned, plopping into a chair. How could I explain that I'd forgotten about the ring because I'd been listening to this strange man play guitar? I'd sound like a teenager, or worse.

Some frothy concoction was set beside Lizzie's chaise. "What are you drinking?" I asked. "Let me have a sip?"

Lizzie stretched to offer me her glass. "Piña colada," she said. "My favorite beach drink. So, where's the ring?"

I took a sip. Too sweet a mix.

"You were gone all this time and you didn't get the ring?" Froggy asked, shifting her weight. Jay was starting to crab.

"I know," I said. "After all that, I guess I left it there." I set Lizzie's drink beside her.

"You dingbat," Lizzie said with a smile, her eyes closed.

"I don't understand how you could have left it. Wasn't that what you went there for?" Froggy's voice gathered annoyance at the quickening rate she bounced Jay on her knee. He started to wail.

I didn't know how to respond, so I asked, "Where's Damien? Where is everyone?"

Froggy stood up. "The men took the kids to play miniature golf." She patted Jay's back and he cried louder. "I've got to put him down," she said and strode into my cottage.

"Like an old dog," I murmured.

Snickering, Lizzie levered herself upright. "So tell me!" she insisted as she reached for the piña colada and took a gulp. "Come on, I know when something's up with you."

I smirked and pulled my chair closer, lowering my voice. "Nothing's up. Well, not really." I took her glass once more.

Lizzie laughed, a short bark, and leaned closer. A wisp of amber curl clung to her lips. "Amanda," she said. "Three hours, no ring, and I *heard* the motorcycle."

I took another swig of her drink—God, I was thirsty—and then I remembered I shouldn't be drinking. I still couldn't think of myself as pregnant. I set the piña colada at Lizzie's feet and squeezed my eyes shut. The combination of strong sun, skipped lunch, and surging guilt made my head swim.

"My period is late," I told my sister in a near-whisper as my throat grew tight.

"Oh, God!"

"And I think Keith is leaving me."

Lizzie squeezed my arm and smiled a sad, tight smile of acknowledgment. "Oh, Amanda," she said. "You must be miserable."

Sunday night's dinner was an ordinary barbecue—hamburgers, hot dogs, and potato salad Froggy had prepared at home—and it was late by the time we got the grill going. The men and kids had returned from miniature golf near five o'clock, and then Jeremy had insisted we all go down to the beach. This was the best hour, he argued, and I agreed, even though, after several hours stretched out on the deck in the hot sun, I'd felt too lazy to get off my chair. Still, I'd gone—we'd all gone, even my father—and it really was the most enchanting time, with the sun low and the tide high and the water a mirror of silvery light, sparkling as though the world were new.

By the time we got back to the cottages, showered and got the charcoal lit, it was nearly dark. A late dinner suited me, since I had filled up after I'd returned from Michael's on potato chips and handfuls of the sugary cereal Lizzie's kids ate. I'd told my sister as much as I could about my situation with Keith and our week's separation until Froggy rejoined us and the conversation turned to childbirth and babies. I never got to tell Lizzie about Michael or the glass house. Just as well, for the time being, as I wasn't quite sure how to describe the experience—nor how I felt about it.

After dinner, Ryan fell asleep on a chaise, covered with a beach towel. The three older kids, Damien and the twins, were running round the cottages with Crosby and a girl whose family had just arrived, playing some East Long Island version of "Manhunt." The adults sat around my picnic table sipping drinks and taking in the vast, blue-black sky, watching for August's renowned shooting stars.

Eventually Rick produced a box of cigars. Jeremy selected one, as did my father after a perfunctory protest, and the three men lit up and sat back. In the hope that we could continue our talk, I was about to suggest to Lizzie that we carry Ryan to her cottage when Athena appeared, still wearing her white dress, looking like a messenger in a school play.

"Good evening," she said with her slow semi-smile. She addressed us all, but fixed her gaze on me. "I trust the good doctor was able to adjust your ring to fit?"

"Yes," I answered. "He was very nice." I cringed inwardly at my words, wondering what Michael's niceness had to do with anything.

"Let's see how it looks," Athena requested. Why did I suspect she knew I didn't have it on?

I shook my head. "I don't . . . Well, I left it at his house." I heard Rick snort behind me, perhaps from cigar smoke.

"Aah." Athena nodded. "But Michael did size the ring for you?"

"Yes." I saw her point. "So I do need to pay you for it."

"No real hurry," Athena said in a way I knew meant she wanted what was owed her as soon as possible.

"Do you need money?" my father asked me, reaching into his pocket. I leaned to stop him. "No, that's okay." His arm felt thin beneath my hand.

The screen door to my cottage creaked open and slammed shut, and Froggy emerged, carrying a sleeping Jay. "I'm putting him down for the night in our cottage," Froggy announced as she lumbered past Athena and headed down the path. Jeremy looked up, cigar between his teeth, but said nothing.

"Will you take a credit card?" I asked Athena.

Athena smiled, her mouth a wide slash. "Of course," she said. "But you'll have to bring it to my office."

"I'll get it," I said, pushing myself up, hurrying into the cottage to find my purse.

For once, my cottage was empty. Inside was quiet and still, a counterpoint to the vibrating, cricket-filled night outside. I sat on the edge of the sofa bed and imagined what it would be like to stay here for a week by myself, alone. Sleeping till I'd slept enough, eschewing regular meals to eat when and how I chose, listening only to the sounds of gulls and wind and waves and the unraveling of my own thoughts. Facing whatever I had to face about my marriage—and myself. I craved solitude with a sudden physical clench that jolted me. I would do this, I decided. I'd arrange a way to spend a week alone.

The idea delighted me, and I allowed myself to imagine taking off right then, slipping out the window of Damien's room, stealing through the shrubbery to where my rental car was parked, and driving down Old Montauk highway to the next resort. Maybe I'd stop at the Memory Motel and have a drink with Keith Richard, who'd just happen to be in town. He'd be looking for a violinist to sit in on a session. I'd call Athena and ask her to tell my family something had come up; ask Lizzie and Jeremy to please watch Damien; and I'd be back on Friday. Would anyone really mind?

Rick's mocking laughter pierced my reverie. I located my purse beside my violin case, grabbed my wallet, and forced myself back toward my obligations.

Athena sat at her desk, the tips of her fingers perched at the edge of the credit card machine in front of her. A single hanging light bulb covered with a white paper lantern swung in the breeze as I closed the door. Odd shadows wobbled across the floor and walls.

Wordlessly, Athena accepted my VISA and ran it through the machine, then presented me with the paper slip to sign. As I took my copy of the receipt, Sunshine appeared, padding over to me from one of the back rooms, and I bent to pet her.

"Well, hello, girl," I said, my nose close enough to her snout to feel the warm puffs of air she breathed. "I suppose your brother will be visiting soon."

Athena rose. "We enjoy having Homer with us whenever he comes," she said, deliberately vague. I smiled, amused, and looked around the room. Its limited appeal increased slightly with shadows and the coolness of night. Again I was reminded of the basement of my parents' home and I wondered whether this place was a re-creation, consciously or otherwise, of something in Athena's own past. I felt kindly toward her, suddenly, because of that and because she seemed to live so easily in solitude among strangers.

"Is it just yourself and your son living here?" I asked, not caring whether she thought me presumptuous.

"Just the two of us now," she answered, sliding the credit card machine into the desk drawer.

I smiled at her coyness, reminded of the way Jeremy and I had spoken to each other during adolescence. *Guess,* we'd always seemed to be saying to one another. *What do you think?*, as though even the simplest concerns were mysteries.

"This place brings me back to another time," I told Athena.

"Really." She crossed the room toward the kitchen. "And do you have time now for a little something . . . a glass of wine?"

"I suppose," I said, knowing I shouldn't drink.

"Come."

I followed Athena to the kitchen. Sunshine brushed past us and settled under the kitchen table with a sigh.

Athena pulled open the refrigerator, took out a nearly full bottle of white wine, and held it up. "Does this suit you?" Before I could answer, she turned to pluck two blue glass goblets from a shelf and began pouring. "It's from one of the local vineyards, owned by a friend of mine. Overpriced, but I didn't pay for it."

I reached for the goblet she extended. I would just take a sip or two. Hadn't my mother and her entire generation smoked cigarettes during their pregnancies? Hadn't they drunk coffee all day and cock-tails before dinner? *Anything in moderation,* my father had often said.

"This way," Athena directed once more, and I followed her out of the kitchen to a small hallway onto which three doors opened. For a moment I imagined I would be asked to choose a door.

But, of course, Athena chose and led me through the first door into a dark bedroom, her room, I gathered. Instead of turning on a light, she lit several large candles scattered across a bureau. Then she moved a hurricane lamp to a low table at the foot of her bed—really a quilt-covered futon on the floor—sat cross-legged at its edge and motioned for me to do likewise.

The quilt was a patchwork of satins and velvets and angoras and silks, odd-shaped scraps of the most sensual fabrics. As I settled myself and my wineglass, Athena slid a large water pipe from under the table. A hookah—wasn't that what it was called—a kind of bong? Probably twenty years had passed since I had seen one.

I laughed nervously and confessed, "I feel like Alice in Wonderland," reminding myself of Michael and how I'd compared him to the Cheshire cat. I remembered his broad smile and his soft eyes and the sound of his guitar. I needed to say his name, to talk about him.

"Will Michael be bringing Homer to stay with you when he goes back to the city?" I asked, directly this time.

Athena nodded, reached under the table and brought forth a small box made of inlaid wood from which she extracted a baggie half filled with marijuana. "We have an arrangement," she told me. "Michael is free to leave Homer here any time." She began filling the bowl of the pipe. I wondered how long the water had been in there.

"It was stupid of me to leave the lapis ring at his house," I said and took a sip of the not especially good wine. I wouldn't be tempted to drink much of it, just the few sips necessary to avoid explaining to Athena why I shouldn't drink.

Athena waved her hand at me, her bracelets dangling. "Don't worry," she said. "Michael will return your ring."

Of course he would. But I realized that what I wanted was to get it from him myself, to see him one more time. I wanted to measure my already slippery memory against his solid actuality.

Athena removed a lighter from the box, lit the bowl, and inhaled deeply on one of the two tubes that hung on either side of the pipe. Holding her breath, she turned to me and smiled with her lips pressed closed, her eyebrows raised, and offered me the other tube.

I accepted it—intending to take only the shallowest hit—and inhaled. How easily the water-cooled smoke filled my lungs. I'd indulged in the occasional joint over the years since college, but I'd forgotten the singular pleasure of smoking from a water pipe. Suddenly my lungs exploded and I lurched forward in a fit of coughing. My shallow hit. Athena watched me like an indulgent aunt, then handed me my wine.

I sipped as little as possible, embarrassed, and avoided her gaze by looking around the room. My eyes had adjusted to the darkness and a painting above the bureau caught my attention. In it a large owl perched on a branch, preparing to swoop down, its stare fixed on something beyond the bottom of the frame. Painted on a rectangle of wood, it was simply yet powerfully executed. This bird wasn't in any way cute, unlike many owl images, but it commanded admiration. Hung as it was above the flickering candles, the painting took on the aspect of a shrine. I felt certain the artist was the same person who had painted the laughing gull on the office door. Athena herself?

"That owl," I said as Athena inhaled again and slid the pipe toward me. "It's wonderful."

"Mmmhmmm." Athena held the smoke in her lungs.

I took my turn, mostly pretending to inhale.

Athena exhaled toward the ceiling, then informed me, "The owl is my symbol, the symbol of Athena, goddess of wisdom, arts, and warfare."

Of course. I nodded, containing a small amount of smoke in my chest, feeling its effects swirl through my brain. I could have been seventeen again and this room could have been my old room, the one I'd shared with Lizzie until I left for college. Instead of an owl painting, a wavy mirror had hung above our dresser, and posters of movie stars and rock bands covered the walls. But our curtains had been sewn from an Indian paisley tablecloth, as Athena's were, dripping candles lined our bureau, too, and the pungent scent of marijuana permeated the room, no matter how much incense I burned. Nobody but Jeremy seemed to notice, though, and he claimed not to care how many brain cells I destroyed.

I took another tiny sip of wine, worse tasting now. "The artist," I asked, gesturing toward the owl. "Is it the same person who painted the gull on your front door?"

"Very good." Athena rose and stepped over to a bookshelf constructed of wood planks over cinder blocks. I'd built such shelves, too, in my old room, and lined them with paperbacks and record albums, incense burners, and interesting rocks, and topped them with a monstrous spider plant whose offshoot descendants flourished even now in my father's den.

I closed my eyes, remembering my old room, remembering getting stoned for the first time with Sally Carter, my best friend. When Lizzie caught us at it, I warned her not to tell anyone; a few years later I was passing her the bowl. She never really took to getting stoned, though. She didn't like the feeling of being out of control, whereas I'd yearned for it, almost required it.

Speakers crackled, and then the room filled with Joni Mitchell's youthful soprano singing "All I Want," the first song on the *Blue* album. I opened my eyes. Athena turned from a tape deck on the bookshelf and returned to thump down beside me.

"Regarding your question," she began.

I looked at her features, softened now around the edges, tapering where they had been sharp. What question? I'd forgotten.

"The painter of the owl and the gull is—*was*—the same person," she explained. "My mother."

I took another hit, forgetting my decision to pretend-inhale, and the rush made me dizzy. My head jerked in an involuntary swoon, and I leaned back in an effort to concentrate.

Athena began to laugh, a throaty chortle punctuated by snorts. She laughed and laughed, the kind of laughter often described as contagious, though I didn't catch it. I sat there, dumbfounded, staring at her.

"You're so transparent," Athena said as her laughter subsided.

I smiled wanly, embarrassed for this character flaw. "I'm sorry," I said, trying for a touch of irony. But the words came out sincere.

Athena took a sip of wine and frowned into her glass.

"This stuff is borderline undrinkable," she said, then fixed her dark gaze on me. "You can't envision me having a mother, can you? Well, in a sense you're right. I was adopted, and now she's dead. So, actually, I don't have one."

"My mother is dead, too," I said. "A car accident, last summer."

"Ah. I'm sorry." Athena peered into her glass. "Mine died of cancer. Six years ago."

I nodded, kept nodding, watching the curved lines around her mouth form and reform as she spoke. "What was it like?" I asked. Was I stoned?

"The cancer?"

"No, having an artist for a mother."

Athena rose. I felt dizzy watching her.

"Aaah," she said. "*Was* she an artist? It's true she painted birds, had a great feeling for them. But mostly she was a real estate agent. Do you want something else to drink? Water?"

"Oh, yes," I answered, grateful. Why hadn't I thought to ask for some? My mouth was lined with fuzz.

Athena left the room and I lay back, turning to rest my face against the quilt. My cheek touched satin, cool and slippery; my fingers stroked velvet, soft and warm. I remembered once, as I lay on our leather couch wrapped in my oldest blanket, my mother had told me she found the voices she heard interesting. "They're like characters in a play," she had said, blowing cigarette smoke above me, and I'd wondered whether she found them more interesting than her family, whether her voices were a choice. I had wrestled throughout my adolescence with that question—could my mother control her illness, or at least her behavior, to any degree, and if she could, why did she repeatedly choose illness over us, Lizzie, Jeremy, and me, her children?

As an adult, of course, I knew better. Schizophrenia wasn't chosen; it was a matter of brain chemistry. I had reminded myself of this regularly, hoping someday my greedy heart would believe my judicious brain. But with that reminder came the frightening possibility of my own genetic frailty. My mother had succumbed to her illness relatively late in life—most schizophrenics were diagnosed in their teens. What would it take for insanity to claim me, and would I know if it had?

Now as I lay in a half-stupor on Athena's crazy quilt, I pushed the demon worry into a dark corner of my brain and contemplated whether my mother might have shown a kind of brilliance in creating her own complex alternate reality. The artist as madwoman wasn't a new concept, yet I had never really considered it in relation to my own mother. I had been too busy trying to keep my distance from her illness. But I liked the idea of my mother as an artist.

I heard Athena return with two clinking glasses of ice water. I meant to sit up—I was so thirsty—but for some reason I continued to lie on the bed. She set the glasses on the table and then stretched out beside me. Or at least I felt her stretch beside me; I kept my eyes shut. Not unpleasantly, I smelled the salty mustiness of her cottage coming off her body, her hair, and her clothes.

"You're not used to smoking dope," she said with concern, and for a moment I panicked, thinking she had put something other than marijuana in the pipe. Then I recalled that in the 1960's and 1970's, we'd all called pot *dope*. What did kids call it now, I wondered, and made a mental note to ask Isabella.

"Mmmm," I murmured. "Plus, I'm premenstrual." *Or pregnant*, I added silently. What troubled part of me wished for that to be so?

"Ah," Athena said. "And the moon is nearly full." I felt her weight shift—closer or away from me? I couldn't tell.

"And I've been under stress lately," I added.

"I thought so," Athena said. I felt her sit up and I opened my eyes. She was adding pot to the bowl, lighting the pipe again. I propped myself and reached for the closest glass of water.

"I was a real estate agent for a while," I said. "I loved looking at houses, imagining the lives they held, but I didn't enjoy the rest of the business."

"My mother was a natural," Athena said, offering me the pipe.

"No kidding," I said, shaking my head to refuse it. If I saw Michael again, I would ask him whether a few hits of pot were harmful in very early pregnancy.

"Mother bought Laughing Gull Cottages and various building lots along this road, bought whatever she could because she knew there was value here."

"There would be," I said, feeling my words come slowly. "By the ocean."

"My mother sold Michael his land, actually," Athena continued. "When she got sick, I came out from California to be with her. She offered me this place. I'd just split with Crosby's father, so I took it."

"The Last Time I Saw Richard" began to play. As Joni sang, "All romantics meet the same fate someday," I remembered the endless discussions Sally and I had once had about song lyrics. Now, at forty, I was engaged in just that sort of rambling conversation, babbling and smoking pot and listening to music in a room reminiscent of my old room. A part of me remained that same silly, over-serious girl.

"I left home at sixteen," Athena was saying. "I traveled cross-country in a VW van with a group of friends and lovers." She smiled, and light from the hurricane lantern glinted on her crooked front tooth. "So, until she was dying, I hadn't spend a lot of time with my mother." Athena shrugged. "But she was cool, knew how to take care of herself, and it turned out Crosby dug her." She leaned her head to one side and her braid brushed my arm. Her hair smelled of muffins. "And your mother? What was she like?" Athena asked.

Right away, I said the word. "My mother was a schizophrenic." I stared at my knees until they swam out of focus. "She started hearing voices when I was eleven, and was in and out of mental hospitals from that point on."

"Unfortunate," was Athena's plain response. But perhaps fate was that simple. My mother was the odd one out, drew the bad card. So it went. The song ended and silence covered the room like a rolling fog.

Finally, Athena spoke. "Are you hungry?"

"Starving," I said, surprising myself.

"I thought you might be." Athena searched beneath the table. "I don't keep a lot of munchie food." She pulled out half a bag of blue corn chips. "These shouldn't be too stale."

I reached for them, and again I was transported to my old room, leaning across the space that divided my bed from Lizzie's. But it wasn't Lizzie I was reaching toward; it was my mother. She was wearing an apron.

"Oh, God," I said to Athena as I cradled the bag of chips in my lap. "I just remembered the time I got my mother stoned."

Chapter 12
Long Island, 1972

I WAS SIXTEEN WHEN I DISCOVERED THE EXQUISITE MISERY of sexual love, the transporting eloquence of the violin, and the soul-freeing pleasure of smoking pot. The three were intricately related, I felt sure, and I spent hours alone in my room considering their connection while Lizzie went to skating practice and Jeremy took apart small motors in the backyard. If only others realized what I knew—that love and music were all that mattered—the world might finally achieve harmony.

Marijuana was, of course, the essential key to cosmic understanding. While LSD might provide a swifter route to higher consciousness, a rocket ship to the soul I intended someday to board, such a trip posed risks and required preparation. Pot on the other hand was a stroll through Strawberry Fields, a blessed relief from daily dread. Pot made life tolerable—it made my life tolerable and therefore, by extrapolation, would do the same for anyone. I figured the world could reap great benefits from increased tolerance. As Bob Dylan put it and I interpreted, "Everybody must get stoned."

I expressed these opinions to Sally Carter, my best friend since fifth grade, and the only person outside my family who knew the truth about my mother's illness, as we hung out in my room one afternoon.

"I don't know," she drawled in a spacey voice. We were splayed across my bed, listening to Jackson Browne's despondent crooning. "There are some people I just can't see getting high."

"Like who?" I asked, staring at the broodingly handsome face on the album cover in front of me, feeling one with his sorrow.

Sally inched her way to the window, where a small wooden pipe sat on the sill beside a purple Bic lighter. She lit the bowl, drew in deeply, held her breath, and blew the smoke out toward the ancient oak in my backyard. She fanned the air with her hand, then gasped, "Madame Hélène!"

Our French teacher. I burst into giggles, and Sally joined me, wheezing with delight.

"*Pas de tout!*" I replied, spitting out the syllables. "*Madame Hélène est très . . .*" I searched for the French word for cool. "*Froid!*"

Sally was beside herself; she rolled on the bed, pushing into me, bumping me into the night table and knocking my high-intensity lamp to the floor. Luckily, it hit the scatter rug and didn't break. But it clattered loudly.

Two sharp knocks on my door, and then Jeremy's recently deepened voice rumbled from the hall, above the sounds of our laughter and Jackson's lamenting lyrics. "Cool it in there, hippies!"

I sat up and stuck out my tongue. Sally gave the door the finger. She'd had a crush on Jeremy for years, impossible to admit because he was both my brother and a grade younger.

"Maybe him," I considered, snickering. Jeremy's footsteps thudded down the stairs.

"What?" Sally stood up and examined the center part of her long, blond hair in the mirror over my dresser. That her hair be absolutely perfect was crucial to her; in fact, her hair was all I could think of that was crucial to Sally these days.

"Maybe my brother is the one person I can't imagine getting high," I said. "Mr. Straight. He's beyond hope."

"Mmm," Sally answered, lifting a pale strand. "But you have to admit, you're lucky."

"I am?"

"Definitely. God, Mandy, you can get stoned right in your own bedroom and no one knows or cares."

I shrugged. Jeremy kind of cared.

"You have so much freedom," Sally said, frowning into the mirror. "Your parents are never around."

I stared at her. Of course she was right. My father was always at work, and my mother, even when she was "well," didn't seem to notice what I did, or mind. I had been forging her signature on my report cards for more than a year, even though my grades were good. She never asked for them. I was lucky! Why then did I so often wish she be magically replaced with a normal version of a mother?

"Yeah." I moved to refill the pipe from the film canister on the window ledge. "Luckiest girl in the world, that's me." I lit the bowl and looked down into our rather forlorn yard. Suddenly I missed Princess, our dog, who had died a few months earlier. I blew out smoke through the window screen. Jackson sang, "I am a child in these hills," and I turned from the view.

"Well, I guess I gotta go," Sally said, looking at her watch, a fancy diver's model left over from her swim team days. "My mother will have a conniption." She had quit the swim team around the time we'd started getting stoned. Her mother had been heartbroken.

Poor Mrs. Carter. Sally didn't have much use for her mother these days, but I still thought of her as I always had, with affection and longing. True, she had a lot to say about what Sally did, but that was normal, wasn't it? Couldn't Sally guess how envious I was of *her* life? Of her cinnamon toast for breakfast and Rice Krispie treats after school? She would *have* to guess: I didn't speak about such things.

I followed Sally down the stairs, through the kitchen to the back door. Only grownups and strangers ever used our front door. Sally yanked her knapsack from beside the radiator and, with a quick "Call you later," left through my yard. I watched her strut past Jeremy, who was working on our lawn mower near the garage, her chin high and her hair swinging. He ignored her.

I turned toward the pantry and considered a bowl of cereal with sliced bananas. Or maybe a banana spread with chunky peanut butter. There was the ubiquitous box of bakery doughnuts, the powdered kind, which my father had brought home the night before. Maybe I would start with one of those. I reached toward the half-filled box.

"Mandy." My mother appeared in the doorway of the basement stairs, carrying a laundry basket. The cigarette dangling from her hand threatened to ignite my father's clean undershirts. Her face wore that stricken look I'd come to recognize, and she was making that weird chewing movement with her mouth. I closed the doughnut box.

"I need you to pick up a prescription for me from the drugstore," she said and she set the laundry on the kitchen table.

"Now?" I groaned. I didn't feel like going up to the turnpike, where our drugstore was. I didn't yet have a driver's license, and I hardly ever rode my bike anymore. It wasn't cool. (In college, bicycles would become de rigueur, and I would regret having sold my black English racer at a garage sale.) Besides, I was stoned and going to Tulip Hill Drugs would bring me down.

My mother reached for her black vinyl purse on the counter, then pushed it aside. "Just tell him to charge it to my account," she instructed without looking at me.

A stale sweetness from the box of doughnuts in my hands made my stomach turn. "Daddy said no more charging," I reminded her.

My mother walked over to the sink and put out her cigarette under the faucet. She threw the soaked butt toward the overflowing trash, where it bounced out onto the floor. I let it lie there. She shook out another smoke from her pack and moved toward the stove.

She lit the cigarette off a gas burner and looked up at me with one squinting eye. "Please, Amanda," she said. "I need the medicine. I'm in pain."

Oh, no. I knew what that meant. She was filling another of my grandmother's prescriptions. My dead grandmother. Maybe this would be the time the pharmacist figured it out. Or maybe he didn't care, wanting only to make money.

"Fine," I said without looking at her. "But I need shampoo."

She didn't answer, and I knew that my little extortion meant nothing to her. For all she cared, I could charge myself a case of shampoo as long as she got her drugs. I did it—bought myself something every time I agreed to one of these favors—just on principle. She was staring at thin air now, blowing smoke, and I knew she was listening to the voices. I could almost hear them myself.

As I pushed through the screen door, she called to me, "Mandy, pick me up a carton of cigarettes."

I let the door slam and hurried past my brother. Maybe I could catch up to Sally, walk with her at least part of the way to the turnpike.

At the corner, however, I slowed down. I didn't want to walk with Sally. Even though she "knew" about my mother, she didn't really understand. Hadn't she just told me how lucky I was? My chest burned with anger. How dumb Sally was!

The only reason she even knew about my mother was because she'd been there, had been at my house in sixth grade one time when my father had to practically drag my mother to the hospital. (Most times, thank God, Mom actually wanted to go, would *ask* to be taken to the hospital when the voices got bad.) Even after five years of friendship, Sally had no idea what it was like to have a mentally ill mother. Then again, I conceded, how could she? It was something I myself couldn't explain.

When Kim Parker's father had had a heart attack freshman year, I had been envious; his was the kind of sickness you could talk about. Teachers would let you out of homework and understand if you were quiet in class. Kids would feel sorry for you, but not too sorry, not like you were from another planet or had a contagious disease.

"My uncle had a myocardial infarction," someone at the lunch table would say and ten people would nod knowingly. Diabetes, arthritis, even a tumor—anything was better than what my mother had, what she was—a schizo. Until she went to the hospital that first time, even I had thought *mental illness* was a euphemism for *retarded.*

A spring rain had soaked everything earlier, and now in the low-slanting four-o'clock sun, leaves glistened against slippery-barked trees. A movement in a branch caught my attention, and I stopped in my tracks, focusing. A sleek, gray-and-white mockingbird peered at me, almost at my eye level. Our gazes met and we both froze. I suddenly remembered the mockingbird in our yard that had learned to sing the first seven notes of "The Ode to Joy." That summer, the summer of my first piano lessons, I'd played the same song over and over. That summer I was eleven and my mother was gone.

Now, stoned, I convinced myself this must be that same mockingbird, trying to tell me something.

With a sharp cry the bird flew away, and the tightness in my chest liquefied into sorrow. I ran the rest of the way to the store.

*   *   *

My father was angry when he found the receipt I'd left on the kitchen counter. "I thought I told you not to charge anymore, Barbara," he chastened my mother during dinner. She was serving us, walking back and forth from stove to table to refrigerator to table, dropping cigarette ashes across the floor. She wasn't sitting down to eat with us. She wasn't hungry.

"*Barbara*," my father said again as he reached to help himself to the largest pork chop. "Please sit down." Lizzie was spooning applesauce onto her plate, licking the spoon, and then dipping it again into the jar.

My mother didn't answer. She dropped the butter dish onto the table and left the room, her slippers scraping the floor as she walked. A bad sign: the sicker she felt, the less she lifted her feet. But she still somehow almost always managed to cook us dinner.

"Skizzie, you're disgusting," Jeremy complained. "Nobody else can eat that applesauce now. Your saliva will digest it."

Lizzie looked up, ingenuous. "Oh," she said. "Sorry." Then she licked her spoon.

"You should know better than to charge things for her," my father said without looking at me as he sawed his pork. "Your mother isn't responsible for her actions, but you need to be."

How could I respond? I had come down from my high, had an awful headache, and wanted nothing more than to smoke another bowl. But I didn't risk it with both Lizzie and my father home. I thought of Princess, missing her again. Walking the dog had always been the perfect excuse to get out of the house. I could light up as soon as I turned the corner.

"What did she buy?" my father asked me.

"What?"

"Your mother. What did she buy this time? More useless junk?"

"Medicine," I said, staring at the milk in my glass, trying to see through it to my fingers on the other side.

"Which medicine? Not her regular medicine."

"I don't know," I said, annoyed. Sometimes his density bugged me more than my mother's craziness. He shook his head and switched his attention to green beans and potatoes.

"I have a Rotary meeting in an hour," my father said, chewing. "Try to get your mother to eat something later. At least do that."

"Yeah, right," I mumbled under my breath. Jeremy shot me a glance. He didn't like me to provoke my father. In his own weird way, my brother watched out for me.

"*Gone With the Wind* is on tonight," Lizzie announced. It was her favorite movie, but I didn't see why, since I knew she identified with Melanie. What was the point of the story if not to imagine yourself as Scarlett?

"Like wow. *Groovy,*" Jeremy said mockingly, though I knew he liked the sound of the word. "But Mandy won't watch anything with *war* in it. Like, peace, love, and understanding, man." He beamed at me.

I made the requisite beleaguered face, but he had given me an idea.

I cleaned the kitchen alone that night, not bothering to insist on help. By the time I was through, Jeremy had shut himself in his room, Lizzie had settled herself in front of the TV with the sound turned up high, and my father had left for Rotary. I climbed the stairs and drifted down the hall to my parents' room.

My mother was sitting on the edge of her rumpled bed, smoking a cigarette, tapping her fingers between puffs. I walked over to her dresser and sifted through the tangle of necklaces in her open jewelry box, extracting the blue beads that had always been my favorites. I gazed at them, my back toward my mother as I spoke.

"Are you still in pain?" I asked.

"It's the smoking," she answered. "Louis says the pain comes from the cigarettes." Louis, I knew, was one of her more recent voices. Like all of her voices, he was "real." That is, my mother knew an actual man named Louis and it was his voice she said she heard. Just as she had heard Gloria, our next-door neighbor, and Selma, the woman from the A&P.

"You could stop smoking," I said half-heartedly, rubbing a perfect blue bead between my thumb and forefinger.

"I can't," my mother answered, as always.

I glanced up into the mirror and saw her reflection rocking back and forth on the edge of her bed, still wearing her apron. She held the stub of a cigarette between her fingers; she had smoked it to the filter.

"What kind of pain is it?" I asked, though I'd asked before. Neither

her internist nor her ob-gyn could come up with any physical cause for the sharp abdominal pangs she claimed to experience.

"Inside here," she moaned, clutching her belly as she rocked. "The voices come from down here and they hurt me."

I turned toward her. She hadn't ever told me that bit about the *voices* coming from her insides before. Somehow, that made everything worse—and strengthened my conviction in what I was about to do. "I'd like you to try something," I said, watching her face contort.

"I need another pill," she whispered. "But Daddy took them. He's sick."

"You need to quit the Percodan," I said. "It's addicting. Besides, those prescriptions were Grandma's."

"I can't stand the pain," she said.

I winced. I knew my father had taken her to doctors, and they'd convinced him that the pain was "in her head," that if she took her medication, her antipsychotic medication, she'd get better. But when? And how, I wondered, could he go to his meeting and leave her in agony? He had given up on her. He pretended, as each of us did when we hadn't the fortitude to do otherwise, that my mother didn't really exist, at least not as a full-fledged member of the human race. We went about our lives as though she were a piece of embarrassing heirloom furniture we were obliged to keep.

But maybe I could help her now.

"Have you ever smoked pot?" I asked.

My mother rocked, her eyes glazed.

"Are you hearing the voices?" I asked.

She nodded.

"Can you make them stop?" She rocked faster. "Mom?"

She looked up at me and smiled thinly. "I'll listen to you instead," she said.

I reached for her and wrapped my hand around her upper arm. "Come to my room with me."

She rose. "Maybe you can find where he hid the pills."

I led her into the hallway. She walked like an old woman, shoulders bent, legs shuffling. She was only thirty-nine. "I want you to try something," I said. "Something else." I took her into my room and shut the door.

My mother stood in the middle of my room, tentatively fingering her apron as I pulled open my underwear drawer and slid my hand all the way toward the back. I drew out the fake book that held my pipe, lighter, film canisters, and rolling papers.

"Can I smoke?" my mother asked, looking around. When had she last been in here? Perhaps it had been years; the thought made me feel like crying.

"Smoking is what we're going to do," I told her. "I want you to try some marijuana, see if it helps the pain. You've got to get off the painkillers."

She patted the pockets of the apron till she found her cigarettes.

"Here," I said, handing her my purple lighter. I decided to roll a joint rather than use the pipe, even though the pipe was more efficient. I figured she would be more comfortable smoking a joint.

As she lit her cigarette and I rolled, my mother continued to glance around my room. I took that as a good sign. If she was looking at things, she probably wasn't overwhelmed by her voices.

The ash from her cigarette dropped on my floor, but my mother didn't notice. I ignored it and went to sit on my bed near the window, lifting the sash. On the ledge perched a large clamshell, one I'd found at the beach the summer before.

"Here," I said, offering her the shell. "It's an ashtray."

She sat at the edge of Lizzie's bed. I exchanged the shell for the purple lighter and lit the joint.

"This is how you smoke it," I demonstrated, speaking in that constipated voice one used when trying to talk without exhaling smoke. "You hold it in as long as you can."

Across the space between the beds, I passed my mother the joint. She slid it between her fingers, like a cigarette, and puffed.

I turned to exhale through the screen. "No," I said, patting the bed. "Sit here, by the window. Inhale deeply and hold, then blow the smoke out the window." I took the joint from her and took a hit as she switched seats, then I handed it back to her. This time she pinched it between her thumb and index finger. She was paying attention. Another good sign.

"It's strong," she said, coughing. "It tastes the way it smells."

I smiled at that and stood to take a cone of incense from a shelf.

Coconut: sweet and potentially sickening, but it would cover the pot smell.

"How do you feel?" I asked. I was already buzzed, but of course it didn't take much for me, especially since I'd been high just a few hours earlier. I looked at the Jackson Browne album cover on my pillow. Should I put on some music?

"I don't really feel anything," my mother said, but her eyes looked different, more alert.

The joint she had lain in the clamshell ashtray had gone out. I picked it up and relit it, taking a quick drag and then passing it again to her.

"Marijuana is an excellent painkiller," I explained, authoritatively. "Plus, it makes you mellow. And no bad side effects." I giggled at the way I sounded like an advertisement. Maybe when I had kids, I thought, pot would be sold by brand names. Ace Acapulco Gold, Zippy Zowie Maui, Sensational Sensimilla . . . on sale this week at your local drug store. At Tulip Hill Pharmacy. A happy thought.

My mother stood up and began pacing the short distance between the bookshelves and the beds. She'd finished her cigarette in between hits of the joint and now she lit another. She slid my purple lighter into her apron pocket and shuffled toward the dolls on Lizzie's side of the room.

"Uh, Mom," I said, extending my hand, "you took my lighter."

My mother looked at me as though she'd forgotten I was there, eyes clouded, and my heart sank. I'd been so sure the pot would help. Hadn't it always soothed me?

"In your apron pocket," I said disconsolately.

She reached into her pocket and found the lighter. I took a roach clip out of the fake book, slid the remainder of the joint between its teeth, and lit it again.

"Here," I said, offering her the smoldering roach. "I'll hold it for you. Just take a drag."

My mother's mouth was working in that way it did, spittle collecting at the corners of her otherwise dry lips. I felt sick at the thought of her saliva gooking up the roach. "You finish it all," I said.

She took a quick hit, then a long drag on her cigarette and blew out a mouthful of smoke. "I think I'll just go to bed," she said. Her voice was thin, as though she'd already half gone.

The room had grown darker with smoke. My mother turned, scuffed over to the bedroom door, and disappeared. A long squiggle of smoke from the burning incense wavered in her direction, as if to follow her.

Through my open window, I heard the howl of a neighbor's dog and then the crunch of my father's car coming up the driveway. I walked into the hall and leaned over the banister, listening for the TV. Scarlett was arguing with Rhett; the movie still had a ways to go. With Lizzie downstairs, my father would stay down there, too. He'd probably get a snack in the kitchen, then go into his den. What did he do in there? What could he possibly do? Not that I cared, as long as he didn't bother me. I went back into my room, closed the door, and lay on my bed.

Night air sifting through the opened window soon chilled the room, and I kicked off my Keds and slid under the covers, not bothering to undress. I thought of putting on an album, but I didn't move to get up. I thought of lighting another stick of incense, but the coconut lingered. I closed my eyes and tried to imagine myself someplace tropical, someplace out of a magazine. But all I could think of were the East End beaches we visited every August.

Every year the question loomed—would my mother join us for vacation, or would she be too sick? Kids we met at the beach frequently assumed our parents were divorced, that we were visiting with our father for the summer. It was easier to let them think that. If only the truth were quite so simple. I tried to guess what condition my mother would be in this coming August, and had to admit the chances of her joining us in Sag Harbor or Bridgehampton or Shelter Island weren't good.

I wondered whether the pot had had any positive effect. Was she asleep? Did that mean the pot had helped? I thought of Jeremy, only a room away—had he suspected what was going on? Would he despise me if he did?

What did my brother do in his room by himself those rare nights when he wasn't off somewhere? I understood why he played baseball and was class treasurer and volunteered for every community clean-up committee. I wondered if he understood it himself.

And what about Lizzie, not quite eleven, the age I'd been when our mother had first started hearing voices? Lizzie barely remembered Mom "before." Was she better or worse off than Jeremy and I? Having a schizophrenic mother—my father had explained what he could of the doctors' diagnosis—was that tenable for Lizzie? Did it seem to her somehow "normal," since it was practically all she'd ever known? Lizzie didn't appear all that bothered by our lack of ordinary mothering, but I had read some psychology and knew that could be a "defense." Lizzie-the-littlest, brown curled and sweet tempered and slightly oblivious. We were each so different—or were we?

We were like atoms, I thought, like the protons and electrons I had learned about in science, zooming paths around a common nucleus but never bumping each other. Each of us was completely separate, isolated, and differently charged. Was this the condition Sally considered fortunate? That although we were by name and blood a family, our orbits never really had to intersect?

All I had to do was make it through to the end of high school, I reminded myself. That was it, just two more years. After graduation, I'd be gone. Out of here. Then my life would begin, my own life.

And what if the atomic particles did collide? Would our world crash in upon itself, our nucleus implode? I recognized how pathetic my attempt to get my mother stoned had been. Why had I thought I could do anything to save her? I'd be lucky to save myself.

The front door slammed and I heard my father's heavy footsteps cross the house all the way to the kitchen. He was so predictable. A knot twisted in my stomach. I cursed my parents. They deserved each other! I would never live such a disconnected life, ever.

I turned over, my face to the wall in case anyone looked into the room. I was sleeping, as far as anyone was concerned. I was sleeping, and I wouldn't awake until the day I left for college.

CHAPTER 13

*T*HE RISING MOON CAST A NARROW CONE OF LIGHT through Athena's window. She stood with her head to one side, her cheek lambent, her hair fused with shadows. She listened as I finished the story of attempting to "cure" my mother with marijuana, then closed her eyes, nodding.

Though grateful for Athena's silent acceptance, I ended my narrative with a bitter laugh. Years had passed since I'd thought about the events of that night or that period in my life; now, reconsidering my adolescence, I understood my actions differently than I once had. I ached for the desperate girl I'd been, but I ached for my mother, too. I wished I could have simply loved her, instead of always wishing to fix her.

If only I'd come to that conclusion while she were alive.

"Oh, God," I sighed. There was so much I might have done, or been.

Athena turned to her box of tapes, sorting through them.

"God?" She repeated it as a question, her back toward me, her white dress otherworldly in the radiance of candles and moonbeams. She selected a tape and held it up to read its label.

"I was thinking how much easier it is to see backwards," I said.

"In retrospect?" Athena rewound the tape.

"Yes." I ached with longing and regret. Half believing Athena could read my thoughts, I pushed them away as I'd pushed my mother away so often, and changed direction. "I was thinking how differently the three of us—me, Jeremy, and Lizzie—how differently we each react to the same experience."

"Such as your mother's illness?" The tape stopped and Athena pressed start. It was Jackson Browne's first album. Of course.

"What a crush I had on Jackson," I said. "His wife committed suicide. I wanted to comfort him, to be the one to rescue him from himself."

Athena turned and took a step toward me into shadow. "Your brother and sister had different reactions to your mother?" She led my thoughts back.

"Well, yes, I think so. Maybe because I'm the oldest, Lizzie's the baby, Jeremy's the middle child and only boy. I always thought I was the one who truly understood how bad the situation was." I rubbed my forehead. "Now I don't know."

"You all suffered a lack of mothering," Athena pointed out, "but you think you took it hardest." It wasn't a question.

"Yes. Well, no. It's just that I had to get away. They didn't seem to. I went away to college, married young, moved out of state."

"You tried to escape your pain."

A slam at the back door made me jump. Crosby's ragged, pre-pubescent voice called out, "Hullo?" Athena turned down the volume of the stereo and moved to her bedroom door just as Crosby appeared under its arch.

"What's up?" Athena asked her son, blocking his entry with her hands grasping both sides of the woodwork.

"Nothing. Damien had to go in, so I came home." Crosby bent beneath his mother's arm, his hair flopping into his eyes, and entered the room.

"He did?" I stood quickly, angling my body to shield the water pipe from Crosby's view. I wobbled.

Three long steps brought Crosby to the bag of blue corn chips that had fallen from my lap to the floor. "Bong night, huh," he stated, rather than questioned. He turned toward his mom. "So, Amanda's cool."

"She's cool," Athena replied, a smile crossing her lips and inflecting her voice. Her fingers spread on her hips.

"Why did Damien have to go in?" I asked, feeling surreally unlike anyone's mother.

Crosby stuffed a fistful of broken chips into his mouth and looked up at me with butterscotch eyes. Not Athena's earth-brown eyes; so whose? I wondered.

"His uncle made him go to bed," Crosby answered me, crunching.

I massaged my temples. Which uncle? I wanted to know, but didn't ask. It had to be Jeremy. Sunshine appeared, her tail sweeping the floor in a low wag. She went straight for the crumbs at my feet. Crosby swung a leg over the dog, straddling her, his fingers grasping the scruff of her neck.

"Pony dog," he sang, bouncing on his knees just above her back without putting his weight on her. Sunshine wagged her tail with increased enthusiasm and continued licking up blue corn chips.

"I've got to go." I was suddenly aware of how long I'd left Damien alone. All day, and now tonight. I'd forgotten to be a mother.

"Good night, then," Athena said as I crossed the room.

"Thanks," I told her as I left, having no idea what I meant.

"Where have you been?" Jeremy's rough whisper chided me as I reached the deck of my cottage. *My* cottage, but he was there, lying on the chaise in the darkness, the glowing end of his cigar brightening and fading like a firefly as he inhaled.

"I'm sorry," I began, then stopped and began again. "You know where I was. I went to pay Athena for the ring. She offered me a glass of wine."

"Your son was running wild." Jeremy sat up, his expression masked by smoke.

"Where is he?" I had the urge to take Damien and leave tonight.

"Inside." My brother gestured with his cigar. When had he begun smoking them? "He's asleep. Exhausted from his busy day." This last was said with irony.

I sat on the picnic bench in a gesture of surrender. "You all knew where I was," I repeated. My brother could have come looking for me, but I was glad he hadn't. Just like when we were kids, when he left me alone with Sally and then was grumpy afterward. It had seemed a reasonable price to pay.

Jeremy balanced his cigar on a sand-encrusted clamshell and swung his legs off the chaise. He sat next to me on the bench and sniffed the air around my hair. Another old behavior, from our high school days, but given the events of this evening it didn't surprise me.

"Uh-huh," he said, puckering his lips. "Aren't you a little old for smoking reefer, Mandy?"

"Never too old for sex, drugs and rock 'n' roll," I offered lamely.

"Ha." My brother scowled. "What was your first clue you'd win Mother of the Year?"

Ouch. Hot tears sprang to my eyes. "That's not fair," I said, shaking my head, gathering my hair in my hand and pulling it to one side, away from him. The rules of our game had changed.

"No?" Jeremy asked, his head tilted back, his eyes lifted toward the night sky. "Maybe not. But your son needs supervision, needs attention."

"I know that," I said. I stood, turned toward the deck railing, and leaned out to face the ocean I could hear but not see. "For God's sake, Jeremy, I've been a mother for a long time. Don't start to tell me I don't know how it's done. You've no idea."

I heard him snicker softly. "Yeah, I know. I'll soon find out all about it." He was backing off. Somehow my brother had never learned how to really be mean.

"They're easy at Jay's age," I said. "Just wait." The ocean roared. Clouds had begun to roll in. Oh, not more rain.

"But Mandy, Damien *was* running wild tonight. He woke up the baby."

"I'm sorry," I said. "I'll speak to him about it." And when I did, Damien would ask why we had to go on vacation with a stupid baby anyway. And how come—Dad hadn't come?

"I've spoken to him," Jeremy said. "We got it straightened out. He's not used to being around infants."

"No." I could imagine Damien's reaction if I told him he might soon have a competing sibling of his very own. Or that his father had another woman.

"But, you know," Jeremy said, "with his father not here, and with you running around like a teenager . . ." My brother reached for his cigar, gone out now, and stuck it between his teeth to chew. "I just think you should pay attention to your son. I mean, whatever is going on between you and Keith."

"Keith stayed in Atlanta to work," I blurted out, my defenses rising. "I told you that. He's just started a new business."

"Yes, so you've said." Jeremy mouthed his cigar like an actor.

"You don't believe me?" My fear sounded like outrage. I didn't want to discuss my separation from Keith, because doing so would make it real.

"Mandy, calm down. Of course I believe you."

I hated being told to calm down, hated that those words, inevitably, produced the opposite effect and proved their own point. "I *do* pay attention," I said. "I'm not *her*."

I knew I didn't have to say *Mother*, to remind him of the times she had not been fully there when she was there.

Jeremy puffed, listening to the surf. "We turned out okay."

I snorted.

"Maybe better than okay is too much to ask," he said. I didn't know whether he was speaking to himself or to me.

"So when did you start *that* disgusting habit?" I pointed at the cigar, which he took from his mouth and examined.

"The cigar? Just on special occasions." He smiled. "Like family vacations."

He was ready to be nice, but I wasn't. "Yes, well, I'm on vacation, too. So cut me a break, okay? I didn't think it would be so horrible for Damien to spend a day with his extended family."

"You're right," Jeremy said.

"His family whom he hardly *ever* sees. Who never visit him in Atlanta, but wait till *he* comes up north to see them."

Jeremy whistled. "A bit hostile, are we?"

"Well, I'm sorry if Damien has been too much trouble for you."

"That is not what I meant, and you must know it. It's great to hang with Damien. I just want you to hang out with us, too, that's all. Not avoid us."

"I'm not avoiding you." I checked my shorts for my wallet, afraid that I'd left it at Athena's. But it was there in my pocket, along with a crushed shell.

"Mandy, if you need to talk . . ."

I knew what such an offer cost my brother. He was not one who liked to delve deeply, not one to pry. I was touched and volunteered what I knew he'd understand. "So much is different this year."

Jeremy nodded and turned his cigar.

"Look, I have to go call Keith."

Jeremy touched my bare arm. "Your skin is hot," he said. "You're going to get skin cancer."

"Oh, shut up." I groaned without bitterness and crossed the deck.

"Tell him hello for me," my brother called.

I heard him strike a match, probably relighting his cigar, then I skipped down the steps, and ran toward the moonlit stones of the path. When I returned, only minutes later, the deck was dark and empty as though he'd never been there.

I evaluated my options for explaining to Keith why I was calling so late. It was near midnight, hardly my usual hour to check in at home. I could lie—say we'd gone out for a late dinner, or had a bon-fire tonight—but I didn't lie. I couldn't remember the last time I'd lied to Keith, about anything. So how could I make the truth sound reasonable? I chewed my lips as our number rang. There were, I knew, degrees of deceit.

I was so unprepared to get our answering machine, I momentarily mistook Keith's recording for him. "Hi, it's me," I began before realizing the voice at the other end was instructing me to leave a message at the beep. I hung up.

The shingled wall of the laundry building, once painted white, had weathered to a flaking gray. Bits of paint fell to my neck and shoulders as I leaned against it. My eyes burned with tears. I squeezed them shut and jammed my fist against my lips. Athena's back door was not more than fifty feet away. I didn't want her to hear me sob, to see me shaken, to come to me. I didn't want to talk to her or anyone.

Where the fuck was Keith? Not home after midnight on a Sun-day—actually Monday now? That could mean only one thing. He had to be with her, with Sarah. Even though this separation was supposed to be about coming to terms with our marriage, with me, his wife, it was about being with her. The certainty hit me like a closing door.

He had to be sleeping with her. My stomach fell the way it did in elevators. Bitterness engorged my throat and the quick, watery sensation in my mouth let me know I was going to be sick. I gagged, my hand clamped against my lips, my guts in spasm.

Sharp-tasting bile pushed up through my teeth and I spit it to the ground, but no vomit followed. I breathed deeply through my nose—a *cleansing breath* from Lamaze class—then blew the air out in a slow measure through my mouth. That helped. Another deep breath. I wiped the tears from my face and exhaled rage.

My head was pounding, aching with marijuana and desolation. I gazed up toward the moon, hidden now behind a cloud, and tried to pray like a pagan. I searched for something in the sky to pray upon—a star, a planet, a night-flying bird—but the clouded heavens were dark and empty. What would I pray for? That my husband wouldn't leave me? That I wasn't pregnant? That I wouldn't become my mother and leave my children unprotected? That I could have her back?

I tried an old childhood ritual, the one I'd called "the worst possible thing." Think of the worst possible thing that could happen, I would tell myself, and think it through to its logical conclusion. In comparison, anything less than the worst wouldn't seem so bad. As a child, the worst possible thing was always a version of the same: I would be alone, and I would die. Of sadness, or an unavoidable accident, or slain by some horrible monster my parents never realized lurked just out of sight. But if I died, I reasoned, I would no longer exist. And if I didn't exist, I couldn't feel anything, which would be all right. On the other hand, if I didn't die, if I survived, well, then I would exist. And as long as I existed, there was hope for something better. Existence therefore was less than the worst possible thing.

The moon slipped from beneath the cloud and shone like a spotlight on the path before me. What was the worst possible thing that could happen to me now? Aside from disaster—a tidal wave, a tsunami, my recurrent childhood fear, washing over the entire East End without warning—and aside from tragedy—Isabella or Damien contracting a fatal leukemia or senselessly murdered in a parking lot—aside from such dramatic upheavals, what was it I feared?

I envisioned myself from the moon's point of view. (Good grief, was I that stoned?) From the lunar surface, looking down, I saw Amanda Kincaid slumped into herself like a bag lady in a New York subway station: her face streaked with dirt, her breath stinking of bile, pathetic, revolting, alone. I saw her as a woman a husband would rebuke, miserable and self-loathing under a wide, starless sky. Alone in a magical place she couldn't appreciate, could barely endure. Foolish and self-pitying, squandering gifts beneath a moon nearly full.

Abandoned. Which was exactly what I feared most.

Chapter 14
Mid-July, Atlanta

BEFORE KEITH WAS OUT OF THE SHOWER on the morning of his resignation from Stone, I made a pot of coffee and carried a mug of it to the yard. I imagined him facing himself in the gilt-edged mirror above his sink as I focused my attention on neatening my garden beds: deadheading, pruning, weeding, snipping off the yellowed leaves and dried up stalks while he flossed his teeth. When I'd reached the old pink roses, the deep growl of Keith's ten-year-old Audi vibrated through my thin cotton robe, but I wouldn't look up as he drove past. The whoosh of warm air against my neck might have been from the closing of a door.

Keith was on his way to changing our life. Sarah had already resigned from Stone and taken three weeks to visit her mother in Florida. When she returned to Atlanta in August, she would set up office in the space she had rented for the newly formed Kincaid, Stein, LLC. By then, I would be in Montauk, stewing under an unforgiving sun over a woman whose face I'd never seen, whose Southern-lilted voice (not Atlantan) I'd heard by dialing her home phone number (extracted from the Stone directory) and listening to her answering machine. She had the voice of a girl who'd played tennis in high school.

Keith had invited me to meet her once—at the last minute, for dinner, but I'd declined in order to keep a date with a friend—and he never made the offer again. I suppose I could have requested a second chance, but I didn't. Though curious, sometimes insatiably so, I had never been ready to face Sarah. What if I liked her? I couldn't possibly swallow food in front of my husband's "new partner" just yet.

I tossed a thorny branch into my wheelbarrow and wiped my forehead with the back of my arm. Which tie had Keith chosen for his day of reckoning? I wondered, envisioning him in his darkest blue suit. Would he wear his red tie, the raw silk? The old Keith would have. What would he wear to work now, in his new company? Khakis? Jeans? Would he grow a beard?

A cardinal called to his mate from the branch of a dogwood tree. I looked up, blinded by the sun. Already the air was thick with heat and humidity. Already the annuals were wilting. I decided to water the impatiens, which were especially thirsty, in the planters that our sprinkler system didn't reach. I lifted the worn, green hose from under the water spigot at the side of the garage, and turned to fill the watering can.

At the sound of gushing water, a neighbor's marmalade cat darted out from under an azalea, startling me. I dropped the hose, and it sprayed my legs as it whipped to the ground. I let out a yelp, but the drenching felt good, reminding me of the long summer afternoons of my childhood, of hours spent running through the spurting water of our rotating metal lawn sprinkler.

Although our tree-shaded house was cool, we weren't supposed to play inside during the summer. "Get some fresh air," my mother would say each morning after breakfast, even on the dankest days. Meanwhile, she sat at the kitchen table, smoking cigarettes and drinking coffee, staring out the window, but never acknowledging us when we waved. Sometimes we'd hear her voice, low and angry, through the screen, and we'd assume she was on the phone, arguing with our father or perhaps her father. Later, we learned she rarely was.

My own two children's summers had been very different, but I wondered now whether they had ever been lonely. I watered my flowers and thought about Damien, who had spent the night at a friend's. How much did he sense of the strain between Keith and me? A week's vacation in Montauk would be good for Damien, I'd told Keith last night, hoping a reminder of my imminent departure would spur him to reconsider our separation. Perhaps he'd ask whether I could send Damien to vacation with my family by himself. *We need the time alone together,* I'd imagined him saying. But he hadn't. *We need the time apart,* was what he'd said.

When I finished watering, I pushed my wheelbarrow full of garden debris toward the compost pile at the bottom of the property. I loved composting. Plants were always somewhere along the continuum of their life cycle, always in some process of growth or nourishing growth. Unlike humans, who were so frequently in stasis. People had to choose growth, I decided as I dumped branches and leaves behind a large magnolia. Maybe that was what Keith was doing, what this sudden upheaval in his life was all about. Plants didn't have midlife crises, though, I thought snidely. Or who knows, maybe they did. I was willing to be convinced of anything, if only someone was inclined to convince me.

Keith wasn't trying to persuade me to go along with him; he had just gone on without me.

An aching hollowness reverberated like an echo in my stomach. At this moment, perhaps, Keith was perched at the edge of a slippery leather chair in Tripp Stone's office, reviewing his letter of resignation. First, Tripp would make light of it, tell Keith he couldn't be serious; later, he'd grow impatient, accuse Keith of "holding him up," demand to know how much more money he wanted.

But Keith wasn't playing any such game. He didn't want more, he wanted out. The certainty with which Keith had changed his life frightened me. How, in a matter of weeks, could vague dissatisfaction progress to deliberate action? Keith's state of mind seemed fixed at a distant point, a place foreign to me, to our marriage.

I accepted that Keith wished to restructure his life so that he answered only to his clients and himself—how many times had we rehashed that point over the past six weeks?—yet I feared what underlay this desire, and where it might lead or had perhaps already led. I feared Keith's desire for change, especially because I hadn't seen it coming, because it had hit me like a sudden ocean wave and knocked the breath out of me.

I hadn't felt this way since the accident that had killed my mother. She had been having an extended "good" period—no hospitalization in over two years—and the loss of her shocked my family to our bones. That her illness hadn't been responsible for her death was surprising in itself, since we'd always assumed, one way or another, the disease that had taken so much of her from us would one day claim all of her. No, she'd been feeling well, she'd been taking her medication. But we didn't know and would never know where she was going that day when a teenage boy ran a traffic light and hit her head-on at forty-five miles an hour. She had died either at the scene or the next day when we removed the life support system, depending on how one determined it. Even the moment of her death was obscure.

Eventually, I came to see my mother's death as the last logical step of her illogical life. Her most unpredictable, bizarre behavior nearly always arose out of the most ordinary of circumstances. I should have known—hadn't my childhood taught me?—that chaos inevitably struck whenever order lulled.

Now, a rustling at the edge of the woods caught my attention. Bare-legged, wearing only rubber thongs on my feet, I froze. Some hidden creature was moving, rippling the dry tips of long grass in my direction. A snake? Copperheads and cottonmouths proliferated in the suburban forests of Atlanta. My hairdresser, serpent phobic, kept a mental cache of stories of friends and acquaintances who'd been bitten on a front porch or found a nest of vipers in a mound of pine straw.

"They're more afraid of you than you are of them," my father had always told us regarding anything that bit or stung. Like most wild creatures, snakes would strike only when threatened. But all that meant to me was that they were easily threatened.

The grass parted an inch from where I stood and I leapt back. A huge green frog, the biggest frog, in fact, I'd ever seen, catapulted out of the grass and landed atop a rock. I laughed out loud, suddenly aware that panic was only one of a number of possible reactions to surprise. Attention was another. Sometimes, apparently, snakes turned out to be frogs.

By noon, I still hadn't heard from Keith. Surely his meeting with Tripp Stone couldn't have lasted this long. I'd expected Keith to call me at the first possible moment to tell me how the meeting had gone. That was how things were with us. Or had been. Maybe they weren't like that now. I'd deliberately avoided him that morning, and I questioned my judgment. He was probably angry, punishing me.

At one o'clock, I decided to treat myself to a glass of wine with a Caesar salad. To distract myself, I perused the morning paper as I ate, glancing through the real estate listings. If I someday lived alone, I decided, I'd buy a cottage in Garden Hills, near the art cinema and the pizza dive. I poured a second glass, picked up the phone, and pressed Lizzie's number.

She answered on the seventh ring. Quick for her.

"Hello?" She was out of breath.

"Phone Bar," I said.

"It isn't cocktail hour yet!"

"It is somewhere," I explained. "London."

Lizzie laughed. "I just got home from taking the kids to the pool. Hold on." She didn't bother to mute her phone as she called, "Girls, get upstairs and out of those wet bathing suits, now!"

I waited as she acquiesced to Ryan's request for a video, searching noisily till she found it. "Sorry." She breathed heavily.

"Did you pour yourself a drink?" I asked. "Phone Bar" was our name for drinking and chatting on the phone as we prepared our families' dinners.

Lizzie laughed again. "I'll have a beer," she said. I heard her refrigerator door open.

"Well," I said, "Keith resigned from Stone today."

"Yeah?" She took a long swig. "So now he starts his own business, right? Welcome to the club."

I bit my cheeks. *Club*, indeed. Lizzie's husband had been handed the running of a well-established if not overly profitable bakery machine business from our father, who had been handed it from his father-in-law. Hardly what Keith was about to do. Of course, I hadn't yet mentioned to Lizzie the minor detail of his partner, Sarah.

"It's a little different, in our case," was what I said.

"I know." Lizzie tried to be sympathetic—she *was* sympathetic, always, about everything. She just didn't anticipate danger the way I did. She never had.

"We have Keith's stock options; we can live off them for a while," I said in a reassuring voice, as if to demonstrate for my sister the appropriate tack.

"See?" she said. "You'll be fine, Amanda; you always are."

Not this time, I wanted to admit. Instead, I proved her right and moved on. "So, did you get my check for the Montauk groceries?"

Lizzie laughed. "Yes, and I spent it already! We didn't buy the food yet, but there was this patchwork throw at the country store I've been dying to buy. It looks so good on the rocker in my den." Enter my sister's house, and you'd swear you'd time-warped to a nineteenth-century New England farm.

"Lizzie . . ." I began.

"Don't worry, I told Rick I saved for weeks out of my grocery money, which is sort of true, except the weeks part. I'll put the Montauk groceries on my VISA."

What was the difference then? I wondered for a second, then I understood her method: when the credit card statement came through, the charge would be for the grocery store rather than the country store, and Rick would let it go.

I sighed. "What does the design look like?"

As Lizzie began to describe the quilt, my call waiting beeped through.

"Let me get that," I said. "It's probably Keith. I'll call you later."

Lizzie rang off cheerfully. But it wasn't Keith; it was Isabella.

"Mom?"

Isabella had two phone greetings, both ending in rising inflections: "Hello?" meant she was in the mood for a chat; "Mom?" meant she had important news or needed money.

"Yes . . ." I said, wary. On the phone, we telegraphed our messages through intonation, my daughter and I. When we were face-to-face, we often didn't even need words.

"I've been meaning to call you all week," she said. This wasn't about money.

"Go on."

And then Isabella told me about Jeff Freeman, the senior she'd scrambled to arrange a summer internship to be near. She had moved in with him, a month ago. She figured it was time we knew.

The afternoon sun spilled hot across my face and for a second, before I opened my eyes, I believed I was already in Montauk. But I had fallen asleep on the sunroom sofa, the empty, green wine bottle next to me explanation for the dull ache throbbing at my temples. The glass-topped table across the room refracted light in a way that forced me to shade my eyes as I lifted my head, effecting a kind of frame around the frame of the snapshot of Isabella on the table's edge.

I crossed the room and lifted the photograph. In it, Isabella was three years old, her flower of a face opening with delight at some birthday present she just that moment had received. The camera had caught her golden curls mid-bounce as she squealed, her pink, unraveling hair ribbon hanging pale against the flush of her cheeks. Abruptly, my eyes stung with longing for the child Isabella, for the gorgeous babyness of her, and I set the frame down on the glass table and whispered, "I miss you."

I missed my little girl, missed her physically, the comforting roundness of her limbs and the damp, sweet cookie smell of her head. If only I could gather her once more into my lap and gaze down at the astounding perfection of her features in repose. I had never given myself so entirely to another person until my daughter, and I never did again until my son—though with Damien I'd remembered, had known what I was in for. Isabella had so surprised me, so transformed me, so altered my life, she had obliterated, at least for a time, everything that was other than pure devotion to her being.

For Isabella, I'd given up playing violin in the chamber orchestra, exchanging my lifetime passion for a passion without constraints, a mother's love for her child. I hadn't known; how could I have known, that I would love my daughter more than my life, that in her I'd see myself reborn?

And then of course she grew, and as Isabella struggled to define herself as independent from me, I struggled as well. I struggled to live without her constancy, without, at times, even her acceptance. I struggled to exist in a place beyond motherhood, the place that was me before her, to become me after. I struggled as though I were the child. And when my daughter pulled away from me, she rent my heart.

And now, my heartbreaker, now she was living with a man. Part of me thrilled at the rapture I knew she felt, the headiness of first love; part of me was fearful for her happiness and safety, dreading the inevitable pain that lay ahead. But mostly, I was worried about how

Keith would react when he found out. Her timing was either brilliant or disastrous, or possibly both.

By four, Keith still hadn't called, but Damien had. He was spending another night with Scott, if that was okay. It was fine. At least something was. Better for Damien not to be present for his father's homecoming this particular evening. That is, if his father came home! He could have taken a suitcase with him this morning, for all I knew. Could be on his way to Sarah and her Floridian mother—if she *had* a mother. If she *was* in Florida. Suddenly, I didn't trust anything Keith had told me in the last six weeks. How could he not call?

I decided to begin packing for Montauk. In the same closet where I kept my suitcase lay my violin case, high on the shelf where it had slept all these years as though under a spell. I took it down, and opened the case. The day's events, underscored by the wine, had left me feeling powerfully unsettled. I longed for the solid comfort of curved wood beneath my chin. So I carried my instrument in my arms like a sleeping child, sat in the sunroom's slanted light on my favorite chair, and began unwinding pegs to loosen strings.

Changes in temperature over time had caused a certain amount of warping and the bridge had fallen. When I'd loosened it enough to manipulate it, I moved the bridge to an upright position and started tightening the pegs. Suddenly, the D string popped and hit me in the face, scratching me, drawing a fat drop of blood. I wiped my stinging cheek with two fingers, licked them clean of blood, and checked my case for an extra set of strings. A set was there, as I had always kept it, as though no time had passed.

I restrung the D, carefully tightening the peg, then proceeded to tighten the A, hitting the tuning fork against my knee for the perfect note by which each perfect fifth would follow. By the time I had finished tuning each string, half an hour had passed and the sun had moved behind the trees in the yard.

After tightening the horsehair against the spring of the bow, I lifted the violin to my chin and closed my eyes, breathing deeply of the resinous wood. I remembered the day I'd lifted my neck above the chin rest for the first time.

I'd been playing piano for six years and had long since declared my intention to study music in college, when one brilliant winter afternoon my mother presented me with the pretty French violin that had belonged to her and to her mother before her. I had known, of course, that our piano had belonged to her and that, while she was reputed to have been the most promising pianist of her class, she had given up playing years earlier. I'd never heard her. She hadn't, however, ever mentioned that she also played the violin.

"Why have you kept this a secret for all this time?" I asked the day she took the instrument down from the attic, furious at the wasted years I could have been studying.

My mother lit a cigarette before answering. "I just now thought of it," was what she said, smoke curling between us.

Now in my Atlanta sunroom, I drew the bow across the strings, and the sound that squawked out hurt my ears. I couldn't recall the last time I'd played. Suddenly, I was angrier with myself than I'd been with my mother, who after all was ill and couldn't be held accountable for forgetting an old instrument in an attic. What was *my* excuse for neglecting this part of me for so long, for this callous malnourishment of my spirit? This violin had been my mother's greatest gift to me.

When Keith finally arrived home around seven, he caught me in a rapture of concentration. Light from the garage flooded the kitchen as he opened the door, startling me where I sat in my chair in the darkening sunroom. I had been playing the violin virtually nonstop for almost two hours, sawing away until my fingers were aching and deeply grooved. Practicing and practicing, I had not allowed myself the pleasure of a melody. I had played nothing but scales.

CHAPTER 15

DAMIEN AND I STOOD BAREFOOT ON THE COTTAGE DECK, throwing breakfast crumbs to the speckled gull. We had developed a ritual, this bird and I, and I was happy when he showed up halfway through our meal. Funny how one living creature could transform a strange place into somewhere familiar.

I felt Michael's arrival before I saw him, a low rumble in the ground I at first mistook for thunder. Then I heard the deep purr of a motorcycle, and I dared to imagine he was riding near. Finally, I recognized the silhouetted shape of him as he strolled up the path, the sun at his back, his silver helmet glinting in his hands.

I pressed against the deck railing and waved. Damien looked to me, scowled, and asked, "Who's that guy?" And the speckled gull, as if insulted by our abrupt lapse in attention, lifted off the grass with a sharp cry and flew toward the west.

Michael caught sight of us and waved back.

"Do you know him, Mom?" Damien asked, splaying fingers on his hips in a territorial gesture.

I smiled and smoothed my son's hair. "Yes," I said. "He's the man who fixed my ring."

"Good morning." Michael reached our cottage. "Looks like another fine day." He stood two steps lower than I stood at the deck railing, thus at my eye level. I stifled an urge to brush hair from his damp forehead.

Instead my hands raked to my own unkempt mop, and I cursed myself inwardly for not running into the cottage as soon as I'd seen him coming. Except for brushing my teeth, I'd done nothing yet this morning in the way of grooming.

"It's probably going to rain," Damien informed Michael in response to his greeting.

Michael chuckled, laid his helmet on a step, and extended his hand across the railing. "I think you're right about the rain. Hi. My name is Michael."

"Dr. Michael Burns," I said.

"Damien Keith Kincaid."

Michael caught my eye. "Pleased to meet you," he said, shaking Damien's hand. "Have you had your breakfast?"

"Yup," Damien said.

"We just finished," I added, tugging at my T-shirt. "I'm afraid you've caught us at our morning worst."

Michael cocked his head to one side. "I wouldn't say that."

"I look the same as always," Damien agreed. He was wearing his all-purpose soccer shorts. "Except I broke a tooth."

Michael glanced at me.

"Yes, he did break a tooth," I said, embarrassed. "Our first day here. But he's okay."

Damien elaborated. "I'll get it fixed when we go home. The dentist says I can wait."

"Well, good," Michael said. He reached into his pocket, letting his hair fall into his eyes. "I've come to deliver your ring."

He held up the small silver circle and then, when I reached for it, took my wrist in his hand to slip the ring on my finger. I thought he held on a few seconds longer than necessary. Or was that my own wish?

"Thanks," I said, admiring the flecked blue stone. The tiny bits of gold flashed like planets in a night sky, like possibilities within a dark universe.

"I'd hoped to invite you to breakfast," Michael said. "But I guess one has to get up pretty early in the morning to catch you."

Disappointment must have broadcast from my face, because Michael's mouth twitched. I wanted to say I'd really not eaten much breakfast at all, that I could go for another cup of coffee at least, but I didn't.

"Anyway, it was nice to meet you," Michael said.

I spoke as though my voice were independent of the rest of me. "I'm free for lunch."

"Lunch," Michael considered. "Sure. Ever been to Lunch?"

"Well, of course I've been—"

"Sorry! I meant the restaurant they call "Lunch," just down the highway. Its name is really The Lobster Roll—and it serves terrific lobster rolls, among other things. There's a big sign outside advertising lunch, so everyone refers to the place itself as Lunch."

"Oh," I said. "I think I've passed it. . . ."

"We're having a cookout on the beach," Damien interrupted. "Uncle Jeremy promised Crosby could eat with us. I don't want to go out for lunch."

"Another cookout?" I asked.

"Yeah, but chicken wings this time!"

"Sounds good," Michael said to Damien, then looked at me. "Can you live without chicken wings? Might I tempt you with a lobster roll and a cold beer?"

I remembered Keith's unexplained absence the night before. "Sure," I said, "tempt me. That is, if Damien doesn't mind a few extra chicken wings for himself."

Damien shrugged and stepped down to examine Michael's helmet.

"What time do you have to leave to go back to the city?" I asked.

"Actually," Michael said, meeting my gaze, "I've decided to stay here through Saturday. My office manager was able to reschedule most of my appointments and I have a colleague taking over the rest." He looked away. "I figured why not enjoy the weather."

Minute ripples ran down my arms, as though something in the air had changed. And, in fact, a cloud momentarily obscured the sun. I watched a large, gray mass gather above the dunes. Damien was probably right about the rain.

"So, I'll come for you about noon?" Michael asked. "Do you mind riding on the bike?"

I shook my head, then nodded. "Yes, I mean, the bike is fine. Noon." And then there it was again, that incredible Cheshire-cat smile.

*   *   *

Though the sun slipped in and out of clouds, our morning at the beach was unusually calm and pleasant. Since the surf was rough, Damien and the other children were content to splash along the shore. Uncharacteristically, they cooperated as they built an elaborate sandcastle, leaving Lizzie and me free to catch what rays we could. My father sat near the children, reading his newspaper and offering the occasional word of grandfatherly encouragement, his low beach chair sinking in the wet sand.

Damien assigned each cousin a task: Ryan filled buckets with water; Lindsey collected shining stones and pieces of shells; Lauren filled and packed the plastic castle molds with damp sand, carefully depositing each one according to Damien's specifications. And Damien, as overseer, designed and adjusted and directed their efforts.

I thought to intervene, to warn him to be fair and not bossy, but I held back. If the kids had discovered a dynamic they found comfortable, I reasoned, why should I interfere? Especially when that dynamic allowed me peace to sunbathe and think. I lay back and let my sadness slow bake, and contemplated the deteriorating state of my marriage under an intermittent sun.

Around ten, when baby Jay awoke from his morning nap, I asked Froggy whether I could change his diaper. She agreed, though with perhaps slightly less enthusiasm than one might expect from an exhausted new mother. I remembered the overwhelming sense of responsibility, and my irritation with her dissipated into a chastened empathy.

"You know, Keith brought me to a place near here the summer Damien was born," I told my sister-in-law as I swabbed her son's florid penis with a baby wipe. Even under the shade of an umbrella and moderate cloud cover, the ocean glare was too bright for Jay and he kept his eyes tightly shut. But his lids flickered at the sound of my voice and at my touch, evoking in me a warm rush of affection.

"Yes, Jerry told me about that place," Froggy answered, watching me.

"I had postpartum blues pretty badly after Damien," I reminded her. "Everything made me cry. Even happy things. *Especially* happy things." I powdered Jay's bottom with cornstarch and slipped a blue-printed disposable diaper beneath him.

"I see." Froggy wasn't easily engaged. I wondered again what, other than her abject devotion to him, my brother loved in her? Perhaps that was enough.

"So, how are you doing, Frances?" I asked. "You seem to be adjusting to motherhood." I lifted Jay and cuddled him against my neck, stroking the soft, colorless down of his head, smelling it. How I loved the smell of a baby's head—it was up there with puppy's breath.

"We've adjusted," she answered, looking toward Jeremy tossing a Frisbee to Rick.

"Good," I said, giving up, perhaps too easily.

Jay began sucking his fist. Froggy reached to touch his arm, obviously eager for an excuse to reclaim him. "Oh, it's time for his bottle," she said, glancing at her watch.

"I could feed him," I offered.

Froggy smiled indulgently. "Thanks, but it's Jerry's turn to feed him. I know he wouldn't want to miss it." She turned and called to my brother.

I held Jay close and allowed myself a moment's longing.

Jeremy sprinted over to the edge of my blanket. Lizzie, who had been sunbathing with her eyes closed, lifted her head from her chair, turned toward me and announced, "I'm going for a walk. Wanna come?"

Had she been listening? Waiting for the right moment to get me alone? "Sure," I said, giving Jay a quick kiss before handing him over to his father.

After prevailing upon Rick to keep his eyes on the kids, Lizzie and I headed east along the shore, ankle deep in foam. I wondered how far we'd need to walk before we came upon the soaring angles of Michael Burns's glass house, and I began to tell my sister about the mysterious doctor-musician I'd just met, and of our plans for lunch at Lunch.

My shoulders burned during my long walk with my sister, and I remembered how my mother always warned that you got the worst sunburn through haze. Lizzie and I never did find Michael's house. Instead, we lost track of time, and I was left with only minutes to run back to my cottage, shower, and dress before Michael picked me up.

I wished I'd packed with more care the way I usually did, taking pleasure in selecting outfits for a trip. I generally spent an entire week trying on, ironing, and folding clothing. I might make a last-minute shopping run for an essential accessory. But not this time. I had thrown together Damien's and my suitcases the day we left, too pre-occupied—with Keith, with my late period, with my uncertain fu-ture—to care about my wardrobe.

There was a lesson in this, I told myself as I selected and shook out a white cotton halter dress that buttoned down the front. One should never be so preoccupied as to ignore her wardrobe—wisdom along the lines of *never leave the house wearing torn underwear*. "You never know when you might have an accident," my mother would say, as though shabby lingerie was of primary concern in an emergency room. I remembered the plastic bag of my mother's belongings the hospital had given to me that last night. It had seemed so little to take away.

I held the halter dress against me in the wavy mirror. I couldn't wear a bra with it, but at least my sunburn wouldn't chafe. And the smooth, white fabric would show off my tan. I chose the rest of my outfit quickly. Strappy sandals, dangling moon-and-star earrings, sheer berry lipstick, a quick smudge of eyeliner: this was beginning to feel like a date. Was it a date? I was glad my father and brother were still on the beach.

When I had finished blow-drying my hair, I put on my watch and noticed the time. Twelve-fifteen! I hoped Michael wasn't a stickler for punctuality. But he was a physician; he would need to be. Then again—I thought of my customary three-magazine wait for my an-nual exam—maybe not.

I found him stretched out on the chaise on my deck, his long legs clad in creased khaki slacks, the sleeves of his white linen shirt rolled up to his elbows. I blushed as I greeted him. We'd both dressed for a date.

"Have you been waiting long?" I asked.

"Not long." He rose slowly, smiling slowly. "You look very nice."

"You could have knocked or something," I said, starting down the steps toward the path. I was eager to leave the Laughing Gull property.

"I did knock," he told me, catching up in a few strides. "You didn't hear me over the sound of your hair dryer. I didn't want to just walk in."

"I'm sorry," I said. I smelled something vaguely familiar as he walked closer to me. Not cologne, but pleasant. Shampoo?

"I'm not sorry," Michael said. "I'm delighted. Thank you for having lunch with me."

I raised my eyes to heaven.

"Really," he said. "I've spent most of the summer brooding. This is a treat."

Fish soap. The scent was of the fish-shaped soap I'd used in his guest bathroom.

We reached the bike and pulled on our helmets as though we rode together regularly. This time, without hesitating, I wrapped my arms around his waist and breathed him in. I hoped the restaurant was a million miles away.

It wasn't. We were there within minutes and seated immediately. The lunch crowd, just beginning to arrive, was dressed mostly in bathing suits and cover-ups. Michael must have known how casual the place was; clearly, he had dressed for me, to put me at ease. He had guessed right about me, obviously trying to score points I couldn't help but grant him.

I ordered a lobster roll (which turned out to be a tasty lobster salad on a hot dog bun) and a glass of ice tea. Michael asked for a beer, two lobster rolls, and a dozen clams on the half shell. I smiled at his appetite. Keith sometimes ate like that, though not around me recently.

Our conversation flowed easily, a marked contrast to the months of strained talk with Keith. Michael told me about his family: his father was a physician; his mother a nurse; and a brother and a sister, both younger, resided out of state. He was curious about my family, about *any* family, he said, that could bear a week's vacation together. I found myself speaking openly about my siblings, my history, everything short of the details of my mother's illness. I told him things some of my friends in Atlanta didn't know.

He was surprised to hear I lived in Atlanta, surprised at the reason I gave for Keith's not being with me.

"If he's in business for himself now, couldn't he have planned at least a few days to join his family at the beach?" Michael asked.

"He could have," I agreed, averting my gaze and then, when he continued to sit silently across from me, finally meeting his. If I had to pick a moment that I acquiesced to Michael, that was it. "We're having a separation."

Michael nodded, but said nothing. We concentrated on our food for a while, then Michael wiped his hands on a napkin and reached across the picnic table.

"I love this ring," he said, lifting my hand with the lapis.

I supposed I knew what he meant: he was glad we'd met. "Me, too," I said.

My hand lay open in his as though I were his patient and he were treating me for some rare ailment. I enjoyed the thought of placing my care quite literally in his hands. And then I imagined the reverse, myself taking care of him after an injury, healing rather than blaming him. When had that ceased happening for Keith and me?

We left the restaurant just as it began to rain. I wondered later whether different timing might have led to different consequences. If it had been raining hard, we probably would have stayed at the restaurant until the rain let up, waiting awkwardly perhaps under the blue-and-white-striped awnings. If we'd left just a few minutes earlier, we would have made the short distance back to Laughing Gull before the downpour. But neither of those possibilities occurred. We mounted the bike at the moment the first drop fell, and we were riding fast when the sky opened up. So Michael decided to turn in at the house of some friends, which we just happened to be passing near.

We parked under a vine-covered trellis and ran to the back of the white saltbox house. A green-and-white awning dripped rain over a moss-laced brick patio. Michael tried the back door, then knocked, then peered in through the kitchen window. He pulled off his helmet and rubbed his forehead.

"They must've driven back to Garden City," he said.

"Who?" I asked, removing my helmet and shaking out my hair, the ends of which whipped wet against my bare shoulders.

"Dennis and Charles," he said. "Both lawyers. Charles was a patient. Gave me a bottle of '78 Lafite after I did some minor surgery on him, and proceeded to teach me everything I've now forgotten about wine. We've been friends ever since."

"You seem to have interesting friends," I said, wrapping my arms around myself. "You and Athena."

Michael laughed. "Athena does have some very interesting friends," he agreed. "Present company included."

I started to disclaim myself as her friend, then reconsidered. Perhaps last night had been the start of a friendship.

Michael led me to a wrought-iron bench beside the back door. "We can stay here under the awning until the rain lets up," he said as we sat side by side. His damp linen shirt clung to his chest. I turned my eyes straight ahead, watching the rain in the garden. The muscles in my legs grew tight with the effort to keep from touching his.

I surveyed the landscape, the terraced flowerbeds and lush borders of evergreens. In the distance, beyond the cultivated sections and a copse of pines, flickered a glint of blue.

"Is that water?" I asked, pointing through the trees. I knew it wasn't the ocean, for we had turned off on the opposite side of the road.

"It's Fort Pond," Michael said. "A good spot to watch the sun set."

I shivered, from the rain or from a sudden urge to watch the sunset from his arms, but I said, "I always get cold after I eat. My metabolism kicks in, I guess."

Michael smiled, reached his arm around me, and rubbed my shoulder. "Mmm-hmm," he said softly. "And a wet dress doesn't help."

Embarrassed—because my dress *was* wet and dark against my skin—I turned my face away and inadvertently bumped my cheek against his hand. He drew me close, cupping my head, and brushed his chin across my hair. Are we actually doing this? I asked myself, half dreading what would happen, half longing for it. I closed my eyes, breathed, then opened them and pulled away. I suddenly couldn't sit still.

Michael shifted to face me and I touched a finger to where his chest showed in the V of his open shirt.

"What's this?" I asked, just to say something; my finger traced the jagged raised line of a scar. The sound of rain was like a fine shattering of glass.

"I had heart surgery," Michael said. His voice was low, without irony.

"What?" I looked up, stunned. "But you're, you must be so young."

"Forty now," he said.

"My age," I said, sitting up straight. "I'm forty."

Michael smiled. "I told you we have much in common."

"But how?" I asked. "Why?"

"Why?" Michael inhaled deeply, then exhaled, shifting forward again. "Who can answer for a simple quirk of fate? A patch of wet leaves on a mountain road I knew well and drove expertly. The bike went down with me beneath it."

"A *motorcycle* accident?"

"I know." Michael's voice was resigned. "You'd think a doctor wouldn't take such risks."

"And you needed heart surgery?" I asked, shifting to face him.

"Yes," he said. "Ruptured aorta. Broken bones, too, but you don't want the gory details."

I placed a hand on his arm. I did want them, but I couldn't ask.

Michael touched my hand as he spoke. "It was such a long recovery. I spent a lot of time alone in a hospital, thinking about what was important to me." He looked out toward the sliver of Fort Pond, his eyes narrowing.

"And what was?" I wondered.

"Being a good doctor." He turned to me and smiled. "Music. Nature."

My priorities were similar. Being a good mother. Music. Nature. Perhaps as a reaction to the chaos of my childhood, I had early on developed a reliance on the calming powers of pleasing form.

My garden—with its borders of blue cornflowers, delphiniums, and hollyhocks; its trellised roses; and its rock garden of creeping thymes—had, for many years, been my consistent source of serenity.

I looked at the flowers around us, dripping wet.

"But you ride a motorcycle, still," I realized.

"True. The bike was one of the major issues between Linda and me," he said. "One of several major issues."

"Linda? Your wife?" The forlorn sound of a gull pierced the heavy air.

"Yes," he said. "We'd only been married six months when I wiped out." He sat quiet for a moment, then added, "She never forgave me for riding again."

"Why did you?" I asked. The rain had slowed to a light drizzle.

Michael stood up, stretching toward the sky. "Because I like to and because I'm good at it. Really, except for that once, I've never gone down. And I'm very careful now."

"That's true," I agreed. "You didn't risk riding in the rain."

"See that," he said. Then he cocked his chin toward the garden. "The rain is beginning to stop."

I stood beside him, rubbing my arms. The air smelled of grass and pine and sea.

"I'm sorry about your accident," I said. "And your marriage."

"Well," Michael said, "I survived both."

For a moment he sounded like Keith, which had the odd effect of both alarming and stirring me.

"Would you like to walk through the woods?" he asked. "We're already wet."

"Sure," I said, staring at the place in his chest where I imagined his damaged heart lay, the place my lips came up to. "Why not?"

Michael took my hand; we stepped off the awning-covered patio and strolled along a redbrick path that led past beds of roses, zinnias, and other sun-loving flowers. The thin rain stung my skin at first, but then it grew pleasant, almost warm. I lifted my face to the sky and opened my mouth, trying to catch droplets. Michael smiled and did the same. His mouth was wide.

"No fair," I complained. "You're taller. You'll catch them all first."

He took me by the waist and lifted me like a ballerina till my head was higher than his. I laughed and threw back my hair, letting the raindrops tickle my face and neck. I felt ridiculous and charmed.

Then he set me back on the ground. We rejoined hands and

continued our walk. Where the brick path ended, a pine nugget path began. The plantings here were those suited to partial shade, hostas and impatiens and ferns. Large and tiny garden ornaments, stone toads and purple-glass gazing globes shimmered through the rain-glossed leaves. Soon we were at the edge of the cultivated garden, at the border of the natural wood. We hesitated only a moment.

Neither of us spoke as we entered that bower of filtered light. Our footsteps careful, we entered the woods, the air beneath the pines redolent and hushed. I felt Michael next to me as though we pressed more than hands, but our bodies didn't touch.

Everything that had happened in my life so far had led me here, to this moment in time, of that I was certain. Yet I was equally certain that this place was as separate from the rest of my life as the moon from the earth, as the Georgia Piedmont from the eastern shores of Long Island.

The rain picked up with a sudden burst of wind. Michael stopped walking.

"Should we go back?" he asked.

I raised my face to a wedge of heavy sky between pine boughs. "No," I said, closing my eyes. I couldn't go back.

Then he was kissing me, his lips sliding onto my wet cheek, reaching for my mouth, his fingers cradling my chin. I savored the inevitable but unexpected taste of him. When he pulled away, I opened my eyes. A raindrop traced a path down his forehead, and I followed it with the tip of my finger along the slope of his nose, down the indentation that my children called the "sweet spot," over the curve of his lips. His lips parted and I slipped my finger between them to find the edge of his tongue.

He groaned softly, sucking my finger and pulling me close. "Amanda." He breathed the syllables against my ear.

I began to unbutton his shirt. "I want to see," I whispered and I caught him wincing; then he helped me peel the wet linen from his chest and revealed his scar. It was brutal, a vertical slash through the middle of his chest, with two small arms on either side of his rib cage, like an upside-down Y. I bent my head to kiss the raised flesh, and he raked his fingers through my hair. I ran my tongue down the length of it, stopping to kiss the place where it came to an end. Then I lifted my head and smiled at him and he grinned.

"Hi," he said.

The rain beat harder, noisily through the pines, the only other sound on earth. I answered him. "Hi."

"My turn," Michael said softly as he fumbled with the buttons of my dress. I reached up behind my neck to untie the halter straps, letting them fall to my shoulders. But Michael didn't tug them down; he undid each button to my waist.

"You're lovely," he said without touching me. But the damp air soughed against my skin.

Michael knelt and undid more buttons until my dress fell to the ground. Gently, he pulled my hand till I knelt in front of him, and then he sighed and licked raindrops from the hollow of my throat. I arched back, my fingers propped behind me in the soft pine straw, and Michael gazed at me, hair dripping in his eyes, as he unbuttoned his pants. Then, leaning forward, he extended his tongue so it barely reached the fat raindrop pooling on the end of my left nipple. His tongue flicked and wiggled till it coaxed the droplet to his lips and as I moaned with pleasure, he pressed himself on top of me and I lay back against my strewn dress.

We kissed, deep and long and hungrily, our bodies slipping against each other. At last Michael lifted himself up to wriggle out of his pants. Seeing him naked I surprised myself with a sudden urge to say, "I love you." But I didn't speak.

His body excited me, and I wanted to touch him everywhere. Though his physique was imperfect—similar to Keith's actually in its middle-aged concessions to gravity—my own forty years showed on my body, too, and I desired Michael all the more because we were equals in that way.

Michael lowered his boxers to reveal a long, appealingly curved cock, glistening with rain and urgency. How different men were from each other, I thought, suddenly realizing I hadn't seen any man but Keith naked in twenty years, at least not in this situation.

"I can't do this," I whispered, as he bent over me.

"We don't have to make love," he said, kissing my neck.

I reached down to touch him and felt that primal ache deep within me. We did have to, I knew. We would.

"Rain is nice," I said. Then I pushed his shoulders so that I could climb astride him.

"Ouch!" Michael yelped and I leapt off him.

"What?" I was sure I'd hurt him where he was vulnerable, that somehow I'd pressed too hard on his chest.

Michael reached behind him and held up an offending pinecone. "Damn," he said, and I started to laugh.

He laughed, too, and then we were both laughing, great, heaving, gut-emptying paroxysms that left us gasping and hugging each other and rolling in the rain. Pine needles prickled me, but I didn't care.

"You're wonderful," he said when our hysteria subsided. "I knew it the minute I met you."

"Did you?" Of course, I'd had the same reaction to him. I tasted salt on my lips.

"Of course I did. I dreamt about you last night," he said, his features recomposing themselves. His fingers brushed a pine needle from my cheek.

"Hmm." I traced the line of his jaw, slipping a finger inside his mouth again. I couldn't keep away from his mouth.

"I want to make you wet," he said, nibbling my fingertip. "But this is ridiculous."

I laughed. Michael lifted my chin, then he reached behind my shoulders to grasp the ends of my wet hair, slowly pulling my head back to expose my throat. "God, you're sexy," he murmured, and then softly bit my neck.

Inspired, I lowered a hand between my legs, spreading my own lips with my fingers, touching myself. "You're right," I said. "I am ridiculously wet."

Michael grabbed my wrist and brought my fingers to his mouth, licking them, sucking them. He closed his eyes, and I moved down to take him in my mouth. He grabbed my head, slid himself deep into my throat and then pulled out.

He rose above me, dripping with rain, his scar an angry red hieroglyph of flesh. "I want you," he said. "But the decision is yours."

"Safe sex," I began.

"Believe me, I've been tested," he said.

"I believe you, but I warn my daughter not to do this; how can I?"

He lowered his head between my legs, gently spreading my thighs with his hands. He licked me long and slow, the full length of my labia, and lingered on the knob of my clitoris till I gasped with pleasure, my hands clutching at pine straw. Several quick laps and then another meandering one, his tongue probing.

Michael lifted his head and I almost pushed it back down. "I won't come inside you," he promised in a rough voice as he licked rain from my navel. "But I want to *be* inside you."

"Kiss me," I said.

He slid upward, raised his mouth to mine, and as I tasted myself on his lips, his cock pressed hard against my thighs. We kissed and he cupped my breasts in his hands, first one then the other, rubbing each nipple between two fingers until I moaned.

"I want you," I told him, and before I'd taken a breath he was pushing into me, igniting each molecule along the way, and I was wrapping my legs around him. His thrusts were long and slow, pulling nearly all the way out before entering me again. My arms fell from his shoulders as I pressed up into him, leveraging myself against the ground. Lifting himself above me, he gathered both my wrists in his left hand and pulled my arms above my head. His right hand slid between our bodies, caressing me as his thrusts gained momentum and I cried out. By the time I came, my flesh had turned to liquid, spasms rippling through my body like the tidal waves I feared.

Michael came on my belly. Immediately I thought of Keith, my throat tightened, and tears filled my eyes. But as Michael hugged me and I held him and the pine needles embossed our flesh, the rain stopped. The loud, hard thumping of our hearts together were our only conversation as we lay listening to the active silence that comes after rain. And though the world was sodden and the sky was heavy and gray, we looked up between the tree limbs at a narrow band of light breaking through the clouds, and its timing was so perfect that we laughed.

CHAPTER 16

*T*UESDAY'S SKY DAWNED OVERCAST and the offshore breeze carried an early hint of autumn. This was the east-end weather I remembered: summer as short and intense as a love affair, progressing swiftly into dropping temperatures and falling leaves, every bright, cool morning a warning of the deeper chill to come. August was the month of never getting enough, where any day at the beach could be the season's last.

Today wasn't a beach day, and I lingered over coffee with Lizzie, allowing myself only tiny, intermittent moments of flashbacks to the afternoon before. She was trying to decide whether to go into East Hampton, trying to persuade me to join her if she did. I knew I wouldn't be an enthusiastic shopping companion today, as all I wanted to do was think about what had happened with Michael and what it might mean. What had I done to the fragile chance of saving my marriage? Had I been reckless and completely selfish, or had something happened I hadn't known could be possible?

"The thing is," Lizzie was saying, "I really should lose a few more pounds before I buy any new clothes."

I frowned at her. "If you need something, you should buy it," I said.

"Well." She smiled as she put down her coffee mug. "What do I *need?*"

At that moment Crosby arrived, dressed in yesterday's T-shirt, coming to say I had a phone call at Athena's cottage.

Michael, I thought, and then immediately my stomach clenched. *Keith.*

Crosby ran off and Lizzie went into her cottage to check on Ryan.

Pebbles rolled into my sandals as I walked the path, and I had to stop to shake them out. I had wanted to speak with Keith, but now I dreaded it. I was afraid he would hear in my voice that something had changed.

It was Michael. "I hope I didn't wake you," he said and I flushed, turning my back to Athena, who sat at her desk flipping the pages of a ledger book, bracelets jingling.

"Oh, no," I answered. "The ring fits fine."

"I'm glad," Michael countered without hesitation. He'd realized this conversation was taking place in front of Athena. "I was concerned for you yesterday."

"Hmmm." I leaned as far away from the desk as the phone cord would allow. "I appreciated your concern."

Athena stopped flipping pages; I felt her eyes, but didn't turn my head.

I continued in code. "It seems the rain didn't cool much off, though."

"I know the feeling," Michael said. The tonal colorations of his voice were deep and mellow. "What are your plans for today?"

He wanted to see me. I was thrilled and confused. "Lizzie and I were just discussing that. Have you any recommendations?" I shifted position in order to glance at Athena. Her head was bent over her book, but her hands were still.

"In fact I do." Michael's voice rose slightly.

My forehead tightened.

"Come visit me," he said.

I reciprocated his directness. "I should be with my son."

"Come visit me and bring your son."

I flashed on the cadences of a poem I'd loved in college: *Come live with me and be my love/ And we will all the pleasures prove . . .*

"I have a couple of Suzuki dirt bikes," Michael said. "Two-fifty's, very easy to handle, that Linda and I used to ride. Bring Crosby along and they'll have a blast."

"Oh," was all I could manage in response while I considered. I understood that when I moved out of this moment, something new would be decided.

"Want to call me back?" Michael asked, and his insight into my situation sealed my decision.

"Not at all," I said. "It sounds like fun."

"Good." I heard a smile in Michael's voice, a brightness around the edges of it. "Do you think you can get a ride over here?"

"Yes . . ." I said, strategizing. Rick and Jeremy had taken Lizzie's van to play golf. If I left Lizzie my rental car, she could drop us at Michael's and pick us up later. She would want to see his house, I knew. And she would judge me least.

"Very good," Michael said, a touch of bedside manner in his voice.

Athena stood up behind me.

"Well," I touched the underside of the lapis ring with my thumb. "See you."

"See you *soon*," Michael said. "Say, an hour or so?"

"Right," I answered, pressing the ring between my fingers. " 'Bye."

I leaned to replace the phone in its receiver and Athena reached for my hand. Her long fingers felt light and surprisingly cool and I stared at them, as if to watch what they would do next. "This ring really does suit you," Athena said, lifting my wrist.

"Thanks." I withdrew my hand. "But you know how it is, I'm still so aware of the feel of it on my finger."

"Oh, I do know what you mean," she said, smiling her crooked-tooth smile. "I bet you're so used to your other rings, you don't even remember you have them on."

She was right; I turned my hand until my diamonds caught light. "Well," I said. "I *feel* them, but as though they're part of me."

Athena nodded, eyelids lowered as though she knew better, and turned toward the kitchen, skirt swishing. She was wearing green today, a dappled rayon that suggested changing patterns of light. "Come have a cup of tea," she said. "Something to settle the stomach."

*   *   *

At Michael's house I again drank tea, this time iced, a special fruity blend given him by another of his patients.

"People are always giving you things," I said as we sipped from tall green glasses on his deck under a swollen sky. Without the sun's sparkle, the house looked less majestic, less substantial. Lizzie had been impressed by it, but she'd refused my invitation to get out of the car to see more.

"Patients give me things," Michael answered. "But they're not the same as *people*."

I frowned at him and he grinned, teasing me again. This was a man who enjoyed his own results.

He was dressed in a T-shirt and bathing trunks, and I wished he would take off the shirt. I wanted to see his scar again, from a different perspective. But of course he would keep his shirt on: the pallor of his chest was testament to his privacy. He leaned to pick up his iced tea, his shoulder brushing my arm. With the boys here I was proscribed, I could not give in to temptation. We couldn't even kiss.

Crosby and then Damien thumped by on Michael's twin red Suzukis, following a path beside the dunes. As it turned out, Crosby had ridden Michael's dirt bikes before, and he acted the enthusiastic tutor to Damien.

"I'll show you the line," he had said with an endearing swagger, and Michael explained that that meant he'd show Damien where to ride, how to take the hills, how to circumnavigate the obstacles. "With knobbies you can ride most anywhere," Crosby had assured me.

"Tires," Michael had leaned over to whisper, his breath a feather across my skin.

I wondered about the other times Crosby had ridden Michael's dirt bike. He seemed very comfortable with it, with all Michael's things, a familiarity he shared with his mother. I pictured Athena stretched out in this chair as Crosby sputtered through the dunes, watching him—or perhaps not watching? I discarded the thought.

"Where's the sun?" I complained.

"I thought you liked the rain?" Michael was teasing again, but he was questioning, too.

I smiled, but didn't reply, teasing back with my eyes.

Then I lay back, concentrating on lying still. I had been nervous about seeing Michael again, but I had wanted it. I breathed deeply. The scent of the ocean was strong today, thick as incense. I liked hearing it without seeing it, calmed by its predictable beat as by a mother's heart.

The ocean had soothed me all those summers when my mother was in the hospital, had soothed us both last summer, two weeks before she died. It was the last important sound we'd shared. "I love the voice of the sea," I said.

The boys passed again, the quick, loud beats of their engines like drums. I sat up and waved to them.

"Come inside with me," Michael said softly. His hand rested on the arm of my chaise, ready and willing, I knew, to touch me.

I leaned forward, closer to, but not touching his hand, and looked across the shrinking space between us. "I can't," I said. "I have to watch the boys."

"Of course, you're right." Michael drank his tea. "Damien is a quick learner," he said. "Like his mother."

I turned toward him. His eyes were hidden behind mirrored sunglasses. "How do you know that?"

"I can tell," Michael said, shifting toward me.

I reminded myself that Keith was with another woman, that unlike me he didn't have his son around to inhibit his behavior.

"Hey, I've got a gig tomorrow night," Michael said, his mouth full of tea as though he had to speak the words the moment he thought them.

"Where?" I asked, sitting forward to reach for my glass.

"The Jaw Bone," Michael said. "Just a dive in town, a local blues bar. The regular band lets me sit in."

Again the boys thumped past, this time riding closer to the dunes.

"Sounds fun," I said. "So is that why you didn't go back to the city, because of the gig?"

"Nooo," Michael said. "In fact I called the drummer this morning. After I spoke to you. Knowing I'd see you put me in a musical mood."

I visualized Michael in a smoky bar, his guitar slung low in front of him, as I watched Damien follow Crosby's zigzag almost exactly. My son was a quick study, as Michael had said, like his father.

I had a sudden urge to pee, and with it the sudden attendant urge to know for sure whether I was pregnant. I hadn't really wanted to know before, hadn't wanted to face what either result might mean, but knowing now seemed essential. How could I continue a relationship with Michael—if we were to continue it—while carrying another man's child? My *husband's* child.

"Come hear us play?" Michael was offering me another excuse to see him.

"I don't know." I hesitated. "Maybe." I stood up and made a visor over my eyes with my hand. The boys were stopped, conferring, straddling their bikes with their engines running. Damien held his shoulders back, obviously proud of his new skill. "It's not that I don't want to," I said.

"Bring your sister, your brother, bring whomever you want, if that makes it easier," Michael said, smiling up at me. "Or come Thursday; we're playing Thursday night, too."

"You're sweet," I said and considered the idea: Lizzie, Jeremy, Rick, and Froggy all listening to Michael play guitar in some beachy dive. Risky, but not without a certain appeal. Making a family event out of it was one way of getting to see Michael perform. The more I thought about it, the more I longed to hear his music.

My bladder protested its neglect, and I spoke up. "I need to use your bathroom."

Michael stood and gestured for me to proceed. With a light hand on my shoulder, he led me past a soundly napping Homer to the glass doors.

"How long can you stay?" he asked, reaching for the latch.

"A couple of hours," I answered. "Lizzie is going to pick me up around lunchtime." In the glass I could see the reflection of Damien and Crosby riding by, side by side this time.

Were the boys racing? I don't know why I didn't call to Damien to be careful. Watching him in the glass was like watching a film, a story made by someone else. Later, I remembered wondering about the gulls, why there weren't any around. But it was one of those perceptions just beneath the surface of thought, the kind that when recalled proves that you should have known in the first place.

Michael turned me to him. "I mean here in Montauk, can you stay another week after your family leaves?"

"I have to leave on Saturday," I said. "I have my plane ticket, and anyway Athena has the cottage booked for next week."

"All easily changed," Michael said, his fingers tracing a circle on my shoulder. "You can stay here with me, and I'll take care of your ticket."

I looked up at him, alarmed and thrilled.

"But Keith . . ." I said, his name like a knife, not sure what I meant by using it.

"Your estranged husband." Michael slid open the door and led me into the house. "Tell me how it is between the two of you."

I groaned, shifting on my feet.

"Okay, go to the bathroom," Michael said. He removed his sunglasses. "We can talk about it later."

I pantomimed my relief and turned, not sure where the bathroom was.

"Straight ahead," Michael directed.

Unlike the powder room or the other upstairs rooms, this little bathroom appeared well used. Michael had meant it when he'd claimed to spend most of his time down here. Signs of him were everywhere, from the raised toilet seat to the remnants of a shave in the sink to a crumpled, dirty T-shirt on the floor. I buried my face in it as I squatted to pee, just as I'd once done with Keith's discarded shirts, and the full force of my betrayal filled me as I breathed another man's scent. And yet I kept the shirt to my face, taking my fill.

When I came out, feeling more emptied than relieved, Michael was waiting within reach.

"I want to kiss you," he said, moving me away from the glass doors into a shadowed corner.

I lifted my face to his, willing to go along with anything he had in mind. Abdicating judgment to trust. The taste of him was strangely foreign, almost exotic, and then I realized I was tasting tea and wondered whether we'd been drinking one of Athena's herbal mixtures, whether she'd been his "patient." Michael pressed me tighter. I tasted him beneath the tea.

Then we heard the screams.

We were running—through the door, over the deck, down through the dune grass and the scrub pines with Homer keeping pace beside us—and still we couldn't see them. But I heard Damien calling, "Mom, Mom," and my heart beat crazily in my chest.

"They must have crossed the dunes," Michael said, pointing to a narrow path between sandy swells. He was right: we saw them as soon as we rounded the hillock. Homer raced ahead of us, and by the time we reached the scene of the accident, I saw Damien's arms draped around the dog and I knew he was all right.

Crosby was lying on his back, next to where the two red bikes lay tangled, and he kept his face turned away from us. When Damien saw me, he began to cry.

"I'm sorry," he sobbed as Michael dropped to the sand. Homer stood alongside his master and sniffed, his tail brushing the sand in a low wag.

"I know you are," Michael said, quickly scanning him for injuries. Then he turned to examine Crosby.

I knelt beside my son and held him, wiping sand from his face. Blood streaked his forehead from a gash just above his left eye.

"Muffler burn, second degree." Michael jumped to his feet. "I'll get ice and be right back." He pointed a finger at Crosby. "Don't move."

I watched as he sprinted away, Homer behind him, watched as he moved through scrub trees and dunes until what I thought was Michael was only a shadow. The sky seemed lower, the ocean nearer, and for a moment I felt as though I were stranded on some abandoned island at the end of the earth. Then Crosby muttered a string of curses.

"What happened?" I asked, checking Damien all over. In addition to the cut on his forehead, he was scraped and bleeding at the knees and elbows, and the abrasions were filled with gravel and sand. But Crosby was obviously worse off, the creamy flesh of his inner thigh bright red where he'd burned it. His eyes were shut tight and leaking tears, his face was screwed up in pain, but he made no sound. I touched a hand to his bony shoulder.

"We crashed," Damien snuffled. His curled fingers lifted reflexively to his broken tooth.

"Duh," Crosby said. He pushed himself up on his elbows.

"Dr. Burns said you shouldn't move," I reminded him, then softened my voice. "Does it hurt bad?"

"It hurts like hell," Crosby said with an accusing hostility in his voice.

Homer bounded from the dunes and Michael followed, carrying a cooler of ice and a medical bag. His face was red and he was winded, and I wondered about his heart.

"Are you all right?" I asked quietly as Michael applied a bag of ice and water to Crosby's leg. Crosby winced and sat up straighter.

Michael glanced at me. "I'm fine. Are you?"

I might have laughed, but I swallowed and my mouth tasted sour. "Tell me what I can do," I said. Homer licked my hand.

Michael was moving Crosby's arm above and below the elbow. "Anything else hurt?"

Crosby shook his head. "I wrecked your bike."

Michael lifted Crosby's uninjured leg above the knee and manipulated the joint. "The bike isn't important. What's important is that you guys are okay." He turned to me. "In the bag you'll find some sterile cotton and a bottle of hydrogen peroxide. You can start cleaning Damien's abrasions. Oh, and there should be a tube of silvadene cream and one of neosporin."

I placed each item on top of the cooler and began to soak a large piece of cotton. Damien tensed. "Will it hurt?"

Michael turned to Damien and smiled. "Not for a tough guy like you." He turned back to Crosby. "Okay, no broken bones. Just keep the ice on it. I'll call your mother."

Michael took a cellular phone from his medical bag and stood up, walking away from us as he pressed numbers. I watched him raise the phone to his ear.

"Ow!" Damien said as I wiped his knee. Homer sniffed his leg.

Michael called to me over his shoulder. "Just pour the peroxide from the bottle, Amanda." It was only the second time he'd said my name. Then he bent his head over the phone and I couldn't hear his words. But I kept watching, staring at the back of his head, at the way his hair looked almost silver in the muted light, thinking that he knew Athena's phone number by heart.

Later, when they were bandaged and medicated and resting in front of Michael's television as we waited for Lizzie to come get us, the boys told me that there was nothing anyone could have done to prevent the accident. Even if I'd been watching from the deck, or standing in the tall grass just yards from where they rode, the same thing would have happened. Crosby had hit the brakes to avoid an obstacle—something long and dark, an animal he thought at first, but later he said a piece of driftwood—and he'd spun out the rear of his bike, his tire knocking sideways into Damien's.

That's how accidents were, Michael told them as he served them Cokes, accidents just happened. I let them believe him. I didn't say that sometimes accidents could be prevented, that in this case, especially, my need to have Michael want me had put us all in danger.

I waited for my sister by a long window, watching the moving sky while Michael chatted about music videos with the boys. An older video came on, one of Isabella's favorites. I missed her suddenly. Michael came to stand beside me.

"They're fine," he said, "really. But I'm so sorry this happened."

"I know," I said.

"Can I see you later? Can you come back tonight?"

Something twisted beneath my ribs. As much as I wanted to be with Michael, I knew I couldn't indulge myself now. Another accident had happened when I wasn't looking. My eyes felt heavy in their sockets. "I can't," I told him. "I can't think how. I'm sorry."

He touched the window glass with his fingertips, leaving ghost prints that quickly vanished. "All right," he said.

And I wondered whether some fine sweetness had dissolved between us.

CHAPTER 17
New England, 1977

*I*SABELLA WAS BORN ON A DAZZLING SUNDAY morning a week before Halloween. Keith coached me through my labor, strong and tireless but deeply frightened. In those days, prepared childbirth was still in its early days of acceptance, and the obstetrics night nurse disapproved of having a nonmedical male presence in the delivery room. Stoically, Keith ignored her mumbles and glances and guided me through the heights of the worst pain I had ever experienced to the depths of my greatest joy. And Keith got to see what I never did, our first child's perfect face framed in the oval aperture of my flesh, that split second before she slid into the world.

"So this is who you are," I said to my daughter as I held her and, with a prodigious effort, she opened her eyes for us to see each other. She was the most distinct person I'd ever known.

On Wednesday, we brought her home to our apartment on the ground floor of an old but fairly charmless house in our college town. Keith photographed her in the wicker laundry basket we'd made up as her first bed. He photographed her artfully backlit by a narrow window in the green plastic infant seat he'd picked out of someone's trash and washed with Lysol. He photographed her in bed with me, and I photographed her in bed with him. For two days we did little but adore her and wonder how we'd ever lived without her. We also wondered how we'd ever have a life again.

My mother came to visit us on Friday. She took the train up

from Long Island because my father didn't want her to drive alone the four and a half hours to the college campus where we lived. But though her mental state was, Lizzie had informed me, *borderline*—a change of seasons or an important occasion would invariably set her off, and both had occurred—my father never objected to her making the trip. "A mother should be with her daughter at these times," he had said. It didn't occur to him that a father's presence might be warranted as well.

My mother arrived carrying a squat, deeply lined pumpkin, and wearing such bright makeup and clothes, I thought at first she was dressed in costume.

"Helloooo," she said, her voice deep in her throat so that it sounded almost a growl.

I looked up from the sagging, thrift-store couch where I lay smelling Isabella's head after nursing her. The sight of my mother's face jolted me. Mascara had smudged in two gray half moons beneath her eyes, and her passionflower pink lips twitched every few seconds, a side effect of her medication. I wanted her to go away; and I wanted my mother.

"Hello, Grandma," Keith greeted her as he took her coat and purse and suitcase and looked around the apartment for a place to put them. My mother held on to the pumpkin. He decided, finally, to stow the purse and suitcase in a corner and drape the coat over a chair as though its owner wouldn't be staying long.

My mother's mouth stretched into a clown smile. "I'm Grandma," she agreed, handing Keith the pumpkin.

"Look, a large, orange gourd," he said, then added at her frown, "a great pumpkin." He set it on a table by the door, on top of a week-old stack of mail.

I kissed Isabella's head, avoiding the soft, downy spot that pulsed with her heartbeat. "Isn't she perfect?" I said as I levered myself into a sitting position. My mother stepped toward us, her hands outstretched but her arms close to her body. A child might think she was a monster.

"Let me hold her," she said and then lifted my sleeping daughter from my embrace.

"Please." I clung to the baby. "Wash your hands."

My mother gazed at her fingers as though they were smeared with grime.

"You've been traveling," I reminded her.

Her eyes seemed to turn inward then, and I recognized the look of her listening to a voice from within. Her lips moved soundlessly, and I had to glance away. I felt an old, double-edged pang of anger and remorse.

She turned toward her purse. "I'll have a cigarette first."

My mouth opened, wordless; Isabella stirred.

"Out," my mother said as though directing herself, walking to the door without her coat. "On the porch."

Keith looked at me as the door closed behind her and the pumpkin wobbled on its perch. "Oh boy," he said, shaking his head. "Three days?"

My mother decided to cook us dinner in the wok, though she had never used one. "This is an interesting pan," she'd said.

Isabella lay in her basket, her tender face against a thin, white cotton pillow my mother had embroidered for her with flowers and rabbits. From my bed, I could hear her tiny sucking movements, and wondered whether she was dreaming of my breast.

Keith was out, at his class—he was a graduate teaching assistant and had already missed four days—and I lay under the chenille quilt that had been his grandmother's, trying to nap. "You should sleep when the baby sleeps," my mother had instructed as she chopped onions on the kitchen counter, the only parental advice she'd offered so far. It was a good though impractical suggestion. I needed to sleep, but I couldn't sleep. I hadn't really slept, it felt, since Isabella's birth. The closest I'd got was a kind of semi-alert twilight, a drifting state of exhaustion that offered rest but not restoration. To sleep seemed to abandon; how could I?

Twilight glimmered outside the window now, a silvery October dusk that made the world seem small. And twilight seemed to describe the darkening descent of my mother's condition, a state where it was difficult to see the real shape of things. Her mind was, for the most part, still with us, but as though slightly obscured in lengthening shadows.

I lay motionless, wishing for sleep and fearing it, but also wishing to be drinking tea at the cast-off patio table that served as our kitchen table, my mother—a normal mother—across from me, passing on her wisdom and experience, telling me the stories of my own infancy. Instead, I remained alone in my room as she fixed another of her silent meals. It was her way, I knew, of caring for us, for me. The very way, I thought bitterly, that consoled me least. "I'd rather order in Chinese," I'd told Keith, "or deli sandwiches, than have a mother who cooks good food while listening to voices."

He had shrugged as he'd gathered his papers, half listening to the lament he'd heard from me so many times. "I like your mother's cooking," he had said as he leaned to kiss me good-bye. "Isabella will get her first taste of it, what, about four hours after you do."

I'd smiled. Another first.

Now I propped up on an elbow and listened: my mother was humming in the kitchen. A good sign. Maybe a signal. I decided to make myself some tea and talk to her as a daughter. I grabbed a pillow and made my way out of the bedroom, pausing first to bend over Isabella and listen to her breathe, leaning closer until I thought I could feel the tiniest brush of her breath on my cheek.

In the hall, the smell of frying onions grew strong, a familiar smell, an appetite-whetting smell, but one that now raised my ire. Had my mother given any thought to the fact that I was nursing and should be eating bland foods? Did she remember—or ever know—anything about caring for infants? I'd have to pick out the onions.

I stopped in the hallway, partly because my stitches ached and my insides felt as though they were about to fall out, partly to compose my surging emotions. Once again I was close to tears. Hormones, I told myself. I didn't want to be upset with my mother, though almost everything she did annoyed me. I wanted—what was the phrase the books used?—to feel our bond. She was, after all, my mother and I had just borne her first grandchild.

She began to hum a melody I recognized, "Once I had a secret love." Hope sprang up in my dark mind like a mushroom. She couldn't be hearing voices and humming that tune, the song that had always meant she was happy. A warm excitement tingled in me, as though I had been given an unexpected gift. All I wanted at this moment was to be somebody's child and to marvel at the miracle of my own.

My mother hadn't turned on the light in the kitchen, and it was after sunset, but my eyes were adjusted to the dimness. She didn't turn as I shuffled into the room. She stood at the stove, lowering chunks of breaded chicken into sizzling olive oil, still humming. The oil in the wok was three inches deep.

"What are you doing?" I cried out, startling her. She turned toward me abruptly and dropped the plate of chicken into the wok. Boiling oil spattered up across her left hand.

I screamed.

My mother didn't, but she held out her reddening palm.

I rushed to the sink and turned on the cold water. "Quick!" I ordered her. "Get your hand under the water."

"Sssh," my mother warned as her face contorted in pain. "You'll wake the baby."

Isabella slept and slept. "Is this normal?" I asked my mother, willing to believe whatever she told me. We were sitting on the porch with the door ajar so we could hear the baby's cries, but though I strained to listen, Isabella remained silent. She had been sleeping for four hours.

My mother drew on the cigarette in her right hand; her left hand lay in her lap, wrapped in ointment and gauze. "Babies sleep," she told me. "Be thankful she's a good sleeper." She tilted her chin as she smoked.

"But she's not," I said as I watched a set of headlights turn the corner, hoping they were Keith's. Isabella had been waking up every couple of hours, all night long, since we'd brought her home. Admittedly, that had only been two days ago. The headlights belonged to a giant-tired car with ridiculously high suspension, some townie's.

"This is my last cigarette," my mother said. "Then she'll wake up."

I looked at her, huddled in a creaking lawn chair under the yellow porch light, the light a miniature moon beneath the half-hidden hunter's moon in the sky. The index finger of her burned hand was tapping out some pattern on her lap.

"How do you know?" I asked, hoping for maternal wisdom: *infants under four weeks of age rarely sleep more than four hours at a time,* rather than superstition: *if I finish this cigarette in three puffs, the baby will wake*—or worse.

"Ssh!" my mother lifted a finger to her lips, and I thought she had heard the baby. I leaned an ear toward the door.

"I hear whispers," my mother told me, whispering.

My muscles coiled tight, ready to spring toward the door and my slumbering child. The child I knew so little about beyond the fact of the raw, protective love I felt for her. Who was there? I listened, but heard nothing beneath the ordinary night sounds of engines and electricity. Fear leapt in me.

"I hear whispering," my mother repeated, rocking in her chair. "And I know who it is."

Like the gas flames on the stove I had rushed to lower earlier, the high, quick heat of my fear immediately reduced, simmering rather than boiling that familiar stew of anger and incomprehension.

"What?" I asked, clenching my teeth. "Who?"

My mother crushed out her cigarette against the metal arm of her chair. "If I only smoke when they tell me," she explained, "Isabella will stay safe."

This was the first time she'd said my daughter's name; until now she'd referred to her as "the baby." Another first. I winced. My breasts throbbed; my milk was coming in.

Keith's car pulled up in front of the house and then I heard Isabella cry. I jumped up, knocking my pillow cushion to the floor, wanting to rush to him, wanting to rush to her. For a second I swayed on my feet.

"I'll get the baby," my mother said, pushing herself up.

"I will!" I snapped and took off in my awkward, shuffling way past her and through the house.

In the dark bedroom, I lifted my daughter against my shoulder, careful to support her heavy, wobbly head. She continued to cry, an insistent, angry sound that I thought must be caused by hunger and sleeping so long. I had never heard her wail this way, and part of me was glad, for my breasts burned full. It wasn't until I got to the sofa in the living room, and settled with her beneath the lamplight that I saw the bright red line across her cheek.

Keith followed my mother into the room. "I smell something good," he said. He cupped my shoulder and bent over Isabella. "And I don't mean you, Stinky." He kissed her forehead.

I glared at him. I didn't like this nickname for her he'd begun using. "Look," I said. "She's scratched herself." I hadn't yet mustered the courage to cut her papery fingernails.

Keith examined Isabella's face as I opened my shirt. I could hear my mother in the kitchen now, opening and closing cupboards. We had agreed to wait until Keith got home to eat her deep-fried wok chicken and vegetables.

Keith frowned, his eyelids lengthening. "She's bleeding," he said. He lifted Isabella's tiny, curled fist. "Her nails are not that sharp."

He was right. My eyes met his, panicking, as Isabella's rose-petal mouth latched on to my nipple. Something—or someone—had hurt her. "But how?" I asked, my stomach rolling into a tight fist. She sucked like an animal.

Keith straightened. "Something in her basket," he said and strode to the bedroom.

Isabella's sucking was painful, like a punishment. I knew before Keith returned with it in his hand that it had to be the pillow. He came back carrying it, shaking his head.

"What?" I asked, so tired the blood slogged in my veins.

"Look at this," he said, holding a sewing needle under the lamp, a thin, pale thread dangling from its eye. "Someone left a needle in this pillow. It could have stabbed her eye." His voice trembled with fury.

Someone. My crazy mother. *I guess you didn't smoke your cigarettes in the right order,* I wanted to hiss at her. But I looked up and saw her standing in the doorway, her hands clasping a tattered dishcloth to her chest, her eyes so large and liquid they reflected light. And I knew that there would never be a trick to keeping children safe.

CHAPTER 18

"I'M SORRY TO IMPOSE ON YOU."

The voice was muffled, remote, not meant for me. I turned over in bed

"Am I too early? Today is Wednesday." Wednesday. I opened my eyes. Montauk. Wednesday! Today my father was moving into my cottage. I jumped up.

I opened the screen door, shielding my eyes from the sun. My father stood before me, his head bent down toward his worn leather suitcase so that my eyes looked onto the top of his fishing hat. "What time is it?" I asked, squinting past him. Outside, another boldly beautiful morning proved August could not make up its mind.

My father heaved his suitcase through the door. "I got up early," he said. "No point in hanging around that other cottage."

He pulled his suitcase down the short hall to the room he would be sharing with Damien, who was still asleep. I moved groggily toward the coffeemaker. What time had I got to bed last night? Midnight? After?

I'd eaten dinner with Lizzie's family, and afterward, while Damien and the twins played gin rummy, Rick went down to the beach to night fish, and my father left us to pack up his cottage, Lizzie and I had sipped our tea and indulged in sister-talk. I told Lizzie, without explicitly telling her, about Keith and Sarah, and eventually about Michael and me. I needed to speak his name, needed to say things about him. But then I felt foolish. Even softened by half-lies of omission, my story felt predictable and small.

"I feel as though I'm a stranger in my own life," I'd rationalized as Lizzie leaned her chin above the citronella candle between us. "I'm watching myself from a distance, wondering what will happen next."

Lizzie looked straight at me then, her hazel eyes flickering with compassion. "We're all still grieving," she said.

I hadn't considered the possible connections between my mother's death, my problems with Keith, and my yearning for Michael, but for the rest of the night her words haunted me. I dreamed of my mother behind a screen door, always vanishing when I tried to let her in.

Now I heard Damien's voice and then Damien himself appeared. "Get dressed," he said in reply to my good morning. "Grandpa's taking us to breakfast."

I spooned coffee into the filter. I didn't want breakfast.

My father came down the hall, hitching up his sagging khakis. "Your brother wants us all on the beach by eleven for the family portrait. I saw him on my way over here and he said today's the day."

"Okay." I nodded, but I wasn't sure I wanted to be part of a photograph that would only serve to remind me of who was lost.

In last year's photo, Keith stood with one hand looped around my waist, the other hand making rabbit ears behind Damien's head. I'd groaned when I saw it, but Damien had laughed and promised to get his father back next year. Which, of course, was this year, only Keith wasn't here.

Nor was Isabella.

Nor, of course, my mother. I wondered whether my father could bear to look at that group photograph from last year. He and my mother had each worn T-shirts she had picked up at the gift shop: my father's, white with a navy blue lighthouse; my mother's, navy with a white lighthouse.

"I don't think I'm hungry," I said, watching the coffee drip. "Maybe I'll just stay here, shower, and play my violin a bit."

"Suit yourself." My father rubbed his forehead. "Are you playing seriously again?"

"No," I joked defensively. "This time I'm determined to play frivolously." I reached for the glass beaker to pour the coffee before it had finished brewing, and the machine hissed and spat at me. I swore beneath my breath.

Damien pressed his lips against his hand and blew, making one of his favorite rude sounds. I shot him a look.

"I'm going to check on how Crosby's doing," he said. "Grandpa, I'll meet you at your car in the parking lot."

We both watched the screen door thud to a close behind him.

"Thank God he wasn't hurt yesterday," my father said.

I opened a grimy cupboard in search of ersatz creamer, then shut it a little too hard.

"Damien must miss his father," he continued.

I frowned. "Yeah."

Keith had finally telephoned yesterday afternoon. Damien, playing cards with Crosby in Athena's cottage when the call came through, spoke first, bragging to his father about his riding skills and exaggerating the drama of the accident. By the time I was summoned by Athena and got to speak, I could have strangled my son. Keith was furious.

"A chipped tooth and a motorbike accident in the space of not half a week's time?" Keith said to my hello.

I took a breath before answering. "I know."

"Evidently, you're focused on your own preoccupations." I hated the voice he was using, measured ice.

"Unlike you," I replied.

"Amanda, my *preoccupations* have to do with putting together a business, to earn a living, to support my family."

Athena swished past me in her long, chiffon skirt, tinkling softly. I turned my back toward her and curled over the phone.

"You were supporting your family just fine." I made my voice low and it sounded hoarse.

"The point is," Keith said in a way I knew meant his jaw was clenched and jutting slightly forward. "The point is, you've let Damien get hurt, twice."

"I let him!" I spun around to catch Athena quickly turning her head toward a shelf she was rearranging.

"Calm down," Keith intoned.

"I *am* calm," I said, my voice cracking on the sharp edge of my anger. "Maybe you should give some thought to whether Damien might have benefited from his father's presence during his summer vacation."

"So it's my fault," Keith replied bitterly. "You agreed to this separation, Amanda." Yes, I'd agreed, lacking any choice. But I would have choices ahead.

I was rigid when we finally hung up, and I didn't care that Athena had been standing there the whole time. If anything, I felt or imagined some empathy—and thus vindication—in her silent regard as I walked out her door.

Now my father turned from his contemplation of the torn screen door and sighed. "I wanted to go back to that other place, you know," he said. "The place from last year. But your brother wouldn't permit it."

I ripped open a humidity-stiffened packet of powdered creamer and dumped it into my coffee, swirling it in with my pinky. "Ow!" I'd burned myself.

My father shook his head. "Amanda never could keep out of hot places," he said, as though speaking of a third person we both knew.

"Ha, ha," I answered. I blew air against my reddened fingertip and considered. "I suppose I would have gone back to that place," I said. In fact, Jeremy had wanted Shelter Island, but I'd insisted on Montauk. I'd told him that this year especially I needed to be at the absolute end of the island, not in between.

"I think Frances told your brother it was a morbid idea to go back to the other one," my father said.

"Yes, she would say that." I blew across the coffee's surface. "What did Lizzie say?"

My father stuck out his lower lip, his pantomime for thinking. "I don't think the discussion got that far." Lizzie was always the last to be consulted. Maybe she was lucky.

I held up my coffee. "Want a cup for the road?"

"No, thanks," my father replied. I realized I'd dismissed him. "One cup is my limit these days." He turned toward the door.

He looked back at me, then flipped down tinted lenses over his glasses. "Enjoy your morning alone. We'll see you on the beach at eleven."

＊　＊　＊

Engrossed in my violin, tranquil with the playing of it, I forgot about the group photo. I played each song straight through, as though in concert, pretending to myself that the people in the pool outside my window were my audience. No one sought or interrupted me, not even Athena. And I managed to keep the spectres of both Keith and Michael temporarily at bay. Only my friend the speckled gull dared to gape at me from his perch on the deck rail, as though he would watch and snag any errant notes that might float off my bow.

It wasn't until I noticed the time and was on the dune path to the beach that I recognized I'd been subconsciously waiting for Athena to call me to the phone, waiting to hear from Michael.

Froggy was annoyed at me for showing up late. She and my brother had timed the photo between Jay's feedings, and I had messed them up. I apologized, but then added that I didn't see the point in taking a picture with so many of us missing. Damien chimed in to request that Crosby take Isabella's place, and before anyone could think of a reason to say no, he'd run to invite his friend. Athena returned with them to offer her services as photographer, then went back to her office as soon as she'd taken the shot. She didn't pull me aside to slip me any message.

Irritable, I settled my blanket just far enough from everyone else so that the ocean's voice rose above the human voices, and I surrendered my senses to the tempo of the tide. I tried to think of nothing, to concentrate on breathing, to attune the rise and fall of my chest to the rhythmic surf. In the back of my mind, however, I was keenly aware of the progression of minutes toward night, toward the moment Michael would pick up his guitar and smile at the Jaw Bone customers. I imagined walking into the club dressed in something thin and flowing so that when Michael looked up from his guitar he'd see me through the smoke as not quite real.

All afternoon I stayed on my blanket, stayed even after everyone had gone back up to the pool, stayed until the sun sank behind me and Lizzie came back down with Ryan in tow and a beer in each pocket of her cover-up.

She handed me a cool, sweating bottle and dropped to the sand beside me. Silhouetted against the sun, her soft curls and curves formed a flat, dark stencil.

"Thanks," I said, realizing how thirsty I was. "I'll just have a sip."

"Oh, that's right." Lizzie smoothed a spot for Ryan to sit next to her. "I keep forgetting. So, do you know you're pregnant?" Ryan began filling a bucket with sand.

"No," I said, savoring the sharp taste on my tongue. "For all I know, it could be menopause."

Lizzie snorted, spraying beer. "Oh, God," she said, wiping her mouth. "Hot flashes and morning sickness, what a charming combination. But . . ." Lizzie paused.

I knew what she was thinking. I didn't bring it up, but in a moment she did.

"Didn't Mom . . . ?"

"Yeah." I nodded "She had a so-called change-of-life pregnancy which, fortunately, she miscarried." I realized what I'd said and quickly tilted the beer to hide my face. I remembered the low wails coming from my mother's bathroom the night she lost the baby. I remembered thinking I had never heard any sound so sad.

Ryan dumped sand from his bucket and handed it to Lizzie. "You do," he said. "Make castle."

Lizzie dug for wet sand and spoke without looking at me. "Why do you say that?" she asked. "I wanted a new baby brother or sister. Remember how I cried when Daddy told us there wasn't going to be one?"

I remembered. She had cried to my father, whined as though she'd lost a doll. Digusted by what I perceived to be her childish selfishness, by my father's fawning, by them all, I had stayed stoned the entire weekend. "I guess I'm following in Mom's footsteps," I said aloud, then caught myself.

I handed Ryan a shell for his castle. He examined it, turning it over and over as though I'd given him a rock from the moon. Then he put it aside.

"Not you," Lizzie said as she tapped her mound of sand firm. "I'm more like her. I'm the one with two girls and a boy, like she had."

I watched a curl drop over her eye as she bent over the sand. "Your girls are twins; that doesn't count."

"Of course it counts. There're two of them." She looked up at me, wiping her forehead with the back of her sandy hand. "And my husband works the family business. I'm closer to living Mommy's life than you." She turned her shoulders slightly toward the water.

"Are you?" I wondered, gazing at my sister's profile, superimposing it, in my mind, over my mother's wedding picture. "You do look the most like her."

Lizzie found a paper cup to fill for a turret. More hair fell into her eyes as she worked and she pushed it away with the back of her arm. Ryan refilled his bucket. "I have her coloring," Lizzie said as she fortified her castle walls. "But you know who looks the most like Mom?"

I did know, but I waited for her to tell me.

"Isabella."

I pressed the cool, green bottle against my cheek. Worse than my having inherited my mother's genes would be for my daughter to have them. But Lizzie was right: Isabella's face was much like her grandmother's, the rounded chin, and short, fine nose, and downward-sloping eyes. I looked toward the water. Why was there such consolation in an expanse of blue?

It was that time of day again when the ocean shimmered, when its surface gleamed dark as the night sky, and sparkled as if dotted with stars. Days at the beach had such symmetry, such perfect rhythm. The sun rose up and sank; the tide slipped in and out. Anything that ended would eventually renew; anything lost could return in a new place, in a new shape.

I thought about my mother's eyes, ever-changing hazel, remembering the way they dulled when she would start to get sick, as though she were observing inward, seeing nothing outside herself. Her eyes were always the first to give her away when she hadn't been taking her medicine. First her eyes changed; then came increasing irritability, even belligerence. Her face would get hard with it.

"Sometimes I'm afraid I have it," I said, speaking the fear aloud so as to focus the risk on myself, away from my daughter. My eyes were almond-shaped and green like my father's, but sorrow transformed them. All my crying, Keith had once teased, washed the color out of my eyes.

Lizzie brushed sand from her hands. "You make the rest now," she told Ryan and turned her face to me. "You mean you're afraid you inherited the gene for schizophrenia?" She stretched her legs and rubbed sand from her knees. "I know. I worry, too."

We had spoken these words before. "I think I'm too old now," I said.

Her eyes met mine above the top of her upturned beer and she swallowed wrong. She coughed, turning away, hacking over the sand to the side of her.

"Are you okay?" I was reminded of the smoker's cough that I'd been sure would someday kill my mother. But it hadn't.

Lizzie looked up at me, her eyes watering. "Nonsmoker's cough," she said hoarsely, smiling at her joke or her ability to read my mind.

"Right," I said.

I recalled the portent of illness that had sounded in my mother's voice when she would begin one of her bad periods: the distracted way she spoke. Even a hello, even on the phone long distance, often had been enough to alert me. Something about the thickness at the edge of her words, the timing of her pause as she dragged on a cigarette. I pressed my memory for clues and I searched for signs of my own.

Did my mouth move in that funny way my mother's had? Did I tap my fingers distractedly? Did I pace the rooms of my house like a caged cat? No. If anything, even my most troubled demeanor was more resolutely sad, more like that self-destructive friend of my mother's from the mental health group.

"Remember that friend of hers who . . ." I glanced at Ryan, not wanting to say the word.

Lizzie nodded. "She was sad," she said. Then she raised her eyes to me and they caught a bit of fire from the sun. In a low voice with a trace of a smile in it, she added, "She needed to get laid."

I laughed, leaned back in my chair, and shut my eyes. The sun warmed my forehead, my eyelids, the bridge of my nose. "That's not exactly my problem," I said.

The wind picked up after dinner. Even on the deck, the sand blew into our hair, burned our eyes, and stung our skin. "Bees!" Ryan cried, slapping at his arms, and we giggled as the wind buzzed through the cottage eaves like a horde of insects. By eight o'clock, we'd had enough and had all gone to our separate cottages.

Damien went into his room to play a video game, and my father settled down to read. I had never in my adult life spent an evening entirely alone with my father. Everything about it felt wrong.

I went into the bathroom and opened the clear plastic case that held my makeup and jewelry. I tried on the earrings I'd brought from home, testing for the way each captured light, wanting something that shined against the dark of my hair. I settled, finally, on the first pair I'd tried, long silver drops Keith told me looked like genie bottles. They pressed against the hollow place below my ears when I turned my head.

Damien poked his head through the partially open door and my hands flew up defensively. I was embarrassed at being caught "getting ready." Was that what I was doing?

"Come look at something, Mom."

I followed my son into his room, the genie earrings bumping softly against my neck. Across the nubby blue bedspread, Damien had lined up his games in order of declining preference. He intended to play them each in turn. Behind us, my father's voice joked that we'd be listening to beeps and buzzes until morning. He was nervous about sharing Damien's room, I knew. His sleeping habits had become erratic since his retirement.

"You don't have to play them all tonight," I said.

Damien scowled. "What else is there to do around here?"

My father followed me down the hall. "I'll make him stop playing whenever you want to go to bed," I told him. He picked up the newspaper, though there couldn't be much of it he hadn't yet read.

"I'm fine," he said, taking a chair.

Damien shut the door to his room, muffling the game sounds, but amplifying the close physical reality of my confinement. A small gurgle of panic welled in my throat, and for a moment I considered leaving the cottage right then, just announcing I was going out. I'd get to the Jaw Bone early and sit at the bar. I'd drink lemon water.

My father lifted his glasses and squinted at me, then rubbed his eyes. A low rumble I'd thought was wind grew loud and close. Almost in tandem, my father and I turned our attention to the cottage door, as if someone or something would come driving through. For a moment my heart froze and I thought, *tornado,* but the roar sputtered to a stop and I realized immediately what it was, and who.

CHAPTER 19

ICHAEL STOOD ON THE OTHER SIDE OF THE DOOR, helmet in hand, his smile fuzzy behind the screen. I stepped backward to let him in and watched his expression as he saw my father. An unspoken question flickered across his eyes, his lips parting a barely detectable extra second before he greeted me.

"Hello."

I tried for an even tone of voice, modulated syllables. The genie earrings swung against my hair as I raised my chin. "Hello."

Michael set down his helmet and moved toward my father, hand extended.

"Michael Burns, sir," he said. I turned away, feeling myself flush. He might have been calling for a date to the junior prom.

"Vincent Sinclair," my father mumbled and pushed himself to a stand.

He shook Michael's hand, started forward as though on his way somewhere, then abruptly stopped and ran a palm across his forehead. I knew this time he was stuck.

During my dating years—years which had coincided with my mother's most volatile period—my father would invariably disappear into his den each evening. It was my mother, therefore, who was present to greet my friends and dates when they called. She might sit silently as Lizzie or I answered the door, drawing contemplatively on her cigarette as though alone in the room. I'd usher my date out quickly if I could, before he got a chance to notice anything strange. Sometimes, however, she would snag him with questions, and I never knew whether they'd be reasonable inquiries ("What are your plans for tonight?") or humiliating barbs.

"What does the word *stub* mean?" she'd once asked a boy who was shorter than I. He'd answered with a careful, dictionary definition, probably thinking she was working some kind of puzzle. I tried to nudge him out, but she waved her cigarette at him. "That's my word for you," she'd told him. "Stub."

I blamed my father, not her. He'd left me at her mercy.

Now, however, I took little satisfaction in having my revenge. Here in the cottage, there was no place other than the bathroom for my father to escape. He turned in place like a dog, eyeglasses perched crookedly atop his freckled head.

"I came by to invite you—all of you—to come listen to my friend's band." Michael glanced from me to my father and back to me. "I'm sitting in. We're playing at the Jaw Bone, a local club in town next to the ice cream place."

Did he think I had forgotten? Or was he expecting me to ride to the club on the back of his motorcycle, to lean my body into his and press him forward. I heard my own breaths. Michael's presence in this room seemed to take all the air out of it.

"Go ahead, Amanda," my father offered. His voice sounded more resigned than I thought it should.

Was he testing me? I shook my head; the genie earrings swayed heavily on my ears. "I was planning to stay home with you tonight," I lied.

Michael shifted his weight, took a step back, and surveyed the room. He spotted my violin lying in its open case. He picked it up and plucked a string. "Beautiful."

I watched his hands, remembering how his fingers glided down the neck of his guitar, remembering my beach reverie. He wasn't supposed to summon me, except through his music; I was to simply appear as he played. What was he doing here?

Michael looked up over the bridge of my violin but didn't quite meet my eyes. He seemed instead to focus on a space between my eyebrows and the start of my hair.

"How's Damien doing?" he asked, then adjusted my violin beneath his chin. Just below his ear a muscle moved. I remembered the surprising softness of his throat beneath my mouth.

"He's fine," I answered, looking down. My eyes caught blue and I twisted the lapis ring. "I think the salt water worked the last pieces of sand from his knees."

Michael plucked a few soft notes, then replaced my violin in its case. "Salt water is nature's medicine," he said. He picked up his helmet. "I checked on Crosby earlier. Stoic little bugger."

I nodded. Had he invited Athena to the Jaw Bone?

My father stood between us, his hands hanging at his side. To my surprise, he spoke to Michael. "What do you play?"

"Blues guitar," Michael said with a quick smile. He glanced at his wrist. "We start around nine-thirty. Tonight and tomorrow night."

"Very good." My father nodded approvingly, almost wistfully. I wondered whether, in the early days of their courtship perhaps, my mother had played piano for him. I had never asked.

I twisted my ring in the opposite direction and stared down past my hand, toward my sandals. I was wearing not a long, flowing skirt, but a short, denim one. My knees looked funny, too red, too bumpy.

Michael moved toward the door. I felt the space between us lengthen as though something beneath my feet had shifted. I wanted to move with him, touch his arm, breathe in the scent I knew was redolent of particular skin and soap. Instead, I bit the nail of my pinky, the one I'd burned with coffee, and said nothing.

"I should get going," Michael said, his hand reaching toward the door handle. "Feels like a storm. Maybe tomorrow will be better for a night on the town." He winked at my father, then opened the door.

"I hope so," I said, folding my arms across my chest against a gust of wind.

Michael waved. "Good night," he called and the door blew shut behind him.

I went to fasten the latch and pressed my face against the screen, but I could see only the blurred edges of Michael's shape as he mounted his bike. My earrings bounced off the mesh.

"You'll have a checkerboard on your nose," my father warned as he had when, as kids, we'd pressed at the summer window screens waiting for him to come home.

I rubbed my fingers against the fleshy end of my nose, feeling for dents. A tic-tac-toe game for fairies, Lizzie once had described the imprint.

"So, that's the doctor, the one with the motorcycles?" my father asked; the sound of Michael's engine faded.

"Yes," I said. I could ask him, right now, *Do you mind if I go?* and he would say, *Go ahead.*

"Go listen to his band, if that's what you want," my father actually said, creasing a page in his newspaper, marking something.

I felt my face burn and hoped it didn't show through my tan. For my entire life, my father had had a knack for making me want to do the opposite of whatever he said. "No," I said. "That's okay." Or perhaps the knack was mine.

He nodded and sank back down in his chair. With a funny jerk of his head, he slipped his glasses back down his nose.

"I think I'll make tea," I said. I turned toward the stove and began to fill the kettle.

"This dampness goes right through you," my father said as I lit the stove. It was the kind of thing my mother would have said, but for a very different reason.

"Whenever you want to go to bed, go ahead," I urged, allowing myself a moment's fantasy of sneaking out later. "You can even turn on the light to read. Once Damien's asleep, he's out." I was making things up, trying to convince myself.

My father made a small sound of acknowledgment and said, "I think I'd like to have a cup of whatever you've got." He stretched in his chair and slipped off his shoes.

I looked away from him, toward the door as though I could will myself through it. Did he want to talk? I didn't. The battered kettle began to vibrate.

"Have you brought a good book with you?" I asked, feebly hoping to remind him of something else to read. I opened a drawer in which I'd seen a stash of fast food sugar packets. I knew he took his tea sweet. He might take his tea to his room.

"Two," he answered. The kettle whistled. "Two sugars *and* two novels." He chuckled and stood. "One book I've finished; the other I can't seem to begin."

"I know the feeling," I said. There were several kinds of tea in the cupboard. An unexpected luxury. Without asking him, I selected a regular black tea for my father and green for myself. I poured his tea water, then mine. I added his sugar, milk, a spoon.

He crossed the room in his stocking feet, and I averted my eyes; something about seeing him shoeless felt amiss. I held out his mug—pale blue with a painted osprey on it—and he took it with the spoon still in and carried it to a card table that had been painted lavender.

My mug, red with white letters, advertised The Lobster Roll restaurant. I set it down and tore open another packet of sugar.

"You've got a stolen mug," my father pointed out.

"Maybe I'll take it home," I replied, thinking of it as a memento of my lunch with Michael. Home to what? I wondered. I dumped sugar into my tea.

"You know I can't approve of such a thing," my father said, startling me for a second. *"Pilfering."* There was a smile in his voice.

"Yeah, well." The air went completely still. Even the waves outside seemed to have grown silent. I felt queasy. Maybe I could use some night air. I gazed at the door and, as if in reply, the wind suddenly picked up, rattling the screen. I realized I was stuck here. I carried my tea over to the table, careful not to slosh.

All week I'd been avoiding my father—all my life, in fact. And now here he sat, a flat purple surface away from me, having just met my lover. My lover! Wind shook the door like a stranger wanting to be let in.

"Yikes," I said. I thought of Michael on his bike.

"Are you still afraid of lightning?" My father leaned toward me, his hands cupped around his mug.

"That was Lizzie who was afraid." I blew across my tea.

"No, that was you, too. And Jeremy. You'd all come running into our bed at the first thunderclap."

"Maybe when I was two," I said irritably. What was the purpose of this?

"You'd count between the flash and the boom to see how many miles away the storm was. Remember that?"

"Everyone did that," I said. The wind growled around the windows.

"Not your mother. She said it made it worse to know." He stirred his tea and scraped his chair closer to the table.

I'd never known that about my mother. "That's funny," I said, though I meant *odd*.

"Your mother did have a sense of humor," he agreed. "When she was well."

I sipped my tea, considering my mother's humor. In her rare moments of levity, her wit had been startling. I was seldom more pleased with my mother than when she wisecracked or teased. She liked to say something ridiculous—"I'm having dinner with the mayor tonight"—and watch my father's face fall in alarm before she'd tug his arm and tell him she was kidding.

A sharp crack against the house made me jump.

My father cocked his head. "Probably a chair blown off the deck," he said.

I shuddered and reached for Damien's discarded camp sweatshirt lying beside my chair. A muffled rumbling vibrated through the floorboards. Thunder. I hoped Michael reached the club safely. If it rained hard, he might not be able to ride his motorcycle back. Who would give him a ride home?

"It's gotten so cold," I said. I took a gulp of tea.

My father rubbed his head with his hand, and for a moment I was afraid he'd read my mind. He always seemed to be evaluating me, but I never had a clue to his thoughts. A bitter taste soured my throat.

"Your mother was always cold," he said.

Was he comparing us? The bitterness washed over my tongue. I got up to get another pack of sugar.

With my back to him, it was easier to speak. All at once, I knew what I had to say. "You never left Mother," I said, holding the square paper sugar packet between two hands, staring at it. "But you knew, didn't you, before we were born? You knew she was mentally ill, even then."

My father made a sound in his throat and I imagined the thin, taut line his lips made. I reached for the kettle and added water to the tea I'd made too strong.

"They didn't know much about schizophrenia then," my father said finally.

I frowned. "We don't know much about it now." The wind blew a fine shower of sand against the front window. "So why didn't you leave her before you had children? Or just not have children?" I had followed this line of reasoning before, alone. I squeezed my eyes closed before muttering the last, obvious thought. "Of course, if you had, I wouldn't exist."

"Marriage is difficult," my father said, as though that were an answer.

"Yeah." The wind rattled the door again, and I walked over to it.

"I was not a saint," my father said, his voice serious, suggesting something more.

I touched my finger to the tear in the screen. "I never even entertained the thought."

"In fact, when your mother got worse, those years . . . I was probably the cause." The moan of the wind obscured his last word.

"What?" My finger poked through the metal threads.

"It was my fault."

"What are you talking about?" I withdrew my finger, pulling it back, scratching my skin, making the tear larger. "You can't blame yourself for her schizophrenia. It's brain chemistry." I put my finger to my mouth, embarrassed to have hurt myself again.

My father sighed, and my irritation flared. I walked back to my mug of tea, folding and unfolding the top of the sugar packet. What was this self-recrimination of his except pathetic self-pity?

I ripped open the packet and poured half the sugar into my mug.

"I blame myself for certain things," he said and I looked at him, at the resolve I saw him mustering. Suddenly I knew I would not want to hear what he was about to say. I held the sugar packet upright in mid-air.

"I retreated from your mother. From her illness, from my own inability to make things better."

I stared at the back of his head, trying to find the mole that looked like Texas. "You retreated from *us*," I said. In the distance, thunder growled.

He shook his head over his mug. "Never from you children."

"You did!" I said, feeling myself grow small inside my son's sweatshirt. I wanted to throw something, to see something splatter, to hear something break against a wall. I still held the sugar packet.

"How? How did I retreat from you?" My father's voice was low and brittle, the voice in which he might once have asked, *Where have you been?*

My heart pounded. Didn't he *know*? "Well, I mean, you were always in your den or at the office. Always working. Never around. We never knew what to expect, what she might do next, and you never controlled her."

"I couldn't control her," he said, his voice wavering. He turned his mug so its handle faced away. "I couldn't control myself."

I breathed deeply, greedy for air, wanting to clear my head, but not ready to let him off the hook. "I would get so mad at you."

My father removed his glasses, adjusted them, wiped them, then held them to his ears. I braced for his words, though not the ones he spoke. "Were you angry, Amanda, about my relationship with Gloria?"

"What?" Gloria Price had taught me to play the piano, redirecting my adolescent pain and fueling the fire of my nascent passion for music. Eventually, she'd moved away, but not before she'd made me promise to pursue my talent. Part of me, I think, had always known there was something more going on, but I still couldn't allow myself to see it.

I remembered how my mother used to hear her voice. Gloria's voice was the first auditory hallucination my mother had ever described to me. Gloria "communicated" with her; Gloria threatened her. At first I'd believed her—I'd been only eleven—and Gloria had frightened me, too. But eventually I'd learned my mother was "sick" and thus not to be trusted.

"Gloria," I repeated.

Suddenly, as though I'd been physically struck, I realized what my father was saying. "What do you mean?"

His fingers rubbed the bridge of his nose beneath his glasses, lifting them till I thought they would fall off, but they stayed. He dropped his hands to his lap.

"Gloria and I," he said softly.

My stomach quivered, as though the low, rolling thunder outside had slipped in through the screen and become particles of air. My mouth grew watery, a sign I was going to vomit. I moved to lean toward the sink and as I did, sugar spilled out of the torn packet, pouring across one of my father's shoes. My head pounded and my stomach heaved.

I bent over the sink and coughed a sour reflux into it.

My father's chair scraped against the floor and he was at my side.

"Amanda," he began, reaching his hand around to my forehead. I slipped away from him and grabbed a wad of paper napkins, held it under cold running water, then pressed it to my face.

"It's the tea," I said without looking at him. "The acid." I dumped my tea in the sink and filled my mug with cold water. I gulped it.

My father retreated toward the table and sat back in his chair. He began again. "Your mother and I never discussed Gloria," he said, picking up his spoon and dropping it into his empty mug. "Not in any rational way."

I recalled my mother's accusations. Gloria was her enemy, trying to harm her, trying to steal her children: all said to be hallucinations, all dismissed as evidence of illness. Now it turned out my mother had been right after all. She'd been right and she'd been ill, both at the same time.

No one had believed her.

"So . . . you had an affair." I stood with my hip pressed against the stove and watched my father's face crumple.

He nodded. The wind tumbled something across the deck.

"How long? How long did it last?" I heard another echo of myself with Keith.

"A year, two years, off and on. I always felt your mother knew of my . . . that she knew I was a cheat." He winced at his word. "And that it drove her to the brink of her illness."

I closed my eyes and shook my head against unwelcome images of my father with a full head of dark hair bent over blond Gloria Price, the small of her back pressed against the edge of her piano. "Oh, God." I stepped away from the stove, closer to the door, closer to the table where my father sat.

"I blame myself for your mother's pain. I always have," he said. A window over the sink rattled. "I've wanted you to know. But I haven't wanted to cause more pain."

My eyes stung and I pressed my lids with my cold fingertips. "You son of a bitch," I whispered. The air hung thick and cold between us. I waited for him to rise and slap me.

Instead, he sat stone still, a vaporous, red-tinged aura seeming to spread around him like a choking mist. I had to move, to breathe. I propelled myself toward the hall, kicking his shoe out of my way. Sugar flew up out of it, startling me, stopping me.

My father rose, his face drained. The folds of skin beneath his eyes were as dark as the dregs of his tea. I met his gaze and the spell broke between us. He bent, picked up his shoes, and set them neatly under the table.

I had to ask. "Did you love her?"

My father's face sagged into his neck, into his shoulders, into his chest. "I needed her," he answered, and I knew that meant that he had loved her. And he had suffered.

I didn't want to hear more, afraid I might be spurred to a confession of my own. "Okay," I said. "So now I know." I turned my hands palms up. "What good does it do?"

My father wagged his head. I thought of Homer.

"Just selfish of me, I suppose," he said as he sat again. "Sharing my burden." He looked up, his spoon clinking against his tea mug as he turned it purposelessly in front of him. "And maybe sharing yours."

My mouth tasted cottony and dry. "Mine?" I sounded guilty to my own ears and quickly gulped a mouthful of water that smelled faintly of salt.

My father shrugged. "I wanted to ask about you and Keith," he said.

"What is everyone's problem about Keith?" I crossed the room to the window. The world outside was pitch black except for the sky, a moving palette of charcoal grays. "Don't change the subject," I admonished with my back turned. "And don't think because you dump your confession on me that I'll return the favor with my own tale of marital woe."

"All right," my father said, accepting my harsh treatment. Asking for it? Was this supposed to settle the score between us?

I shut the window, trying to slam it, but the old wood was warped and difficult to budge. It moved in small, begrudging increments.

"It's only that you've seemed distraught," my father said evenly. "Even before tonight."

"Have I?" I intended irony, but my inflection acknowledged him.

"Yes. You have." His voice fell.

"Yeah, well, I had a screwed-up childhood." I turned now to see his reaction.

My father frowned and made a noise in the back of his throat. "Well, I'm sorry for that," he said. "In fact, so did I."

I thought of how little I knew of his childhood. Had we ever asked him about it?

"Your mother was all I ever had. When things started to change, when *she* did, I didn't know where to turn."

"Okay," I said, waving my hand to stop him. "Okay."

"I was afraid I might go crazy myself." He appealed to me with the bloodshot, watery green eyes that were the molds of my own.

I pulled my hands up into the sleeves of Damien's too-small sweatshirt and slumped against the wall. Despite myself, I felt my anger cracking into a puzzle of pieces, a hard taffy slapped against a table. I couldn't give it all to my father.

I listened to the wind, matching it to my breaths. My father had loved my mother, I knew he had, and he had needed more. Keith and I had loved each other, sometimes fiercely, and yet we'd come apart. Did that make us equal now, my father and me? Did it mean we could forgive each other, or only that we understood?

A sudden tap at the door, and then my father was opening it and Lizzie was in the room. Her hair was in a ponytail and she shook it the way she'd done since she was a little girl. The sight of her made me long for my home in Atlanta, for the comfort of my own favorite things. I wanted nothing more and nothing less than Keith's faded shirt, a cup of mint tea in my over-sized mug, the smooth feel and sharp, clean smell of my own washed sheets.

"What a night," Lizzie said, dropping a paper grocery bag onto the table. "Look what I've brought."

"Doughnuts," my father guessed. He sat in his chair.

She reached into the bag and pulled out a plastic container filled with brightly colored jelly beans and chocolate eggs. "Easter candy!" she announced happily. "It's still good." She reached in again.

A gust of wind blew the screen door open and shut with a *whack!* and the lights flickered. "Whoa," Lizzie said, and I went to refasten the latch.

Lizzie unloaded half a fudge-swirl pound cake and a box of chocolate-chip, macadamia-nut cookies onto the table beside the candy.

"A moveable feast," my father noted.

"Death-by-chocolate," I said, taking my seat.

"No one's forcing you," Lizzie teased, pulling a folding chair to the table. A fierce gust of wind shook the room.

"I'll force myself," I said.

Lizzie smiled, unwrapping the cake. The wind grew silent for a moment and then a crash of thunder split the air. We both jumped.

"Better sprinkle some crumbs on the ground to appease the goddesses," I said. I envisioned Athena scattering tea leaves.

Lightning flashed, illuminating our family tableau as though we were blocked in a scene from a play. "Ibsen?" I wondered aloud.

My father raised his eyebrows quizzically, the creases of his face tightening into folds as though pulled by a string. Then his eyes narrowed as he understood. "Don't be melodramatic, Amanda," he said. "I think Chekhov."

I snickered and he smiled and Lizzie rolled her eyes, shaking her ponytail. "You two never let up," she said. Outside the sky split and rain poured in a deluge, drumming against the roof. I looked up toward the ceiling, checking for leaks.

"Everyone's asleep at my cottage," Lizzie said, selecting a foil-covered egg from the candy jar. "I thought I'd be nice and bring you some dessert."

"I might have some stashed," I said.

"Do you?" Lizzie asked. She peeled purple foil from the chocolate and flattened it with her fingernail.

"No," I admitted.

"Thank you, Lizzie," my father said. "Very thoughtful. I'd like a piece of cake."

Lizzie took a knife out of the cake box, cut a slice, and handed it to him on a napkin.

I took a cookie, ravenous for something sweet.

Another flash of lightning lit the room, followed quickly by the crack of thunder. "The storm's directly above us," I said.

My father smiled and broke off a corner of his cake, and I realized I'd caught myself in a lie. I'd *counted*. The cottage shook. Rain was splashing in through the open window, soaking the couch. I jumped up to close it and saw, in the distance above the dunes, two simultaneous forks of lightning blanch the sky and illuminate the sea.

I left the window open an inch.

Wind pummeled the cottage, tossing deck chairs and pool toys like skipping stones.

"Mom would have hated this," Lizzie said as I sat again, pulling my chair closer to hers.

"I know," I said. "But I wish she were here."

My father grumbled a cough. I looked at him to find his eyes were glistening.

"Cake stuck in my throat," he said. His fingers tapped his glasses, which lay beside his tea mug. I glanced at Lizzie and she returned my look. Neither of us spoke.

I picked up a chocolate egg and peeled its foil, laying the shiny irregular shape on the table in line with Lizzie's row. She took it to smooth wrinkles with her nail.

"Where was she *going*?" my father spoke finally, as if it were the next logical question.

Lizzie pressed a hand to his shoulder. "She wasn't going anywhere," she said.

"But she *was*," I insisted. "Not anywhere important, probably, but the point is she was going someplace and not one of us has a clue where."

Thunder exploded, surrounding us, deafening us; a simultaneous blaze of white and then everything went black. For a moment no one spoke, and the sound of rain might have been a river we'd plunged into, the entire cottage dunked in darkness as though for a washing, or a ritual.

"Are there any candles?" my father asked.

"Just the citronella one, outside," I said.

"It's long gone," mumbled Lizzie.

Another flash, then a few moments passed before the thunder rolled. The storm was moving away.

"I remember the hurricane of '38." My father's voice sounded surer in the dark. "I was a kid, and I thought it was exciting. But it destroyed this end of the island, wrecking everything in its path north. Six hundred people killed in Providence, Rhode Island."

"Stop scaring us, Daddy," Lizzie whimpered.

"No, it's true. People were going down to the beach at the point to look at the waves; then it came and took everything."

"When?" I asked. "What month?"

"September 21," my father said. "The autumnal equinox."

My eyes were adjusting to the darkness and could make out the shape of my sister's hand clutching my father's arm.

"The rain's slowing down," Lizzie said. "No hurricanes this early in August, right?"

"Mmm, probably not," my father said. "Want to hear a funny story?"

The thunder was rumbling now, complaining rather than raging. "Do we have a choice?"

My father ignored me and began. "During the storm of '38, one Providence family hid in their attic. When the hurricane hit, it sucked the house right out to the Atlantic Ocean. The attic floated all the way across the sound to Montauk—with the family still in it." He paused for effect. "They all survived."

I felt more than saw our three smiles.

A soft, greenish light appeared behind the screen, and then the door handle rattled and Jeremy's voice called from the other side. "Hey! Open the door. It's me."

I touched my way to the door, in the direction of the glow.

Jeremy stepped into the cottage and lifted a green Coleman lantern. "I bring you light."

Lizzie blinked. "Thanks," she said.

Jeremy placed the lantern in the middle of the table and took the fourth folding chair. "Not that anyone thought to invite me to your party," he said. I considered the ways we were the same with one another, the routines we'd worked out, the defenses. Of all the people in existence, my sister and my brother were the most like me. I felt suddenly that I could, if I chose, explain everything to them—explain Keith and Sarah and Michael and the baby I might be carrying, explain the disorder of my life that scared me to death. But I didn't need to.

"We knew you'd show up," I said. "What's it like out there?"

"Oh, the usual aftermath. Chaos and mass destruction." Jeremy grinned at me, impish in the flickering lamplight.

I poked his arm.

"Not too bad." He shrugged, popping a jelly bean into his mouth. "A bunch of leaves and branches and overturned chairs strewn around. And the proverbial silver lining, of course: probably some really cool surf at Ditch Plains beach."

I wanted suddenly to hear the sound of waves from the back of Michael's motorcycle, and I was reminded of what I had missed tonight. I felt an ache that had nothing to do with my mother's illness or death, my father's infidelity, my husband's betrayal. I ached to hear Michael play blues guitar at the Jaw Bone, to lightly touch his arm as he came toward me from the stage, to find again the shining in his eyes where I liked the way I saw myself reflected.

Light from my brother's lantern flickered across our faces. I looked at my father's shadowed eyes and wondered whether he'd ached for Gloria all these years.

CHAPTER 20

THURSDAY MORNING'S DAWN WOKE ME out of a dreamless sleep. I opened my eyes and clutched the blanket to my chin, imagining for a moment that my father and my sister and brother were still here, that I had just dozed off for a few minutes. But the room was empty; even the tea mugs had been put away.

A watery light spread across the bed, and I wanted to feel the cool brush of it on my skin. I rose, used the bathroom quietly, and dressed in layers—sweatshirt over polo shirt, light cotton drawstring pants over bathing suit. I scribbled a note for Damien and my father instructing them not to delay breakfast for me. As I boiled water for a thermos of instant coffee, I gazed through the window above the sink and saw the sky newly lit, the day just begun, a milky glow thinning to crystal blue as it spread from east to west. I couldn't wait to smell the ocean after the storm, and when I tugged open the cottage door, even the kettle on the stove seemed to quiver in the sweet, quick blast of morning after.

Slick, flattened leaves and sodden clumps of pine needles plastered the deck, and pools of oily water created moats around the paths. But the shabby little cottages of Laughing Gull Resort somehow seemed brighter in their sogginess this morning, like shiny-skinned children after a bath. I capped my thermos and pulled the screen door softly shut behind me.

I had slept deeply and I felt rested and alert. Though the confrontation with my father had shaken me, some tension in me had been released. I hadn't wholly forgiven him, any more than I wholly forgave myself. But I'd begun to feel I could.

I headed down the dune path, breathing deeply of air tangy with beach plum and the drying detritus of the sea. Pitch pines dripped last night's rain onto my head and coarse, wet sand squeaked beneath my rubber thongs. The only other sounds were singing birds and breaking waves.

I climbed the rise that afforded the first sweeping view of the sea and paused to take it in.

The ocean crashed in front of me, breaker upon breaker, sparkling like liquid ice against the shore. Awesome, Damien would say. I hugged myself, rubbing my chin across the neck of my sweatshirt, in humble awe of the Atlantic and her dual nature—brimming at once with life and potential destruction, with beauty and terror. How easily Damien, or any of us, could be swept away.

"Eros and Thanatos," I said aloud, remembering as I crossed the dunes the two, identical goldfish with those names that Keith had won for me at the Spring Carnival our junior year in college. Predictably, they'd lasted only a few weeks, and we'd argued over which of them had been the first to die. I'd insisted Eros had lived longer.

The wind stung my eyes, and the muscles in my shoulders tightened. This time last year Keith had stood with his arm around me on a dune much like this one—the last time I'd come for an early morning walk along this ocean, the last time I'd seen my mother alive. Had he still loved me then, last August, or had our marriage already begun to fail? The sudden, sharp realization of that possibility thudded against my chest.

I lifted my face, and the wind licked away the very tears it caused. Something sank inside me; I pressed my hands to my belly, trying to feel some sign of the child I thought might be growing there. My last child. Keith's last child. All my children were Keith's children; I'd never have any others. I turned my back to the wind.

Last night I'd yearned for Michael. Michael, who had no children but seemed instinctively good with them. I groaned aloud. What was I thinking? My God, what was I doing? I looked up at a laughing gull, chortling on his way to catch breakfast, gliding above me.

I turned again and began to walk in the direction of the point. I walked in the way I'd walked earlier this summer in Atlanta, as though the act of moving my body through space would in itself create a destination. Or, if I were lucky, maybe a hurricane would sweep me to Providence.

By the time I returned to the cottages, the sun was high and half the morning gone. I dreaded the chastising looks of my father and brother and sister-in-law, but by now I was ready for them. Amanda was acting wayward this vacation, so be it.

So steeled was I in my defensiveness against family disapproval, I didn't immediately recognize the slight woman who sat at my picnic table, bumping baby Jay on her knee. Then she shook her head of thick, short hair and I thought of Isabella, though Isabella wore her hair long. Her hair was beautiful, unusually multicolored, each thick, gold, chestnut, or amber strand as shiny as nylon, with as improbable a texture. It glinted in the sun.

Suddenly I realized that it *was* Isabella sitting there. She had cut her hair. She had come to Montauk.

When I got close enough to hear her speak—explaining to Lizzie that she'd flown from Boston straight into MacArthur airport—I realized my daughter had left her new lover behind. Something was wrong.

But Isabella was smiling as she turned at the sound of my approach. "So, she appears at last."

I could feel Lizzie's questioning eyes, but I didn't return her glance.

Instead I exclaimed, "What are you doing here!" I circled my arms around my daughter's thin shoulders.

"Aren't I invited?" she teased. "Is there no room to spare at the inn?"

"Lizzie always has room," my sister said. "You can stay in our cottage if you don't mind sharing a piece of the floor."

I ruffled Isabella's hair. "I like this," I said. "But what a surprise." Isabella had worn her hair in long, unruly waves since she was three. Now a deep wedge tapered to her neck and angled across her jaw. Very sophisticated. She arched her head away from me.

Baby Jay grunted as he flopped on Isabella's chest. "Look at you!" she said, lifting him up and out. "Flying baby."

Froggy came out of the cottage, carrying a bottle. "Good thing you didn't fly in last night," she said to Isabella as she reached for Jay. "I think he's the only one who slept through that storm."

"He's adorable," Isabella said, handing Jay over. "He looks like a little-old-man version of Uncle Jeremy, doesn't he?"

"Ha," Lizzie snorted. "Jeremy says all babies look like Winston Churchill."

Froggy let the comment pass. She sat on a bench to feed Jay his bottle. "Speaking of sons . . ."

I cut her off. "Where *is* mine?"

"Your father went out on some errand, so Damien had breakfast with us. Now he's with that boy."

"Crosby," I said, and Froggy nodded. She bent over her baby and sniffed the air, wrinkling her nose.

"Crosby?" Isabella wondered.

"That's right," I said. "His mother is Athena, who owns the cottages."

Froggy stood up, popping the bottle out of Jay's mouth. "I'm going to change him, so I can put him down as soon as he finishes eating." She didn't wait for a response, but turned and let the screen door slap shut behind her. Jay began to cry.

"Isn't this *your* cottage?" Isabella asked.

Lizzie snickered.

"It is," I said, rolling my eyes. "It's also Sinclair Central."

"Oh," Isabella said. Her hand reached up to touch the skin of her newly exposed neck. "That makes sense."

"Here they come." Lizzie jerked her chin toward Rick and the others trudging up the path. "No doubt starving for lunch." She squeezed Isabella's shoulder and headed off toward her family.

"So," I began, trying for an offhand delivery. "Is everything okay with you?"

Isabella ran her fingers through her clipped hair and cast her eyes toward her lap. "I'm okay," she said. "I just couldn't bear to miss vacation this year."

I stood quickly so she wouldn't see the concern in my eyes. "Let's go find your brother."

I took Damien and Isabella to lunch at Lunch, and we all had lobster rolls.

"How fun," said Isabella when she spotted the hot dog buns. She was acting as though she had meant to come to Montauk all along, and I couldn't probe her decision now.

"I think hot dog rolls with lobster are weird," Damien said, taking a huge bite. He had accepted the arrival of his sister with a grin and a shrug, as though she had merely shown up late. I wondered whether he hoped Keith would follow suit.

"So, what's been going on?" Isabella asked her brother.

"Nothing much until I met Crosby," Damien answered, and recounted for Isabella the stories of his broken tooth and motorbike adventure, tales that were already beginning to take on mythic overtones.

She in turn described her misadventures with a certain rat named Joe 22 during her internship in the Psych lab, the first five weeks of which had just ended. "I've decided not to go back for the second five weeks," she announced casually, reaching for ketchup.

"Oh?" This was the source of why she was here.

"I'll tell you about it later."

"Okay." I sipped iced tea with my teeth against the glass, and my eyes scanned the outdoor deck where we sat. I was looking for Michael as much out of dread as eagerness. If I saw him in front of my children, would I give it all away? As far as I knew, he hadn't called or tried to contact me yet today. I was glad of it, but also wondered what his silence meant. Had my father scared him off? Had I?

Damien began to tell a joke he'd learned from Crosby, something that required him to lower his ordinarily exuberant voice. But I didn't hear the words; I was listening for the sound of Michael's motorcycle, wondering whether he'd ridden it home from last night's gig, whether he'd been alone. But Michael didn't appear, and by the time Damien and Isabella were laughing at his joke, covering their mouths with their hands, I was jittery with wishing he'd walk in.

Damien sipped the last of his soda noisily, as though getting away with something. Isabella wiped the corners of her mouth with a folded napkin.

"In case you're wondering," she said to me, "Daddy paid for my plane ticket."

Did Keith's stratagems lay behind Isabella's arrival? I looked at her face and asked, "So this was planned?"

Had Keith sensed that the potent combination of our marital estrangement and our geographical distance might lead me to disaster, and sent Isabella as a foil?

"Of course, this wasn't planned," she said.

No. I knew that as much as I might want to imagine Keith plotting to win me back, he would never do so. If he'd wanted to be with me, he'd be here. I rubbed my eyes and breathed into my hands. The other tables seemed suddenly much too close.

"I called Daddy yesterday and told him I wanted to come down. Well, needed to—as in a break. He said okay, so I flew standby. I spent the night at Logan."

"Cool," Damien approved while I frowned.

"Don't worry, it was fine. A zillion people around."

"I'm sure," I said, imagining my daughter curled vulnerably on an airport bench.

"Frances is funny with the baby, isn't she?" Isabella said, switching to the safety of family gossip.

I went along. "She even has a method for heating up his bottles on the beach," I said.

So we went on like that, exchanging intimate trivia. I wanted to believe that she didn't blame me for Keith's absence, that her warm banter meant she hadn't sided with him against me. We talked about everything that didn't matter, hairstyles and movies and news from home. After lunch, we played miniature golf, then shopped at a few of the Amagansett outlets until Damien could bear no more, and returned to the Laughing Gull in time to join the others for magic hour at the beach.

I felt, with my daughter beside me, a lessening of the sting of Keith's absence. I hadn't fully realized how self-conscious I'd been about it, how shamed. How lonely. Whatever the reason Isabella had come, it felt good to have her. Although we'd confided nothing to each other, I sensed she and I shared a covert understanding. We were women in trouble with our men.

The entire Sinclair crew went to Gossman's restaurant that night. We sat outdoors near the railing, so the children could toss bits of bread to the ubiquitous gulls while the adults sipped frothy summer drinks and watched the fishing boats come in with their day's catch. Rick caught sight of a large swordfish hanging from one of the charters, and he rushed off to the seafood market next door to put his order in. Tomorrow, Friday, was our final night in Montauk, the traditional *last supper*.

My father, who had ordered frozen daiquiris for us all, was as animated as I'd seen him in some time. He was pleased to see Isabella, to have all his grandchildren around him, but it was more than that. He was talking about my mother, describing funny moments from past vacations as though something in him had been released.

"Remember the T-shirt she made me wear for the picture last year?" he said as the waitress brought our salads. "Have you ever known me to wear a T-shirt? I put it in the pile for the Goodwill when we got home but she . . ." His expression changed. "Your mother was gone before they came for the pickup, and I took it out."

Jeremy nodded and reached for his menu. Lizzie turned to look toward the specials board.

My father reached for the basket of bread. He was wearing his usual plain white sport shirt tonight, creased in the places where the laundry had folded it. As he stretched across the table, I noticed something dark showing through the fabric, and I made out the distinctive shape of a lighthouse. He was wearing the Montauk lighthouse T-shirt beneath his sport shirt.

He met my gaze as he leaned back in his chair, but I said nothing and pretended to sip my drink. The folds under his eyes were soft and powdery, his irises nearly colorless in the gray shadows his skin cast. Everything about him seemed to be fading. How could I have expected miracles from someone so clearly mortal? I slid my tomatoes onto his plate, knowing how much he liked them. These were thickly cut, a deep, wet red. Locally grown, they'd be delicious.

"I'm going to the ladies'," I announced as I rose, taking my drink with me. "Order me a lobster if the waiter comes."

Once out of view of our table, I stopped at the bar and placed down my drink.

"Is something wrong?" the young bartender asked.

For a moment I thought he'd read trouble in my face, but then I realized he meant the drink. "Could I exchange this for a nonalcoholic version?" I asked. "I'll be right back."

Then I really did use the bathroom. My insides were jittery, as though my body perceived things my mind had not. I wanted to see Michael; I wanted to talk with Isabella. What if I were pregnant? When I returned to our table with my new drink, my father stood and pulled out my chair. He had eaten the tomatoes.

After dinner, Lizzie and her girls wanted to walk around the shops at the dockside mall. As they checked out the Irish store for sweaters, the rest of the group stopped at the ice cream vendor, and I took the opportunity to ask my father whether he would mind taking Damien back to the cottage in his car. He didn't question me or hesitate at all. He only said, "Be careful," then he took my son's order.

It was still early when Isabella and I got to The Jaw Bone; though the sun had set, a reddish glow clung to the fading light. I sipped an O'Douls and Isabella a draft beer, and we watched people nibbling ice cream cones pass by outside the grimy window.

"I finally feel like it's summer," Isabella said. "You can't imagine how sick I got of cleaning those rat cages in a basement."

So now we would talk. "Is that why you left Boston?" I asked. "To get away from rats?"

She looked up at my smile, her hazel eyes glistening, reminding me again of a photograph of my mother as a young bride.

"You could say that," Isabella said as she fished a pack of Camel Lights out of her drawstring satchel. She tapped out a cigarette, picked up a matchbook from the table, and lit up.

"When did you start smoking?" I was sickened at the sight of it.

"Oh," Isabella exhaled quickly. "Just recently."

I looked at her through a smoke and dust-mote haze. With her saucy new haircut and the pouty drags on her cigarette and the hurt in her eyes, she was a prime target for some predatory male. A pair of them had just walked past us on their way to the bar and eyed her.

"I wish you wouldn't," I said, gesturing with my chin at the cigarette.

She fanned the air with her hand. "Does it bother you?"

"Yes, but that's not what I mean. It's so bad for you."

"Well, it's just for now," she said, blowing smoke away from me. "It really is. Just till I get through this crisis."

"Okay," I said, sipping my pretend beer and turning slightly toward the view of the small stage in the corner. "Tell me."

"Jeff and I are fighting, to put it mildly. I needed to get away. We were living in his apartment, so I had nowhere else to go." Her voice cracked.

I wanted to tell her that was absurd, to remind her of the money we'd given her for summer living expenses, but apparently that wasn't the point she was making.

"What happened?" I asked. Someone dragged a microphone across the stage.

She wiped her eyes with the back of her hand, singeing her hair with her cigarette. "Damn it!" Isabella squashed the cigarette in the middle of the faded shark-jaw logo on the ashtray. A sharp, acrid scent wafted across the table.

"He's just so selfish!" she went on. "I didn't think he was a typical male, but, God, is he!"

She hadn't taken long to tap directly into her anger. Maybe she would get through pain more efficiently than I had in my life. I waited as she fumed, vaguely aware that the place was beginning to fill up around us. People were moving tables together, scraping chairs across the floor. I wondered whether Michael would notice me in this corner.

"The bottom line is, he's going to graduate school in California," Isabella said, lighting a match and dropping it in the ashtray. "We weren't really together at that point, when he was applying, but still. I would never do that to him."

"Do what? Go to graduate school?"

"Move cross-country. Without me! Without even giving me the option of joining him."

"You would switch schools?" Would she put her own life second to a man's?

"I don't know." Isabella tapped out another cigarette, but didn't light it. "I might have. I probably wouldn't, but I would have liked to have been asked." Her voice trembled. "To have been wanted."

Futile as her line of reasoning was, I knew what she meant. I wanted to put my arms around her, to tell her I too had felt that pain, felt it still. But I knew she needed me to be strong. Before I realized what I was doing, I was blurting out something I had never told her, about a time I had not thought of in years. "Daddy did something like that to me once," I began.

"But you two graduated college together."

"Yes, but the summer before our senior year I had a job playing violin in a small chamber orchestra in upstate New York. It had been planned for months, and I assumed he was going with me, that he would get work there of some kind. We'd talked about it, and I thought it was settled." I must have missed clues, I realized now but didn't say.

Isabella leaned toward me, holding her unlit cigarette like a dart. "What did Daddy do?"

I drained the O'Douls, wishing I hadn't brought this up. "Well, he didn't come with me," I said, but my attention was caught by movement across the room. I knew before I saw him that Michael was there. He stood loose-limbed on the stage, as though he belonged. He leaned to help the guy setting up, stretching so that even in the dim light I thought I could see the sinews move in his arms, and my heart fell straight to my stomach as though someone had cut it loose.

"What happened with you and Dad?" Isabella followed my gaze. "Do you know that guy over there?"

I turned to her, wondering how I could ever prevent her from hating me. "Yes," I said. "I know him; he's a friend of Athena's."

That satisfied her, or she didn't want to know more. "So, you and Dad?"

"What happened that summer was that instead of coming with me, your father left with two of his friends to go visit a buddy in Ohio for a couple months. Figured I had my plans, so it was okay if he just did his thing."

"Wow," Isabella said as she lit the cigarette. "You must have been really pissed at him."

I nodded. "Devastated," I said. Then I caught myself and smiled wryly. "But histrionics run in the family."

Isabella frowned, not quite sure how to take that. "So, then what happened?"

There was a reason I'd forgotten this story. "When your father came back at the end of August, he found me throwing up into the toilet. I told him I was two and a half months pregnant." I tried to smile. "With you. And the rest is history."

"Huh." Isabella turned her head toward where the band was setting up. Was she avoiding my eyes?

"I wanted you very much," I said, knowing that the words sounded false. "So did Daddy, as soon as he knew." And we had, hadn't we? We'd loved her beyond our dreams.

She narrowed her eyes, Keith–like, her body still angled toward the stage.

"I mean, I could have, uh . . ." I didn't want to think about the possibility of not having Isabella, nor focus on my current possibility. "We really did want you."

"I understand," she said, still turned away.

"His leaving that summer was awful," I continued, moving my empty bottle to the edge of the table. *And this summer*, I thought. Though Keith was still in our house, I felt more and more that our separation would continue after my return. "But, of course, he didn't understand what I was so upset about."

Isabella swung her head around. "I know!" she said. "Jeff is the same way. 'What's the big deal?' As though people who love each other leave for a year here and a year there all the time."

"But if *you* did it . . ." I began, grateful for the shift from history to commiseration.

"Oh, please! If I go out to a movie with my girlfriend, he's all hurt and lonely when I come back."

I laughed then, and so did she. I thought I saw Michael lift his head from his guitar tuning. Recognizing my voice? I felt the draw of him as surely as though he'd crooked his finger.

"Oh, Mom," Isabella said. "Are they *all* like that?"

He isn't, I wanted to say, wanted to believe, though of course I really didn't know.

"Let's go up to the bar," I said, needing suddenly to see Michael up close. "We can get another drink and sit nearer to the band. I hear they're good."

"Sure," Isabella said, rising. "Hey, isn't that new?" She touched the ring on my right hand.

I nodded. We made our way toward Michael and the stage, and I told her about the legendary properties of lapis lazuli.

CHAPTER 21

"WHY AREN'T YOU DRINKING?" Isabella asked as the bartender set another O'Douls in front of me. I was trying not to stare at the stage, but in my peripheral vision I watched Michael tuning up.

"I'm off alcohol at present," I told Isabella. "Not permanently."

I didn't want to lie to her, but I simply couldn't tell her I was late with my period. Not now, especially not after our conversation.

She nodded and sipped her beer. "You and Daddy drink a lot."

"At times," I answered. We did drink a lot, never more so than during the past year. I hadn't thought much about it because I hadn't wanted to. Now that I did, I realized that the worse things got between Keith and me, the better our wine became. Aside from that, my current state and situation were much the same as they'd been when I was twenty: estranged from Keith and carrying his child. Had I grown up not at all?

"Well, it's good for you to clean out your body once in a while," Isabella said.

A stocky, red-bearded man in his late twenties climbed onto the stage, picked up a guitar, and leaned into a mike. "Hey," he said to the crowd. "We're Bo and the Bone Daddies." He strummed a minor chord. "And I'm Bo."

A few whistles and laughs and *yeah*s came from a group near the stage.

"Welcome to the Jaw Bone," Bo told them. "Drink up." He launched into the opening bars of "One Bourbon, One Scotch, and One Beer."

Bo sang and played lead guitar, lit from above by the one house spotlight, as the other band members joined him on stage. Michael played rhythm guitar to the right of him, his head bent and his hair hanging in his face like a boy's. A small black woman on the other side of the stage plucked a bass guitar that looked too big for her, but she laid down an assertive groove. Behind them all was the drummer, a broad-shouldered guy with a silhouetted halo of curly hair.

Isabella swayed to the music. "He's cute," she whispered, and I wasn't sure whether she meant Bo or Michael or the drummer. I just nodded, hoping she didn't suspect I was here to see Michael. I worried Isabella would discover or at least sense the truth about Michael and me as soon as she saw us together. And that Michael would interpret my having towed my daughter along to his gig as a sign that I didn't want to be alone with him. I risked alienating them both.

The song ended and the crowd clapped with enthusiasm. Bo hopped back as Michael stepped forward into the Jaw Bone version of the limelight. He adjusted the mike, played two test chords on his guitar, and looked into the crowd through a shock of gleaming hair. Smiling, he scanned the faces and nodded at those he seemed to know. "Hi, people," he said into the mike, and I felt a slow burn begin in the pit of my gut. I couldn't tell whether he was looking at me or past me, but I couldn't look anywhere else but at him.

The brash opening notes came as a surprise after such a coy greeting, and Michael launched into "I'm Ready" as though he'd been playing half the night. I held my breath through the first verse, stupefied by the rasp in his voice and my conviction he was singing a message directly to me.

Two young women at a front table got up and began to dance, their shoulders and hips shaking in time to the walking bass line. Michael did a deep knee bend toward them as he slid into a guitar solo.

"He's good," Isabella murmured and my chest went hollow.

Bo came up beside Michael and joined him on harmonica, the two of them trading riffs. Michael kept time with his whole body—

tapping his foot, rolling his hip and shoulder, and nodding his head. My body moved in time with his. I imagined myself up there with him.

A very tall man and a very blond woman got up to dance, and then someone at another table began clapping on the offbeat. Possibly a Southerner, I thought, remembering the adage that New York is a 2/4 town and Atlanta is 1/3. By the time the song ended, a dozen people were bouncing at the foot of the stage.

Bo clasped Michael's shoulder. "Give it up for 'Doc' Burns, ladies and gentlemen. The Doc on guitar." Michael raised his hand in a half-salute and the crowd whooped.

"Lady Bird MacKenzie on bass." Bo gestured toward the bass player, who bowed elegantly. A group near the wall cheered.

"And last but never least, Thump Marullo on drums." Yet another section bellowed as he waved his sticks. Apparently, this band provided its own fans. Was that why Michael had wanted me here?

"I have to go to the ladies' room," Isabella said. She slid off her stool.

"I'll go with you," I said, not wanting to miss any of the set, but feeling the weight of my own bladder. I grabbed my purse and glanced back toward the stage.

Bo slapped his harmonica to his mouth and began to play and then sing "Hoochie Coochie Man" as we wound our way through the tables. I was wearing all white, not a gauzy dress, but a simple white T-shirt and white cotton slacks, and I wondered whether I stood out against the dark.

"So this is your kind of music," Isabella said as she pushed through a door that said FIRST MATES.

"I guess it is," I said. As we entered the wet, smoky restroom, I remembered my mother telling me about going to see Billie Holiday sing at a speakeasy with a boyfriend before my father. "The blues is for everyone."

A deeply tanned girl in a halter top sat on the ledge of the sink, passing a joint to a pale redhead leaning against the wall. The first girl grabbed her purse as I walked by, then relaxed when I paid her no attention and headed for a toilet stall.

The seat-liner dispenser was empty, so I bent to line the seat with paper the way my mother had taught me as a child, and as I did I felt slightly dizzy. The smell of the sweet-burning reefer made me queasy. I held my forehead and, to distract myself, listened to the girls muttering softly. One spoke with the soft Irish brogue common to Montauk summer help. I wondered whether these girls knew the band, knew Michael, and whether Michael knew I was there.

Much as I felt he must have seen me sitting at the bar, I couldn't be sure. From the stage, faces would be shadowy, or obscured by the lights. I wanted him to see me, but I felt anxious about what would happen when he did.

I waited for my bladder to relax, trying to clear my mind.

"Mom?" Isabella was peeing in the stall next to me.

"Mmm?"

"You haven't told me what you think. What would you do if you were me? Would you break up with Jeff?"

"Well . . ." I'd never met him; I didn't want to advise her out of selfishness.

The girls at the sink had apparently switched to regular cigarettes, and the added stench of that smoke in the damp, confined space made me suddenly ill. I heard the Irish girl giggle and say, "But he likes it that way." Then my stomach lurched so sharply, I leapt off the toilet and tugged up my pants, dropping to the floor just in time to throw up my dinner into the bowl.

"Mom?" Isabella's voice was urgent, young.

"I'm okay," I rasped. My fingers clutched more of the rim than I'd covered with tissue. The music grew louder and then muffled as the smoking girls opened the door and left. I wiped my mouth with toilet paper and flushed, then sat again, and pressed my forehead against the cool, hard metal of the stall, willing my stomach to settle. I lifted my shirt to my nose and breathed cotton-filtered air.

"Bad shellfish?" Isabella asked when I met her at the sink.

I scrubbed my hands under the hottest water I could coax from the tap. "I don't think so," I said. "Though I guess something didn't agree with me."

"Are you okay?" Isabella combed her hair with her fingers. She sucked in her cheeks. "Are you just trying to avoid giving me advice?"

I smiled. "That's it," I said as I ran the water cold. I cupped my hands to splash my face and rinse my mouth.

Isabella stared at herself in the pitted mirror, tugging at her hair, adopting poses.

I frowned at my face, sallow beneath my tan as though it were a mask. I looked away, down toward the sink, and saw that the knees of my pants were dark and damp. "I can't believe I knelt on that floor," I said, brushing at them.

The door opened and I recognized the blond partner of the tall man from the dance floor. The band went into "I Just Want to Make Love to You," as the blonde disappeared into the last stall and blew her nose.

"Actually," I said, swallowing the bitterness in my mouth, "if you want my opinion, you should just play it out. Don't act out of anger or pain." I turned away from Isabella as I spoke, searching for my lipstick. I couldn't look directly at her eyes, nor at their frank gaze reflected in the mirror.

"So, you think I should stay with Jeff?"

"Not exactly," I said as I reddened my lips. "He's going to California; you'll be in Boston. Continue your relationship if you want, but be open to other things."

"Other men, you mean." She shook her head. "I can't. I'm either with him or I'm not."

Just wait, I thought to myself. "Well," I said.

"I thought you of all people would tell me to follow my heart," Isabella said, watching me in the mirror. "I didn't expect such pragmatism from you."

I scrubbed my teeth with my tongue.

"But that's good," she continued. "You make sense. Play it out. See where it goes."

I nodded.

She was satisfied. She moved toward the door, then turned toward me with a devilish half-smile.

"So this cute guy fixes your ring and then we go see his band," she said. "What will Daddy think?"

We took an empty table near the stage—someone had folded a wad of bills under a half-drunk glass of beer and left—and if Michael was surprised to see us, he didn't let it show. I wanted to dance, but felt that to display myself at Michael's feet would be vulgar and, besides, Isabella wouldn't want to dance with her mother. She seemed to enjoy the music, though, nodding and smiling at the play of open-hearted lyrics against the soulfully bent notes. By the end of the second set, I was leaning back in my chair, eyes half closed, the better to focus on Michael. I wanted his performance to never end, but soon enough it did.

"Back in ten," Bo told the crowd with a wink. The musicians laid down their instruments and dispersed toward various corners of the bar. At the first break, I had wondered whether Michael would speak to me, but he'd disappeared, returning to the stage only as Lady Bird floated through the bass line of "Mustang Sally." I'd been disappointed, but relieved. He'd settled it for me, choosing prudence over peril.

So now, at the second break, I didn't expect him to approach us. In fact, I'd turned to Isabella to ask, "Should we go?" when I felt the air behind me grow faintly warm and tinged with the scent of fish soap.

Isabella was gazing up above my head, her eyes widened, her lips half curled as if considering a smile. I swung round to Michael.

"'Evening, ladies," he said. "Are you enjoying yourselves?"

My heart pounded so I could barely hear his words, and my cheeks flamed with something that was almost anger.

"Very much," Isabella answered, holding back on the smile.

"We haven't met," Michael said, leaning across my shoulder to extend a hand to her. The heat of him enveloped me. "I'm Michael Burns."

"Isabella Kincaid," she said. "I thought you were called Doc." Now she smiled, her classic, nose-crinkling Isabella smile.

Michael laughed. "Stage name," he said, moving his hand along the back of my chair. "For the fans."

The skin along my upper back prickled, and I was afraid Isabella would sense the charge in the air. But of course I had wanted him to come over; he was the reason I'd brought Isabella here. I turned to him.

"Glad you could make it," he said. He squeezed around the table so he could face us both. Tableside manner.

"You seem to have a following," I answered, trying to sound insouciant, but the words came out tight, accusatory, much the way they did when I asked Keith where he'd had lunch. I regretted them immediately.

But Michael grinned. "Not I," he said, feigning modesty, his fingers splayed across the tender place on his chest. "But the band is pretty well known with the summer crowd."

Under a thin film of perspiration, his skin glistened and the hair at either side of his neck stuck together in a fringe of damp curls. I breathed as deeply and as quietly as I could. He turned toward me and caught my eyes.

"I have a favor to ask you, Amanda." When he said my name, its syllables reverberated in the hollow place beneath my throat.

"We'd sure like someone to play fiddle on the next song, "Summertime." Simple, but apropos, you know? I was hoping you would agree to sit in."

"I can't," I answered as immediately and reflexively as though he'd asked me to jump off a cliff.

Michael raised his eyebrows, still gazing at me, refusing to spare me. It occurred to me he'd made that ridiculous request just so he *could* gaze at me, so he'd have a reason to. Would he do that, or was that something *I* would do?

"Oh, Mom," Isabella said. "Too bad you didn't bring your violin in the car."

Michael snapped his fingers softly. "No problem," he said. "We have one. Bird has one with her. She's got to play the bass, of course."

"Still," I said, pulling my eyes away from his to examine my hands. "I couldn't." I had been practicing for weeks, however, and in fact I probably could. Or get away with playing very little.

Michael touched me then. In front of Isabella, though she didn't react. He laid his long fingers over mine till the warmth of them seemed to pass through my flesh and my tendons and my lapis ring, to my bones. Then he squeezed, gently but firmly the way he did, until my hand felt part of his.

"I won't press you," he said, his words belying his body. "But it's an easy tune, as I'm sure you know, and it'd be fun to play together."

I laughed then, at everything, and I agreed.

*   *   *

Twenty years had passed since I'd held any violin other than my own, and Lady Bird's instrument felt awkward in my hands. Her bow was heavier than mine and she used no shoulder pad. When I asked for one, Bo produced a bright bandana, which I folded and wedged under the instrument, but it still felt not quite stable as I tuned the strings. I played a quick scale to warm up, then wiped my clammy hands against the sides of my white cotton pants. I glanced at the spots on my knees where I'd knelt on the bathroom floor, but in this light I could scarcely see them. Then I worried: what if my stomach heaved again while I was onstage?

The thought made me shake my head, which Michael took as a sign I was ready. "Howdy," he said into the mike, and—to my relief—without introducing me, gave me my first notes.

I played it straight as Thump brushed the snare drum and Lady Bird drifted in and out between my lines. Michael followed my lead with simple strumming, and by the end of the first verse, I was ready to play for real.

Jumping up an octave produced a more plaintive, penetrating sound, and my heart, which earlier had seemed to plummet to oblivion in my gut, rose in my chest. This felt good.

I glanced out into the audience to gauge Isabella's reaction, but I couldn't see her, couldn't see anything in the fuzzy glare of the lights. Which meant Michael wouldn't have seen me till the lights were dim. But he had seen me, somehow, and he had summoned me onstage, and we were making music.

I started to slide late into my notes, adding an arpeggio here and there to let him know I could play. Michael strutted across the stage to face me, grinning and nodding as I played slurs. I began to improvise, my improvisations fading seamlessly into his till I let him anchor the melody. How could I have refused this?

At the turnaround, we switched back again, and I began to play off the minor, reaching for that elusive note between the notes. Michael shook his head at me and laughed, hunkering down on his guitar as though digging in for the long haul. I laughed, too, and our eyes locked and we finished the song that way, swelling up and down the scale, holding on to each other's gaze.

The audience burst into applause and Michael threw his arm

around me. Something in me opened then, and I filled with satisfaction, rising like helium air. Bo announced my name into the mike and I stood there, heart pounding, cheeks aching from smiling, breathing in the sweet, dank smell of Michael until finally I realized I should leave the stage so they could continue to play.

As I floated my way back to our table, I reveled in my fleeting celebrity, looking at the faces around me for approval. Michael had offered me this. Aside from the births of my children, I couldn't remember a time I'd felt so elated.

At the table I found my daughter in tears.

We were quiet during the ride back to Laughing Gull Cottages. Isabella had been astonished at my performance, not because it was good, she said—though it *was*—but because I'd done it at all. She'd seen me transformed up there on stage into a person she hadn't known her mother could be. I was flattered, of course, and thrilled, and also worried a bit, knowing how children dislike surprises from their parents. The tears, though, had been all for Jeff, brought on by the song's stinging sadness against her own fresh wounds.

"It's very weird," Isabella said. "To have your mother play music that makes you think about your boyfriend."

"Only if she plays it right," I joked, still elated, but feeling now the small, ragged edge of regret, remembering Michael's face as I turned to wave good-bye.

We'd left the Jaw Bone shortly after my performance, while the band was still playing. Anything I could have said to Michael then would have seemed anticlimactic, redundant, and it was getting late. I'd blown him a kiss from our table as we stood and he'd saluted me, fingertips touching his chest in the place I imagined his damaged heart to be before his hand traveled back to the neck of his guitar.

He would call me tomorrow, surely, and somehow I'd find a way to see him alone. "Summertime," my version, played and replayed in my head the whole way back to the resort. And in the space of a song, we were there. All of the cottages were dark when we drove into the parking lot.

"Did you come to this place with your family as a little girl?" Isabella asked as we locked our doors.

"Not here," I said. "Different places every year, some very close to here, but never this one." We began crunching our way up the path.

"Why always different places?"

I stopped as a cloud cleared the moon and its light spilled around us. Isabella looked up at the sky with me. "I don't know," I answered finally. "Every year was different. Some years, my mother was with us, some years she wasn't—because she was in the hospital."

Isabella looked at her toes. "The mental hospital," she said with quiet understanding.

"Grandma was a diagnosed schizophrenic." I had never spoken those words to Isabella, and she'd never asked.

Isabella bent to pick up a small, pale stone. "I didn't really know exactly what was the matter with Grandma," she said as she turned it between her thin fingers. "For a while, I thought she had 'female problems,' which is what some of my friends' grandmothers had." She smiled sadly.

"Female problems," I repeated.

She shrugged, closing her fist around the stone. "I didn't even want to know really, and then one day, I just figured I did know."

"I'm sorry," I said. "Somehow, especially once we lived so far away, it was never the right time to explain . . ." I stopped myself. Could I ever explain?

"I didn't really want to know." Isabella wrinkled her forehead. "It must have been really sad for you."

The compulsion to deny welled up in me, but I let it evaporate. Isabella put the stone in her pocket. We began to walk again. "I just never knew what to expect," I said.

Isabella sighed beside me like an adult. "Who does?"

The white stone path to the pool glittered with moonlight. "It's like a fairy tale," Isabella said, pointing ahead.

Impulsively, I ran toward the pool. "Let's swim!" I called. The gate was locked, of course, but the five-foot, chain-link fence wasn't difficult to climb. I scaled it easily, proudly, poking my toes through twisting vines as I felt for the spaces in the fence. A sweetness of crushed honeysuckle filled the air.

Isabella followed me, climbing quickly, pausing to balance for a second on the top bar, arms outstretched. Then she leapt to the ground. Smiling, but silent, we stripped to our underwear. In the moonlight, the stains on the knees of my pants disappeared.

The night temperature was cooler than the water temperature; a lacy mist of warm air hung above the surface. We dove through the vapor into water so still our dives barely rippled the surface. Water closed over our heads like the slick skin of a pudding, so that entering it was like being swallowed or like shooting through a cavern, our bodies dark missiles of skin and bone. Weightless, my body felt its strongest. I swam laps underwater until my lungs ached for breath.

I surfaced and lay back in a float and the big, black sky seemed suddenly close. The clouds slid apart, revealing stars scattered thickly as sugar crystals. The moon was all but full.

Isabella paddled gently beside me. "Look," she whispered as if afraid of waking someone. "You can see stars in the water."

It was true. Hard points of light shone on the pool like openings into another universe. If I squinted, the sky and water seemed to merge, and we were suspended in celestial liquid.

CHAPTER 22

Montauk

August—One Year Earlier

O N OUR LAST DAY OF VACATION, KEITH AND I DROVE east along Montauk Highway. We traveled in silence, my window open, his closed, the air conditioning on full blast. I slouched sideways in my seat without a seatbelt, which I knew annoyed him. But I was sunburned and sullen, already mourning the end of a vacation I felt had hardly begun. I stared at Keith's profile and tried to will him to look at me.

He was sunburned, too, in blotches where he'd missed with the sunscreen. One side of his neck was so pink, it looked unfamiliar. I wanted to touch his skin, to feel the heat of it, but I sensed he would recoil if I reached for him while he was driving.

Through the window I saw a sign for a scenic overlook just ahead.

"Oh, Keith. Could we please pull over?" I hoped for enthusiasm, or some small acknowledgment that he might enjoy a moment alone with me.

But he frowned as he flipped up the turn signal and changed lanes. "Why stop here?" he asked as he swung our rental car into the nearly empty parking lot. "We're on our way to the point. What more of an overlook can you possibly need?"

"I want to see the cliffs," I said. I had a mental image of Keith and me balancing on the edge of a windswept precipice, holding on to each other, laughing.

We were en route to the Montauk lighthouse, a Sinclair family excursion for which we would typically be the last to arrive. Keith had received a call from Tripp Stone just as we'd been about to leave the motel, so the others had gone ahead, including Isabella and Damien, who had ridden with my parents in their car. We were to meet them on the north side of the lighthouse for a picnic on the beach.

"Each diversion makes us later," Keith pointed out as he opened his car door. He was referring to my earlier insistence that we stop at a liquor store for wine.

"*You* took the call from Stone," I reminded him as I slid out my side. "That's why we're late."

Keith let his door slam shut. "You weren't nearly ready. You're always late when we're to go somewhere with your mother."

Was that true? As though he relished yet another group activity. He'd excuse himself to find a phone ten minutes after we arrived, I knew. He had forgotten his cell phone at home and had been irritable all week because of it.

"Oh, come on," I said. "Does it really matter when we get there?"

Keith leaned against the hood of the white Taurus, crossed his red-brown arms over his chest, and looked at me from behind his sunglasses. His eyebrows arched above the frames. "Your call," he conceded.

I scanned the woods edging the parking lot: no view, no sign, nothing but trees and sky. "I don't see an overlook," I said.

Keith shrugged and recrossed his arms, glancing casually at his watch.

At the far end of the lot, a narrow break in the underbrush indicated a path. "Must be through there," I said, pointing toward the dark space. I headed toward it.

Keith followed and then passed me, ducking beneath a branch as he disappeared into the woods. A pinprick of hurt so familiar I almost didn't notice pinched behind my eyes. For more than nineteen years he'd been doing this—walking ahead, never beside me—and each time I felt the quick sharp pinch, like a sewing needle. I hated shopping with him for this reason; he was always losing me. "We waste so much time trying to find each other," I would protest, appealing to his logic. He never argued the point, but he never changed.

He stopped under a canopy of oak, but when I'd almost reached him, he pressed on down the narrow, sloping path. He held aside branches for me, sharp holly and jutting mountain laurel, but he didn't turn to speak to me until we'd been walking several minutes. In my sandals and shorts, I wasn't dressed for hiking, and I'd started worrying about ticks. As if catching my thought, Keith stopped and turned. I nearly collided with him.

"Do you want to keep going?" he asked as he reached for my arm to steady me.

His fingers circled the flesh high up my arm, squeezing slightly. I wanted to feel them tighten until they hurt. I held still. Light from an invisible sun filtered through branches in abstract patterns, dissonant visual phrases. The air was rich with scents: pitch pine and bayberry and crushed acorns and the mulchy soil that probably never completely dried out. I wasn't ready to turn back.

Keith released me and put both hands in his pockets, his posture telegraphing his impatience.

We hadn't had a conversation alone since we'd come to Montauk. We hadn't even gone to sleep at the same time.

"I want to see the cliffs with you," I said, moving closer. I said the words to please him, then heard the truth in them. I rested my cheek against his chest. "I want to do something with just you." I'd been so caught up with my parents and siblings—when I was with them, I was a Sinclair, and everything else faded.

"How can we be going toward cliffs when this path seems to lead down?" he asked reasonably. He removed his sunglasses and folded them into his shirt pocket.

I pulled open the plackets of his unbuttoned shirt, pressing my lips against his bare skin.

"Montauk is an Indian name for *hilly country.*" I spoke into the muscle above his heart as though I could physically direct my words inside him.

The low thudding in his chest seemed to quicken. For me? I'd grown so accustomed to our separate lives. Wasn't that how everyone I knew lived? He was preoccupied with work, I with family. Lately, especially, I'd been consumed with preparations for Isabella's going away to college, and had spent the summer, in fact, in a kind of pre-mourning of her departure. Meanwhile, Keith had been campaigning hard for increased responsibility at Stone, so caught up in it I'd stopped asking him about work.

Without realizing it, I'd been missing him.

I reached up to pull his head down, to kiss him. His neck was surprisingly cool after all. He *could* have been a stranger. A trickle of fear, like a drop of icy water, traveled through my veins. I trembled, kissing him, almost afraid of him, almost thrilled.

Keith slid his hands out of his pockets and under my shirt, slid them up either side of my waist to my ribs, then around, slipping them under the band of my bra. He sighed into my mouth as his thumbs brushed my nipples. I lifted up on my toes and pressed my hips into his. He dropped one hand to my hip, pulling me to him. I felt giddy, as though we were sneaking around, and I swallowed a giggle.

Underbrush rustled and we froze. Something moved close to us. A fox? How wonderful it would be to encounter a wild creature here, in its element. Perhaps it had been drawn by our scent. I held my breath. Keith dropped his hands from beneath my shirt and rested his chin on my head as I turned slowly toward the sound.

A walking stick appeared first, rising up over the dip in the path, and then the arm and the person attached to it, a gray-haired woman dressed in army fatigues, binoculars hanging from her neck. Behind her trudged a similarly clad man toting a long-lensed camera. Keith stepped back, apart from me.

"Hello," the woman gasped as she approached us.

Keith grunted a greeting and I forced a smile. She stopped in front of us, breathing hard.

"Hello. Did you see the cliffs?" I asked.

Her companion—husband?—handed her a water bottle, which she tipped to her lips.

"Didn't see cliffs," the man said. "Quite a few birds, though." He gestured toward the treetops.

"But where's the overlook, then?" I asked. The woman wiped her mouth with her hand and shook her head.

"Never got to an overlook," the man answered again. "We walked in about twenty minutes, stopping here and there, then we turned back. The way back's harder, mostly uphill. Longer, give or take a few minutes."

The woman was breathing easier now, staring at my bare legs. "Watch for poison ivy," she said as she thrust her walking stick forward.

The man lifted his hat—perhaps he only adjusted it—and they moved on. I watched till they were out of sight, then I turned to Keith, smiling, but the weary look on his face dissolved my mirth.

Could his desire for me be so easily disarmed? I touched his cheek. His eyes were the color of flint.

"Let's go," he said. He turned to head back up the trail, and I felt as stunned as though he'd physically pushed me aside.

"There must be an overlook," I insisted, almost to myself. "It's just too far."

My mother waved to us from her beach chair. She squared her shoulders and I noticed her T-shirt, as I was meant to. It was one I hadn't seen before: navy blue with a white outline of a lighthouse, *the* lighthouse.

"See what I got at the gift shop!" she announced, pulling the fabric out from her chest with both hands. "And your father's is the reverse!"

I looked to the rocky shoreline where my father stood next to Jeremy. His shirt was white with blue graphics.

"Like a photograph and its negative," said Keith.

"Oh, I'm the negative, of course," my mother said with her halfsmile.

I frowned at Keith, but he didn't notice. He bent over my mother, showing her the wine we'd bought. The sort of thing I would never think to do.

"What a pretty label!" she said, touching the watercolor estate rendering with a fingertip.

Jeremy called to us. "Something's out there!" He was pointing toward the horizon.

Keith called back. "No doubt something is."

My mother took the wine from Keith and nestled it beside a bag of food. I looked around. The lighthouse beach, a popular attraction, was sparsely occupied today.

"Where is everyone?" I asked, half rhetorically.

Jeremy began to make his way toward us, my father trudging behind him. Now I could see the blue lighthouse on his shirt. In thirty-nine years, I'd never known my parents to dress alike. I thought of how mortified Isabella would be to be seen with them.

"Where are the others?" I asked, directing my question toward my mother.

She was lighting a cigarette, cupping her hands around the match, not listening.

"Mom? Where are the kids? Where's Lizzie?"

"Hmm?" she jerked the match to put it out, then buried it in the sand. "Lizzie and Rick and all the kids went into the lighthouse, to the top. Frances is in the ladies' room. Or . . ." My mother lowered her eyes as she took a puff of her cigarette. "Maybe Frances went to the gift shop." She took a long, self-satisfied drag, as though no one could fool her, certainly not her daughter-in-law.

"Yo, Kincaids-come-lately," Jeremy greeted us. He ruffled my mother's hair. "Have a smoke, Ma. Don't want to shock the lungs with too much sea air."

My mother smiled up at him and I wondered at the ease between mothers and sons, even *my* mother and brother. Part of me envied it. Would Damien someday treat me with that effortless combination of affection and protection? Did I want him to?

My father lowered himself into the chair next to my mother. She showed him the bottle of wine and he nodded.

"Everything okay at the office?" he asked Keith.

"The office is closed. It's Saturday," I pointed out.

"Tripp Stone phoned me to discuss a client," Keith reminded me in an impatient tone. "To prepare for Monday's meeting. Nothing unusual." He looked at his watch. "But I will have to make a few calls in a bit."

"Business calls on Saturday," I noted, then turned toward my father. "I like your shirt, Dad."

He made a face, thinking I was teasing him. "It was your mother's idea," he said.

I fixed my gaze on the lighthouse rising to my right. Isabella and Damien might now be at the top looking down at us. I couldn't see them if they were—the observation deck was enclosed—but I wished I were up there with them, taking in the broad view.

Jeremy dropped onto the blanket he and Froggy had set across from my parents' chairs, their clean sneakers anchoring each corner. "Soon as they get back, we'll take a family photo," he said. "The entire group, the whole fam-damly."

My mother's lips moved, but she said nothing.

"Okay," I said to him. "So what did you see out there?"

"I'm not sure," my brother answered. He flipped on a baseball cap. N.Y. YANKEES. I remembered the spring he was ten, when he'd pitched a little league no-hitter. Lizzie and I had seen it, but my father had worked late at the office and my mother had been in the hospital. His team had been called the Yankees that year.

"It could have been almost anything," my father said.

As the afternoon wore on, the sand grew too hot for bare feet. I shook my head at the surprise on Keith's face as he hopped his way back to us after nearly an hour of making calls from a booth. *Serves you right,* I thought. For what? For forgetting his cell phone? For not finding the way to the cliffs? *For not even pretending to pay attention to me.*

However, I had spent the last hour gossiping with Lizzie, exactly as I would have whether Keith had been there or not. My father had gone fishing with Rick and the boys. And my mother had listened to our banter, smoked, laughed occasionally, and coughed. She didn't join the conversation. Although I wanted to talk with her, knew that I should since this was our last day together, the best I could manage was to try to be entertaining for her benefit. So I acted out the parts of the Atlanta socialites in my stories, exaggerating the drawl that New Yorkers always found so funny. In turn, Lizzie told stories about the people from our old neighborhood: who had become fat, who divorced, who sick.

"Yikes!" Keith hopped onto a beach towel. "When did the sand get so hot?"

"Shows how long you've been gone," I said, lifting my head from my beach mat.

Lizzie was sunbathing beside me, with the back of her swimsuit unhooked; she edged over and kicked my foot. Earlier, she'd teased me about provoking Keith. *See,* she was telling me, *you're doing it again.* She didn't know about the overlook, about a lot of things. I returned the kick and sat up.

My mother laid down the magazine of Froggy's she'd been thumbing through. Maybe because of her medication, she didn't have the concentration to read very much. She adjusted her position in her chair and lit another cigarette.

Across from us, Isabella was braiding Lauren's hair the way she'd done Lindsey's and her own. "Daddy!" she admonished Keith now. "That's my towel you're getting all sandy."

Keith sat down in my father's folding chair, next to my mother. Then he lifted Isabella's towel. "Here, take it," he said, flinging it toward her.

Isabella held up a hand to block her eyes from flying sand. I cringed.

For months, especially these last few since her high school graduation, Isabella had been finding fault with everything Keith and I did. Correspondingly, she was hypersensitive about our treatment of her. I had spent the summer walking the thin line between her disapproval and her need. Now she probably wouldn't speak to Keith for the rest of the day. Damn him. Damn him for ruining what was left of our last day of vacation.

Isabella's expression was horrified, but she made no attempt to pick up her towel. Instead, she turned her back.

"You can use my towel," my mother offered. "Here." She tapped cigarette ashes into the sand, reached into her bag, and pulled out a frayed, green bath towel I recognized from my childhood. Isabella glanced at it and quickly looked away.

"That's okay, Grandma," Isabella answered in a too-nice voice that I knew translated along the lines of *You just don't get it, Grandma.* "Let's go, girls," she said to the twins. She snapped an elastic band around the end of Lauren's braid. "Let's check if anyone has caught anything."

My mother folded the green towel onto her lap, as though to save it in case Isabella should want it later. Isabella took Lauren and Lindsey's hands, one on either side of her, and the three of them set off toward the rocks. People would mistake them for sisters, I thought with a familiar twinge of regret as I watched their sun-gilded braids bounce off their backs. Isabella would no doubt find that satisfying. She judged other families superior to her own, other parents preferable. Aunt Lizzie made the best French toast, she often said. Uncle Jeremy knew how to tell a joke. Keith and I were useless.

Keith began lathering himself with sunscreen, and the act of it repulsed me. How could he be so conscientious about some things—his skin, his job—and so inattentive to others, to me? Was he cruel or merely oblivious, or did they amount to the same thing?

"Here come the lovebirds," my mother said. She had spotted Jeremy and Froggy returning from a walk along the north side of the point. They stopped to talk with Isabella and the girls.

Froggy knelt on her blanket and reached for her camera bag. Her long legs curved gracefully—annoyingly—into the curve of her smooth, high butt. No wonder she had such power over my brother; Jeremy had always been a sucker for perfect form.

Lizzie pushed up onto her elbows and followed my gaze. "Just wait till she has kids," she murmured, motioning for me to hook up her bathing suit.

I smiled at the thought of Froggy with a sagging belly and dimpled thighs. "She never will," I said into the back of Lizzie's head. Secretly, I worried Froggy would never give my brother children.

"Hey, homeys," Jeremy greeted us. "I just told the girls to round up the rest of the posse. It's time for the family picture."

"I'll take it," Keith offered.

"But then you won't be in it," I protested.

"No," Jeremy said. "We'll get someone on the beach to take it. People do that all the time on vacation." He bent over his wife. "Frances and I met some fairly interesting characters that way on our honeymoon."

Froggy was looking through the camera lens. "The light is good," she said. Though she'd met Jeremy working in the college bio lab, I'd never heard her speak of anything remotely technical.

My mother lifted her head toward the sky—checking the light? Keith stood and pushed his feet into his sneakers so that his heels crushed and hung over the backs of them. He stretched his arms and gazed at the ocean, which was surprisingly calm.

"A disappointing week for the surfer set," he said.

Jeremy chuckled. "Got some killer surf in Atlanta, do you?"

My mother moved her feet in the sand, back and forth as though she were rubbing something from the bottoms of them. "The calm before the storm," she said, watching her toes.

"I don't think so, Ma," Jeremy said. He pointed his chin to the faultless blue sky.

Lizzie, who would not be photographed in a bathing suit, was tugging on a terry-cloth cover up. "You never know," she said.

"Yes, you do," Jeremy said. "About some things, you do know."

"Storms can come up suddenly," Lizzie said. "Especially here."

Not that suddenly, I thought to myself. But then, as if to prove Lizzie right, a large blond dog came loping through the sand toward us, apparently out of nowhere. A golden retriever, wet all over except for its head. It ran up to my mother, perhaps attracted by the motion of her feet or, more likely, by the food in the bag beside her.

"What news do you bring us?" my mother asked oddly as she patted the dog between its ears. Her feet stopped still, half covered in sand. The dog panted loudly and wagged its banner of a tail, then lay its big head on the green towel in my mother's lap.

The scent of wet dog wafted over to me, reminding me of Princess when she would come in from being left in the yard in the rain. I had blamed my mother for leaving her out those days I arrived home from school to find my dog soaking wet, never thinking that Princess might have liked the rain. But now I breathed in the rich, boggy smell and I knew that, of course, she must have liked it. She liked being outside in the rain, *and* she was happy to come inside when I came home from school. Both things could be true.

I leaned toward my mother and the retriever. The dog was grinning, wrinkling its jowls. I remembered the hard, velvety feel of Princess's snout as she'd push against my hand, remembered how I worried the first time her nose had been warm and dry instead of cold and wet. How if the two of us were in the same room, we had to touch.

I regretted not having a dog for my kids. Keith was allergic. Besides, he claimed, we traveled too much to keep a dog. But it was he who did most of the traveling; even at home, when he took up weekend hobbies such as bicycling or kayaking, it was he who wandered away from us.

A sharp whistle pierced the air and, as quickly as it had arrived, the retriever lifted its head and took off, summoned by a master I did not see. The dog disappeared over a dune and I looked back toward my mother, at her hands smoothing the towel in her lap. Her eyes met mine. She winked.

I smiled at her. "I wish today wasn't our last day," I said.

Her face softened as something—a memory?—flickered across it. I wished I could see her thoughts projected onto her forehead like a movie.

"Me, too," Lizzie said. "Back to bills and laundry, ugh."

I looked toward Keith. He hadn't even turned around. I studied the slope of his shoulders, wondering what he was looking for, or whether he saw anything at all in the low tumbling surf. I was angry with him for his remoteness from me and for his roughness with Isabella, embarrassed that my family was witness to his neglect. Seeing my husband through their eyes, I was someone to be pitied. I couldn't help but compare my husband to my brother, so devoted to his wife, or even to my brother-in-law, at least playing with his kids.

But I didn't believe, then, that Keith could ever be lost to me, no matter how at odds we might be. He was my one constant, as integral to my life as my own personality. From the moment we'd decided to share a tiny studio apartment in college, we'd inhabited a circumscribed, two-planet universe.

"Here they come," Lizzie said. The fishing expedition was returning, sans any visible fish. Damien led the way, digging his pole into the sand like a walking stick.

"Anything?" Jeremy asked as my son shuffled sand onto his blanket. Damien grumbled, "Nope."

"Nah." Rick carried Ryan over to Lizzie and sat him in front of her. "He needs to be changed."

Lindsey and Lauren ran up behind Rick, hands full of clam and crab shells. Lizzie laid Ryan on a towel and removed his sodden trunks. "Mommy," Lindsey said, "a lady told us about a manatee."

"It's ugly, but it's nice," Lauren elaborated. She dumped her shells next to her brother.

"I guess that's right," Lizzie said, holding a squirming Ryan with one hand, shaking baby powder between his legs with the other.

Lindsey made her pile of shells separate from Lauren's, on the opposite side of the towel. Rick foraged through their cooler for a beer. "So, this manatee's been hanging around Montauk Harbor, over by West Lake," he said to Lizzie.

"Hmm," Lizzie said, wrapping a disposable diaper around Ryan. He rolled over and reached for a crab shell.

"What's that?" my mother asked. My father dropped his fishing pole and sat in his chair beside her. She poured lemonade from a thermos into a plastic folding cup and offered it to him. He drank it in one gulp.

"A manatee," Rick repeated, scowling at the can of beer in his hand. Not his brand; I wondered why Lizzie had bought it.

"A large sea mammal, kind of looks like a walrus without the teeth," my father said and pressed his cup down into itself.

"Tusks," Damien said. Lauren giggled.

"I thought they lived down south, around Florida, though," my father said. My mother took his cup, wiped her finger around the rim, and returned it to her beach bag.

I nodded. "So did I."

"Welp," Rick said, then took a long slug of his beer. "I guess this guy's from out of town." He grinned and Lizzie rolled her eyes. Ryan bit a crab shell and spit the pieces into the sand.

"Ryan! Mom, stop him!" Lindsey whined.

Lizzie grabbed the shell from Ryan, who started to cry. She stood him on his feet.

"The manatee must be on vacation," Lauren said.

"Animals don't *go* on vacation," said Damien. "They migrate."

"People are animals," Lauren said. "People are even mammals."

"Duh," Damien said. He tossed a small stone toward the water, but it fell short. Ryan ran over to him and put his hand out. Damien handed a stone to Ryan, who immediately tossed it and laughed.

"Frances and I saw manatees off the coast of Florida, didn't we?" Jeremy said. Froggy nodded.

"This manatee's lost his place," my mother said.

"The woman did say it had a bunch of fresh scars," Rick said. "Those things are slow moving, so they get hit by boat propellers."

Lizzie shook her head. I knew she was thinking, *Did he have to say that?*

Lauren and Lindsey looked at each other. "Will he find his way home?" Lauren asked softly.

Rick swigged on his beer. "Not sure what might happen to a manatee in the wrong place," he said.

Froggy handed Jeremy the camera. "Okay," Jeremy announced. "Time for the Sinclair Family Beach Photo."

While Jeremy explained the operation of his camera to the silver-haired man in a Speedo suit he'd commandeered to take our photo, we arranged ourselves in front of the ocean. Keith, the tallest, anchored the back row, his arm around Damien to his right. He held his left arm out to me. Without meeting his eyes, I settled myself beneath it. The breeze off the ocean blew my hair around my face. I caught it in my hand, grumbling, as Lizzie stood beside me.

"The windswept look is in style," she said, balancing Ryan on her hip. Rick ambled next to her, beer in hand.

Lauren and Lindsey settled in front of their parents, beginning a second row. Isabella placed herself to the left of them, away from Keith and me. She would look like part of Lizzie's family. I reached toward her shoulder and she allowed my hand to rest there a moment before finding a reason to turn her body and shrug me off. "Your hair's sticking up," she told Damien.

He ignored her.

My mother, meanwhile, was seating herself and my father at the bottommost row, sitting in the sand.

"Why are you two down there?" Lizzie asked as Ryan squirmed in her arms. Rick took Ryan from her and hoisted him up onto his shoulders.

"I want my lighthouse to show," my mother said, pulling at her shirt.

Jeremy and Froggy squeezed in front of us next to Isabella and the twins. They crouched so as not to block our faces.

"All set?" the silver-haired man called.

Jeremy flashed a thumbs up. "Everybody say seaweed."

I felt Keith's weight shift and glanced over at him. He was making bunny ears behind Damien's head.

"Keith," I groaned. "Must you ruin everything?"

His mouth twitched into an angry frown.

"Amanda," my mother whispered, as though we were in church. She had turned to look up at me.

"Forgive, if you can," she said and the camera clicked.

CHAPTER 23

S WIMMING UPWARD FROM THE DEPTHS OF MY PSYCHE, my mind faster than my body, I broke through the surface of consciousness, a dream still with me. I opened my eyes. Dust motes swirled like miniature living creatures in a rippling brook of sunlight. Unfamiliar objects puzzled me. For a moment, I thought I was home in Atlanta. Then I recognized the sound of waves.

I had been dreaming of my mother, a dream in which she was alive. In it, we sat in a windowless room, at a small, round table. I reached toward a blue china teapot, startled to find it icy cold to the touch. I looked at my mother. She began to grow lighter, brighter, and almost buoyant, and I reached for her over the cold teapot. My mother was expecting a baby. Suddenly, I knew that. She let out a quick, sharp cry and expelled a tiny, shining object from between her lips. She held it out in her hand: Damien's tooth. "Isn't it lovely?" she said.

Now I shivered in the morning air. I blinked, bringing into focus the shape of the speckled gull on my windowsill. I yawned. The gull cocked his head, peered one eye at me and comically—mockingly?— stretched open his beak. Then he flapped his wings and lifted away, taking the last of my sleep with him.

Wisps of unarticulated dream remained, that "fuzzy" feeling of one's brain wrapped in wool. I sat up on my knees, leaned toward the window, and gazed into a morning as sharp and clear as the stars had promised the night before. I filled my lungs with salted air like liquid.

Awake at last, I hopped out of bed, relishing the now familiar feel of the smooth, cool floor.

I didn't want to waste any of my last full day in Montauk.

I hurried to the bathroom, quickly peed, washed, and brushed, the usual ablutions. Then, after I finished, I stopped to listen outside Damien's and my father's door. No awake sounds. It was still quite early; I had time to myself and I was greedy for solitude. I pulled on my sweats, grabbed my violin and headed to the dunes. I would play an ode to the sunrise. I would play "Summertime." My head was still full of it.

Although I'd slept fitfully—half-consciously reliving my performance with Michael again and again—my body hummed with energy. Last night, on stage, I had felt completely and luxuriously alive. Music had reclaimed me, and I was drunk with the joy of it—and with the excitement of what might be to come.

Maybe I could stay on in Montauk a little longer. Maybe I could play another gig. And another. When I went back to Atlanta, I could find musicians to play with there. Why had it taken me so long to see what was so obvious? That loving others—a husband, a child, children—didn't have to mean giving up all other passions.

A green sign at the entrance to the path warned against disturbing the dunes, but today I was heedless. Today, I acknowledged no obstacle. I climbed to the top of the largest mound and, carefully laying my case on a mat of grass to avoid picking up sand, extracted my violin. I quickly checked my tuning and began to play.

The first, sweet notes brought tears to my eyes, or maybe it was the wind off the ocean, or the memory of Michael playing beside me. I wanted to play *this* violin for him, my violin, the one that had been my mother's. Then I thought how I had never heard her play, and my heart ached with the loss of her.

I closed my eyes and sawed sightlessly, played by feel and memory and longing. The music I made was loud in my ears, though the wind ate it up, and I didn't hear or see anything except the notes that filled me. I played the way I'd played at the Jaw Bone, though, of course, without Michael's obbligato, and when at last I was through and I heard my name, I turned with the absolute conviction that Michael stood before me. But he didn't.

Instead I saw Keith climbing the dune.

My heart plunged through my gut, a falling elevator. I held my violin to my chest and spoke his name.

He stopped slightly downhill from me, his back against the sun, his frame silhouetted against the too-blue sky. I squinted into his face; because of the dune's slope, we stood at roughly the same height, eye to eye.

" 'Summertime,' " he said, nodding.

I wanted to snatch the word out of the air, to take it back. How dare he approve of me now?

My face must have broadcast my reaction. He stepped forward, his eyes on my eyes, rising. "I'm sorry to interrupt your playing." His eyes moved to my violin. "It was haunting."

I stared at him, not comprehending why he was here.

"I followed you," he said, taller now, almost his full height. "I mean, I got out of the cab and was paying the guy, just as you entered the dunes. Then I heard your music."

I gazed at the ocean the way one might look across her own living room during a guest's visit, with smug territoriality. This was my place. I turned back to him. "Why are you here?" I asked.

Keith frowned, slid his hands into the pockets of his khakis and looked away. A muscle tightened in his jaw. He spoke with his eyes on the ocean. "I'm on my way to meet with a former client in the city, hoping to get his business."

So he wasn't here for me, or was he using his client as an excuse? Either way, I didn't like it. I was angry with him for appearing so suddenly, for interrupting my small moment of triumph. For invading the solitude I now realized I craved, or required.

I lay my violin in its case, clicked it shut and started past him down the dune. Keith picked up a suitcase he'd left on the path, the blue one he'd had for years. I'd planned to buy him new luggage for his birthday in the fall. We walked toward the ocean in single file. "Taking the scenic route to Manhattan?" I asked, turning my head sideways as he bumped along behind me.

"No, Amanda, taking the opportunity to be with you, to talk."

I stopped and groaned in frustration. "You *had* the opportunity! You chose not to be here. You chose . . ." I bit the inside of my cheeks as my eyes filled and burned. Why now? I began to walk again.

He followed, then stopped a few yards from the tide line. He set down his suitcase and removed his shoes and socks. I placed my violin case on top of his suitcase. We walked together in silence to the edge of the surf. I wanted to tell him I might be pregnant, scared myself with wanting to tell him, but I couldn't—I wouldn't—let that determine our fate together.

Over Keith's shoulder I saw an elderly couple on an early morning walk. The same couple who swam laps in the pool each day. I recognized their orange college sweatshirts. Did they have a child at Syracuse? Had they themselves gone to school there and been together ever since? I wondered at the kinds of pain they'd managed to get through.

"I've got to catch a train into Manhattan soon," Keith said.

I exhaled. "Fine," I said.

"But I can be back this afternoon." He calculated the hours. "Get there by nine, nine-thirty, leave by one-thirty. I'll be back here by four, at the latest."

The lap-swimming couple approached us. They weren't all that old, after all. Maybe ten years older than we were. All the times I'd seen them, I'd never really looked close.

We greeted each other and I dropped my eyes, wondering as they passed whether they talked casually about me ("She's the one whose boy broke a tooth. I've never seen the father around.") as Keith and I might have spoken about them.

A heaving wave sent quick, rolling foam across our feet, splashing up against our legs. Keith jumped back.

" 'I grow old, I grow old/I shall wear the bottoms of my trousers rolled,' " Keith recited. He stooped to roll his cuffs.

"The Love Song of J. Alfred Prufrock." In college, Keith and I had composed a jazz piece for piano and violin based on Eliot's poem, our senior project. We'd performed the music as my roommate, Diane, an English major, read the words aloud.

I recalled the next line and spoke it. " 'Shall I part my hair behind? Do I dare to eat a peach?' "

" 'I shall wear white flannel trousers, and walk upon the beach.' " Keith's eyes were brilliant with remembering. He held out his hand.

We moved toward each other. Keith took my hand and placed it on his shoulder and then took my other hand as though leading me in a dance. But neither of us moved.

"Khakis," I said and pressed my face into his shirt. "You always wear khaki trousers."

By the time I got back to my cottage, my father and Damien were gone. A note on my bed in Lizzie's rounded script informed me she was fixing a big family breakfast at her cottage. "P.S.," it read. "Look under your pillow."

I slid my hand beneath the pillow, expecting to find a doughnut wrapped in a napkin or a candy bar. But my fingertips touched the pointed edge of a cardboard box. I lifted the pillow.

A pregnancy test kit sat squarely on my wrinkled sheet. My stomach tightened. I had to face this. I smiled to think Lizzie had usurped my role; she was acting like the big sister. I told myself I would do the test before Keith returned from the city, that it was important I knew the results before we spoke again. But I had just peed. I snatched up the box as though there were someone around to see and hid it in the bottom of the plastic garbage bag that held my dirty laundry.

My stomach felt cavernous. I needed food. I headed out the door just as Athena was coming up the steps.

"Hello. You had a call while you were out this morning," she said.

Michael, I thought. My reaction, not one of pleasure as it would have been two hours earlier, but of anxiety, was not lost on her.

Athena smiled with just the corners of her mouth. "Another friend of mine," she said before I could ask. She stood with a hand on either railing, blocking my path.

Another friend? I looked past her toward the pool where two yellow dogs sniffed through the flowers. Sunshine and Homer. Had Michael gone back to the city without saying good-bye? My heart froze.

"It was Betty MacKenzie," Athena said. "Otherwise known as Lady Bird."

"Oh!" Homer leapt at the fence after a squirrel and Sunshine followed with the slo-mo version. I was pleased and disappointed. Would Michael not call me?

"Bird wanted to thank you for last night." Athena's mouth curved minutely upward.

I felt my face flush. "How nice," I said, trying to hide my thrill. "I sat in with her group last night."

"Yes, I know," Athena said. Of course she did.

She moved off the step to give me room. She was wearing pants today, loose cotton pants the color of weak tea, with a shirt to match. The outfit accentuated her pallor; paradoxically, it also made her look less ephemeral.

"Shall I call Lady Bird back?"

Athena turned up her palms. "She didn't ask you to, but why not?"

"I'm on my way to breakfast at Lizzie's cottage," I told her. We began to walk. She jingled beside me. The dogs ran up to us, their wagging tails fanning the air with redolence of honeysuckle. I stopped to pet them.

"Michael hasn't left yet," Athena told me without my asking.

Was she speaking out of kindness, sensing my interest, or playing some kind of game? I decided it didn't matter. I was grateful for the knowledge. We continued to walk.

"Would you like to join us for breakfast?" I asked as we came to the path that led to Lizzie's.

Athena smiled with her whole mouth this time. "Thank you. I would."

"And if you have it, I'd like Lady Bird's number."

"Of course," Athena said. "In fact, I have it here." She handed me a slip of memo paper stamped with the image of the laughing gull from the door. She had printed Bird's phone number in small, precise numbers.

I laughed.

"That gull," I said, folding the paper and sliding it into a pocket, "from your door. I expected to see it everywhere, as a logo. But this is only the second place I've seen it."

Athena touched my shoulder with the tips of her fingers, a gesture both intimate and distancing. "I keep the image for my personal use," she said.

We sat on Lizzie's deck finishing our omelets and coffee while the children, zigzagging across the lawn like the colorful moving pieces in a kaleidoscope, raced into puffs of wind, striving to send kites aloft. My father trailed after Ryan, disentangling string behind him as he went. Isabella was helping the twins add ribbons to their kite's tails, having taken up a boys versus girls competition instigated by Damien and Crosby as to which of their kites would fly highest.

I scraped the last of my eggs from my dish.

"That was delicious," Athena said as she wiped her fingertips on a napkin. The gracious tone was new to me. She had spoken little during the meal, even as Rick scowled at her sideways, and her presence had lent an awkward cast to our conversation. I was waiting till she left to tell Lizzie and Jeremy about Keith's arrival. Of course, I thought wryly, she probably already knew.

Lizzie shrugged. "Thanks, Athena." She lifted the coffeepot and her eyebrows. "More, anyone?"

"Wheee!" Ryan sang as his kite, in the shape of a seagull, quickly lifted and then quickly dove to the ground.

Jeremy stretched across the table with his Styrofoam cup. "Can't ever have enough caffeine." Baby Jay lay asleep across my brother's lap. Froggy reached to shield him.

"Not with the baby on your lap, Jer, for God's sake!" For once I agreed with her. Lizzie had been burned by hot coffee as a baby. I wondered whether she remembered.

Froggy rose, hefting Jay to her shoulder. "I'm going to put him down and take a shower."

I glanced at Lizzie to see her reaction—Froggy was once again leaving the table without offering to help clean up—but Lizzie was shading her eyes with her hand, watching the kite-fliers. Damien and Crosby had gotten theirs up, a green and purple-spotted flying fish. Now Crosby was expertly letting out line.

"Okay," Jeremy said, tilting his face sunward as his wife walked away. "Man, I don't want to leave this place."

"That's gratifying to hear, but I'm afraid the cottages are booked for next week," Athena said, jingling as she crumpled her napkin. Jeremy laughed.

Rick sprang up from his chair as if to a bell. "I'm going to town to get the paper." He nudged Jeremy. "Should I check to see if we can get on the course for nine holes this afternoon?"

Jeremy considered. "It's our last day. . . . What do you girls want to do?"

"Oh, you know," Lizzie said. "Clean up, watch kids, cook meals . . ."

Athena stood. "I must get back to the office," she said. "Thank you for including me."

"Sure," Lizzie said.

Her word choice struck me, and I understood that, apart from Crosby, Athena had no family. Maybe her odd manipulations amounted to little more than an attempt to feel part of something. She had done me no harm, even some good. She had brought me to Michael, who had brought me to the Jaw Bone. I glanced at the lapis ring. Had she somehow summoned Keith as well?

Rick threw his keys into the air and caught them in his fist. "I'll see what's available, bro," he said as he strode off toward the parking lot.

Athena paused in front of me. "Come by to use the phone whenever you like," she said. I knew that she was thanking me for the breakfast invitation, for being open to her friendship.

"I will," I said.

Lindsey and Lauren shrieked. Their butterfly kite was soaring above Damien and Crosby's fish. Isabella cheered, her arms raised in victory. I smiled at her easily won pleasure—and her strength. She would be okay.

Alone with Lizzie and Jeremy, I wanted to tell them about Keith. But some confusion in my mind kept the words from flowing easily. For so long, all I'd wanted was for Keith to love me again. But now my goals were not so simple. I didn't want to chase the impossible; I wanted to discover what was possible. I wanted love, but I also needed to please myself. I wanted my family around me and I needed to be alone. I wanted to play my music, to focus on it at last.

"Late night?" Jeremy asked.

"Not really," I answered. "But I had a good time. I played violin with a blues group."

"Thanks for inviting us." His words were light, but his expression was surprised.

"It was spur of the moment," I said, lightly smacking his arm. "I got asked to sit in on a song."

"With that doctor?" Lizzie asked.

I nodded. "Michael Burns."

"He's also the one who fixed your ring," Jeremy recalled.

"Doctor, jeweler, musician . . ." Michael sounded like a fantasy. I chuckled and added, "Indian chief?" I didn't say *lover*.

"What was Isabella's reaction?" Jeremy asked. Lizzie kept her eyes averted. I wondered whether they had recently discussed me.

I shrugged. "She said I sounded good. I think she was surprised I had it in me."

"Of course you do," Jeremy said. "You always have."

I smiled at him, grateful.

Shouts rose from the lawn as Damien and Lauren raced alongside the pool fence, kites soaring behind them. My father had tied Ryan's kite to an Adirondack chair in which they both now sat, like kings presiding over a joust.

"Mandy, what's going on with you?" Jeremy asked.

I looked at Lizzie and she shook her head. "I haven't said anything," she insisted. To Jeremy, she added, "I don't *know* anything."

"I just hope you haven't put your marriage in jeopardy," he said.

My cheeks flamed. "What do you know about my marriage and who's jeopardizing what!"

Jeremy held out his hands, palms down. "Very little."

"Very little," I repeated. Pangs of guilt constricted my throat.

Lizzie began to clear the breakfast dishes from the table.

On the lawn, Damien was attempting to run backward. He tripped into Lauren and both of them fell, letting go of their kites. Isabella went chasing after the errant strings while Crosby and Lindsey exchanged insults. Jeremy took a long gulp of his coffee and stood.

"Looks like my cue to go fly a kite," he said.

I sighed and he touched my shoulder as he squeezed past my chair.

"It's only that I care what happens to you, Mandy."

"I know," I said. Then I told him, "Keith's here."

Jeremy frowned. "He's been avoiding us?"

"Of course not, he just arrived. He's in the city and will be here this afternoon."

"I'm glad," Jeremy said. "It's good he's come."

Was it? It was true. Keith's arrival compelled me to look at our marriage from a changed perspective.

Jeremy turned and started down the deck stairs. Damien and Lauren stopped arguing as he approached. He raised his hand in a victory sign, or a peace sign.

"So Keith came after all," Lizzie said quietly as she piled silverware onto a plate.

"Yeah," I said, not bothering to disguise my bitterness. "He had business in New York."

Lizzie nodded. "What will you do now?"

I winced. "I don't know." I needed to see Michael before Keith returned, that was first.

"Did you get my little package, by the way?" she asked.

"Yes, thanks," I said. "I haven't taken the test yet, though."

Lizzie looked at me squarely. "Yeah, well," she said. "I have."

CHAPTER 24

"YOU KNOW HOW IT IS," LIZZIE WAS SAYING as we watched the kids splash in the pool. All of the kites were now tied along the fence and Jeremy had organized a game of water polo, boys versus girls. "You know how it is when you're worried you might be pregnant."

"Uh, *yeah*," I answered. "I do." The wind had picked up and the kites were flying high. But the air was still warm and soft against my skin.

"Even if you really don't want to be, when it turns out you're not, you're always a little sad."

"True." The butterfly kite dipped below the fish, narrowly missing entanglement.

"You're always a little sad because"—she searched the air between the kites and the water for the right words—"it's as though some *possibility* is lost."

She'd got it exactly right.

She pushed a curl off her forehead and turned to me. "I didn't want to be pregnant again. Wouldn't even have thought of it, probably, if it weren't for you. I don't keep track half the time."

"You should, though," I told her. I looked at a shadow falling across her cheek. For all her easiness, Lizzie had her own demons. She had rarely burdened me with them.

"I know I should," she said.

"Maybe that's why I haven't taken the test yet," I said. "Maybe I still want anything to be possible."

Lizzie tilted her head and laughed. "Amanda, you've always wanted *everything* to be possible."

Her laughter rang through me like a bell. What was possible; what was desired. How long had it been since I'd allowed myself to consider either? But if I had another child . . . would I be repeating my past, the life that had taken me to here? Or was there another way?

"I need to talk to Michael," I said, now acutely aware of the few hours before Keith's return.

Lizzie smiled at me, her expression half distracted, half solicitous, and for a moment she looked so much like my mother. "When I grow up," she said, "I want to have as much fun as you."

I called Lady Bird and thanked her for her kind words, and she told me the group would love me to sit in again. Though the group was named for Bo, Bird was its leader. I pressed her for a specific time, and we agreed on the following Thursday at the Jaw Bone.

Gratified but nerve-wracked—what if my playing last night had been a fluke? What if I couldn't repeat it?—I called Michael. "Can you meet me in town?" I asked when he picked up the phone.

"I can do that," Michael answered after a moment's hesitation. "How are you today?"

"I'm fine," I said. I felt my whole body pull up toward his voice. "Quite fine. I'm on my way to the market to pick up a few last-minute necessities for this evening's feast." I realized he probably expected me to say something about the night before, about playing onstage together. I wanted to, but I would wait till I saw him. Then I would tell him I was scheduled to play again.

We agreed to meet within the hour in the parking lot of the grocery store. In the meantime, I guiltily began to pack up what I could of Damien's things. I wanted to stay on here, but I worried about how to do that without making my son feel abandoned.

Keith would have to help; he wasn't the only one who required "space."

I spotted Michael immediately as I wheeled my cart into the parking lot. He was leaning against his motorcycle, arms crossed against his chest as though to protect it, that shock of hair falling across reflective sunglasses.

He spotted me, too, and walked over to meet me. "Hey," he said, "didn't I see you play violin last night at the Jaw Bone?"

I turned my face up to his and saw that his sunglass lenses were coated in something almost oily looking, perhaps mercury. They didn't reflect my face the way I expected, but produced dazzling swirls of color in the light.

I loaded a grocery bag into my car. "Must have been someone else."

He bent closer to me. "I don't think so."

I smelled his soap scent and felt the air between us grow dense. I loved that we were in public and couldn't touch, relished the sweet, aching thrill of denial.

But he reached for me, and lifted a handful of hair from my neck. "Let's see," he traced a curve with his finger. "I think you held that fiddle right about here."

The line he drew on my skin vibrated. "Michael." I pronounced his name as a warning.

He let my hair drop through his fingers, let his fingers trail down my arm. I looked at him, my eyes even with his mouth, holding my breath.

"Oh, I'm sorry," he said and he lowered his voice. "I thought you were someone I wanted desperately to fuck."

I let out my breath, half laughing. "You're something!"

He grinned. "So are you, Miss Amanda. You were hot stuff last night."

I felt the blood rise to my face. "You were, too."

He laughed. "Yeah. *We* were. I knew we would be."

"Look, Michael . . ." This time his name was a plea. I glanced at my watch.

"I know, I know. You don't have much time."

I surveyed the weekend scene around me. I had come here to tell him face-to-face about Keith's arrival, but I couldn't put his name between us yet. "I'd like to talk somewhere."

"Come back to the house."

I shook my head. "Just talk."

Michael shrugged. "We can just talk at my house." He crossed his chest with his hand. "Cross my busted heart and hope to die."

"You're impossible."

"Improbable," he corrected as he straddled his bike. "But remotely plausible."

"All right," I said as I opened my car door. "Lead us on."

I parked my car behind his bike and followed him onto his deck. The wind blew a fine layer of sand in delicate lines across the wood planks, settling in the cracks. I walked over to the trough of sunflowers we'd planted, finding them dry.

"Where's your watering can?"

Michael pointed to a spigot near the door under which sat a galvanized watering can. "Be my guest." He moved a chair close to the sunflowers and lowered himself into it. He'd taken off his sunglasses, and he squinted, watching me. Something was different. Here was his physician self, I thought. Cautious.

I tended to the bent-headed blossoms, surprised to find small weeds already poking through the soil. I plucked them and made a neat pile of leaves and roots next to the planter.

"You've been neglecting these," I said, turning to Michael.

He hung his head, mock sheepishly. "Can you forgive me?"

"I think I can," I said evenly. Forgiving—and being forgiven—was becoming a specialty of mine. I lifted my eyes to the dune grass swaying in the docile wind. The pastel colors were more beautiful even than I remembered. Suddenly, I knew this was what I wanted, being here.

"I'll let you make me a deal," I said. I brushed the soil from my hands.

Michael reached for my hand, but I drew back. "No, seriously. Listen to me. When do you go back to the city?" My mind's gears cranked into action.

"When you force me to."

"Michael . . ."

"Tomorrow?"

"And what happens to the house after that?"

He shrugged. "It lies temporarily fallow, a monument to capitalist greed and everything that's wrong with American health care providers."

"Hmmm." I was only half listening to his words, anxious to set my plan in motion.

"Then, after Labor Day, I either turn it over to Linda or I rent it till my lawyer—Charles, I believe you've met his lovely garden—till he tells me what to do. Recently, I've been having second thoughts about impulses of generosity unbecoming to a physician."

"Rent it to me," I said.

"What?" The wry humor on his face shifted into a puzzled scowl.

"Rent the house to me! I want to stay; I'm not ready to go back to Atlanta."

Michael sat forward, as though straining to hear something.

I blurted my news: "Lady Bird invited me to play again this Thursday."

"That's great." Michael seemed pleased, but there was something held in check beneath his smile.

"And she told me about Saturdays," I continued.

"What about Saturdays?"

"How any of a whole slew of musicians might show up to play, how it's kind of one big jam session."

Michael's expression was thoughtful as he reached for my hand again. This time I laced his fingers through my own. "That's right," he said. "Whoever is in town and feels like playing can show up. We sometimes have ten or twelve musicians on that stage at one time." He shook his head. "It can get crazy."

Was he trying to temper my enthusiasm? Why?

"So you want to hang with musicians," Michael said, strumming my fingers against his lips as he spoke. "It's great. Intense." He looked into my eyes. "You have to have a lot of confidence to hang with that crowd. Did she tell you Keith Richards sometimes shows up? Billy Joel?"

She hadn't, and I must have revealed as much because Michael laughed and nipped at my fingertips. "You'd believe anything, if you wanted it badly enough."

My stomach felt as though he'd pulled the plug from the bottom of it. Was I a fool? Was he making a fool of me? I withdrew my hand.

"I'm just teasing you, Amanda," he said, but something burned in his eyes. "The Jaw Bone *is* that kind of place. I've been there on a Saturday and played on one or two songs. There have been times I've sat there and not played at all, just listened to what was going down."

I watched as a small black speck dived between waves, a cormorant working for its lunch. I stood in silence, one hand shielding my eyes. I imagined lying next to him, his breath against my face, warming my skin like sun. "I love it here," I said. "And I'd love to live in this house while I sort things out." I looked at Michael.

A ripple of pain washed over his features. "It wouldn't be for long," I said, but I didn't want to coerce him or even persuade him. I could see my wishes did not match his, and disappointment drained through me.

Michael gazed to where the cormorant flew, nearly indistinguishable now from clouds.

"Will you rent it to me?" I asked one last time.

He lowered his chin. "I can't."

I grasped my own fingers, the ones he'd held. "Why not?"

He wagged his head. "Amanda," he began. Then he leaned forward, brows furrowed, and pointed through the dunes. "Look out there, in the water. Do you see that?"

I followed his gaze, heart pounding. He was refusing me. He had told me no. A dark spot on the water moved left. "I don't know what I see."

Michael stood. "Let's go up to the tower. There's something out there."

From the tower, I could see beyond the flat blue sheet of sky to where gray clouds moved in from the east. The wind was strong up here, and the hairs on my arms lifted my skin in tiny bumps.

Michael adjusted the eyepiece of the telescope and peered through, then offered it to me. "There's a major school of blues out that way." He pointed to a cloud that, observed through the telescope, turned out to be a huge flock of seabirds.

"Is that what you saw downstairs?" I asked, lifting my head. The wind was biting against my neck.

He considered. "No, what I saw was something with a large tail."

He took my shoulders in his hands. "Maybe a mermaid." He smiled, but he looked grim. What was going on? He had been teasing in the parking lot.

I rested my cheek against his chest, listening for the sound of his heart. "I hear your bass line," I said.

"That old out-of-tune thing?" He smoothed my hair with his hands, his fingers large and warm against my skull.

"How's it doing?" I asked, moving my face across the rough cotton of his shirt.

His arms tightened around me, his hands cupping my head like an infant's. "It's strong," he said. "But vulnerable."

I slid my hands to his waist, hooking my thumbs through his belt loops the way I did when we rode his motorcycle. Whenever I was with Michael, it seemed, there was wind at our backs.

"Anyway," Michael said. "All human hearts are the same—simple pumps and valves. Only the voices change."

Voices. I looked up at him, the wind slicing at my eyes. I remembered the voices my mother heard and realized that her own voice had been within them. I had never known how to hear it.

"Why are we up here?" I asked. For a second I imagined he wanted to throw me off the roof.

He brushed his lips against my forehead. "I like the broadest possible view."

I squinted up at him, my eyes tearing.

"And," he added, "it gives me an excuse to hold you in my arms." I closed my eyes, dampening his shirt. "Do you need an excuse?"

Michael didn't answer. I heard his heart as a thudding counterpoint to my own. I pressed my face against his chest, trying to feel his scar. *Remember this moment forever.*

I had said those words before, the first time at the age of ten.

One afternoon on my way home after school, I'd stopped as I occasionally did to visit my grandmother. She kept candy in her cupboard, special kinds she knew I liked, Heath bars and chocolate kisses. As I'd stood in her living room tracing the design on her Oriental rug with the tip of my sneaker, that ordinary moment of waiting for her to return from the kitchen had seemed suddenly to represent all the ordinary but pleasant moments of anticipation I'd experienced in my life. In those moments, when something good was about to happen, the world seemed just the same as always. Only I knew it wasn't, and that was happiness.

I wanted to remember. Wanted to remember every detail of color and scent and shape, so that I would always have them. And I wanted to remember the soft, folded skin and powdery scent of my grandmother herself, my mother's mother who, though I didn't know it then, had less than two years to live. *Remember this moment forever,* I'd told myself as the afternoon sun illuminated my grandmother's green silk drapes. And I had.

When her mother died, my mother's deep and silent grief seemed to take her, too, away from me, and I was struck with the adult knowledge of the inevitability of loss.

"I don't want to leave," I said now as longing welled in my chest. *I don't want to lose you.*

"And yet, you can't stay," Michael said, resigned.

I pulled away, tears streaming down my cheeks. "If you'd rent me your house . . ."

Michael shook his head as though shaking ideas out of it and pressed back against the railing. Over his shoulder, I caught a flicker of silver out where the water was calm.

"That's not the way," he said and his words sounded bitter. "I can't become . . . what you want. Not now."

I didn't understand. "I should just go back home."

Michael grimaced. "If you want to go home, then yes, you should."

I threw up my arms. "Keith is here in Montauk!"

"I know," Michael said quietly. "Athena came by to get Homer early this morning, and she told me she'd seen you two."

"Goddamn her!"

Michael stared at his fingers, twisting the telescope. "No, she had to tell me. I was about to come ask you to breakfast." He snorted a funny little dry laugh. "To celebrate last night."

I winced. I had tried not to hope that Michael would come for me at breakfast. But he had wanted to after all. Perhaps I understood. "You won't rent me your house because my husband's here?"

"I won't rent you my house because your husband"—he bit off the word—"*exists.* You're still married. You aren't free."

"I'm separated," I said.

"As am I. Neither one of us is in a position . . ."

"Ha!" I stamped my foot and then was mortified. "You invited me to stay here only days ago."

"Don't be such a damned greedy child!" His voice cracked on the words, and I knew he was sorry for them even before he pounded the deck railing with his fist.

But I felt the tight cords of hope in my chest fray apart. So that's how he saw me. I dragged the palm of my hand along the railing, unmindful of splinters.

"I hate you," I said, and my voice broke, too.

"I hate *you*," he answered.

We looked at each other, saw the wretched absurdity of our words in each other's eyes, and slowly began to laugh.

"Amanda," he said, breathing deeply.

I looked at the ocean, trying to compose myself. "Thank you for last night," I said. "For 'Summertime.' " I didn't say *For changing my life* because it sounded melodramatic. But last night had made clear to me that what I wanted more than anything else was to reconnect with my violin.

Michael lifted his chin to the sky and spoke as though addressing it. "I loved playing music with you." His hands gripped the railing behind him for balance.

I nodded; a tear dripped from my chin. He was right not to rent me his house. I had so much to figure out and no right to ask anything of him—at least not without offering him something of myself in return. But I wasn't able to do that, not now. It wasn't fair to try to solve the problem of my pain through him.

Michael held out his arms to me and I folded into the warm bulk of him.

"I'm glad I met you," I said. I leaned against his chest and listened to the syncopated thumping of heart and sea.

Michael held me for a long, sweet moment, then he slid apart from me. "I made this for you," he said, extracting a cassette tape from his pocket.

I accepted it and read the hand-penciled label: *Instant Ocean (Just Add Water)*.

A memento.

I turned the plastic box over. In the same, neat, undoctorlike hand two columns of songs were listed, a compilation of recordings to conjure summer by the sea. And to say good-bye.

My eyes rested on the last title, "Corcovado." I knew the song, romantic in an edgy way that appealed to me. A song about a room beside the ocean, and finding love.

"I thought you might listen to the violin parts," Michael said when I looked up at him.

I felt my face crumple. "Thank you."

Michael's hands were in my hair, his lips at my neck and my ears. He covered my head with kisses and whispers. *Remember this moment forever.*

"I think the weather's changing," is what I heard him say.

CHAPTER 25
Long Island, 1967

"D O YOU EVER HEAR VOICES?" MY MOTHER ASKED.

I looked sideways at her standing beside the kitchen table and continued eating my breakfast, Cheerios with sliced banana. In the hand nearest me my mother held a burning cigarette, in the other a deep blue coffee mug.

I shrugged, half looking at her, half looking at the edge of my pajama sleeve dipping into my cereal. I said, "I don't know."

It was Saturday morning. Outside, a spongy, gray mist pressed against the window. All spring, the weather had been confusing and unpredictable. I was hoping for snow, so that school would close Monday. Our sixth grade teacher, Mr. Georgi, gave a lot of work and I was behind on a report. But I couldn't tell how cold it was out.

Lizzie was inside watching cartoons; Jeremy had gone to baseball practice. I usually walked the dog on Saturday mornings, but my father had stuck his thin, pale face into my room to tell me he'd already walked her while he'd waited for his coffee to perk. He hadn't walked the dog in months.

I hadn't expected my mother to be around when I came down to the kitchen. She was sick. She heard voices that made her stomach hurt, that had made her run away. My father was taking her to the hospital at eleven o'clock. But she had come downstairs after me and taken a cup of coffee from the pot my father had put up.

Now I watched her right hand. The lengthening ash on her cigarette threatened to drop onto the floor. "I hear *your* voice," I said.

She lifted her cigarette, dropped the ash, and blew smoke over my head. "You do?" She tapped her forehead with her index finger, her cigarette resting against it. "Do you hear my voice in there?"

That wasn't what I meant. "No," I said. "I just hear you when you speak, like now." I looked at my sleeve, soaking up milk.

I focused on my spoon, on the puffy oat circles floating in the tiny white pool. Maybe the Cheerios were tiny rafts, sailed by creatures too small for me to see but that I could hear, faintly, if I leaned really close. An entire universe in a spoonful of milk. I leaned forward and ate them all.

Guiltily, I looked up at my mother. "Maybe I do hear some," I reconsidered.

"Oh." My mother set down her mug. Was she surprised? Why did she have to talk about this stuff, make a big deal out of it? She walked over to the sink and back again. Back and forth, from table to sink, trailing smoke. She seemed excited or nervous. Probably about going to the hospital. I ate the last two slices of banana, the last banana in the house, actually. Would my father do the grocery shopping while my mother was gone? He never remembered fruit.

My mother stopped in front of me. "What do they say to you?" she asked. She picked up her coffee mug once more, but didn't drink. Behind her, the radiator beneath the window hissed.

I tilted my cereal bowl to my lips and slurped the last of my milk. A few drops dribbled down my chin. I bent my head, wiping my mouth and chin on the neck of my pajama top. "Huh?" I said.

She ignored my bad manners. "The voices. When they speak to you, what do they say?"

I squeezed a small drop of milk out of my sleeve back into the bowl.

"Do they threaten you?" she asked. She set her coffee mug on the table.

"Um." I lowered my cereal bowl to the floor for Princess to lick. Her dog ears heard the click of the bowl and she came padding into the kitchen, probably from her spot in the dining room under the table.

"They don't speak to me," I said finally.

My mother walked to the refrigerator, then the sink, taking short, smoky puffs from her cigarette. "But you said you heard voices sometimes." She seemed to need to know this, like it mattered. Did she want us to be the same?

Princess looked up from the licked bowl, thanking me. I petted her and she wagged her tail. I picked up the bowl, thinking that I could just put it back in the cabinet, it looked so clean. Anyone would be fooled. "I sometimes can hear different sounds," I said as I carried the bowl to the sink. "They don't talk *to* me, though."

Princess trotted back to the dining room. My mother paced past me and turned again. "Whose voice do you hear?" she asked. "Do you hear hers?" She cocked her chin toward the back door. I knew whom she meant.

I crumpled my wet sleeve in my hand. "I don't hear anyone's."

"She tells me things," my mother said in a dropped voice. "Terrible things that will happen."

I knew this. Gloria was communicating with her, mentally, she had said, and it made her feel sick. Gloria's voice had even made her run away. Yesterday, she had slipped out of the house and taken the train into the city without telling anyone. It took us a while to realize she was missing. We were so used to her being here, the house seemed to contain her even after she'd gone. Now, though she stood beside me, it seemed that part of her was still away. And soon she would be gone for real.

My mother told us she had gone to the city to get away from Gloria, from Gloria's voice, but her voice had followed my mother to the city anyway. So she'd found a pay phone and called my father. After he found where she was waiting on a bench and brought her home, my father called the doctor. Then he said my mother needed to go to the hospital. It would be like when Lizzie was born, only for a longer time. He wasn't sure how long.

I had heard my father on the phone talking about how the hospital might give my mother something called an electroshock. That's the only part of the conversation I heard—I went downstairs to practice piano—but when I thought about it later, my stomach felt wobbly, the way it did when I'd traveled too long in a car. How did they shock a person? Did they actually plug her in? Would she smell burnt afterward?

"Do you still feel sick?" I asked. I hoped my mother wouldn't have to have an electroshock. I would never have one.

My mother's cheeks pulled in, though she had finished her cigarette and stubbed it out in my cereal bowl. "She's making me sick. I can't sleep. I feel so anxious, it gives me pains."

I nodded. She had told me this, too, though my father said her pains weren't real. My mother wasn't pretending, I could tell, but I wished she would be quiet. Even though this time we would know where she was, I didn't like her going away. Our house wouldn't have a mother.

"Do you want a doughnut?" I asked. Doughnuts were my mother's favorite food.

She didn't answer, but looked toward the thawing window. I saw that her eyes had turned dark and strange. Something mean worked its way down her face and pushed at her mouth.

"Bitch," she said in a ragged voice. "Whore."

The words twisted out of her mouth like smoke.

I felt my eyelids pull up in surprise, and I almost giggled. Except for *damn* and *hell,* I had never heard my mother curse. I wished Jeremy were here. He'd never believe this.

Her arm shot past me suddenly, as though to slap someone. I jumped back. A streak of blue flew by my head and crashed, shattering against the stove. Coffee pooled on the floor. Her mug.

"I know the game!" my mother shrieked. "I know the game!" Her fingers were curled hard like claws.

Don't listen to the voices, I wanted to say. *Just don't listen.*

Down the stairs came the quick, heavy pounding of my father's footsteps. I turned toward the doorway as he stomped into the kitchen in his terry-cloth bathrobe, his legs dripping water. He had just come out of the shower. I didn't like to look at the wet hair on his feet.

"Barbara!" he said sharply, as though yelling at Princess, telling her to get down off the couch.

My mother reached for her pack of cigarettes on the counter. "I know the game," she said in a new voice, low and hard. She lit a match and held it. The sulfur smell made me dizzy.

"Barbara," my father repeated, softer.

I wanted to leave, but couldn't move, as though only my continued presence would prevent total disaster.

My mother lit her cigarette, but still did not blow out the match. She raised it, peering into the blue center of the flame as it burned down to her fingertips. She held it close to her face and I imagined she was listening to it. I thought of a match head universe like my Cheerio universe, tiny creatures like the ones I'd eaten going up in flames.

My father lunged toward my mother, swatting the match from her hand, extinguishing it. Then he yelped and jumped back, hopping on one foot. Bright drops of blood dotted the floor, forming an uneven pattern around the flattened ash.

"For Christ's sake," he said as he sat in my chair and lifted his bleeding foot. He had stepped on a shard of broken coffee mug.

My mother walked out of the room, smoking. The stairs creaked softly as she climbed them. I waited until I heard her door close, then I bent to pick up the pieces.

We were lying around on my bed, all three of us, doing nothing. Five minutes earlier, my father had driven away, taking my mother to the hospital. We had each kissed my mother good-bye at the front door and then run up to my room to watch from Lizzie's and my bedroom window as the car disappeared.

Down in the basement, Mrs. Paladino—a neighbors' grandmother who lived around the block—was doing our laundry. Here to care for us until my father got back, she had decided to "do something useful" and headed toward the laundry room before my parents were even out the door. I had a ghost of a memory of someone—my mother?—once describing Mrs. Paladino as "nuts when it came to laundry."

"Sing me 'Kiddie Car,' " Lizzie asked now. Her head hung off the end of my bed and her feet rested on Jeremy's lap. He was half sitting horizontally across the bed, his shoulders pressed back against the wall. My head was on my pillow; my arms hugged my pulled-up knees.

Lizzie was asking for a baby song. Oh, God, she would be a brat with my mother gone.

"I forget how it goes," I said.

Jeremy started humming some other song about a car, something he had heard on the rock 'n' roll radio station. He drummed his thighs with his hands.

"This is it," Lizzie said. She pushed up on her elbows and began to sing the words.

Lizzie looked back and forth between Jeremy and me. Jeremy groaned and rolled his eyes.

"Now you sing it to me," Lizzie said. She tugged on the hem of my jeans.

I poked Jeremy with my toes and sat up. We might as well humor her for as long as we could. Otherwise, we would pay the price of her whining and crying. Jeremy could just go to his room and shut the door; I had to share my room with a five-year-old. As it often did, this struck me as unfair. But I said, "Okay."

I began to sing in my best school chorus voice, and suddenly, my head was filled with the memory of my mother singing us to sleep, her voice filling the dark spaces in the room and wrapping around our dreams. It was almost as though the walls still contained the sounds of her songs, and would always. When I'd gotten to the chorus, Jeremy joined in. He ended on a too-high note, like an opera singer, to show it was a joke. But I knew he felt it, too. The sad feeling.

Lizzie sighed loudly and closed her eyes, dropping her head off the bed once more, stretching her neck.

"How was practice?" I asked my brother. He looked at me as though I had just landed from Mars.

"We had a game," he said. "We won."

"Oh," I said, picking up a puff of brown Princess hairs from my yellow bedspread. "That's good." My parents had long since stopped going to his games. No penciled reminders circled the dates on a calendar the way I'd seen in other kids' kitchens; our house didn't have a calendar.

Lizzie pulled herself up, chin first, grunting. She swung her legs off Jeremy's lap and hopped down from the bed. "I have homework," she said, pulling out her red schoolbag from beside the dresser.

Jeremy snickered, reached into his pants pocket, and extracted a Superball. He threw it against the closet door; no one would tell him not to. *"Homework,"* he said. The ball bounced wildly and disappeared. Jeremy didn't budge to retrieve it.

Lizzie dumped the contents of her bag across her bed: drawings and loose crayons and kindergarten work sheets, PTA notices and bright activity fliers and crumpled newsletters. She spread the papers until she found the one she wanted, a mimeograph of capital and lowercase *E*'s, with a box for a picture.

"I wanted to do *L*, for Lizzie," she explained seriously, "but the teacher made me do *E*, for Elizabeth. So now I have to draw an elephant instead of a lion."

Jeremy plumbed deeper into his pockets and came up with nothing. "Does it have to be an elephant?" he asked. His interest surprised me. "Or just something starting with *E*?"

"E," Lizzie answered. She was tracing the purple dotted lines of a row of letters. I could see her writing was wiggling, because she was doing it on her lap.

"Put something underneath," I said, standing to reach for a large piece of blue-and-white cardboard on her bed. It was an envelope. "What is this?" I turned it over.

"Egg," Jeremy said. "Escalator. Electricity."

I shot him a frown.

Lizzie looked up, the tip of her tongue sticking out between her teeth. "Oh," she said. "That's my school picture."

Jeremy lunged for the envelope. "Let's see it."

He snatched it out of my hand before I could protest. "Creep," I said as he drew out a sheet of photos. He always had to be first. I watched his face cloud, his eyebrows crunch together. "What?" I said.

He turned the sheet over, not giving it to me. "When did you take this picture?" he asked Lizzie.

She had finished her letters and was peeling the paper from the worn-down end of a gray crayon. She kept her head bent and looked at him sideways. "I don't know," she said.

I grabbed the pictures from Jeremy. They were all the same shot, three medium size and nine wallet size: Lizzie, from the chest up, smiling shyly into the camera in front of a backdrop of swirling blue, fake clouds or something. Her hair was in braids, as usual, and as usual they were frayed and coming undone. Then I noticed that, in the photograph, she was wearing her pajama top.

I reached into the envelope for the second sheet I knew would be there—the class picture—and in that, too, Lizzie was wearing her pajama top, the soft one with the tiny pink roses, and a plaid skirt. She was standing in the second row between a girl with red curls and a boy with glasses.

"Lizzie?" I asked. Jeremy had stood and was looking over my shoulder, as though trying to figure something out.

"Hmmm?" She was coloring in the bulbous outline of an elephant, going over and over the same spot, as if scrubbing in color.

"You're wearing your pajama top in your class picture. Look."

She raised her head, her lips parted as though about to ask a question. I turned the sheet so that she could see. She shrugged, then said, "So?"

Jeremy pointed to a chalkboard behind the group shot. The date, written in careful print in the upper left-hand corner, was October 8, 1966. Lizzie had been carrying this around for more than five months. "Where were we that day?" Jeremy asked softly, as if I would know, as if it were up to us to dress Lizzie for school. Well, now it would be. I didn't answer him.

Lizzie, biting the end of a braid, was still looking at us. She seemed to be waiting for some kind of pronouncement.

"You look younger in that picture than you do now," Jeremy said, dropping to his knees. His head and shoulders disappeared under Lizzie's bed.

Her face lifted, brightening. "I know!" she said.

Jeremy slithered out from under the bed, holding the Superball in one hand, slapping the dust and dog hair from his shirt with the other. He walked around the bed to the far side of the room. "Catch!" he called to me as he lobbed the hard, black orb across the room. And I did.

CHAPTER 26

"CRAZY WEATHER," LIZZIE SAID, referring to the bank of clouds that had moved across the sky during the last hour and was now breaking up. I watched as smoky wisps pulled free of the mass, floated to the east, and disappeared, piece by piece.

The speckled gull landed on the railing next to me, his curved, scaly feet angled forward so that I saw them up close and thought at once of a gargoyle. I pushed forward in my chair and he took off as abruptly as he'd arrived, with a great, lifting flap of his wings.

Lizzie, Jeremy, Froggy, my father, and I were hanging around Lizzie's deck, catching our last afternoon of sporadic sun. Sinclair Central had somehow shifted from my cottage to here. We read the papers, sipped our drinks, and listened to the children's calls as they played tag on the lawn beneath their airborne kites.

Rick was fixing a marinade for the swordfish steaks—something requiring a long list of ingredients. He came out of his cottage wearing a makeshift, beach-towel apron. "Anyone up for making a run to town?" he asked. "We need soy sauce and ginger."

Not me, I thought.

To my surprise, Froggy rose from her chaise and offered to pick up the supplies. "Pay attention to the baby monitor!" she instructed Jeremy as she strode off with Rick's list.

I stared at the words on the newspaper page, but my eyes refused to focus. Instead, my attention turned inward to my mind's movie screen, where I played and replayed the morning's scene with Michael, trying to convince myself we had actually said good-bye. I touched the lapis ring he had fit to my finger. I knew the blue stone would forever remind me of this place, this sky, this ocean. My talisman of possibility.

Jeremy was the first to spot Keith walking up the path. "Ahoy, there, Cap'n Kincaid," he called, and I snapped my head up to see my husband trudging along the path as though he'd been here all along.

Keith raised his hand to his eyebrows, a gesture that was both mock-salute and an effort to block the sun's glare. He had forgotten to bring sunglasses, I realized and smiled to myself. He never packed for a trip without reciting aloud, to me, the list of what he'd gathered. "What about tennis shoes?" I'd remind him, or, "Don't you need another tie?" But invariably, he left something behind at the last minute.

"Da-ad!" Damien switched directions mid-stride in his pursuit of Lauren and ran toward his father.

Keith bent to embrace—and buffer himself against—his hurtling son. Their dark heads together set off a swift constriction in my throat, and I looked away. By the time I turned my eyes back, Keith was before me, Damien beneath his arm at his side.

"Hi," Keith said. He had changed into shorts and a gym T-shirt. His arms and legs were pale, his forehead dotted with sweat.

"Hi," I said. The familiar surprise of his sharp blue irises held my gaze.

Lizzie greeted Keith with a quick hug. My father shook his hand. The girls and Ryan grunted hellos and called for Damien to come back to their game. Rick came out from the kitchen, wiping his big hands on the towel tucked into his shorts.

"Keith," he said, louder than necessary. "You missed quite a week."

Keith glanced halfway in my direction. He said simply, "I'm sorry I did."

"Dad." Damien tugged at Keith's shirt. "Will you come in the pool with me? I want to show you my back flip."

"Not now, son," Keith said. "I have plans to do something with your mother."

Damien bit his lip, reminding himself of his broken tooth. "Look."

He lifted his lips to Keith in a baboonlike sneer and pointed with his finger. Keith peered into his mouth.

"Cool," he said, gently tapping the jagged edge.

Damien apparently interpreted that response as a dismissal, for his temper flared. "Yeah, well, it *hurt*," he said, his voice suddenly tight with emotion. "And no one cares."

"That's not—" Keith began.

"It is true!" Damien insisted. "Mom doesn't care. She hasn't paid attention to me all week!"

Keith looked at me, and heat rose to my face.

Lizzie turned a page of her magazine. Jeremy walked off toward his cottage, monitor in hand, though I hadn't heard any baby Jay sounds. Only my father continued to look straight at us.

"Damien," Keith said in a deep, soft voice, "I'm sorry I haven't been on vacation with you. I'm sorry you hurt your tooth."

Damien sulked. "Yeah, right."

"And I do want to see your black flip," Keith continued. "Because I want to show you a flip of my own."

Damien looked up, his eyes narrowed. "No way."

I searched Keith's face for clues to his meaning.

"Yes, sir," Keith said. "I could do a killer back flip in my day."

I frowned. I had never known him to do a back flip.

"All right," Damien said, his intonation a challenge. "We'll have a contest."

"You're on," Keith said. He clasped Damien's shoulder. "Mom and I will be back in a couple of hours."

Surprised, I stood up. Where was he leading me now? I busied myself gathering the newspaper, putting it right.

"Ha!" Damien said. "I hope you're going somewhere to practice, because that's what I'm doing." He shrugged away from Keith and ran off.

In the distance, a dog barked.

"I'm taking notes on how you handled that, man," Rick said, holding out a sweating can of beer.

"Thanks, no." Keith waved his palm at the beer.

"Are we going somewhere?" I asked. The days of my blindly following were over.

Keith reached for the tea I'd been drinking and helped himself. Ice cubes slid along the sides of the glass as he gulped. I thought of Michael drinking his tea with slow satisfaction and I had to turn away.

"I thought we'd take a sail," he said as he put the glass down. "An afternoon sail to nowhere."

Keith drove my rental car to a marina off West Lake Drive. From the meeting with his former client, Joe Osborne, he had extracted not only the promise of new business, but the key to his Rhodes 19 day sailer. Joe had even called ahead to the dock master, who was expecting us.

Keith and I spoke little on the drive over. I could still hear Damien's accusation, *She hasn't paid attention to me,* and I carried it with me as though it were a bad, unfinished dream. I knew about the kind of wound that first scraped raw and then formed a crusty scab upon one's heart. My mother had been absent from us even when she was with us, had not *paid attention* to the quiet and the not-so-quiet pleas we hoped she would hear. In some ways, the easiest times had been when she was at the hospital, when we could feel sorry for her because she was officially sick.

Could my actual, physical absence hurt my son any more than my emotional distraction had already done? I watched the landscape pass. My mother had loved her children as best she could. She had not chosen to be ill, and she had struggled to maintain her family through tremendous turmoil.

I had behaved far more selfishly than she.

Keith took a beer out of a disposable cooler on the floor. He remained silent, concentrating on drinking and driving. I turned toward the window and watched the late-summer landscape pass. I admired the plants that thrived here, withstanding salt spray and whipping wind and blazing sun to flourish.

At the marina, a lip-pierced dock boy directed us to the Zodiac in which he would motor us out to the mooring. "You planning to take her out of the harbor?" he asked. The silver stud in his lower lip moved, and I wondered whether it hurt him to speak. If so, did he wear it as a kind of modern-day hair shirt? What sins could he have committed so young?

Keith turned as if the length of our journey depended on me. We hadn't sailed for years, since we'd left Long Island for Atlanta, and it was after four o'clock in the afternoon. I shook my head.

Keith nodded. "I don't think so," he said. He stepped into the boat, then reached for my hand to help me in. He placed the disposable cooler between us.

The dock boy started his motor. "Okay, then you're just going to sail in the lake?" They called it a "lake" but it really was a large bay.

"Right," Keith said, in a voice that was slightly too loud, even given the sound of the engine. "Just a couple of hours."

The boy shrugged. He putted away from the dock. "The south end gets the best wind," he said. "You'll want to tack out."

"Of course." Keith shifted and bumped the cooler with his knee.

I felt oddly as though we'd reversed time to an earlier point in our marriage, when we'd frequently sailed. We had almost always tacked out—crisscrossed a route—so as not to get stuck coming back. But those trips had taken the entire day, occasionally longer. Was the point of this excursion, I wondered, to reenact some central marital drama? Why hadn't we just gone somewhere to talk?

The boy cut the engine and pointed at a small, white boat in front of us. "She's all rigged."

"Great." Keith stood, found his balance, and hopped aboard the Rhodes. He reached for my hand, and this time that simple gesture released a vivid memory of his reaching for me across the deck of the day sailer we'd routinely rented out of Port Washington when Isabella was small. I let him pull me harder than he had to.

Keith tipped the dock boy and immediately set to checking out the boat. As the Zodiac sputtered away, I stood still, listening to the rhythmic slapping of the water against the hull and the clinking of the halyards against the aluminum mast. These were sounds I loved and missed in Atlanta. The music of the sea.

Though I'd yearned for the ocean after we moved to the South, I'd never missed the Sunday sails during which Keith and I invariably bickered. My idea of a good sail had always been a leisurely cruise, an expedition whose destination was more often than not the simple passing of a few hours in luxuriant repose. Keith, on the contrary, believed a good sail equaled a good day's work. He was ever preoccupied with wind, with the constant trimming of sails, with heeling the boat as far over as possible till I feared one of us would slip into the Long Island Sound.

"We've always had different approaches to sailing," I said aloud now as Keith unfurled the jib. I watched him for his reaction. He shot me a stony look I couldn't read. He pointed past me.

"Grab the tiller," Keith ordered, then added, "please." He raised the anchor.

Most people would motor out of a harbor, but Keith had always made it a point of pride to use only sail power: engines were for emergencies. Part of a sailboat's beauty, his unarguable logic went, was its quiet.

I steered us out of the mooring area as he pushed off and the jib filled. A small corner of my mood lifted with the sail. On a boat, one's body moved in time with the waves, one's spirits with the air. Whatever reason Keith had brought me out here, I was glad to be on the water.

I glanced at the stern and saw that this boat had no outboard motor. "Where's the engine?" I asked.

Keith was raising the mainsail. He didn't hear or he didn't answer. Instead, he shouted, "Fall off the wind!"

I jerked the tiller, then stared at him till his edges blurred, my eyes transforming his gleaming dark hair to fair, his wrinkled T-shirt into a crisp polo, the dark purplish edges of a scar shining between the plackets of his open collar. My eyes transformed Keith to Michael, who would never shout orders at me. I closed my eyes for a moment to dispel the building ache behind them. Hadn't my vulnerability to Michael, the hole in my heart he'd so easily filled, been caused in good measure by the loss of Keith?

A horn sounded. There was more to it than that. I would have to sort it out.

"Okay," Keith said, the mainsheet slack in his palm. "I'll take the tiller now. You can relax." He smiled at me and pulled in the sails to head into the wind.

We were going to tack to the south of the lake, so we'd have the wind behind us for the return trip. I sat on the bench, but didn't get comfortable. Soon I'd have to move to the other side.

Why were we doing this? I wondered again. Was it only because Joe Osborne had offered Keith his boat? Did Keith have something to say to me, or had another occasion merely presented itself? I glanced down at my hands, at my "sending stone." Whatever Keith's agenda, I had points of my own that needed to be made.

I felt something inside me swell, a too-fullness in the bottom of my stomach. Then I remembered I had forgotten to take the pregnancy test.

"Shit," I said. My insides cramped.

"What is it?" Keith asked softly. He had the boat heeling now, water splashing up over the deck to port.

In lieu of answering, I repeated my question. "Where is the engine?"

Keith shook his head. "We don't need an engine on a day like today."

"But there is one down there?" I pointed to the cuddy cabin where an outboard might be stowed.

Keith shook his head again. "No. There isn't one."

I swallowed the bitter taste in my mouth and gripped the bench. Wasn't this just like Keith, to put me in a predicament without consulting me?

"Ready about!" Keith called and I grabbed the jib sheet in its cleat.

"Ready," I answered; it wasn't a question. But choice was what I wanted. I was ready for choice.

"Hard-a-lee!"

I released the jib and lunged to the other side of the deck, ducking under the swinging boom mast as Keith released the mainsail and jerked the tiller for the tack. The sweet wind blew my hair and filled my lungs, and the little boat swung neatly in a forty-five-degree arc with very little loss of speed. Now I was on the sun's side. I recleated the jib and he pulled in the main.

"Just like old times," Keith said, catching my eye.

"Not exactly," I answered and gathered my spirit.

The boat sailed smoothly, back and forth in a tight zipper pattern across the lake. I could tell when Keith was going to tack, and I would slide across to the opposite seat even before he said, "Ready about."

Though at first I found it wearisome, the tacking became a soothing pattern. Part of me was lulled by rocking rhythms to an ease like the one-time ease of our life together. But that couldn't be reclaimed, or it was no longer enough.

Keith single-handed the Rhodes, letting me sit back. "Just relax," he said. "Collect your thoughts."

So I did, or attempted to. I positioned my head with my face in the sun, but beneath my tranquil posture, my emotions clashed. I had longed for him to want me again, for us to love each other as we so long had, but now that seemed the one thing that was no longer possible.

I sensed Keith looking at me, but I kept my eyes closed. *Collecting my thoughts.* Perhaps this environment had made me stronger. I felt less vulnerable here than I had at home in Atlanta, felt, in this neutral place of simple activities, that I had begun to absorb the effects of what I had already lost—and glimpse a potential I had not yet fully imagined.

Finally—why had it taken so long?—I grasped that the best Keith and I could do for one another was to let each other go.

I turned my cheek to the wind, feeling its measure against the lines of my face. I felt the steady blue pressure of Keith's eyes on me, too, but I didn't flinch. Let him know my thoughts. It was time.

I remembered the tower of Michael's glass house, the blood-quickening effect of the view from up there. Despite his rebuff of me, Michael had changed something. He had made me feel alive in dangerous circumstances, and reacquainted me with parts of myself I hadn't known I missed. Even if I never saw him again, I had caught a glance at myself, through his eyes, from the outside. The thought of him hurt in a good way, like a tongue against a sore tooth. And I knew I was strong.

All my life I had tried to shore myself against the fear and pain of abandonment. I'd grown at times exhausted with the effort, or nearly paralyzed by it. When my mother died and I knew true loss, I didn't know how to mourn. And when my husband began to pull away from me, I'd refused to face the implications.

And then I'd met Michael, who had wanted me and whom I'd wanted.

And I had pleased myself playing music!

Whatever else happened, music would be a part of my future.

I opened my eyes. Keith was still watching me. "Where have you been?" he asked.

I shook my head. I knew I must explain that I had found myself at a juncture in my life, much in the way that he had. He had led me here, perhaps, but from now on I must choose my way. And yet I had betrayed him with Michael, betrayed any hope for our marriage when I might be carrying his child! He had a right to know.

"I've been to Hell and back," I began, but I said it without accusation.

He offered a smile. "I've missed this," he said; his eyes shone with feeling.

"Missed sailing?" I asked, deliberately misunderstanding him.

"Sailing," he agreed. "Quiet. Life gets so full of noise." He lowered his eyes; perhaps he too felt culpable. "And I've missed us."

Had he really? *Too little, too late,* I thought sadly.

I said, "I need quiet, too." I did.

Beneath us, the boat shifted. "Ready about," Keith said, and we tacked.

I looked at Keith's face, my eyes tracing its planes so familiar and yet surprising, now, after this state of having been without him. God, I would miss him.

Keith looked up, his mouth set, but his eyes awash. "I want you back," he said.

I shielded my eyes against the slanting sun and so he couldn't see them, couldn't mistake the longing in them for acquiescence—and so I wouldn't mistake myself. I knew what I needed to do.

I couldn't go back. "I can't return to the way things were," I said.

Keith wrestled with something he did not disclose. "So, your answer is no?"

I couldn't have raised Isabella alone, nor Damien, but I was a different person now. If I was pregnant, I would tell him, of course, but I could manage on my own. "I need to be alone," I said. "For a while. I'm not sure what will happen. So much will change. So much must change."

Keith didn't answer right away. He turned to the bow and we sailed gently beneath the clear blue sky. I got the feeling being apart might be what Keith wanted, too—or not wanted, exactly, but knew was right. In the end, perhaps, what was good between us would remain. "Okay," he said at last.

Soon I felt a settling inside me, a physical sensation like petals falling to a pile and the stillness that follows.

After a while, the wind dropped down, became barely a breeze, and Keith let the sails all the way out in opposite directions, a technique known as "wing and wing," running before the wind. Though tricky, this point of sail made the boat feel as though we were barely moving. Michael had predicted a change of weather—bad weather, I'd thought—but the sky was clear and bright. The rolling clouds I'd seen from his rooftop had blown away, as apparently had most of the wind. The water was luminous, a vast mirror reflecting a serene heaven.

"The sails are luffing," Keith said, changing course. "Get ready to jibe."

We were, in fact, almost dead in the water. "Let's just drift for a while," I said.

So we did. He released the sheets and let the sails flap. We drifted and gazed at the scenery, at the houses and restaurants along the shore, at the colorful Sunfish tied up at the docks, at the few motorboats that buzzed by now and then. Keith got us each beers and though I knew I wouldn't drink it, I accepted one. The bottle felt too heavy in my hand.

Keith lifted his in a wordless toast and took a long swig. His eyelashes fanned against the tops of his cheeks, reminding me of Damien. As though catching my thought—a phenomenon that at one time occurred regularly between us—Keith spoke of our son: "That kid really cracked his smile."

"He did." I remembered my panic the day Damien broke his tooth, how I'd imagined Keith making light of it. Then I thought of Michael after the motorbike accident, the way he'd handled the boys. I realized that his being a doctor had held a strong appeal for me, that by definition he was someone whose nurture could be counted on.

Keith changed his tone. "I understand you're angry," he began. I recognized his ready-to-face-facts voice.

I had been furious, devastated, but the worst of it had passed. I answered only, "Yes, I have been."

"And I know Damien is angry at me, too, even if he mostly takes it out on you."

His words stung, and my eyes filled with tears. "He thinks I don't pay attention," I said.

Keith leaned forward so that our knees bumped and stayed touching. "I know that's not true," he said. The catch in his voice tugged at me the way it always had, but it plucked strings of resentment, too. He hadn't treated me gently in a long time.

I swallowed, concentrating on the familiar press of my bones against his. "It is true," I said. "This week I've been . . ." I blinked. "Preoccupied."

Keith looked down at the tiller, as though he could change our direction without the wind. We had reached the middle of the lake.

"I know how Damien feels," I said, squeezing closed my eyes, my body rocking with the rise and fall of the boat. "It's exactly how I used to feel about *my* mother." I sniffed a bitter laugh. "And my father, in a different way."

"You pay so *much* attention, Amanda. You anticipate his every whim. Before he can say we're out of orange juice, you're returning from the store with it."

I smiled, grateful but sad. "That's not what I mean."

"Well." Keith looked up at the sail, heaving gently as though it were breathing. "We have lives apart from our lives as parents."

Now was the time to tell him about the baby, about the possibility of a baby. Why had I not taken that pregnancy test? I'd been in denial for so long. Still I held back from telling him, as though holding on to some chance the test would be negative.

We sat in silence, alone on the water. The few boats that had been out earlier seemed to have gone in for the day. Keith finished his beer while mine grew warm in my hand. I set the bottle between two cushions.

"Ready to tell me what you're thinking?" Keith asked. His voice sounded startlingly near.

"I've been ready for months," I said, though in fact I hadn't been. "But now I don't know where to begin."

He lifted his hand to stop me—afraid I would cry? "Okay," he said. "I'll start."

From the direction of the harbor, a horn sounded. I snickered at its timing. Let Keith steer the conversation; our sail was coming to an end.

"First of all," he began, "Sarah is gone."

My unthinking reaction was to blurt, "She's dead?"

Keith barked a laugh of surprise. "No. Certainly not to my knowledge." He slid under the shade of the sail. The high-contrast afternoon light had taken on a surreal cast. "What I mean is, we're no longer business partners. She's relocated to Florida and I'm going it alone, at least for now. I think that's wise."

I leaned forward. "Go on." I turned the lapis ring around and around on my finger.

"New ring?" Keith asked.

"Yes," I said. Our eyes met briefly, sharply, in challenge. I rubbed smudges from the surface of the stone.

Keith looked down at his hands, working his thumbnails under the label on his beer bottle.

"Are you sorry you left Stone?" I asked.

Keith frowned. "No. It's the best thing I could have done. But I know you don't forgive me for it."

"That's not true!" I protested. "It wasn't your changing jobs that hurt us."

Keith's face darkened. "Wasn't it?" he asked. "You were furious with me for altering life as you knew it. Even if a change was long overdue."

I shook my head. "No," I said. "It was *you* who changed."

Keith reached a hand toward me and then let it fall. "I *made* changes," he said.

"Yes," I said, "and so have I."

He licked his forefinger and held it up to test for wind. He shook his head.

Did he blame me for everything? For getting pregnant in college, for making us adults too soon? He would never say such a thing—he would probably never think it. But was it true for him, nonetheless?

"What happened with Sarah?" I asked. I pressed the ring. The smooth blue oval felt warm beneath my thumb.

Keith peeled the label from his beer bottle, trying to get it all in one piece. It began to tear and he stopped. "In retrospect, considering Sarah as a partner was a mistake."

"Hmmm." I stared at his mouth, which had hardly moved as he spoke. I remembered the breath mints, remembered that he'd said he "didn't know" whether he would like to sleep with her, remembered how I'd pushed him, how I must have seemed to him. I'd learned a lot about infidelity in the last week, and I knew I had to take responsibility for that lesson.

Keith's relationship with Sarah Stein, whatever it might have been, had had a debilitating effect on our marriage. But that hadn't been the start of our decline. Nor had my affair with Michael been its demise. We had both been unhappy for a long time, despite our love for one another. I reckoned Keith and I were equal parts of this sad thing, this unraveling marriage, paradoxically in it together.

"Why was Sarah a mistake?" I asked.

Keith set his bottle down. His eyes seemed muted, more shale than steel. "Because I'm in a different place in my life than she is," he said. "Because what I'm doing I am doing for me." The inner ends of his eyebrows raised in surrender. "A new partner was not the answer."

It was hard to look at Keith and not feel my heart tear. We had been together twenty years. And we would know each other always, of course, because of the children. I wondered whether he would ever go back to his music.

"I understand," I said.

He stood and surveyed the horizon. A slight pink burn lit his cheeks and the bridge of his nose. "I think we should try to get under way if we want to make it back for dinner."

I glanced at the flat telltales: no wind.

I stood up beside him. And then I felt a quick, warm, heaviness between my legs, and I realized I was not pregnant. "When do you return to Atlanta?" I asked. I held the mast, my hand beneath his as though we were two riders on a New York subway.

"Tomorrow," he answered, leaning close, but not touching me. "With you."

Maybe it was the deep tone of his voice, the sureness of it, or the sequence of his words. Whatever the reason, I was emboldened, finally, to blurt, "I'm not going back tomorrow. Not yet. I want to stay here, by the ocean, a couple of weeks longer." What I didn't say but he understood was that I needed to be without him.

Keith's eyes met mine and held them. "I see," he said, and a thin break in his voice convinced me that he really did.

I realized that at this moment I had begun to let go of my past.

"I'll arrange for Damien to stay with my family, with Lizzie or my father. And I'll take him back to Atlanta in time for school," I said. Keith was nodding after each word, his head turned away from me. "I don't know what I'll decide to do after that."

"Are you ever going to drink that beer?" Keith asked, pointing to the bottle still wedged between cushions.

So that was it, then. "Yes," I said. "Right now."

I squeezed my eyes as I tipped the green bottle to my lips. There was no baby. I was really on my own.

We ended up having to paddle back. I washed myself with salt water and jerry rigged my underwear with a folded paper towel as Keith tried vainly to trim the sails to catch some air. But the wind had vanished, and eventually Keith brought up two oars from the cuddy cabin. This was the time of day for doldrums, I remembered. I figured someone in a powerboat would eventually come out to tow us— though no one ever did—and the pleasurable exertion of paddling released my constricted muscles. Keith and I fell swiftly into a complementary cadence, maneuvering the boat with less effort than I expected, not needing for the moment to talk.

My oar thunked in and out of the water in a satisfying way, and I enjoyed the sense of traveling under my own power.

When we neared Star Island, a peninsula near the harbor inlet, Keith suddenly stopped paddling and motioned for me to do the same. I followed his riveted gaze to a bulge in the water. About fifteen feet ahead of us was a large, elephant-colored creature, rolling lazily across the surface.

"A manatee," I whispered.

Keith turned to me, his eyes lustrous. "Now that's a buddy to do flips with Damien," he said in a soft, constricted voice.

We gaped in amazement at the rolling creature who dipped below the surface and then reappeared. I wished Damien and Isabella were here to see this.

Surprisingly agile for something of its bulk and design, the manatee moved in slow, almost balletic turns. Was it performing for us? With a flick of its spatulate tail, it swam closer to our boat and regarded us with large, dark eyes that I realized were probably the source of the mermaid legend. A profound munificence resounded from its animal gaze: the whiskered, slack-jowled face evinced a comical intelligence. "It's curious about us," I said, delighted.

"Look at those scars," Keith said, pointing to the broad, flat back.

I cringed. One scar in particular looked fresh. "Boat propellers," I guessed.

We were very close to the marina. Our boat was drifting and the manatee drifted, too. I wondered whether this manatee was the same one that had been sighted last year, and had returned.

"Manatees are at great risk these days," Keith told me. "Jimmy Buffett started an organization to save them."

I remembered having read something about that. I wondered whether any local musicians were involved. "What an incredible animal," I said, longing to touch it. I leaned forward over the boat's side and trailed my fingers in the water. Keith crossed the cockpit to sit beside me, and the boat dipped, then righted.

The manatee drifted closer, its eyes bright, its expression quizzical. "It isn't afraid of us," Keith said.

"It is incredibly serene," I agreed. "For a creature that's lost its way."

"Maybe it isn't lost. Maybe it means to be here," Keith suggested.

Those words surprised me, coming from Keith, and I checked his face for wryness, but found none. The manatee rolled again, and a flipper nearly brushed my fingertips. I drew back my hand in surprise, then reached forward into the water, up to my elbow. "Come on," I whispered.

Was it playing with us?

"Do we have something to feed it?" Keith asked.

I shrugged. He had packed the cooler. "Lettuce?"

"No," Keith said, thinking. "I guess not."

The manatee swam closer, then quickly stood upright in the water, tail down, flippers at each side. "Oh!" I gasped. My cheeks ached with pleasure. The big, round, wrinkly skinned head floated toward me. I wiggled the fingers of one hand in the water, and at the same time felt Keith's warm palm press my other hand.

Now the manatee lay back, its body half the length of the boat. My fingertips brushed the hard edge of its leathery flipper. My senses thrummed; the shimmering water seemed to pulse with life.

The manatee twitched so that my fingers slid across its middle, and I realized it wanted to be scratched.

"My God," Keith whispered and his breath warmed my neck. I rubbed and tickled the manatee's bulbous belly, at once incredibly rough and impossibly soft. This was a creature of contradictions—awkward and graceful, homely and beguiling, imposing and vulnerable. Belonging to the sea, but not this northern sea.

I remembered my mother's curiosity about the lost manatee a year ago, and my heart wrenched open, for I recognized something of my mother in this docile enigma. I stroked the gray-brown paunch until I felt a shudder like a sigh.

The manatee tilted its head and gazed at us with grateful eyes. Then silently, contented, it righted itself and swam slowly away. We watched it go, Keith and I, our bodies still and the boat rocking beneath us, until we could no longer distinguish between animal and sea.

CHAPTER 27

WE RETURNED TO LAUGHING GULL COTTAGES at that moment between dusk and nightfall when the swiftly fading light makes the air appear to quiver. Across the lawn, the children were chasing fireflies, more fireflies than I'd seen all summer, flickering through the grass like fairies. For once, Keith wasn't walking ahead of me, but followed me closely up the path.

As Lizzie and Rick set tables for our farewell feast, Athena lit tiki lanterns, moving from one to the next around the pool. She was dressed in an ankle-length kimono of the palest peach and her hair hung loose, in dark and silver ripples down her back.

The last rays of the sun streaked the sky with crimson, and above the dunes to the east, the moon had already begun to rise. Damien hailed us as we came up the path, as though Keith and I were returning from a voyage. I knew he was happy to see us together, and a sharp pang of regret shot through me. Soon Keith and I would have to explain to our children that we were separating. I would not be able to spare them—most especially Damien—that hurt.

For the moment, however, spirits were high. Damien was eager to discuss the diving contest. As we walked over to where Isabella was seated in a low chair, he enumerated the rules he'd chosen. Keith listened closely and asked serious questions.

Isabella was feeding baby Jay his bottle as Jeremy and Froggy showered and dressed. The sight of Isabella cuddling an infant evoked in me a piquant memory of myself, only a little older than she was now, nursing her, and for an instant I felt all time collapse—my past, my future—into this moment.

"So what did you two do?" Isabella asked.

We told of our sail and our encounter with the manatee, absent the sad accounting of our marriage. I explained that I had decided to stay on in Montauk for a couple of weeks, alone, and was surprised and relieved to find that neither child appeared particularly alarmed by the idea. What I had done—what I might do—began to feel real, and I grew excited and a little scared.

First, I would spend time alone, sorting through the emotional journey of the past week. What would my future be? One part of it had to be playing my violin, making music a priority at last. I had an opportunity to play here in Montauk, with fine musicians and a real audience. I was eager for it.

Soon, however, I would have to face not only my own future, but my family's. Where would we live, how would we live? I recognized that choices were mine to make, and I took little pleasure—though I did take a little—in knowing that the balance of power had shifted between Keith and me.

Keith went to the cottage to change into swim trunks, Damien began to practice his dives, and Isabella sang soft lullabies to baby Jay. I seized the chance to speak with Athena at the pool edge.

"Very festive tonight," I complimented her efforts.

Athena smiled. "Always on Fridays," she answered. "And for your family, something extra." She gestured to the sky just above the ocean. "A full moon."

Indeed, it had begun to rise. "Perfect," I said. "Well done."

"I'm keeping the pool open after dark tonight as a favor to your son." Athena reached to light a lantern.

"Thank you." I said. I looked around for the lifeguard.

She read my thoughts. "Your brother signed a liability release, the standard one I use for private parties. An attorney friend of mine drew it up."

"Of course." I laughed and wondered whether the attorney friend was Charles of the fateful garden.

Athena laid her cool hand on my arm. "Your husband is hand-some," she said.

I followed the direction of her gaze. Down at the pool, Keith was leading Jeremy to a chair beside the diving board, no doubt comman-deering him to act as judge for the contest. "He is," I said. And yet I had wanted someone other than Keith.

"This has been quite a week for you," Athena said.

I regarded her face, luminous as a seashell in the lantern light, seemingly free of guile. I believed she had tried in her odd way to help me, though I had sometimes imagined arcane motives behind her acts. I wasn't sure why Athena had done the things she had, but I was grate-ful nonetheless.

"It has," I agreed. "Have many of the guests already left?"

"Yes, or are in process of leaving. And most of the new arrivals don't get here till the morning." She steadied a tilting lantern. "You have the place nearly to yourselves."

"How nice." Part of what I liked about the Laughing Gull was its relative remove from the business end of Montauk; at the same time, one could walk from here to town. I asked, "Do you have any empty cottages?"

She frowned. "Tonight?"

"No," I said, although I realized that I might have asked for a cot-tage for Keith for tonight. But I didn't. I said, "I'd like to stay on after the rest of my family leaves, for a couple of weeks or so. If you have something available."

Athena fingered her bracelets, considering. "I'm booked," she said. "At this time of year . . ." Her voice trailed off and her eyes narrowed. "Unless."

"Unless?"

"One of my housekeeping staff, a young Irish girl, is leaving to-morrow. She's taken a job as an *au pair* with a couple from Connecti-cut. They were guests here. You might say they stole her away from me." Athena's mouth curled.

I stared at her. Was she offering me a job as a maid?

"Come," she said, taking my wrist. "I'll show you the room—she's not in it. They've all gone to dinner. You can see if it suits you."

"You'd rent me her room?" I checked.

"Yes." She pulled one of the torches out of the ground. "I won't be replacing her at this point in the season." Using the torch to light our way, she led me down the white stone path to a bungalow beside the laundry.

A week ago, I'd walked this same path under a lesser moon. I remembered my futile attempts to telephone Keith, my suffering over the state of our marriage, my late period and my chaotic longings. I would scarcely have believed, then, that within a week Keith would be here in Montauk and I'd be preparing to send him back to Atlanta without me; would never have imagined I'd have played my violin for an audience and be eager to do so again. I'd never have imagined I could have a brief, intense affair and move on from it. But I had; I would.

When we reached the bungalow, Athena opened the second in a row of doors, confirming my suspicion that the building was divided into individual rooms to house the help. She flicked on an overhead light—not quite a bare bulb but a fixture almost as unappealing—and motioned me in. Invading someone else's place without her knowledge made me uncomfortable, and I held back. At any rate, I could see everything there was to see from the doorway.

The dark room held a single bed, a dresser, and a table and chair under the sole window. One corner was fitted with a sink and a narrow cupboard, upon which sat a coffeemaker and a hot plate. A tiny refrigerator of the sort one took to a college dorm finished the "kitchen." On the far wall, a door left ajar offered a view of the toilet. Two worn, overstuffed suitcases on the floor made it clear that the Irish girl was packed and ready to go. Nothing of her remained but a balled-up paper napkin on the table.

I heard the sounds of an approach, and turned to see Homer and Sunshine loping down the path. I smiled to think of two more weeks with them. Perhaps they'd accompany me on walks along the beach.

"Seen enough?" Athena asked, and I nodded. She turned off the light and pulled the door shut, then locked it with the key hanging from her wrist just as the dogs reached us, tails thumping.

"Hello, you two!" I bent to pet both dogs and let them lick me. The sight of Homer's winsome expression made me smile. I imagined he felt sorry for me, that he had been rooting for Michael and me.

"So, what do you think?" Athena asked as she began to walk.

I walked beside her as the dogs ran ahead and then behind and then ahead of us. "It's small," I said, making my decision. "But it's fine."

She tilted her chin. "A room of one's own," she said. "That's what you need, isn't it?"

I smiled, surprised to realize she was more accurate than she might know. I'd never had a room of my own, but had gone from sharing a bedroom with Lizzie to sharing a dorm room with Diane to sharing a bed with Keith. "It's exactly what I need," I told her. "For now."

Damien and Keith held their back-flip contest, despite my concern that Damien, or more likely Keith, would injure himself in the process. Neither did, but neither could Keith execute anything remotely resembling a back flip. His attempts were laughable, but he put enough heart into each effort to satisfy Damien and elicit hearty cheering from us spectators. During the last of his allotted five attempts, he took a long running start and bounced high off the board. I caught my breath, thinking he might seriously attempt a flip, but at the crucial moment he twisted his body into a dive—a beautiful, knife-sharp dive—that made me sad.

Naturally, Damien won the contest. For his trophy, Keith presented Damien with a shining Statue-of-Liberty pencil sharpener he'd picked up at Penn Station, and Damien beamed his triumph. Keith turned to me and winked, as though I had been part of his plan to lose the battle but win the war with our son. I knew he'd always do his best for our kids.

Then Jeremy announced a new event, a cannonball contest, open to everyone. Damien urged Crosby, who had been watching from behind the fence, to join them, and soon the pool was churning with splashing bodies. My father bet every grandchild a dollar that he would win, though, of course, he wouldn't. And so the evening progressed in good-hearted foolishness.

Keith slept with me on the pull-out couch, and it didn't feel at all wrong to lie beside him, falling asleep to the symmetry of his breathing. We were exhausted by the time we got to bed—from the boat rowing, from the wine we'd drunk with Rick and Lizzie's farewell meal (the swordfish marinated and grilled to perfection), from the depleting intensity of what we'd said, and hadn't said but soon would have to. Neither of us initiated lovemaking, and though I was menstruating I knew that was not why. Just before I fell asleep, I thought that Keith and I would never make love again, and a pebble of disbelief lodged itself in my chest.

Only time would dissolve it.

I found Keith propped on an elbow, facing me when I awakened.

"Good morning," he said.

"Morning," I answered.

Our eyes met and I saw that we were both uneasy. A breeze ruffled the bed sheet. I turned closer to Keith's body warmth. The weather *was* changing, but slowly. August was a month full of hints of temperatures to come. Keith stretched an arm loosely behind me.

"No air conditioning," he said. "This is great."

I heard Damien in his words, Jeremy as a young boy. Then I heard splashing.

Someone—my father, to judge from the repetitions of the faucet noises—was up, washing in the bathroom. The day was beginning. By eleven, my family would be gone and I'd be settled in a room of my own.

"Do you think you'll come back to Atlanta?" Keith asked, his voice low and private.

I shifted out from him. "Of course I'll come back to Atlanta," I said. "For Damien to start school." I knew that wasn't what he was asking, and I was answering what he hadn't asked.

A faint wash of pain crossed his face. He slid his arm out from under me and sat up. "I'll move out of the house." He said the words as though he were thinking them for the first time, as though they were an answer to a question.

"We can decide about the house later," I said, and I thought of Michael and his wife. No one in this situation would be ready to begin a new relationship. I had thought and thought about my last conversation with Michael, and I was now grateful to him, though my gratitude was bittersweet, for refusing me his house. He had somehow seen beyond our fantasy.

"Yes, there's time to decide about the house," Keith said, turning toward the window. A gull flew past. "I can move into the office meanwhile."

My eyes filled as I envisioned Keith living like a college student, back to where we'd started. "We'll talk about it," I said. There were differences now, of course. We'd changed. That was the point.

Keith rested his elbows on the windowsill. We sat in silence and listened to the morning. "You know," Keith said after a while, "I'm sorry I didn't get to spend the week here."

Didn't get to. I pulled the sheet around my shoulders and closed my eyes.

"I kind of miss your crazy family," he added.

I opened my eyes and let them fill. Keith *was* part of my family; he would always be. We looked at one another and neither of us, at this moment, was angry.

"It's been hard for you, getting over your mother," he said kindly. "Especially here at the beach, I would imagine."

I recalled her face in profile in the group shot, and I realized that for me my mother would always be here, in Montauk. Something gave way in me then and my voice caught in my throat with a creak. "Yes."

Keith drew me to him, and I began to cry. I cried in a way I'd once thought I could never bear.

Jeremy and Froggy were the first to leave. They came to my cottage to say good-bye as I was helping Damien pack. They were in good spirits, evidently pleased with the progress they had made as parents.

"This week seemed to work out for you," I told my brother as we stood on my deck, looking at the water. "Dealing with the baby wasn't too difficult."

"Jay was fine," Jeremy agreed. "This was good for us." He grinned. "Really good. Froggy decided not to go back to work after six weeks." I knew he had secretly hoped she'd decide to stay home with the baby, though he'd made a point of it being her decision.

"I'm glad," I said, hugging my brother, and thought to myself that marriage was a lot about accommodating each other—with as little bitterness as possible. And about taking care of children.

Soon after Jeremy and his family left, the Adamos' van drove up the road to the edge of the cottage path, and the rest of us went down to see them off. Lizzie lowered her window and leaned out to kiss me, while Keith and my father went around the car to shake Rick's hand and the children talked through the back window.

"Well, I'm glad we were both minus," she said, referring to the pregnancy test, although I hadn't needed to take it.

"Yeah," I said. "Froggy can have the Sinclair babies for a while. One a year."

Lizzie and I laughed. The men remained oblivious.

"This was a good week," she said, leaning out the window for a last look over the dunes.

I looked too, toward the road, and thought of Michael riding his motorcycle, then pushed the thought away.

"You know, we should have a girls-only weekend," Lizzie said.

"I'll be staying a couple of weeks; drive out and visit for a night," I suggested.

She nodded. "That's an idea. I'll try to arrange it."

I was pleased. I hadn't spoken leisurely with my sister without interruption for a very long time. We would have a lot to talk about.

Isabella, Damien, and Keith were riding home with my father. Keith would be dropped off at the airport, and the children would stay for the next two weeks with their grandfather. He had announced during our farewell dinner that it was time for him to sort through my mother's things—something that thus far he'd been unable to do, but felt he could now face. It had been his idea to solicit his grandchildren's company and assistance. Both Damien and Isabella had responded with enthusiasm, which pleased me and made me proud. In two weeks, I would pick up my son and return with him to Atlanta.

The five of us said goodbye at the road. I watched as the car drove west and disappeared over a hill, then I headed into the dunes.

The beach seemed too big, too empty. But I couldn't yet face what I'd come to think of as my monk's quarters, not while the sun still shone white in the sky. So I spread my blanket at the crest where the sand dropped into the sea and listened to the tiny sounds, the ones beneath the ocean's roar.

For a while I just sat, trying to empty myself by opening my mind to memory. I thought once more of our group photograph, of my mother's turned up face. *Forgive if you can,* my mother had said to me. I remembered her words. *I can,* I thought, although I knew that I no longer needed to forgive my mother anything. To attempt to do so would be like trying to forgive the moon.

I unwrapped a cheese sandwich Lizzie had given me and ate it in large bites. Later, I read a weekly news magazine I'd discovered in my monk's bathroom. The world had continued to spin and turn while I'd cocooned myself in my sorrows. I was curious about it.

I watched the tide and its rhythms brought my thoughts to my violin. I pictured myself playing with a band, with Bo and the Bone Daddies. I imagined myself onstage next to Lady Bird at the Jaw Bone, then outdoors on a deck beneath a striped awning, then way back in a smoky bar I knew in downtown Atlanta. I made a mental list of songs I wanted to learn.

Before long, I mounded a sand pillow, lay down beneath a folded blanket and fell deeply asleep. For once, I did not dream.

I must have rolled myself up as I slept because when I woke, the temperature had dropped, yet the chill had not awakened me. Athena had accomplished that, somehow awakening me without touching me. When I lifted my head, she was there and the sky was all but dark.

"I fell asleep," I mumbled inanely as I pushed myself up.

"Yes," she said, dropping to the sand, her skirt a perfect circle around her. "I thought I'd find you here. I wanted to make sure you were okay."

"Thank you," I said. "I am. I will be." I lifted my hand to remind her of the lapis ring, the healing stone.

She smiled, then turned her face up to the sky. The full moon shone white like the flesh of an apple. "Look at the moon," she said to me. "Can't you feel its pull?"

"Oh, yes," I answered. I pressed a hand to my middle.

"Lunatic," Athena said slowly. "You'd think the word would connote something everyone would want to be."

I laughed. "Maybe it does," I said. "It just takes awhile to know it."

Athena rose. Her hair was loose, the silver strands shimmering through the dark ones. She lifted her long dress, pulled it over her head, and stood in the moonlight in her underwear. "Shall we swim?" she asked.

For a moment I was taken aback; then I looked at the water dappled with dancing light. "Not too far," I warned as I peeled off my clothes. A shiver ran along the top layer of my skin.

We entered the ocean slowly, as though we were walking into liquid starlight. Neither of us spoke. The water felt warmer than I'd expected, perhaps in contrast to the chill of the night air, and seemed calmer than it had all week. Lulled by the moon.

At the first touch of rock beneath my feet, I dove and swam; Athena followed, but the currents carried us apart.

I paddled past the breakers, aiming for the gentle swells. Luminous creatures—jellyfish?—undulated beneath the surface of the water, lit like lanterns. I steered away from them, and when the current took them off, I allowed myself a brief tingle of fear for what other, more dangerous creatures might lurk nearby. Then I swam on.

I stopped when I sensed I had gone far enough, and my toes just reached the smooth bottom. I stood beneath the rising moon in water up to my neck—solitary, individual, and fragile, but no longer afraid to be alone.

Nonetheless, I looked for Athena, watching out for her as I thought she would for me. I spotted her several yards to the right, floating, absorbing moonbeams. Her hair spread around her like a plant from the sea.

As I watched her I thought of my mother in just such an image—nearby, but separate, floating in her own pool of light. Then I looked toward the horizon and let the image go.

Maryanne Stahl, a native New Yorker, teaches writing at Kennesaw State University near Atlanta. She lives on a lake with her cats, dog, ducks, son, and husband. *Forgive the Moon* is her first novel. She is currently at work on her second novel for NAL, set on Shelter Island, New York. Visit her Web site at www.maryannestahl.com.

FORGIVE THE MOON

❖

Maryanne Stahl

This Conversation Guide is intended to enrich the
individual reading experience, as well as encourage us
to explore these topics together—because books,
and life, are meant for sharing.

A CONVERSATION WITH MARYANNE STAHL

Q. How long have you been writing?

A. I taught myself to read and write at four, spurred on by a desire to understand my older cousins, who lived in the apartment above me in my grandfather's brownstone and who went to great pains to spell out almost *everything* so I wouldn't understand. When my mother saw I could write my name, she sent me to first grade, and I soon became a voracious reader. I started writing my own stories, making up my own lyrics to tunes on the radio, putting on plays in the garage (for a while I wanted to be an actress)—that kind of thing. I also loved to draw. I drew before I could write, and I continue to dabble in visual art.

At eleven, I wrote and illustrated my first novel, *The World Through a Tinted-Glass Window*, on loose-leaf paper. At twelve, I began a collection of short stories inspired by pictures cut from magazines, which I handed in for extra credit to my favorite nun, my English teacher, Sister Jeanne Marie. Shortly thereafter she left the order and was rumored to have run away with a lover, which struck me as the perfect response to my impassioned literary efforts!

Q. Which writers have influenced you the most?

A. Well, of course, anyone I've ever read has influenced me in some way, but I am especially drawn to contemporary women authors. I read almost everything by Elizabeth Berg, Alice Hoffman, Sue Miller, Anita Brookner, Jodi Picoult, Alice Munro, Susan Minot, Anne Tyler, Mary Gordon, Anita Shreve, Mary Gaitskill, Rita Ciresi, Helen Dunmore—and P. D. James. I would love to write a mystery someday.

Shakespeare, Donne, Marvel, Yeats, Joyce, Beckett, and Eliot are among the authors I return to again and again. But my favorite book of all time, the one that made me want to write, is *Wuthering Heights* by Emily Brontë.

I know that I am considered a women's writer because I write from a deeply female perspective. But I strive for what Updike has called "invisible writing," which to me means absolute clarity, words providing a kind of transparency to the imagined world.

Q. How much of Forgive the Moon *is taken from your own life?*

A. There is mental illness in my family, but the novel does not recount actual events. This is a work of fiction, informed by my experience but shaped by the exigencies of story. Readers often assume that characters, especially those in first-person novels, are based on real people, when in fact the process of creating characters is quite complex. I am certainly not Amanda. For one thing, I have no musical training whatsoever, though my grandfather was a musician. But I know Amanda's sorrows and anxieties and thrills because I've experienced sorrow and anxiety and thrills.

All my characters are composites, all contain bits of me as well as bits of people I have known. Of course, the characters themselves make up much of who they are as they play out their stories in my head. And I steal, unrepentantly, from everyone and everywhere. Writers are the ones at restaurants leaning back in their booths and surreptitiously taking notes.

Q. Where did you get the idea for Forgive the Moon?

A. I based some of the characters from this novel on ones in an un-published middle-grade novel I wrote called *Voices.* I had just returned from my first extended-family vacation in Montauk, and a friend in my writing group pointed out that such a setting and situation would provide great material for a story. As I heeded her advice, I found my-self reimagining my characters from *Voices* and bringing them to adult life in *Forgive the Moon.*

When I think of it, many significant turns of events in my life have come about in a similarly haphazard way—and that's a theme that re-curs in my stories: the tension between chaos and control, what's ran-dom and what's caused. Amanda grapples with this from the start, when she feels responsible for Damien breaking his tooth.

Q. What are you working on now?

A. I'm working on a novel now that is the story of two sisters and their relationship with the same man—one is married to him, one in love with him—once again dealing with issues of betrayal and obli-gation and fulfillment. I've set the story on Shelter Island, which is situated between the forks of Long Island and is very different from the rest of the east end. The island location made me think of *The Tempest,* one of my favorite plays, and so I began to experiment with motifs borrowed from Shakespeare. The story keeps evolving as I write it, but I hope that forgiveness will again be a theme in the novel, just as it is in *Forgive the Moon.*

QUESTIONS FOR DISCUSSION

1. The author begins and ends the novel with Amanda standing in the ocean. Why do you think the author has chosen to bracket the story in this way? Discuss the significant differences between the opening and closing scenes.

2. Amanda and Keith seem to be going through midlife crises. Amanda has lost her mother and, symbolically, her daughter, who has gone off to college. Keith is choosing to leave a lucrative job. They are both reevaluating their marriage and their future paths. In your opinion, do most people go through such a stage? What do you think of Keith's and Amanda's choices?

3. What long-term effect do you think living with a mentally ill person has had on the Sinclair family? How does Barbara's schizophrenia affect her reliability as a character in this story? Is everything she says suspect as a result?

4. Do you think Amanda would have found her way back to music without Michael's influence? Discuss the influence he has on her in general and on her decisions about her marriage.

5. How responsible is Athena for what happens to Amanda? Is Amanda too easily swayed? And how much of Athena's power has to do with Amanda's desire for a maternal figure to replace the mentally absent mother she knew as a child?